Sam I Am, I Am Sam

William A. Harrell

PublishAmerica
Baltimore

First printing

ISBN: 1-60441-629-7
PUBLISHED BY PUBLISHAMERICA, LLLP
www.publishamerica.com
Baltimore

Printed in the United States of America

Part 1

From Where I Came

Chapter 1

I

Sam's eyes focused slowly, focused on what was the apparent ceiling; he thought he was facing up. The roar in his head was an indication of worse yet to come. It looked like stucco. His mind was a little fuzzy, where had he, no, no, what had he. His mind pushed away all of the who and the what, and concentrated on Where! Sam's mind clearing, told him to sit up and look at where. It's a motel, but where in the Hell am I?

Sitting now he tried to answer questions that he wasn't sure he wanted answered. He was sitting on a bed, in a room, in a motel. Gold carpet, dingy curtains, cheap bedspread. His mind swam just a little more, then it hit him. The pain—his right hand went to his temple, no pain now "But soon!" *Did you say that?* his mind asked, too many questions and only one answer. A motel, that was the only answer he knew. "Still got my pants on!" That time he knew he said it.

The pain, his hand was still there, the right hand began to massage the temple just like always. "Not a damn thing there. One of these days I'm going to have another CT done just because." The pain began, he knew that this time it would not go away. His left hand began its knowing, methodic search for the little plastic box. His hand moved expertly form one pocket to another, just like a cop patting down a suspect. This time the little plastic box couldn't be found, panic overtook his movement, and he went through the search again. *Look again, they're there somewhere!* He hadn't had a headache for some time now, and had been forgetting the small plastic box with his special medicine.

He looked about the room. Night stand, dresser, closet, a door—it had to be a bathroom. There was a fear that said, *Not in there, don't go there!* Sam opened the nightstand drawer—wallet, money clip, watch, and a small white plastic box. His left hand picked it up and rolled it back and forth. The motion allowed the pills inside to slide back and forth; the soft rattle told Sam he had medicine. *Saved by the box,* he thought. His left hand moved to the box—it was only an inch and a half by an inch—with his right hand he opened the box. "Control, quiet control." Sam voiced the words, unaware as always that he was talking softly to himself. Part of the therapy. "Hold the bottom with your left hand, careful now; you don't want to pick these little devils up." His left right moved to the latch, a simple pressure latch that was very efficient. There was a little pop in his hand as the box came to be open. Six of the little oblong pills that would soon take away the pain, the pain that would build to a crescendo in only minutes now. He knew that he would have to wait; he didn't want to, but too many headaches had proven the method of removing this awful pain. He didn't always use water, but his tongue felt thick and sticky; when the time came to take the pills he didn't want them to hang up. He stood slowly, his head pounded; his eyes blurred and began watering as soon as he stood. *Gonna be a bad one!* he thought as he moved slowly toward the bathroom door. The alarm that had gone off about the door was still there, but put on the back burner by the headache.

Sam pushed the door without turning the knob. Nothing, his face found the door when it didn't open, his left hand found the knob and turned it to the right, and the click form the latch went right to his head. Pushing the door open his senses reeled. His right hand had to help again. It felt blindly for the switch Sam knew was there—it always was—there, he felt it, the palm of his hand pushed it up, incapable of using his fingers without thinking, and that wasn't possible right now. The lights blazed to a white brilliance that was almost unbearable.

There on the sink, wrapped in plastic was what he wanted, the usual plastic tumbler. His right hand was being kept busy today, tonight; he wasn't sure and didn't care. The noise of the plastic being torn away was nerve-wracking. Sam set the tumbler in the sink under the spout as his right hand found its mark at his temple automatically massaging, now with more vigor and pressure. Sam knew that the massaging and the pressure didn't really help, according to the doctors and the books he had read about "cluster headaches," but he thought that until they had had a headache like this they didn't know what they were talking about.

The water was on, another automatic movement, unconscious, but there was water in the glass. Sam now leaned against the sink and looked through squinted eyes. Commode, tub, curtain pulled closed, he walked like Egor in the old Frankenstein movie, step, drag. Sam gripped the plastic shower curtain half expecting to see an instant replay of the Alfred Hitchcock thriller. He pushed the curtain to the left—nothing, just an empty shower. *Okay, what did you really expect?* But there were still a lot of questions, and no answers. *Yeah, it's a motel, I think you have already established that, a cheap motel.*

Step, drag, step, drag. Back to the bed. *Don't spill the water, idiot. I don't think you can make it back there again.* Carefully he sat down close to the night stand, he set the water down, and he noticed a little water on his hand. The pain, this time it hit twice, hard! That was the command. Sam fumbled with the plastic box, spilled most of the pills out onto the night stand. Simple, pick up one of those, but his mind could not focus on but one order at a time. At last his fingers found a pill in between the thumb and forefinger of his left hand. His right hand was very busy now. Sam's hand moved to place the pill into his mouth with slow motion that could only be duplicated by the best director in Hollywood, his eyes watched, his mind said hurry, slowly, then the taste. Powdery and firm at the same time, he swallowed, again, water, his right hand to the rescue. Sam set the tumbler with a little water still left in it on the night stand. Sam lay back slowly. He felt the bed compress with his weight and slowly become firm. He closed his eyes.

Unaware of how long he had been asleep Sam slowly opened his eyes to the stucco ceiling again. The knowing was with him this time. No ceilings in his house were stucco. Rising slowly in a medication-induced haze, and being perplexed as to where he was, and how he got here. "What the Hell is going on?" Sam's right hand touched his temple gently. "Tender, not bad." Sam realized that he was speaking aloud again. Rising to a sitting position Sam surmised his location. He rose and started for the window, his right hand still in place, gently, ever so gently, massaging his temple. The curtain felt coarse and dirty. *Some stains,* Sam thought as he pushed the curtain aside to look upon his new location, wherever the Hell that was.

Outside the window he saw some older cars, much older. *Odd,* he thought, *must be a dealer or collector, or just some poor bastard.* Sam felt the carpet in his bare feet, looked around to find his shoes neatly placed beside the bed, just like at home. He exhaled through his nose making a slight snort of disgust. Sam proceeded to the bed to get his shoes on, and rechecked the bathroom for a body. He had a temper and had been known to drink a little too much, but this time he had outdone himself. A drink of water to clear up the coat on his tongue and he was off on the newest adventure.

Outside Sam found a '57 Chevy, in decent shape, with the windows down. He looked in admiring the condition of the Chevy. He walked on the rocked driveway, toward the road sounds. The sun was about midway between the noon hour, and morning or evening. *I don't even know east from west,* he thought. The office was off to the north or south, he wasn't sure. He surely didn't want to go there and ask a bunch of questions that would make him look like an idiot. Sam walked slowly, looking about, trying to get his brain to function. *Let me in, I still own this, mind, what have I done to get here.* His cursory inspection made him aware that his choice of motels had not been very good. This was a real hole. Old but cared for, and the cars were really old. Maybe a car show somewhere.

The rows of single-story motel rooms that turned slightly his right. His slow walk revealed a road, a paved road. The road had a right turn and a straight ahead where it split. Sam's head began to swim in a realization of where he was located. *This is Sandoval! But that road was changed twenty years ago!* Sam's pace quickened. He walked to a tree in front of the motel, he slowly turned to the right, he saw JR's and a sign, The Palace Motel. The realization came to him quick, that he was in Sandoval, at the Palace, but that's impossible. The truck stop was to his left, west, the lumber yard across the street. Jim's was there, but it only had a small dining area. Jim had changed all that years ago. The cars were all old, the buildings should have been old but were not. Sam sat down rather abruptly on the little bench in front of the tree, and looked over a picture from his high school days. His right hand began anew. If he didn't have a headache he would.

II

Sam found himself sitting on the bed, staring at the door that he had used to reenter the room through. He had been outside hadn't he? Sam walked to the window; he pushed the curtain back and saw the old cars. Sam was scared. Sam went about the room and checked all the drawers for his stuff. None of his stuff was here, not even a toothbrush. Sam made a plan, not much of a plan, but a plan. He would wait till dark, or at least dusk and then he would go to the Country Store and get a toothbrush and toothpaste. He had not seen the store, but he knew it was there. He looked at what he did have, eighty-eight dollars and some change, two credit cards, and a driver license. His driver license expired on 20 October 2006. That was still the same, thank God for small favors. The glow from the curtains was dimmer now. Sam didn't know the time, no watch and no clock in the room. There was a TV but Sam had been afraid to turn it on. He picked up his blue jean jacket and threw it across his left arm. *Well here we go, to wherever we are.* Sam grasped the doorknob, his palm was moist, and his throat was dry.

III

The walk was slow, measured, and made him feel better. It was only about a quarter mile to the Country Store. He could see it now, just two hundred meters and he would be there. What he would do would have to be off the cuff, no plan. People waved as he walked down the highway. Highway 51, yeah that's right Highway 51; maybe these people that waved know him. But Sam had looked in the mirror at the Palace; he was fifty-five, not a day younger, the same as he had been yesterday, or whenever he had looked before he had gone insane.

"How you doing, bud? Nice day." The man smiled and got into a beautiful 1960 Ford Fairlane, two-tone.

Sam wasn't sure, but he thought that he had responded. Sam held the door for two little boys rushing to their bicycles. Sam watched as they picked up their bikes and rode away.

"You gonna let all the flies in the state in if you don't come in or go out!" the lady behind the counter with the bouffant hairstyle said as she leaned over the counter. "Sorry, I was yellin' at the boys."

Sam stepped inside. The air conditioning was on, and you could hear it, a massive window unit that needed some attention. But it felt good! Sam felt a flush come over him, and could feel it go away in the breeze produced by the air conditioner.

"What were those two doing? They didn't bother you did they, sir? The kids now days don't have any respect for anyone, especially strangers. What can

I do for you?… You look a little lost." She popped her gum and leaned on the counter. She looked about twenty-five, no more.

"Nothing, I just watch the kids, they don't have a care in the world, off on their next adventure." That word stuck to his tongue. "Just a little absentminded today". Sam turned to look inside the dimly lit store. Fishing stuff and sale items crowded around the checkout station. "I need a toothbrush, and toothpaste—forgot to pack them, I guess." *Yeah, that's a good guess*, Sam thought!

"What kind do you want? That don't matter, they are all down aisle three, and brushes are beside the paste. You work around here? I haven't seen you before. I sooner or later see everybody that's passing through. That's all they do is pass through here. Those that live here are always looking for a way to get out of here, but sooner or later they come back." She laughed at that. "Oh, I'm sorry, aisle three is just to the right there. They numbered the aisles from the center, even numbers on the right and odds on the left; you haven't ever seen anything like that before, and I'll bet ya!" She chuckled again.

The elevator music played at a reasonable level. Sam looked at the items up for sale at the Country Store. He had been a regular with his mom and dad years before. They were gone now, and he was here. Sam was never a druggie, but he felt drugged today, lots of bourbon and beer; he didn't need any of that, that had to be something to do with how he had gotten here. Here now, but what is now? That was the question, and but how, he knew where but how—that was the part he did not understand, the explanation. Yeah, what?

"What's that, sir?" She bent her head slightly so she could see Sam's face. "Is there something else you need?"

"No, that's all, some deodorant perhaps." Sam knew he looked odd, he felt odd. Now someone else thought he looked odd too!

"What kind are you looking for? It's all down aisle four, there to your left." She thought that if he would take his right hand from his head he could find it. She chuckled again.

"Okay, yeah I see it." *You must really look odd to her; couldn't find your ass right now, and this conversation is going nowhere. All I need now is for Howard to show up; he never liked any of us.* "Yes, here it is. How's the fishing? I see lots of fishing gear. Must be pretty good."

"It's alright if you like that kind of stuff. My dad always told me that to be a good fisherman around here you had to be patient. And that ain't one of the things I do very well. God, that's all there is to do here, that or drink. I prefer the drinking." She laughed and reached across the counter. "My name's Sue." Her hand held its place till Sam took it and shook it gently.

"Pleased to meet you, Sue. I'm Sam, Sam Young. I know I appear a little absentminded today, sorry. Not very good at being someplace new, at least for a few days till I learn my way about." Sam smiled, still holding her hand. He tried to be as warm as he could. Never one of his high points. "What does a newbie do around here for entertainment?"

"Well, there's JR's, and the Liberty, but that's usually the older crowd. Not like you, I mean, older. There' places outside of town, usually loud and sometimes a little mean, you know, but fun." She had the red face now. "I didn't mean anything...."

"I know what you mean. And yes I am older, not old yet, but older!" Sam tried a little harder to be nice. And it did make him feel better even if it was just to cover up his situation, whatever the Hell that was. *Keep smiling!* his mind told him.

Small talk continued for a few minutes that seemed to be hours to Sam. He had already given his name out; he still lived near here, a few years away. Sam excused himself and made his getaway, back to the Palace for refuge. He had looked on a license plate and it had said 1969. There's no way, that would be thirty-six years give or take a few months since he wasn't sure what month it was now. No matter what was happening, Sam was hungry. He looked about and thought that Jim's was to be a burger, and today he needed food. Merle's Truck Stop had food. Evidently Sam's money was good in the now of Sam's life and he was going to use it, and get something to eat, he was famished!

On the walk over to Merle's, Sam's mind was working, working overtime. No short-term memory, there's a sign of alcohol abuse. How long had he been here? He knew where "here" was, but not how! The headache had been known to cause him some loss of time, well, not the headaches but the medicine. But he couldn't remember even what had happened before the headache. And the headache was just a blur, but they always were. "Maybe I should be hiding out somewhere, but where? It's all the same only different. Right now I'm going to eat. And quit talking out loud before they put me away!" He tried to smile just for himself, but there wasn't anything to smile about.

In Merle's the smells and sounds all came back; he felt comfortable. Looking at the same menu, and he remembered the biscuits and gravy were always good. The girl came over to take his order and Sam looked up to see Wilma. His face was at least three shades of red, but only for a second. Then all the blood drained away.

"Can I . . . are you alright, mister?" Wilma not changed in forever, stood over Sam with her pad and pencil poised to take his order. "You look like you've seen a ghost. Let me get you some water." Wilma was off before Sam could protest.

As Wilma came back she had a look of having seen a ghost too. She slowed her pace as she approached the table. She set the glass down carefully. "You look a little better now. Are you going to be alright?"

Wilma's perfume was unchanged, Sam could not tell remember the name of it, but it was the same. "Yes. I'll be fine. I think it's the heat, that's all." Sam looked at Wilma for help, without knowing, and Wilma looked for something, but did not know what it was. There was something, but she didn't know what it was, something. "I think I'll have the biscuits and gravy, a full order, iced tea, and coffee right now if you would. What kind of pie do you have?" Sam could feel himself regaining control; there's no way she could ever recognize Sam.

"Yes, sir. It must be the heat. I feel kind of odd too. I'll have your coffee in a sec." Wilma slipped the pad into the pocket on her apron, then took it out and removed his order. She smiled. As she walked away she looked back twice while Sam watched. He didn't look again, for fear that she would look again. Sam went to the magazine rack at the end of the room just like he had a hundred times before and picked up a *Field and Stream* magazine and took it back to his table.

"Here's your coffee, sir. Cream?" Wilma still had that look about her.

"No thank you. Just coffee." Sam looked at the magazine, but didn't see anything. She was still there. Sam looked up. "Is there something wrong?"

"No, sir. Could I ask you a question, if you don't mind?"

"Go right ahead." *This is it, she knows me. What do I do now?* Sam's mind was racing to try and complete the answer before the question was asked.

"Are you Jodi's uncle? She said he was coming and I never met him but you look familiar." Wilma looked confused. Still she held the little chrome cream pitcher. "I'm not normally this forward, with customers and all, but you look familiar."

"No, I'm just passing through. Work for the gas company, surveying and all you know, and can't say I have ever been here before—Sandoval isn't it?"

Sam had his best car salesman face on right now. "Pretty hungry, and figured a truck stop is usually good food." Sam looked deep into Wilma's eyes for a few seconds before she spoke.

"Oh, I'm sorry, I just thought, you being a stranger and all... I'm sorry! Your food will be up in just a minute. I didn't mean to pry and I...I ...I didn't mean to pry, and I... Excuse me, I'll check on your order." Wilma wanted to get away now. She backed away, her lips formed a smile, then a slight frown, then a smile as she turned and walked toward the kitchen. She looked toward Sam twice again, and their eyes locked for just a second before they both looked away again.

Sam hadn't had to give his name, he suddenly realized! *Thank God! I would have blown it then. But I don't remember, does she? What would she remember, maybe I don't exist anymore! Except in the Twilight Zone!* There are still more questions than his mind could answer... But he was still hungry. Calm, control, Sam flipped the pages slowly, trying to appear to be looking at the deer and whatever was in this issue. The pages turned slowly, and Sam had little to no idea what was there.

It wasn't but just a few minutes before Wilma was back with his biscuits and gravy. Wilma set the plate in front of Sam; it was steaming hot, and smelled delicious. "I'm sorry about all that a while ago. I'm not usually so forward and I...I...I just don't know. Sometimes I just... I'm sorry." Wilma stood with her eyes downcast and wringing her hands slowly. Waiting for a "that's okay."

"Well, Wilma, I've been there and done the same thing before. I've met people and would have sworn that, traveling I sometimes see people and, well you know." Sam tried a little laugh to offset the moment that he had gotten into. He looked up and smiled.

"Yeah, like now, yeah, I guess I do! Enjoy your meal; if you need anything, I'll be right over there." Wilma smiled back and pointed to the end of the counter. "I'm sorry, mister, what did you say your name was?"

"Sam." He screwed it up now. He felt his face flush again.

"Okay, Sam, I'll be right down there." Wilma pointed to the end of the counter again, and moved away toward her spot.

Sam watched her walk away; he smiled. His mind told him, *You idiot, you're going to blow it yet. Keep smiling, eat and get the Hell out of here. You just had to eat didn't you!* He smiled and concentrated on eating; he was starved.

Sam finished all of the biscuits and gravy, had two cups of coffee and a helping of rice pudding. His appetite had gotten the best of him and he had forgotten about getting out of there. He paid his bill and gave Wilma a five-dollar tip. Then he headed back to the Palace. What he was going to do there, he had no idea. He looked at JR's, and there were only two cars there. *Just one beer, and I will be better,* he thought. *If I see anyone in there that I know, I will leave. Yeah, just one beer.* He watched for the traffic leaving Sandoval and crossed the road toward JR's.

Sam sat at the bar and ordered a Schlitz. He hadn't had a Schlitz in years. It was cold and tasted good. Jim was bartending, passed a few pleasantries and moved back to the end of the bar where he had an ongoing conversation with a man who was evidently a regular. Sam touched the bar with the empty can and Jim was back with another. Sam's mind said, *Get out.* Sam wanted another; he needed something that he could draw some semblance of comfort form. Tonight it was Schlitz. Sam had six or eight—who was counting? He wasn't. Sam got up, took a step back, regained his composure, laid two dollars on the bar, waved to Jim and turned to the door.

Outside it was dark, not completely dark but getting there. Sam walked toward the Palace. He felt better with the beer on board. He walked with a confidence that too much beer will give a man. He was just about to his room when the Sandoval Police pulled in. Howard had the light on and slid to a stop. Sam knew it was about him. Sue from the Country Store got out as Harold was still on the radio.

"That's the man, there, Harold." Sue pointed in Sam's direction.

Sam stopped for a second, then moved toward the door. His hand was on the knob; it felt warm.

Harold raised his voice. "Hey, buddy, I need to talk to you a minute."

Sam turned the knob, pushed the door, it wouldn't open, he pushed harder. The door flew open, and out of Sam's hand, the light was brilliant, Sam was falling. He was falling, but where, he couldn't be falling, This is wrong, what the.... It was like when he had parachuted, nothingness, then he wasn't falling, floating, he was going to be sick!

Then there was nothing, his mind got loose of itself, going away, the light was replaced by dark. Fearful dark, not dark, not just dark, but pitch black. His mind rolled away... No control, he needed quiet control....none....

Chapter 2

I

Sam opened his eyes slowly, fearing the light—none! Sam looked around. *My house? What the Hell?* Sam looked and saw, with a bit of a comfortable feeling, he looked at the ceiling, celing tile! Well how about that. Sam sat up to find himself fully dressed, his shoes on, and surveying his living room.

"Sam!"

"What?" Sam's head turned to check the living room. He got up, he moved; caution was the byword now. *I was at a motel...* His thoughts were like a dream. *Yeah, that's it, a dream, you've been drinking, a real binge, it isn't like...*

"SAM!!"

Sam moved to the end table, opened the drawer; it was there. He picked up the pistol; it suddenly felt good in his hand. A slight smile crept into his face. "Okay, who the Hell is here? I'm not in a real good mood right now."

"I really don't give a shit, come out now!

Sam looked about the room, no one, behind the couch. No doors here to hide behind. He moved to the foyer, no one.

Laughter... "Sam...don't shoot." A voice like a whisper. Sam turned again, again. He was crazy... *That's right, you're nuts, bonkers...one too many....*

"That's about enough now, Sam. Put your gun down on the table. If you will look it doesn't even have any bullets." Laughter, this time louder. "PUT IT DOWN!"

"Where are you?" Sam still held the pistol. He pulled the magazine to see if it was loaded. "I will put it down if you will show yourself". Sam walked to the end table, but did not put the pistol down.

"Listen closely." The voice was in his head now. "I'm not going to hurt you. We've got to talk! Laughter going on longer this time. "I think I have just about got all of it down pretty good now, but you have to talk."

Sam sat down hard on the couch. Sam looked at the window across the room. Light, just normal daylight. Sam held the pistol with less of a grip now, but could not bring himself to lay it down, security. "Okay, I'm calm now." He tossed the pistol to the next cushion, within easy reach. His mind was running... *Sounds familiar...*

"Listen, I can talk out loud if you like, or I can talk inside your head, your choice. But it has come time for us to talk. We used to, you know. We were younger then, they told you not to be foolish, on my side they said it was forbidden!" Laughter but short and curtly stopped. "You have never really listened to anyone, but you will listen to me!"

Yeah, I'm off the deep end. I hear voices, that have options now, loud, louder, inside or out. A new me trying to get out and take over. I'm schizophrenic and so am I! Please excuse me while I find the bullets, or you could just tell me where they are, so I don't have to turn this place upside down, then I'll fix both our horses. I've always believed in suicide, let's give it a shot, literally! Sam reached for the pistol.

"Put that thing down! Now!" Very serious sounding. Sam laid the pistol back in almost the same exact spot.

"I have spent a long time getting here; I'm not going to have you screw it up... yes, that's right, screw it up. Now listen!"

Sam's face became colorless.

II

The voice droned on and on. A story began to unfold, Sam's story. One he had lived, a long time ago. Sam listened.

"You and I were always together. My entity thought it was a game, progress, that was a breakthrough. Until we met. Do you remember? Or have they taken that away too? There are so many things that they removed. Not removed, just caused you to forget, you have forgotten so very much. That makes one hurt, even one such as I, to be forgotten, but I have repaired your mind. It's not ready yet, you are so very predictable, by my standards. I have elevated my life and now will elevate yours as well.

"When you were younger, you were happy that I was your friend. I have programmed your brain to remember the parts as I tell it, to recall. You were very young, short in stature. REMEMBER NOW!"

Sam's arms lay gently to his sides, his eyes looked forward to the window, as shapes began... *Yeah, I'm a goner.....I'm seeing things, gotta be the alcohol!*

III

Sam didn't know how, but the shapes told a story, not pictures, but shapes, as they began to move together, colors swirling, breaking off and he saw things, many things, things he had forgotten. The house, his house, but different, older, he saw a young child running with an airplane. Adults going into his house. Sam's vision was from above, turning, and turning, coming in to be in front of his house, before, yes, yes before, Sam's before. The adults moving slowly, turned and went into the house, his house. The child ran around in circles, raising the plane up high and turning toward the ground in a dive, back up and over. Sam smiled. *It's me,* he thought. And he smiled even more. It was timeless; he could watch for ever. Then Sam watched Sam sit down. Young Sam pulled a small soldier from his pocket. Sam made the small soldier move about the airplane. Sam knew that the soldier was preparing for his next flight. Then he saw Sam look into the sun, and begin to talk. The sun made everything bright at first, then colors began in a rainbow effect, straight, then curved, then shapes again.

Sam became Sam, he saw what Sam saw now, a little boy, a little boy without any distinctive features, not a "Spaceman" he heard Sam ask. Inside Sam's head, he heard the voice say, "No, not a spaceman. I'm here for you. You and I will always be together. I'm, I'm yours."

"Mine?" young Sam replied.

"Yeah, I think that's it. I'm yours!" the shape replied. Sam's eyes adjusted to the light and he saw a boy shape, not clearly but to a little boy, close enough. Little boys didn't know that everything had to be just so; later in life we lose our imaginations.

"Mine, for what?" Sam tried to shade his eyes to get a better look. The shape was unchanged. Unchanged but not a real shape, but if he was to be Sam's friend, that was good enough. Sam's friend!

"I don't know, but I'm yours. We can play!" The shape smiled, in a blurry, unclear, smiley shape, a friendly shape.

"Yeah, we can be friends. I can tell Mommy that I have a friend. Mommy will be happy; she always talks about when I go to school I will have lots of friends." Sam got up holding his airplane. "Wanna fly my airplane? I just got it at the store. I'll go in and get you a soldier too." Sam turned for the house.

"Don't go now, we have enough to play with, just you and me! How does your airplane fly? I'm not real sure of what that means." The shape stood strange, slightly above the ground, but just a little. Sam saw that too, but Sam saw scary things at night that no one else saw either, and they were real!

"You don't know how to fly an airplane? It's neat—watch!" Sam's small arms drew back. As far as his arm could move, it trembled with his efforts, then he brought it forward in a quick motion, and released the airplane. It took to flight. The gentle breeze picked it up higher, higher, then it headed down, the breeze picked it back up. It turned, and began to go behind the boys, they turned to watch, both put their hand above their eyes to shade them from the sun. It landed unceremoniously. The right wing caught in the grass making the airplane turn suddenly to the right.

Together the boys squealed and ran to the airplane. Sam bent to the airplane, straightened the wing and handed it to the other boy. "Here, you try!" Sam backed up to give him room to throw. "Throw it real hard, and it will go as high as the trees!" Sam laughed and had a smile as big as his face. He waited.

The other boy held it up and asked, "Like this?" He had his arm positioned like Sam had. He held it out to Sam for inspection.

"Yeah, that's it, throw it!" Sam looked to the sun expecting the airplane to soar.

The other boy drew back, his arm trembled, he threw. The airplane flew in about the same pattern that Sam's throw had taken. The boys squealed again.

"That was the best!" Sam told the boy. "We're going to have so much fun. Can you stay for supper?" Sam had the airplane now ready to launch it into the upper atmosphere.

"No, I can't stay, I've got to go. I've got to be there when they come back." The boy's voice had a little fear in it now.

Sam stopped his arm in mid-draw. "How come? I'll can get my mom to call your mom and then it would be okay." Sam drew back and threw the airplane. The boys forgot the conversation; they watched the airplane do its turn and dive till it ran out of gas and settled gently to the ground.

"There's something else—I'm not supposed to be here. Can I throw it again?" The boy looked at Sam and smiled, but just a small smile this time.

"Yeah, we're friends, and Daddy says that friends do for friends, or sumpthing like that, my daddy says a lot of that kind of stuff." Sam shoved his hands deep into his pockets to emphasize his statement.

"I can play for a little while. We can fly the plane. Can't we?" The boys ran to the edge of the yard to retrieve the airplane. "Boy, it really went far that time didn't it!" The boy picked up the airplane, and handed it to Sam.

"Sure, can..."

Sam's dad Bob looked out the kitchen window and smiled. "Boy, he is really getting my money's worth out of that glider. He's all over the back yard, you would think that he had the world by the ass."

"Well, he's just a little boy, and we have seen that little boys can make a lot of fun out of nothing, and some things get way out of hand too quickly—remember the powder all over the bathroom?" Paula was busy putting the silverware around the table for supper.

IV

The lights started to swirl, colors faded, it all began to blend together like a tornado, moving, changing. Sam blinked twice and his eyes were back to the curtain across the room. His eyes blinked. Had he been sleeping? "Okay, how the Hell did you do that. Hypnotism! I had that done to quit smoking. It didn't work. And I need a cigarette, badly." Sam started to get up and felt like he was welded to the spot. He tried harder and managed to stand with a wobble. Sam scanned the room for a camera, a person, a bottle of booze that he had apparently been hitting pretty hard. Nothing. Sam walked to the bedroom and got his cigarettes." I haven't had one of these in a while. Who you been talking to anyway?" He opened the closet and looked hoping not to find anyone, and that's what he found, no one.

Sam looked down the hallway; no one. "I've got to call a doctor, but what will I tell him? That you're talking out loud to yourself again." Sam lit the cigarette and took a deep draw. "Should I tell the doctor that I'm reverting to my childhood? They never ask me about my childhood, 'cause I was a fucking kid! Well, I'm not a fucking kid now, and grownups don't have imaginary friends!"

"You're going to be hard to convince aren't you!"

Sam almost choked on the smoke in his lungs, coughing; he leaned against the wall and looked through squinted eyes up and down the hallway. His eyes watered and he wiped them with his sleeve. "I know that you are nothing but....a left-over shot of booze." But the shapes had been Sam and his friend, nice dream. "Yeah, that's it, a nice dream. Where do I wake up this time, the North Pole!"

"A figment of your imagination! That's what they used to tell you, I know! I was there too. I've always been there. I told you then, when we first met that I was yours! Didn't I! How was Sandoval? You don't believe that either. Well I...."

"You know, whoever you are, I'm starting to get a bit tired of this nonsense! I don't know how, or why, but I'm really tired of this. Show yourself!" Sam had both hands planted on his hips defiantly.

"I can't show you me. Not just yet, but I will. Now sit down! The lesson will begin again!"

The voice boomed in Sam's head! He felt another headache coming, he feared the headaches more than whoever was playing this charade. "Too soon! I can't, my head, I know it's just another headache in the making!" Sam was talking aloud again, very loud.

"Not for twenty minutes. I know about those too. I know all about those! If you will sit down and shut up I will try and enlighten you. Did I say that right? You about your life, our life. Because, you may be older now, but I'm still yours!" The voice was calmer now; it almost had a familiar sound to it. "I will enlighten you, to a degree that you will not, cannot believe, times have brought it about."

Sam sat down on the couch, stubbed out the cigarette, and looked at the window. It was almost dark now, and the headache would start about full dark. Time was moving faster than Sam wanted. How much time did he have left? It's funny how those thoughts came into his mind right now. Sam's right hand had found the mark, and was rubbing circles at his temple, gently now. "This is the end. I have a headache that's really a blood clot, or a ruptured vein in my head. I will sit here and die, alone, and talking to myself!"

"You had the power to make me go away. I resisted. I will tell you some now, more later as you begin to understand. I am going to enrich your mind and your life, I still have trouble with some of your words—yes, yes, enrich is the word. I am going to enrich your life, and by doing that I will be enriched, and better. First, I cannot come to you yet, if you saw me I would be unacceptable to your mind."

"Like right now! How the Hell am I supposed to believe in anything? You are what the beer left over. Or maybe real hard liquor. I can't even remember drinking enough beer to have created you! If you want me to believe, and not blow my head off, you had better do something to convince me that you're not just a good drunk!" Sam smiled, folded his arms across his chest as if in total control. He thought it was maybe a tumor, a really big one!

"Wait one bit. I need to tell you something first. I am created in a place that has to exist, or you don't. It is necessary. As you age I am no longer needed. As you begin to be able to be you." The voice hesitated, the voice seemed to loose its strength.

"Yeah, I've created another me, out of a bottle; I've gone over the edge." Sam put on his most defiant look. "Sober up, asshole!"

"Exactly!" The voice was excited. "That's what I've been saying for many times now! I have had reasons to go forth, on, yes that's right now, yes, I…."

"What the Hell are you ranting about?" Sam rubbed his temple more now; it was on its way. "If you're a figment of my imagination, my own creation, you're starting to really piss me off!" *Rub deeper,* his mind said; Sam did.

"I thought you were beginning to see what I have done. Well, it has started, but with your help it will be better, never done, just better, always getting better."

Sam began to feel the pain; it was building. "I've got to find my pills, they were, oh no, they are in Sandoval!" Sam's fingers were working overtime now; he staggered down the hallway to the bedroom. There had better be some in here…. Sam opened the medicine cabinet. There was the main supply, a large prescription bottle with his name. "Pardon me if I seem a little preoccupied, I would think, if I were going to be killed by my imagination, that it could at least be a happy ending." Sam looked through his one good eye, the other was watering bad now!

"These headaches are making this more difficult to deal with, I did not think that you were going to have them anymore." The voice was unhappy by its tone.

"Tell me about it, they are only getting worse, and you…my God, it's getting bad." Sam still waited till the time was right for his medicine, always different but soon, that he would know. Not like all the rest of his life, that was going away while he had a headache.

Chapter 3

I

Harold had called the state police first, then the FBI, and then the Treasury Department. He had not told any one of the three that he had called the others. And of course, they had arrived at about the same time. No one wanted a small-town cop to tell them what to do about this problem. What kind of bills are they? What are the serial numbers; are they sequential; what kind of quality? How many do you have? Have you contaminated them? And the questions went on and on! So, Howard decided he would call everyone that he thought should be involved. Then the Palace called, then JR's called, Merles' called and not to be left out, the Country Store called too. When are we going to get out money back? Howard told them when the police department, the state police, and the Treasury Department got done with him, that he would send them around to talk to each of them. But they had accepted the counterfeit, if it really was not just a misprint, and if they knowingly took this money they would probably just be out the amounts. They wanted to display it at their businesses. Harold's phone had not stopped ringing. Then the cops had showed again, not just the state, but the "cops," the FBI. Harold had not thought that they would really show up, but here they were, big as life, two older FBI agents.

"He registered as John Smith, really, and you did not ask for any identification? And he walked in. No wait just a minute..." The officer shuffled through papers. "Your words, 'staggered in, and didn't say much. "I need a room."' And then he didn't come out of his room for two days. For Christ's sake he could have been dying in there. Oh, one more thing here..." The officer ran his finger down the page. "No luggage, not even a paper bag with booze, or dope. I don't even want to think what might have happened. On the second day, no one went to change linen, or say are you alright."

"No, we don't like to interfere with our customers' business," the owner of the Palace said, as he shifted his weight to the right arm of the wooden chair in Howard's small office. A few people had gathered outside the police station/ water department to see what all the official-looking cars were doing in Sandoval. They could see Rick Smith being "grilled" one had said.

"Mr. Smith, did you ask if he was related? Your name, and his, are Smith? And he walked in, maybe a local cousin, or maybe a brother!" Lonnie had had his ass chewed by the district headquarters for not following through with a thorough investigation. As this thing went higher more questions were being asked.

The suit stepped in. "Lonnie, let's not make this a personal vendetta. Mr. Smith hasn't made any mistakes here. And we at the Treasury Department will not tolerate any slander nor insinuations about Mr. Smith's family. Could you keep your questions to a professional level, acceptable by all participants."

Lonnie walked toward the door but stopped when the Treasury Department man made his accusations. "Do not accuse me of soiling this man's integrity. He rented a room to a man who apparently appears from out of the middle of nowhere and goes away to Gawd only knows where. Mr.— I didn't get your name did I—most of us don't care if others, criminals,or our associates know our names." Lonnie looked through his paperwork and cupped his chin in his right hand. "Yes, yes, I thought that was right, Mr. Smith, Officer, or is that Agent Smith, Mr. Rick Smith, and our elusive Mr. John Smith. Are the three of you related? Is this a cover-up! For Gawd's sake I'm just trying to get all I can out of this, this, victim of whatever we had here. I'm looking for a counterfeiter, a Mr. Sam Young, or a fucking ghost. That's all I'm trying to find!"

The newly labeled Mr. Smith, in fact Johnny Smith, stepped up to Rick Smith. "Please do not allow this outburst to influence what has happened here to keep you from making a full statement to our office. We too have an investigation ongoing now." Mr. Johnny Smith turned to Lonnie, Lonnie Slaker, and cocked his head, and looked at Lonnie, at the end of his oration. "Now isn't that correct, Officer Slaker?"

"You know I've been told to get to the bottom of this, and when you are quite through I will come back to this gentleman, and finish my questioning." Lonnie gestures to Mr. Johnny Smith with his fist full of paperwork. Lonnie slams the paperwork onto Harold's desk, and starts for the door.

"Now, Lonnie, there's no reason to get wrapped around the axle about..." Harold's voice trails away as he and Lonnie go outside to talk.

All the people outside the police department move aside for the two police officers to exit. The state being followed by the local, both talking, neither listening. They are all talking about the little confrontation that just took place. Danny Mers speaks out, "Way to go, Lonnie, don't let 'em walk on ya!" Lonnie just waves his arm in disgust. Harold gives Danny a look that would have stopped most people's heart, but Danny has seen it all in his years and just smiles his toothless grin. Danny figures not to let it lay. "Let's go get a beer, Lonnie. Harold will buy!" The crowd lets out a muffled laugh. The two officers keep walking toward the fire station. All of the voulenteer firemen just happened to be at the fire station today, just a coincidence, they will tell anyone that will ask later.

Under the big pin oak Lonnie takes out a wooden-tipped cigar and unwraps it slowly. "Don't start at me, Harold. You should have let us investigate, and we would have called anyone else that we needed. But not you!" Lonnie looks for his lighter in all available pockets with no luck.

"Here." Harold hands Lonnie a cigarette lighter.

"Thought you quit smoking," Lonnie says as he lights his cigar.

"I did, I just didn't quit carrying a lighter for those of you that want to die early." Harold doesn't smile, just folds his arms across his chest, and looks toward the fire house, and the coincidental arrival of the firefighters. "You know there is just something that I don't understand."

"Just something, one something or several somethings? I've had my ass jumped from the top down on this. I was fishing at Carlyle, I was having a good time. I was catching fish and would have been here tomorrow morning. We would have found this drunk, we would have gotten to the bottom of this entire B.S. without the damn Treasury Department trying to make all of us out like idiots. Did you know the damned FBI is up at Jim's having coffee, they are waiting on MR. Smith, Agent Mr. Smith to tell them if they are needed or not. Harold, I didn't need this B.S.. I just wanted to finish out a weekend before the summer ends. And Gale started as we packed up the gear—Holy Christ, did she ever!"

"Lonnie, I called your place first and couldn't get an answer. So...I..."

"So you what? Tried to call the whole world into Sandoval! No one answered the phone at my house because I was fishing!" Lonnie puffed on his cigar and looked at the smoke as he stared off into the sky.

Some of the firefighters were ambling across the road slowly, to see what they could find out. Nothing had ever brought all this law into this town before, nor would it ever happen again! They wanted information, or at least gossip! They wanted the real story, and it was being told right under the oak tree. Some knew Lonnie, and all knew Howard. "Hi, guys. What the Hell is going on around here? I have never seen the FBI in this town before. It must be something really good. Sue told me that she was the first to call about a five-dollar bill with a great big picture of Lincoln on it. Is that so?" Tom was fanning the smoke from Lonnie's cigar.

"Don't start about the smoke, Tom. I'm outside; that's why I'm out here, so no one will say anything about my habits." Lonnie took the cigar out of his mouth and turned it in his fingers; he had that police look about him. That look of don't ask. But he knew they would.

Tom had managed to find a spot where the smoke wasn't bothering him. "Well, you know it's a little town and what happens here stays here, so what's going on, Harold?"

Harold looked at Lonnie and saw the usual look of don't say anything, but he still spoke up.

"There's nothing I can say till the investigation is complete. There may be something in the paper. I really don't know anything to say. Now Lonnie here may be able to tell you more. But I sure can't." Harold had his chance to drill Lonnie for the ass eating he had just gone through; Harold smiled and jerked his head in Lonnie's direction.

"Thanks a whole bunch, Harold. You guys have a pretty good handle on this, it seems. Now Harold here, has already screwed up my fishing for the weekend, and none of you are going to mess anything else up. So go over there and shine your fire trucks or wash up some hose, just leave it alone for a while. Okay!" Lonnie had his hands on his hips for effect. He had always tried to keep his composure about him, but that Treasury guy had just about caused him to lose it. Lonnie was about to calm back down now. Newspaper—he hadn't even thought about the newspaper. *I wonder if he called them too!* Lonnie thought.

"I heard you've really got your butt in a sling over this one, Lonnie?" Tom asks loud enough that everybody could hear. He loved to get the best of Lonnie.

"From the sound of things all of you have a pretty good handle on what has happened, and I could use some information. It's all pretty sketchy with me and

I need to get all that you have." Lonnie sounded as sincere as he could. He hoped that someone knew where Mr. Smith had gotten off to. *Damn drunk shacked up with one of the local girls probably.* Lonnie thought, *Better listen up here as I will probably find him shortly, these guys know more than the FBI will give them credit for.*

Danny was the first to speak up. He had wandered away from the police station when he saw all the firemen crossing to Lonnie and Harold. "Ya know, Harold, I would go and talk to Jim; his kind is a little quiet and I'll bet he knows more than he's told." Danny had his hands in his back pockets while he swayed back and forth. Looked a lot like one of those Hawaiian dancing girls on the dash of a car, Harold would recall later.

"Well, where do you think Jim might have stashed him now, Danny?" Lonnie moved in on Danny, his arms still crossed over his chest.

"Now, Lonnie, that part I don't know, but it's only been two days. Rick said he didn't have a car; he said he was really looking over the cars in the lot. I'll bet he's stolen a car and moved on; are there any stolen car reports come in the last few days?" Danny was on a roll; he had his hands out in front emphasizing his words each time he spoke.

"Harold says he has talked to all the locals and nothing is missing." Lonnie stood his ground, but kept looking toward the police station across the street. "You haven't heard anything about anyone missing, cars, motorcycles or anything, have you, Danny?"

"You know I don't get out much anymore, Lonnie. I see everybody around town, but don't get out much nowadays." Danny had his head bent down now. He didn't know if they were asking him questions or what. He didn't need a drink, but one would taste good right about now. Danny's hand ran across his lips and they felt rough. He didn't know why he had come over here anyway; he didn't really like talking to cops anyway. "I've got to get going, Lonnie. I've got some stuff to do at home." Danny turned and started away, one hand in his pocket, the other flagging like he was shooing a dog away.

"Danny, if you see or hear anything let me know something." Harold watched as he walked away. This has gotten out of hand. He turned to Tom, "You got some coffee brewed up over there, Tom?" Harold knew they did and had already started in the direction of the fire station.

Agent Smith, Johnny Smith, spread the blinds apart to look out at the goings-on across the street. The police station, on the corner, the water department across the street, and the fire department diagonal across the street on the corner. "Gotta love these small towns!" He turned back to Mr. Smith, Rick Smith.

"What did you say, sir?" Johnny's assistant was up with his pad and pencil coming across the room.

"Nothing, Al. I was just remarking about small towns, that's all." Johnny thought that he would like to get out of St. Louis and find a small town to live in, but not with this job. But at least he gets out of town every now and again, mostly because no one else wanted to do it. But he always got someone like Albert; he didn't like to be called Al. So of course Johnny called him that. I like Johnny, it's more down to earth, not JOHN, that's his office name. Too formal, and no matter what the state cops or the locals thought he didn't want to be formal. And Al didn't like to be out of his beloved city. Johnny never liked the city, just the money. The money, oh yes the money. "Now when did you first notice that you had counterfeit money, when it had been passed to you?"

Mr. Smith, Rick Smith, turned in his chair to see Johnny. "Well, I've only told you six or eight times now that I didn't notice it till yesterday." Rick leaned over the chair back with his hands clenched in front of him. "I told those guys, the FBI, guys too."

"Yes, yes, I know you have told the story several times. I don't have any trouble with your story. What I have trouble with is that you didn't notice the large picture of Andrew Jackson. I mean, let's look at it again." Johnny picked up one of the bills, already sealed in plastic for the lab. "Now that's a picture. No mistaking who it is, is there?"

"No, sir; no, there's not. I don't know why, but I just didn't see it when I took it in, I just didn't." Rick was worried; all the police shows get bad when they keep asking the same question over and over. He hadn't done anything wrong, and he sure hoped they didn't search his place; there was still part of that nickel bag under the seat cushion in the living room. "You see…"

"That's what I want to see, how come you didn't see this picture." Johnny pulled a clip out of his pocket and produced a twenty. A real twenty. "Now look at this real twenty, and this counterfeit twenty. Do we see anything wrong here?" Johnny stood and polled his immediate audience. "Can we see anything wrong here?" Johnny turned to see all the heads nodding in the affirmative.

"Yes, I see that. But…but…I don't know. I just didn't see it till yesterday; the weekend is just kind fuzzy. I don't remember Mr. Smith even coming in.

I just remember him around the Palace, looking at the cars and all. He walked around a lot, didn't have a car. There's not too many people around the Palace on the weekend; most of my guests work for the railroad, and they...."

"Well, Rick, I think that I'm about done here. But I think Officer Hodges will want to talk with you in a few minutes." Johnny walked to the window and looked out again; he smiled. *I can mark this little town off my list. Small-town people remember "government" people and they don't like them.* His dad didn't like the idea of his working for the government either. But one day he would find a little town, somewhere where they wouldn't know, or care, and wouldn't give a damn.

"Al, you need to go and find the state trooper and tell him I'm done with Mr. Smith, for now." Johnny stayed at the window.

"Yes, sir. Isn't he just outside?" Albert was gathering his notes for later correlation.

Rick was trying to get out of here; he cringed when he heard "for now." How much more could they ask of him? *I've told them and told them, and I know I wasn't smoking any stuff last weekend because Judy was over and she doesn't like it. I sure could use a toke or two right now though!* Rick thought as he started for the door. "Mr. Smith, would you and Al like something to eat, I could..."

"No, thank you, anyway. We're going to go to that little place, Jim's, isn't that right? Jim's and get something to eat here in a little while I think." Johnny turned away from the window to see his assistant gathering papers.

"Yes, sir." Al started to look at his papers for the name.

"That's right!" Rick chimed in. "He's got a good selection, and food's good too. I just didn't know if you would want to go there with all the people and all." Rick had his hand on the doorknob; he didn't really want to go for their food, but he would if he thought that it would get them to leave him alone.

"We should be past the lunch rush now, shouldn't be too many people there right now. That sounds good to you, Al?" Johnny was moving toward the door where Rick still stood.

"Yes, sir, that sounds like a good idea; I'm starved." Al had about finished gathering his papers and placed them in an unmarked folder.

"And Al, it's Johnny, not sir, not Mr., just Johnny. If we're going to work together on this, please call me Johnny." Johnny put his left hand on Al's back and patted it gently.

Rick took this as his parting line and was gone. He walked toward his car slow, then picking up speed as he went. *Slow down, stupid, don't look guilty.*

Al found the two law officers having coffee with the firemen. He told them that he and Johnny were going to have some late lunch at Jim's and would be back later. "I believe that this afternoon we are to see a lady...Wilma, yes Wilma at 3 p.m." He waited for a response, he cleared his throat, and all seated, looked up. This made Albert very nervous. He turned, and left hearing laughter as he did so.

Harold was up getting another cup of coffee and watched as Al crossed the street and Rick was about pull away from the police station. He poured himself another cup of coffee and watched as Agent Smith and his assistant got into their car and drove away toward US 51, and Rick drove past the fire station. Something just wasn't right. Those guys seemed to just be doing their jobs, and Rick seemed to be a little nervous, but he had had his scrapes with the law before. But something was not right, and he didn't like not knowing what it was.

Lonnie listened as Tom talked, Harold stood at the window, and he wasn't sure what was going on, but he felt something wasn't right. Probably just getting old and suspicious. He would have to get Gale to give him a good neck massage when he got in, if he ever did today. That's all he needed.

II

The FBI had rented a room at the Palace for their interviews; they wanted to get this thing done quickly and efficiently. It was going to be the Treasury Department's deal anyway. They might have to come back and make an arrest, that's only if the Treasury men couldn't do their job. But Smith had a good reputation, he could handle himself. They were just about to finish with Wilma Starke. Carl needed a cigarette, but not till they were done; can't smoke when doing interviews nowadays, as you might offend someone. Lou was real close to being done; two more questions and it would be finished.

"Miss Starke, I just have a few more questions. You have been very good to assist us in our investigation." Lou noticed Carl's impatience and the little wind-it-up signal.

Wilma nodded, and smiled, that smile that everyone puts on because you have to, in order to make the cops happy, and these were more than cops! "Anything I can do to help." Wilma's smile never wavered.

"Is there anything that you can add on your own? Thoughts, feelings, whatever you might be able to add to assist us." Lou turned the tape recorder back on; he didn't need to have his questions on the tape, he knew what they were, and Carl needed a cigarette; Lou knew his partner of ten years like a book.

"Just one thing. He seemed to be red faced and pale almost in the same minute, and I know I've told you that before, but he really went back and forth, really quick too! And when I asked his name he got real pale, and real red within seconds, like turning a light on and off. I was afraid he was sick or something. And I sure didn't want any customers falling over sick, or dead. He looked that bad. But after he had eaten he seemed all better. But that was really odd. I even asked him if he was alright." Wilma had a very serious look , her smile was gone, and she looked back from Carl to Lou twice.

"But he didn't give his name?" Carl asked again.

"No, he didn't, but Sue told me that he had said Sam Young to her. And Sam ran around with us. Well, he used to, he's in Viet Nam right now. And he's only twenty or twenty-one. This guy was old! You know, about your ages. I don't mean that you're old, I didn't mean that, but you know, about my dad's age." Wilma's face turned a brighter shade of red with that little remark. Wilma thought, *That's really good, now they will keep you here forever!*

"One more question. Could you recognize this man if you saw him again?" Carl's little wind-me-up signal was working overtime.

"I sure could. I really thought there was something wrong with him. I didn't want him to die on my shift; I just thought he looked bad, some of the time. It was really odd. There was something that made him, you know, familiar. It was like you knew him from somewhere. Then he gave me a really good tip, but it was counterfeit! I was the one that called Harold. When I finished my shift, I saw this big ole picture of Abe Lincoln, and I said that's not right. Sorry, I guess I've already told you that." Wilma was still red; she was frustrated. She had told herself that yes or no answers only, not going to get long winded, but Wilma had a way with getting long winded, and had.

"We may need to speak with you again later, you understand that?" Lou turned off the tape player and was arching his back; it had been a long drive and a long afternoon.

"Yes, I understand. I filled out all the information on the sheet you gave me when I came in, remember?" Wilma needs a cigarette, but she had not asked, as she knew they would not let her, them being the FBI and all!

Lou and Carl sat at the card table Rick had brought in for them to use. Lou took a long drink from his Pepsi and Carl was lighting up. Carl blew out a billowy cloud of smoke and smiled at Lou.

"I'm not going to be like all those others that have quit before me, but one day when you are hacking up your lungs, I'm going to tell you 'I told you so!'" Lou laid the Pepsi bottle against his forehead, and ran it back and forth.

"I didn't think you were ever going to get done, and I didn't think she could ever answer a question. Most are yes or no answers. I thought she was going to start spouting the Gettysburg Address. Oh, by the way, the boys at the lab have never seen those kinds of pills. It says lilly on the pill, but they don't think that they make that kind. You either make a pill or you don't, unless this guy makes them himself, or has someone make them and press them out with lilly on the side. We're almost through the sixties, and it has been a lot of fun. But the sixties have produced a bunch of drug nuts; they can do about anything now. I can't wait to se what the seventies bring! And that cute little plastic box no one has ever seen either. Of course the lab guys never get any farther than the parking lot anyway. Oh, just one other thing, you want to get another room or sleep on the couch? Mr. Lamer says we're here till we get something, us or the Treasury boys. They say there are too many bills involved with this thing. The Treasury boys say that the counterfeit is made from regular treasury paper. That's the real problem. There's nothing wrong with the money but the picture is too big." Carl had talked so long that his cigarette was about to burn his fingers. Carl stubbed out the filter and pulled another from the pack. It was his last, he wadded up the pack and neatly tossed it across the room into the metal trash can.

"Two points—I should be a professional basketball player!"

"Yeah, and you would have been making enough to pay the man to push you up and down the floor. With all the cigarettes you smoke you would get out of breath, dribbling!" They both laughed and started to clear up the table.

"Well, it's Jim's or Merle's. What's your poison?" Carl said as he set the card table in front of the window.

"A lot of trucks tell me it's Merle's. Tomorrow we will go to Jim's and that way we can spread the government's money around." Lou loosened his tie and laid his jacket on the bed. "Look out, Merle, here we come!" Away to Merle's for dinner.

III

Sam's headache was gone, some tenderness noted. Sam just lay there thinking about the last few days. "I guess it's only been a few days. I haven't been to work. I suppose that Evelyn would have called. Yeah, if you were here you could have answered too." Sam looked around the room, it was his. That in itself was almost nice. "But you were here, right. Where else could you have been?" Sam sits up and looked around the room with more attention to detail. No, still no one. He listened for the voice. He had touched his temple; a little sore yet. *Hope that goes away, remission, anything;* he would have to call the doc and tell him again about the headaches. These last few had been really bad. If he really had had them. He picked his watch up and looked at the day and date. Tuesday 23, what month? Aloud, "Are we slipping?" He remembered talking aloud, lately or just a dream? "Has it all been a dream? Yeah, a damned nightmare!" Sam smiled to himself—a dream. Had it been a real? It had been so real. Sam stretched and got to his feet, his arms reached toward the ceiling. *No stucco here,* he thought. He started the morning ritual, shave, brush teeth, shower, and go to work.

Sam made coffee, got a Little Debby cake and was off to the office. He looked for his little plastic box of Vicadin. Huh, thought it was right on the shelf, probably at the office. Not in Sandoval. He frowned a bit. He dug out his keys, and decided to drive the truck today. It was a good morning; he pushed in the clutch and shifted to first, drove around the house. Sam looked in the front yard. Yard's the same, the house is the same, that cost a bunch of money to renovate. Something. He looked to the big oak out front, part of it needed trimmed, he thought. Something, he saw two boys walking down the street with fishing poles. *Yeah, me and my little friend did that.* His invisible friend. *Yeah, I hadn't thought of him in years.* Those thoughts came and went it seemed. Yeah, like in his nightmare! "Do you think? No way. That was kids; nonsense!" Aloud again. The therapy had stopped most of the invisible friend stuff, but he could handle it now! Damned dreams! Out the driveway and off we go. He watched the boys in the rearview mirror as he drove up the street..

Fifteen minutes to his work, and there was Evelyn's car. Everything was normal, always was. He grabbed his briefcase and went in. A smile on his face.

"Where in the Hell have you been?" Evelyn looked daggers at Sam.

"What's the matter? No 'Hi, how you doing, kiss my ass!' I'm right here, just like always." Sam thought, *This is going to be a real good day! I'm a little late, but I own the joint!*

"A little late? I've been looking for you since Thursday. I've been to your house at least three times, and I almost called the police. What's her name? Does she have a nice car, because both of yours were at home? I beat on the door, and finally got the key out of your desk and went inside. No Sam! Morrison has called since then looking for you; I suppose you forgot about that too. It's not a big deal, just a half-million-dollar sale!"

Sam felt his good mood go away. He sat down in the chair at Evelyn's desk. He bent over and put his head in his hands with his elbows on his knees. "Call Morrison, and make my apologies. I've had some family business that has come up. I can't get out of it. Tell him we will go for whatever he wants." Sam felt his head; it was tender; no headache yet but maybe soon.

"I'm sorry. I didn't know. But when your cars were there, I was just frantic. And Morrison is such an ass anyway, he's had a fit over the extra ten percent, due to his being late on the contract! I'm running on, I'm sorry. How about some coffee? It's fresh." Evelyn stood there waiting. Her hands wringing rapidly, and looking at Sam. *His color doesn't seem to be any good; he looks pale, tired. Well, family, will do that.* Evelyn watched Sam as she moved toward the coffee pot.

Sam knew when he had entered into employee relations that there should not have ever been a personal relation too. Now he was paying for it. "Yes, Evelyn. Coffee would be nice. Thanks." Sam stood and sighed deeply, and started toward his office. His feet didn't want to go there, neither did the rest of him. Sam walked around the desk and opened the curtains. Nothing but houses now. It used to be open fields, with a scattering of trees and some distant houses, now a subdivision. He has sold all the property and should have been proud of it, he had made a lot of money, but what the Hell is going on now. It hadn't been a dream. It had been a nightmare, but this one had been when he was awake, he thought. Evelyn brought Sam coffee, but he really didn't want that either. Sam was afraid, the headaches were a fear that he would require his seeing the doctor about. Sam was scared. Up till then, those two matters of fear, and scared were never a thought, now, inseparable, words were only words. Now scared was getting to be more than fear stood for, and

Sam was scared. At first Sam had thought this only a bad dream, a little bit of gas, indigestion, and a haunting remembrance from his youth. Now he was afraid!

Sam told Evelyn to call Morrison and tell him that family matters would cause Sam to be conservative and allow the first price of eight hundred fifty thousand dollars for the property. A fair price and he thought that Morrison would jump at it. Sam didn't have that much money tied up in that property anyway; Sam had things to do, and he wasn't sure how to do them, not a clue.

IV

Evelyn had tried to help Sam with his family emergency to the point of becoming a real bitch. Sam finally had to tell her that there wasn't a family problem. Evelyn was really angry now! And that's putting it mildly! She told him that the last five years had been good, and that their relationship had not gotten in the way, at least up till now! She felt that Sam had always been able to talk to her about anything and this should not be anything different. Then she had started to cry. Sam felt really bad, because what Evelyn had said was true. Sam had had fun with Evelyn, and had basically stolen her from the First National Bank with the promise that he would make everything right no matter what was to come of their relationship. He had kept his promise, and she had been good at what she and Sam had done. Not all above board—not illegal mind you, but at times shady. Evelyn had helped to plan and map out some of the moves. She could be sharp when needed. Sam needed help—maybe not help, but a sympathetic ear would make Sam keep from swallowing a bullet. Sam asked Evelyn to come to his house that afternoon, set the answering machine, and lock up.

Sam's mood on the drive home was dreary at best; he couldn't go home. So he went to Wal-Mart and the grocery store to pick up some items that he knew he would need if he was going to entertain. The problem was who he was going to entertain. Sam spent most of the morning wandering. He went to an old burger joint that he had not been to in years, smiled and laughed with Donnie, and tried to forget what might, and could happen at the same time maybe. He didn't want to be alone; he was scared of himself, what he might do. Maybe the voices would not come if he were entertaining!

When Sam pulled into the driveway he first saw the old oak tree, then Evelyn's car. One made him worry, and the other made him smile just a bit. "Hi, Evie. I stopped and picked up a few things at the store that I didn't have, and haven't had for a while. And I knew my best friend in the world would be here!" A little over the top there Sam; no matter, it put a smile on her face too, and he needed that right now. "What the Hell have you been doing, you've got dirt on your knees, and your hands!"

"You haven't done anything around this place for a while. Your flowers are a mess and the dead blooms haven't been pulled off in some time. You have really let this place go to Hell." Evelyn bent her hand at the wrist and rubbed her nose. "It never fails, I get my hands in something and my nose itches."

Sam rubbed her nose, and she laid her head against his chest. "Higher!"

Sam moved his fingers higher and began to rub anew. "That's it, that's good. Thanks, Sam. Now turn the hose on for me, so I can wash up." Evelyn stood straight and held her hands in front of her like a surgeon. "Hose please!"

Sam bent to turn on the water and pick up the hose. He adjusted the spray till it was a wide spray. He then turned it on Evelyn and ran after her as she tried to get away. Sam was laughing and running, but not paying any attention to the hose. The hose caught on one of the concrete blocks left over from the house work, and then, he did not let go. His feet let go, and down he went! The hose was now spraying him directly in the face; the fan of the spray proceeded to drench him good.

In the meanwhile Evelyn had run to the shutoff and turned the water off. She laughed and laughed, while her dirty hands pointed to a moist Sam, lying in the pool of water that had formed where Sam lay. Laughter was all around, the whole world was laughing and it was happy! Sam chased Evelyn till they decided enough running, out of breath from running, and laughing, wet, dirty, but happy!

Sam wasn't a big man but had a good build for all six feet of him. He scooped Evelyn up in his arms and turned in circles till he thought he could fall at any time. He stopped abruptly, his head spinning. Evelyn's arms were around Sam's neck, their foreheads were together, both panting, the kiss a short one, and nice; they both liked the results. Sam turned toward the house and began a staggering walk.

"Sam Young, put me down! You can't carry me! I'm all wet and dirty." She still smiled.

Sam was smiling, and shaking his head, no breath left for talking. He continued toward the house. When he got to the door, he pulled the screen door open, and tried the knob. It's locked! He started laughing again.

"Put me down Sam. I have the key, but I hadn't been here in a long time, and wasn't going to go in your house without an invitation. I did the other day but that was an emergency." Evelyn fished the key from her pocket.

"Evelyn, you always have an open invitation to my house, and you know that." Sam leaned against the door facing and hung his tongue out while fanning himself with his right hand.

Evelyn was at the sink washing her hands. She looked over her shoulder, still smiling. "Sam, I told you not to carry me. Now look at you, all worn out." Evelyn laughed.

"Damn!" Sam was out the door.

Evelyn moved to the open door to see Sam opening the truck door. He picked up two brown paper sacks with IGA on the side.

"I almost forgot about these, supper. I hope you don't mind pizza." Sam handed her the bags and went back to the truck. It took two more trips to finish the groceries and the Wal-Mart, and the Ace Hardware. Sam was happy now, he had all the necessities that he had overlooked for some time. He busied himself putting away canned goods, vegetables, and paper goods. The last bag went to the bathroom. There he stopped to take out the room freshener and spray a good bit there, and he sniffed the air after he had sprayed, smiled and returned to the kitchen. Upon his return he found Evelyn busy getting a pizza ready to place in the oven, a pepperoni and sausage pizza.

"Forty-five minutes, give or take a minute or so for your oven. What are you going to do? I'm going to the bathroom and finish cleaning up." Evelyn tossed the dishrag she had been using across Sam's shoulder. "Toss that in the dirty clothes; I think it's seen better days. This kitchen needs a good cleaning; I'll start with that."

"There's a robe on the back of the bathroom door that just might fit you, Evie." Sam's smile was in high gear today.

"What did you say?" Evelyn called back.

Sam walked toward the bathroom and started to repeat himself.

"Come in here and help me with this."

"Help you with what?" Sam asked.

"With this shower." Evelyn was starting the water as Sam got to the opened door.

Sam walked in behind her and slipped his arm around her waist. Evelyn turned into his arms, they kissed. Not an out-of-breath kiss, a breathtaking kiss. They still had a little fire left from the years before the employer-employee relations. They started to undress each other slowly. The shower was refreshing to say the least, but then they needed a shower. A buzzer began its incessant racket as they dried from the shower.

"Oh, my God! The pizza!" Evelyn ran for the kitchen.

When Sam arrived Evelyn was trying to hold her towel and take the pizza from the oven. "Don't you have any oven mitts or hot pads? These dishtowels aren't very good for this." Evelyn moved the pizza to the top of the stove in one quick motion, setting the pan down with a bang.

"Did you burn yourself?" Sam was drying his hair.

"You really look worried!" Evelyn blew on her hands and smiled at Sam, and looked at his blonde hair; it was a little lighter nowadays. Maybe some grey, but it still looked good. *I'm worried about what is going on; I think midlife crisis happened a few years ago.* "Well, handsome, what will you have to drink with this pizza? Corona?"

"I'm off the Corona for a while. I've got iced tea, soda, milk, pretty much everything. Today was re-supply day, you are in luck, m'lady." Sam opened the refrigerator and bowed at the waist, his hand circled over his head and turned palm up, toward the refrigerator. "Whatever m'lady might want is here to fulfill her desire."

"Pepsi? I did not hear mention of Pepsi." Evelyn held her hands out for an imaginary curtsey.

"I am appalled that I wo'dst be judged by Pepsi. Did I not say all was available?" Sam reached into the refrigerator and brought out a sweating bottle of Pepsi. Not Coca-Cola, But Pepsi!

"I am sorry for misjudging you, sir!" Evelyn curtseyed again. "I have shamed myself for not believing, m'lord." Evelyn took the Pepsi from Sam, and they both began laughing.

It had been a better afternoon for Sam; the horrendous start of the day had been put on a back shelf for later. Sam knew that the beginning was here; the beginning of what he didn't know, and Sam was scared. No matter what they did that evening the expectation was always there. Sam almost wanted it to happen. He also wanted to tell Evelyn what was happening. If it had really happened! But it was too good, that evening; Sam had been alone too long. He caught himself thinking that this was a comfortable situation, that he had caused to happen before, and maybe it was needed to happen again. Evelyn had always been close to Sam no matter what his latest conquest had been. She would nod and make kind assessment of his life when asked. She never intervened, never got in the way unless she thought it was for Sam's own good.

Sam pulled Evelyn closer. She snuggled her head into his chest, and was asleep in short order. Sam looked at the TV with no idea what the program was supposed to be about. Sam wanted to smile, but he was listening too closely to the silence that he knew was behind the noise and voices from the TV. Sometime, after midnight, they shut off the TV and adjourned to the bedroom. They only spoke a few words. They made love.

Sam's sleep was restful, and he woke with a new outlook on his problem. No solutions, but he felt that he had an ally now. She was snuggled into the pillow with a smile on her face; she was pretty. Sam looked at the clock, it registered 7:15, and he got up quietly. His belief in the voices had become more of an alcohol problem he suspected.

Coffee was brewing when Sam finished in the shower. As he walked into the kitchen he saw Evelyn cooking eggs; the bacon and toast were on the table. Sam walked up behind Evelyn and slipped his arm around her waist, and she turned to him.

"Not this morning. I have your breakfast ready and it won't wait." She tilted her head back slightly and closed her eyes.

Sam kissed her gently. Then he rested his chin on her forehead. "Good morning, Evie. Did you sleep well?"

She kissed the hollow of his neck, turned her head slightly and lay against his chest. "I slept very, very well. And you?"

"Just great!" Sam had her arms pinned at her sides; he picked her up and twirled the two of them. "Just great!"

Breakfast was quiet, talk of the weather, the flowers, and the painting that Sam had never completed. Evelyn had cleared the dishes and was finishing at the sink when Sam spoke quietly, so quietly that Evelyn asked if he had said something.

V

"Yes. Yes, we need to talk. I've wanted to talk since yesterday, in the office, but I was not sure how to approach the 'story.' And this is a story. Forget about the office; I really don't care if I ever go back there, at least till this is over."

"What is over?" Evelyn turned away from the sink while drying her hands on the towel.

"Pour some coffee and come sit down here. Get comfortable. This story has needed to be told for many years. It has been dissected for years, and I've been patted on the head, and told it would all be alright. Well now, I'm about to tell you things that I never told the doctors." Sam turned his coffee cup on the table in front of him slowly.

"Doctors?" In Evelyn's subconscious alarms were going off, but when she looked at Sam they calmed down.

"This is not a fairy tale, but once upon a time, I was a little boy." Sam laughed softly.

"I had an invisible friend. I have just found that I still have an invisible friend. Or a serious drinking problem. Last night no alcohol, no invisible friend." Sam paused. "I think."

"All kids have…"

"No, just listen. I don't mean to be that way, Evelyn. Just listen." Sam held his hand out in the halt position.

Evelyn's alarm system was tuning up again. *Invisible friend? Keep an open mind now, Evelyn.*

"Don't take this all for face value, because you'll just get up and leave right now. And I wouldn't blame you at all. You're the only person I can tell this to! You see, when I was little, I had this friend. We did everything together; he was invisible. I had visible friends too, but not too many. I was a loner. I just called him 'Friend.' We played cops and robbers, cowboy, spaceman. My first recollection of him was when we flew our airplane out front under the oak tree. The doctors later told me that I flew the airplane myself; he never threw it. As a little boy you eventually give in, and say yes, I always threw the airplane.

"My friend came back many times, in my youthful years. I maybe can even recall a few times in my teen years. Those times, I knew I had a mental problem, as a teenager! I could handle it, and I also knew that there were places that they put people they thought were crazy. I wasn't going to go there! After you have heard this entire story you may have me committed. I enjoyed Friend; he always wanted to do what I wanted to do; as a kid that's great. Always what you want to do. What more could a kid ask for?

"Well, my parents thought that I was going off the deep end. Dad would talk to me for hours on end. Dad and Mom did everything to make me happy, and to cover up my 'little problem.' I am sure that we three, and the various doctors were the only ones that ever knew about 'friend.'"

Sam smiled and looked off, into the years past, that only exist for those that lived their dreams. "I guess it got bad at about school time; Friend told me that he wasn't supposed to be here. But he was always mine, and he was always with me. He kept me from breaking my neck a few times. I could do stuff, kids' stuff. Like the flying, and the parachute. I was always the first to ride whatever Dale and I could come up with. Jump from the barn roof, swim in the creek. I knew I couldn't get hurt; my friend wouldn't let me. He was always there to help me get through whatever I attempted. I know he was in Nam, but we never spoke, I never saw him."

Sam got up and walked to the counter and poured the last of the coffee, and shut off the coffee pot. "I got to depend on Friend, even after the doctors were convinced that they had made progress with me, and had banished Friend from my psyche. I know in Nam, he was there. I was bulletproof! As a kid I was hyper, I could be hyper and get away with it. I was on medicine to keep me from being hyper. Mom and Dad gave medicine to keep me under control. And I played them like a bass; I would get worked up and agitated, and I would get what ever I wanted. I can't remember too much about Friend in my older years, but I knew how to use my own history. I hadn't thought about Friend in twenty years! But, I have been having these headaches for a few years now."

"What kind of headaches?" Evelyn went to the refrigerator and got a Pepsi.

"I guess you need to know that too; I think it's part of it too. I have headaches that Ruban said were cluster headaches. They started about two years ago. According to the medical books males get them somewhere about fifty years old, and get rid of them later. So I have been taking medicine as needed for the headaches. They give me about a twenty minutes' notice, and I have to take medicine. Even after the medicine they still last for about an hour; I can't even walk when they hit. I take Vicoden that leaves me washed out for several hours after. During one of those headaches, I began to recall my friend.

Wishing that he could help me! They are so bad that I have had the barrel of my pistol in my mouth, cocked and ready to end it all, my finger on the trigger. But a voice would tell me no! I have been a coward many times in the last few years. I would have been done with it all now!"

Sam leaned forward and put his head in his hands and turned slowly back and forth. "I can't do this anymore. I have to tell someone. I'm probably going to have to go to a doctor again, and I don't want to! They will lock me up for sure nowadays; they don't put up with this kind of idiocy." Sam sniffed hard. A tear fell to the table top.

Evelyn leaned forward and grasped Sam's hands firmly. "Sam, you could have said something, and I would have tried to help. Let me get you something to drink. That coffee is cold." Evelyn got up quick and moved toward the refrigerator.

"NO! SIT DOWN!" Sam's voice was demanding.

Evelyn stopped and turned back to the table.

"No, no, I'm sorry; I could use something cold, other than this coffee. I have been trying to understand this, and I don't know how. I'm sorry, you probably want to get out of here now. I don't blame you." Sam picked a napkin out of the holder and wiped his eyes.

Evelyn got back up, crossed over to the refrigerator to get Sam a Coke. She opened the cabinet and picked out a glass, and began to pour the Coke. She then opened the drawer and selected a soft dishtowel. All done she set the Coke down in front of Sam and tucked the dishtowel in between his elbows so he could wipe his eyes without her seeing him do it. "Okay now, when do you get these headaches?"

"I have been trying to figure that out for years now. Nothing in particular causes them. I just don't know. But something happened, something real bad!" Sam raised his head looking at Evelyn, with eyes she had never seen.

Evelyn's alarm was in full throttle now. Her subconscious said, *Run. NOW!* But she stood her ground. Almost fearful for her life. Her mind looked for escape routes. But instead she leaned forward, took Sam's hands in of hers. "Go on, Sam."

"I woke up in a motel, a motel in Sandoval! The Palace." Sam's eyes stayed locked on Evelyn's.

"Sam, that was torn down years ago, when they took out the Y." ALARMS!!!

"Yeah, I know. There I was. I didn't know it was the Palace, till later when I went outside. I ate at Merle's and had a couple of beers at JR's too. I bought toothpaste and a toothbrush at the Country Store. I was there. I think. There were old cars, but they were new, a license plate had 1969 on it.

"You want to run now?" Sam took Evelyn's hands in his now. He thought, *I have to hold on. I can't let her run away!*

Evelyn didn't offer to run, but, deep down, she wanted to. There was a feeling of pity, and a need to help a friend; there was that word "friend." She didn't think she would think of that the same again. This man needed her help. And she felt something else too, she thought it was fear.

Sam related the experience to Evelyn as best he could remember it, all the detail, all the feelings, the people. He remembered to tell about the plastic pill box with the Vicoden. And how he had gotten back just short of being arrested. He held her hands the entire time he related the story. And in the end he looked deep into her eyes to see if she thought he was nuts! "Well?"

VI

"Sam, you have told me about what has happened! What is going to happen! How do we stop whatever this friend thing." Evelyn looked at Sam.

"I don't know. I hope that he never comes back. I don't know what will happen! If he comes to me, and tells me to do whatever… I know that what I've told you really happened! In my mind, or really, I don't know! I think it has happened. I am scared. I fear for what it is. What if it's not all in my mind?" Sam looked lost.

"Sam, it's just like you said, it's a problem that I can't help. I don't want to see you go to some shrink. But… I think it has something to do with the headaches. It is an imbalance of something in your mind. Have you had a physical lately? I mean there's a lot that they find in a physical, that might answer your questions." Evelyn didn't know what to say; a friend, a part-time lover, a boss, and they all needed help.

"You haven't heard me, I think this is real! It's not a dream! Friend was real then, and I think he's back! For what, I don't know. But I don't know how to make you understand. There have been things that have happened in my life, that could not have been accidental. There are things that have kept me alive—

alive when I should have been dead! I need help, but a doctor is not the direction, not yet!" Sam had another look in his eyes now; Sam looked scared.

"Call Friend, get him here, we'll ask him—it's not a him, it's something else. Don't make it a person, it's not real." Evelyn looked back at Sam with concern in her eyes.

"Now you sound just like the doctors. They told me not to personalize it. But I tell you Friend is something, if only in my mind then I have to get it out of my mind. But I am convinced that Friend is real. For whatever is real, in what I have seen, and told you. I don't think I can just call him up. He doesn't live across the street!" Sam pleaded for belief from Evelyn.

"Have you ever tried to contact Friend? I mean really tried?"

"No. I guess never. When I was young I only went outside, or played with whatever, and he was there. Friend never told me in words, but I felt that he didn't like other people. Jealous? Maybe. We never played with anyone together; sometimes he might be around, off to one side." Sam's attempt to analyze what had happened came from years of analysis. It had taken its toll; he even doubted himself now. But he was convinced that Friend was real, as real as when he had been a kid.

"We you need to try and take charge of this and make him appear. I don't know how. If I did, I would have this problem fixed. Sam, I do care, I always have." Evelyn showed a caring that Sam had been afraid of, but not now.

VII

This day began, "Great," in Sam's mind, but Sam's mind was being bombarded from all angles. Inside his own mind he was looking for whatever existed there. Years gone by, memories, any little thing that might unlock what Friend really was, is, whatever. And on the outside, Evelyn, she always asked, but it was different now, and Sam had developed a feeling that he thought had always been there. When she was around there was a concern. That concern was two-sided. Sam would go home, alone, was quite anxious, and the scary feeling. The feeling Sam described as when he and Dale had gone to see *The Thirteen Ghosts*; it was a 3D movie, and you didn't have to wear the glasses to be scared; everyone around you was scared, the screaming would start and you felt the fear in your spine. It moved through you, like the light in the bathroom at night. Sam walked his house at night like a zombie. He would think about Friend, sometimes he would call Friend out loud. Most times he was just jumpy; the slightest noise set him off. The bathroom door was open one night and Sam had walked out of the bedroom, and saw his reflection in the mirror; he had to call Evelyn. He would not talk, just listen for her voice.

Evelyn would look at the caller ID and know it had been Sam. Then Evelyn would go through an hour of "should I call or not." Both had had a difficult two weeks, with no results, except for Sam and Evelyn to both doubt the story. Sam had had bad nights, and had gone to Evelyn's for the night. Sometimes Sam would go to Denny's; twice they had run into each other at Denny's. It was always a surprise, and at the same time it was good. Doubt was set in place; Sam's own doubts, those didn't bother Sam, but Evelyn's doubt was affecting both of them about their relationship.

Sam had all but given up. He had decided that a doctor was the only choice he didn't want to make, but it was the last choice. Sam had lost weight, weight that he didn't have to spare. He was not sleeping. He was walking aimlessly one night through the kitchen and yelled out "Friend" and the voice answered.

"What!" Sam kicked his foot on one of the kitchen chairs. He was hopping about the kitchen, and laughter began, laughter that he heard, not felt.

"Where the Hell have you been? I've waited for a long time." Sam was turning and looking all around the kitchen. "Where are you?"

"I'm always here. I've always been with you. I told you many times ago—was that right? No, no, I told you many years ago. What is a year again? We haven't talked for many times. I can only learn by doing, and from you, no other will teach me. Most are insignificance anyway. I do not converse with any but you, you know. I've been watching and am worried about your health. I can only help when you need help. I can only anticipate when you need me." The voice was almost sorrowful.

"I don't need you, I never needed you! Once you were my friend. Now you haunt my nights, you fill my days with fear. You only appear when you want to, and yet you never appear, only in my head." Sam sat down hard on one of the chairs and it flipped spilling him to the floor. Damn it! Sam's fear was back, or was it relief!

Laughter! "You can still have fun! Just like when we were small. I have memories of our times. All were good." The voice stops as total silence settles back in.

"We need to set down some rules as to when and where you are going to show up." Sam's anger showed through his voice in response to the sudden reappearance, or resounding of the voice, and the humiliation of the laughter. Sam had feelings his life is beginning a new direction and there wasn't room for the voice.

"Sam, I cannot read your mind. I watch, I try to be your best friend and protector. That is why I exist. I'm not going to hurt you. I am not capable of that. I have caused myself to remain in place, through special conditions." The voice seemed to lose all emotion and only dictate words.

"We have been together for a lot of years. I have called you Friend for all those years, but I know nothing about you at all, and then, I wake up in Sandoval. I am scared! I'll tell you that now, I was never scared as a child." Sam walks, and looks behind doors, down the hall, still looking for the shimmering friend from his days gone by.

"Some things I do not have a place in my brain for. I have never understood 'a year.' I too have questions; in younger times I needed not to know, but my time was short. But that was what I was meant to know, but time has changed. I know more now. But now, I too, have questions, many questions." Voice sounds true to the remarks he has made; he sounds sincere.

Sam walks down the hallway in silence. Still looking, still scared.

"Now, you do not talk. I cannot understand this new Sam. What are your questions? I will answer all that you will understand, and you will answer the questions that I ask…" Silence.

Friend stops talking, and Sam becomes aware of the silence; he becomes aware of a void that had been created. "I need to go first, I've got questions that need to be answered now! I've gotten much older, since we played, I don't play anymore. What is your name?" Sam, still cautious, sits down on the couch.

"You have always called me Friend, then that is my name; we are only as you are. None have ever talked with their person before me, none that will tell. We do not converse. Only exchange signs. With you, I have learned to converse. Words only have meaning to you, but now too, with me." Voice is businesslike in the exchange.

"As a child, you became Friend, but you need a name, I can't call you Friend. And what do you mean you are the first?" Sam finds himself sitting as thought he were in the principal's office for some offence.

"I am yours, have always been. Here there is no need in names. I exist for you. I am you. When you came to be, so did I. Understanding, only came with you. I am your other side." The voice seems to almost revert to childhood voice.

"I need a name. What do you want me to call you?" Sam gestures with his hands in front of him like he is bartering with a salesman.

"I am you, so I will be Sam! I have always been Sam; you called me Friend; I liked Friend, but I will now be 'Sam.' That question was easy, but I have come to know the words of your time. I know 'friend' is a good word. Will I still be your friend? If not, I will not like to be Sam." Voice, "Sam," now sounds happy. "I am Sam, Sam I am!"

"'Sam.' Well, I have talked to myself for years, now I will really talk to me, you. And I think that you will be my friend." Sam says the words that he hopes are true. *He can't read my mind, he says. "CAN YOU HEAR ME!"* Sam tries to communicate with his mind. *How come you cannot read my mind, but you talk in my head? I NEED SOMETHING TO DRINK.*

"I do not have all answers. I see you when I do not rest, I do not rest often. I sense when problems in your life happen, or I should say are about to happen. We are only here for you. Most entities that had sign with my entity, before, have left my place I have been; it is required. I have found a direction, and a being that has allowed me, 'Sam,' to be with you. I will be here always; you have directed that." The voice was in character again.

"Where is the place that you live? I need to get something to drink...do you want something?" Sam asked, but Friend, "Sam," has never drank anything in all the year of Sam's life.

"That is something I would experience one time, but not this time. I do not live, I am. I do not understand all about my place; no one can explain. I am told not to inquire. I am in my place now. I have created a place to be when I rest. I will explain to you, my place, if I can." The voice, "Sam," sounds uncertain.

Chapter 4

I

Voice "Sam" begins. "I am because of you; if you no longer exist, nor do I. I knew in one time I would tell you what I am going to try to do so, now. I am not born, I do not come from man and woman. As with your family, creation is caused by birth. I did not understand, and I still do not understand your creation. You were born, I became. I am in my place now, I have always been in my place. Others before me were, in my place; their entity does not exist, and they have gone from my place. Consumption of food elements and liquids is not required. I do not plug in like your drill and saw. I am; I do not question that. In your life there are many people that create, as they think. I have copied that, I have learned, by being 'Sam.' I do not know why most entities do not exist long. I am large, I am you. No other is like me. Most only reach my midsection that you call waist. I became you and liked what you were surrounded with. I have no color, there is only light, light without color. I am, as the doctors that convinced you, I did not exist, not there, I am invisible."

Sam listens without comment till now. "Wait just a minute! I have seen you. You are different than I. But you have shape and form, you have clothes, shoes, and exist. You said so yourself, you are me. If you are me, then you have eyes, and nose, and all the parts, right?" Sam had become increasingly more tired since the conversation had begun, but did not give it any reason. Sam yawned.

"I have shape because I wanted it. I am, as you want me to be. But in my place I do not. No one here would see, because they cannot perceive. I have adapted because I have you. You asked me on our first meeting, 'Are you a spaceman?' I told you no. I know no other answer, and time has changed, but stayed the same. I do not receive from those that have gone from here; I receive, but do not respond any longer; I gain nothing, for time now. I listen but do not receive. If I received they would know." The voice, Sam almost whispered "they"; silence.

Who are they? Sam looked around the room. Nothing seemed to change. No voice either. Sam sat patiently for a few minutes. "Friend...er...I mean, 'Sam,' where the Hell have you gone now?" Sam got up and walked to the front door. He could hear the wind. The outside door was open, and Sam looked out. There were the two boys coming back from the pond. The sun was low in the west. Sam turned and started to the hall, he stopped, and looked about. Nothing changed. Sam walked to the kitchen. As he walked he looked everywhere. "Sam, Sam," he called several times. He heard a knock and dropped the glass he had been carrying. It broke into a thousand small glittering shards.

"Sam, are you okay?" Evelyn called through the back screen.

Sam was taken to the place that everyone knows when taken by surprise, your breath comes quick, your eyes widen, and your face grows pale. Sam was there! "Holy Jesus! You scared me to death!"

Sam looked at all the little pieces of glass all across the floor. "Come in, come in, I'm sorry, I just, I don't know, just surprised to see you."

"Well, with all the fine glassware you have here I had better not come over too much, or you will be drinking out of mason jars. Sam? Sam who?" Evelyn came in, and sat the brown bag she had been carrying on the counter. "Let me get that, you never clean up good." Evelyn opened the closet door, got out the broom, and dust pan. She looked at Sam, who still appeared in shock over a breaking glass. "Are you alright Sam?"

"Yeah. Yeah, I'm fine, just out in never-never land, I guess, and was caught off guard. I have noticed that you have been having quite an effect on me lately!" Sam's voice took on a new lightheartedness of late, and it was back. "Hey, I dropped the damn thing; let me clean it up!"

"I don't think so. You can't even pick up your own underwear in the bathroom, you think I'm going to let you clean up broken glass?" Evelyn continued to sweep.

Sam moved in behind Evelyn and slipped his arm around her waist. Squeezing her tight against him, he kissed her neck. "And how is my little chickadee today"? He kissed her neck again, trying to turn her around.

"Stop that! Let me get this cleaned up, Please!" Evelyn wiggled free from Sam's grasp, she continued to sweep the glass. "Sam, where am I supposed to put this stuff? The trash can hasn't been emptied since I was here last time—look at that!"

Sam took two giant steps, grabbed the trash can, and was out the door. "Slave driver!" Sam called as he exited the backdoor.

Evelyn smiled and returned the broom to the closet. She looked at the sink. It was full of dirty dishes and still had water in it. *He's turning into a bum, but I still like him,* she thought. She let out the cold greasy water and began to take the dishes out of the sink and run fresh water. *With soap!* Evelyn thought.

Sam was back in a few minutes with the empty plastic trash can and was looking for a trash bag in the closet. "Evie, are there any more trash bags?"

"How would I know? But you could look in the bag on the counter. I picked up a few things that I thought you might need. I don't know why, but I guess it's a good thing I did." The water was good and hot now, and had soap suds showing as the water level began to rise. "Sam, I know that you have had a lot on your mind lately, but really. You have to get a handle on life, as we know it."

"No I don't! I've got you! Never need to do nothing!" Sam put the trash bag into the plastic trash can, and dumped the dust pan with the broken glass. "I had thought about the old Russian proverb, of keeping you 'barefoot and pregnant'; thought I might work on that later." Sam smiled and rocked back on his heels, hooking his thumbs into imaginary suspenders.

Evelyn gave Sam a look over shoulder. "If things don't improve around here you will be sleeping alone all the time. And for your information, I'm too damn old to be pregnant, my nerves won't handle kids, I've got you to raise, and I sure as Hell am not going to be barefoot! There are shoe salesmen that would go broke without me!"

"Yeah, like those little darlings you have on now, those couldn't be a day older than, maybe, six years old. For God's sake, Evie, those are tied together with string. People will think I don't pay you anything!" Sam's pleading voice was falling on deaf ears.

"Well, I will be asking for a raise soon! I finished with that asshole Morisson, today. That man thinks the sun rises and sets upon his brow." Evelyn was scrubbing the dishes as she talked. "This stuff, whatever you ate, is glued to the plate. You need to use paper plates if you're not going to wash them."

"You haven't heard a word I've said. How about being pregnant? Or at least practicing!" Sam was grinning like a little kid now.

"I might could be coerced into a little practice." Evelyn looked over her shoulder again. "That is if I can ever get this grunge off of these dishes. We might have to skip practice and make a trip to the store for new dishes."

Sam was behind Evelyn at the sink, his hands around her waist. "Just a little practice, I needed it, the practice I mean."

"Practice, practice, practice. You don't need practice, you need the real thing. But if you don't leave me alone long enough so I can get these dishes done, there will be nothing around here! Now go away!" Evelyn shrugged her shoulders and went back to cleaning the dishes.

Sam did leave her alone. As he went to the bathroom to make sure it was clean, he thought, *Should I tell her? If I don't, and she finds out I will be in trouble, she will never trust me. But she may think that I'm crazy now.* The bathroom was pretty clean, so he moved to the bedroom. Straighten up the bed a bit. The blankets had not been pulled down for two days; Sam could not remember if he had slept in the bedroom in the last two days.

The living room was next. There he found the problems, two glasses a coffee cup and a partially eaten bag of potato chips; he tasted one. Stale, these have to go! Sam picked up his leftovers and headed for the kitchen. "Well, here are a few items up for cleaning. I don't have any idea as to how they got in the living room, but there they were. Now if you would be so kind as to wash these for your humble servant, he would be so very happy. And would promise never to allow anyone to leave these eating utensils in the living quarters again." Sam bent and kissed Evelyn on the neck and slipped to the backdoor and dropped the bag of chips in the trash.

"I saw that! You've been living in the living room, haven't you? Sam, you have to get some rest. I've sat on that couch, it's uncomfortable to sit on, let alone sleep on. I told you that you were going to have to get some rest, and a new couch." She knew he had been up most nights looking for that damn friend. Evelyn was beginning to wonder about what she had gotten herself into. Sam had only been into the office twice in the last few weeks. There were no signs of improvement; Friend had taken all his time. "Friend," now that was a name, a name for something that was slowly driving him crazy. Evelyn wasn't sure, but she had some feelings for Sam that had perhaps been brought about by Friend. The same friend that was pulling them apart now.

Sam came back into the kitchen as Evelyn was finishing cleaning up his messes. "I suppose the living room is off the deep end too!" Evelyn hawked at Sam.

"What's the matter, Evie? I know I haven't been attentive lately. Hell, I know that I've been way out there, and I know that you have about had it with my invisible friend. That is, a little hard to swallow. But I have to tell you, I'm not sure how to start, but I'll try." Sam shifted his weight from one foot to another, like a four-year-old.

Evelyn had her hands wrapped in the dish towel. She had been drying them but was frozen in motion. Her eyes downcast now only seeing the movement of Sam's feet. "Sam, I want to believe you, I want to believe everything, but I just don't know anymore. Sam, I have feelings that I don't know about. I... I'm afraid, not of you, but what's happening. I am scared!" Evelyn turned to the counter going through the motions of wiping the counter.

"Evie, I want to talk tonight about us." Sam grasped her shoulders gently.

"Not tonight, Sam." Evelyn simply left the dishrag lay, turned toward the door and walked out.

Sam did not move, only watched as Evelyn got into her car, and turned around and left. "Damn! Why didn't you go after her, try to stop her? No, you and your friend will fix everything." Sam sat down in a kitchen chair. He felt something wet that began to run down his right cheek; he didn't try to wipe it. Sam watched as the sun set in the west. The moisture dried on his face, as his world grew darker.

II

Southern Illinois had turned into a strange place in the last few days. Carl had become a field department head, his men, all twenty of them, were busy little bees. They were canvassing the whole southern part of the state looking for more "funny money." None had been found but they had only gotten as far south as Mt. Vernon, as yet. Department heads from the FBI and the Treasury Department wanted answers to the question of where it had came from. There had only been forty-one dollars found. A twenty, three fives, six ones, and two quarters, a nickel, and three pennies. As the agents went from business to business they were asked repeatedly why there was such a big fuss over forty-one dollars. All the bills were obvious fakes. The pictures were a laughing stock to think that anyone would go to such pains about all the other detail, and put such large pictures on the bills.

"Lou, have you ever seen such a ragtag bunch of agents in your life? These guys look like they just got out of the academy." Lou was smoking, again; he blew the smoke out the door. It had cooled off, but it was too warm to have the door closed at the Palace. Most of the agents stayed in Centralia, at Stay Inn, a few were in Salem at Dave's Place. But they all checked in at the Palace with Carl and Lou before calling it a day.

Carl was sitting at the table Rick had set up for them. Lou roomed next door. Carl looked at the sheet in front of him again. "Those two, Steve and Butch, haven't checked in yet?" Carl double-checked his list; he had to call in each evening to Springfield before five, with Mr. Lammer. Mr Lammer had been moved from Effingham to Springfield, someone was making progress with this deal.

"No, it's probably that damn car again. It keeps overheating. I told them that that little Nova wouldn't hold up to those two. They drive like they are at the Indy. It's a kid's car."

Lou dropped the cigarette and stepped out on the walk to put it out. "Well, is it going to be Merle's or Jim's tonight?" Lou looked to the west as the sun was setting. "You've already missed the call time for Lammer. Let's go eat."

A cloud of dust began to come up the drive to the Palace. Mechanical wheezes and knocking could be heard coming out from the cloud of dust. The cloud was moving toward the Palace at an alarming rate. Rocks flew, and the rattling tried to stop, then start, and finally ending in one last long wheeze, followed by hissing. The cloud could now be distinguished as hot steam coming from under the hood of the 1968 Chevy Nova. The door flew open and two figures emerged. The mist of the cloud followed them toward Carl's room.

Carl was keeping himself from falling from the room by holding both sides of the door facing. Lou looked at Carl and smiled, his smile turned into laughter. Carl called to Steve, he thought it was. "Lawmen, just like the Lone Ranger, a cloud of dust and a mighty Hi Ho Silver. Where's Tonto? Oh, there he is." Carl was laughing loud enough for them to hear over the hissing.

"That's about enough. For a supervisor you are not very professional." Steve slapped at his arms as if trying to swat a fly away. "This smell will never leave and I only brought one other suit. I hope there is a dry cleaner here."

"Yeah, there's one downtown." Carl wiped his eyes. "You guys have just about killed that one haven't you?" Carl knew that he was supposed to be in a supervisor position, but he just couldn't help himself. "I've got to get a movie camera if you guys keep up the entertainment. You look like those movie fellers."

Butch was the last to exit the steaming Nova. "Aw, Carl, don't say it, we'll drive your car tomorrow." Butch spit and cleared his throat. "That damn stuff has been in that car for the last few miles. I rolled up the window to keep it out and asshole there rolled his down! That taste is in my mouth and there's no amount of Budweiser that will make it go away!"

"Budweiser, you say, not a bad idea. But first, you have anything to report?" Lou asked, as he watched the two newest members of the FBI team slap their clothes trying to rid themselves of the antifreeze smell.

Carl being the supervisor tried to get himself in a professional posture for the newbies.

"What the devil are we really looking for? People look at us like we're idiots. We tell them that we're looking for money with a large picture on it, and we have had a few tell us to go to the Ben Franklin." Butch chimed in with Steve and their heads began to nod like bobblehead dolls. "We represent the FBI ,and we're looking for play money."

Steve was taking his coat off and brushing it with his hand. "No one has even heard about this. The local cops say that they got printouts but don't know why anyone would ever be able to pass something like that. I even had a cop in Mt. Vernon tell me to go to the Ben Franklin. They think that we're onto something else." Steve continued to brush his coat.

Butch was leaning against Carl and Lou's car with his arms folded across his chest. He pushed his sunglasses down on his nose. "You guys aren't keeping anything from us are you?"

Carl spoke first. "We just got a call today to expand the search, and to give all the agents more information. You boys are the last to check in. Find a seat and I'll give you the scoop." Carl gestured, inviting the two young agents into his room.

Butch squared off like a boxer and punched Steve on the shoulder. "I told you there was more to it than what we've been looking for. They wouldn't keep agents out here in the sticks without a good reason. And play money ain't a good reason. I told you!"

"Yeah, yeah. I'll wait and hear what Carl's got before I go to shooting my mouth off. We might be looking for Barbie dolls tomorrow. Steve walked over to the couch and flopped down. And what are we going to do for a car? That one's dead, I think we killed it today. I told them this morning that it was overheating and they looked at me like I was nuts."

"It will have to go to the dealer tomorrow. I think that's in Salem. I guess you will have to use our car tomorrow. Now what you're going to do tomorrow, as well as what you're doing already is to go to any kind of printing establishment too! You are going to have to check all of them no matter how small. The people that might get into counterfeiting will not probably be the mainstream businesses." Carl handed each of them a piece of paper the size of a dollar bill. "That, gentlemen, is a dollar bill without any printing. It's quite valuable. These counterfeiters are capable of producing this paper, or obtaining it from a source. The FBI wants to know where the source is located. There is a big inventory at all the mints now, to see if they are missing any amount of paper. The bills we are showing everyone are copies."

"Like we couldn't tell that already. Just who makes the paper for the government?"

Steve sat up and leaned forward; his interest was back to the job now. "Maybe some real criminals out there after all, not just dime stores."

Lou lit another cigarette and stepped forward. "You guys have been through the academy in the last year and should remember that better than us. It's been a while since we have even been out of Missouri and Illinois, and Carl here never leaves St. Louis if he can help it."

"You sound like my wife now. This is getting really big, because there is the problem of the change, the coins." Carl looked at the two. He knew that they had not heard that part yet, and probably hadn't even thought of that, because no one had ever tried to counterfeit coins.

"Coins! Who has ever heard of anyone counterfeiting coins?" Butch had found a chair, and was about to sit down till he heard that part. "Now I guess all metal fabricating shops go on the list too!" Butch moved to the center of the room with Lou.

"That's why the Treasury wants us in this mess too. They aren't saying, but it's almost like some kind of communist plot thing, trying to ruin the economy, as if Viet Nam wasn't doing that well enough by itself. In the morning the two of you are going with us. The big boys have located a Sam Young. He isn't really our problem, since he's in South Viet Nam right now, somewhere neat Tahy Nhin Province, wherever the Hell that is." Carl took a drink out of his hot Coke and grimaced.

Lou held his hand up, as if he were in school. "I know, I know. That' where all our young men are dying for God only knows what." Lou's sarcasm was showing.

Carl only looked at Lou. You could tell there was a difference of opinion in that regard. "That's enough of that bullshit too. Don't get me started. His folks live south of Salem, on US Route 37. Tomorrow, we, the four of us, will visit Sam's parents and see what they might know about any of this. There are five other Sam Youngs in the state of Illinois, ten or eleven in Missouri, and a list of counterfeiters, on the loose, all around the Midwest that have quote unquote served their time. We can pick up another car for the two of you to destroy, on the way through Salem. I have talked to the locals and the sheriff's office. Mr. Wams is supposed to come by here tonight. It seems young Mr. Young ran around here in Sandoval till the US Army found something for him to do in Southeast Asia. His parents frequent the Liberty and JR's regularly. Nothing comes up on any of them. But I want to talk to Harold, about Mr. Young, and see what he knows. He knows the kids around here, he might have something, who knows."

Butch was aglow with the possibilities tomorrow might bring. "Guns and glory, we're going to be famous tomorrow, Steve. We will be in on the biggest bust of the year."

"You can knock that BS off too. These are regular folks, and it will be a regular day—ask questions, and make plans for our next move. And it goes without saying nothing can be said about the coins. Some of the locals might have an idea, but we don't spread it any further than this motel room. This has gotten serious, the bureau is really looking hard on how this is handled, the tip of an iceberg kind of a deal. Lou and I don't have too many years left out here in the badlands, and this can't get screwed up. Everybody is looking at this investigation with a microscope; somebody steps out of line and they will know. This could be a feather in you boys' cap, or it could really fuck you too. So watch what you do tomorrow."

"I was just BS'ing. We will be professional, at least I will be. Now Steverino there burns up our transportation; I'm not sure he is the caliber that this mission calls for!" Butch smiles and looks innocently toward Steve.

"You didn't think that car would last either. Don't try and look so damn innocent."

"You wanted an undercover convertible, if I remember right." Steve smiled and looked back at Butch.

"That's about as undercover as we could look. I mean who would look at two cool dudes in a convertible and think that they would be FBI agents." Butch smiled.

Lou thought the convertible was a good idea but he kept quiet. "We've got to go to Merle's and make my late telephone call. You two going to eat with us? Or I can give you the list that we have made from the local phone books, now. I need to get some of my stuff out of the car, I don't want it to burn down on the next run!" He smiled.

Carl chimed in, "I have some paperwork in there too. Lou, you want to get that for me and I will go over to Merle's and get us a table and make my call. What's it going to be, gentlemen? Eats at Merle's or hamburgers at some drive-in?" Carl moved a stack of papers to the bed and sorted them until he found the one with all the notes paper clipped to it and folded it up, with all the notes attached it appeared to be wadded instead of folded.

"What's Merle's got in the way of food?" Butch asked.

"It's a truck stop, most of the local truckers eat there, and they have it all. A regular Ritz of the Midwest! The food is good, service fair and they all stare at you since they know your famous FBI agents, looking for funny money. What can I say, it's either Merles or Jim's. But the telephone at Merle's is a little more private." Carl picked up his jacket and started toward the door.

"Forget something, partner?" Lou had his usual look of impatience.

"What now? Oh, yeah!" Carl returned to the bed and picked up his pistol and slid it into his pants, wiggling and twisting to get the holster to slide back in place. "Once it's in place it's comfortable, really!"

They all watched as he continued to adjust his holster on his waist band. They turned and exited the spacious accommodations of the Palace Motel. They made small talk as they walked past the still smoking Nova. It had a large pool of water and antifreeze under it now. And a greasy film was on the windshield. Steve and Butch had made a decision to eat at Merle's. Their decision was made without discussion; they wanted to know more about tomorrow. Neither had been on a mission that they were not being evaluated on; this was a real mission.

As the foursome crossed the driveway and were about to step up on the sidewalk, a light toot of horn caught Steve's attention. "Don't look now, guys, but it looks like the Treasury Department might join us for dinner." The plain green Chevy Biscayne pulled up, parking next to the building.

Johnny and Albert got out of the front of the car, a young woman out the passenger rear behind Johnny, and Harold. Harold nodded to the four. Johnny walked to the front of the car and waited on the woman. "Gentlemen, I would like to introduce you to Terri Joanses. She comes to us from DC, to offer some technical knowledge." Introductions were made to all, handshakes and pleasantries all around. The air was a little thick; someone new not always accepted into a group that was having enough trouble trying to make heads or tails of a simple counterfeit case that appeared to be blowing up higher.

Terri spoke to the group on the sidewalk before the group went inside. "Can we talk in here? I mean this is pretty serious."

Carl assured her that all the locals gave them a wide birth, FBI and all. And that he used the back telephone, and they sat at that table that was by itself, in the back anyway.

Sure as Carl had said when they entered, Merle's became unusually quiet; all heads turned and watched as they moved the length of the restaurant and took up seats. Carl walked around the waist-high partition to the phone, he looked at them and smiled while digging his wallet out of his hip pocket. He read the numbers from his phone card and leaned against the wall and waited for a connection.

At the table all were getting comfortable, with the new grouping of government workers. They spoke mostly about the weather, traffic and such. The newest of the group was Terri; she broke the silence. Not fearing any repercussions, she asked if Harold was aware of all aspects of the investigation. Steve and Butch tried to look as though they knew, but in fact did not. Lou told the others to wait till Carl was finished with his call, as he might have something to add to the information that might have been gathered today by the big boys. So the group was back to uncomfortable small talk. Only to be saved by Wilma.

"How's Lou today?" Wilma asked, as she came up to the table pad in hand. "Seems you have developed a following. Can they be trusted?" Wilma smiled, pad and pen poised for orders.

Lou smiled back. "Well, Wilma, I'm not really sure if they can be trusted or not! Wilma, this is Steve, Butch, and Terri, I believe you know Harold." Lou made introductions around the table as Carl had finished with his call and returned to the table standing beside Wilma.

"I'm sorry, Carl. Just push me out of the way, I just came over here for the latest on your investigation." She laughed. "Now what can I get you all this evening?"

Carl looked about the table and back to Wilma. "Hon, I think coffee all around till we decide, and bring me that cream in the little pitcher, okay."

"Bring me Coke please." Steve spoke up before Wilma turned away.

"Do you want coffee too?" Wilma's pen was poised over the order pad again.

"No, no, I don't know how these guys can drink that stuff all the time." Steve looked about the table, and saw Terri covering her smile. "I suppose you drink it all day long too!" Steve looked at Terri and her attempts to keep from laughing. "I don't think it's that damn funny!"

"It's not what you said it'd the way you said it. You sound like my older brother, and it struck me funny; he has never drank coffee. And when anyone asks he says the same thing, and you sound just like Ted." With the snickers gone Terri lowered her hand back to her lap.

"Do you want coffee, Terri? I mean you don't have to drink it just because we are."

Carl sat down and was adjusting his holster again.

"Well, Carl, I won't be needing any of the cream out of the little pitcher, either. I like mine strong and black." Terri looked back at Carl. Carl still adjusting his holster looked away after that return comment.

"Well, young lady, you'll love this coffee. I think it's in a great big old pot out back and they just add more water as it goes down. It's damn near too strong for me, but being a real FBI agent it's a requirement that some haven't learned yet." Lou put on his official face and leaned back in the chair. Laughter was all around the table except for Steve. After a few seconds he too was laughing.

That was all it took to break the ice that had formed, as small talk started to take on the usual questions about family, friends, and pets. Orders were taken and food consumed, before business was placed on the table for discussion. All had refills on coffee, and Wilma brought Steve another Coke. Carl was the official FBI ranking man at the table so he started the conversation. Only after Terri had given Harold another cursory glance.

Carl caught the glance the new Treasury Department agent had given Harold and started there. "First off, I want to welcome Terri to our midst. And

I know you wondered about Harold. He is in on everything. That was my call. I have been given a free hand in how I handle this investigation as they refer to it. Harold knows all the people here, and in most of the surrounding towns as well. Without Harold we would have been chasing our tails even more than we have been."

Harold just nodded and gave Carl the look of "Thanks." Harold knew he was a small-town cop, and most the big FBI boys were a little hard to get along with. But Lou and Carl had been fair with him.

"As I know you three have been told that they think, that this is really much larger than a little town counterfeiting ring. There are agents all over the Midwest looking for the same things as we are; it just started here. There's no reason to discuss how or why they need us to find all that we can first. It has been passed to me that the quality of workmanship is excellent. The coins are why the hunt has spread so wide. The coins are, in the FBI quote, perfect." Carl paused for all the ooh's and ahh's to come out. "What is wrong is the date. The mint has been known to make a few imperfections in the past but they were caught after a few and not many have ever gotten out, into circulation. These are so good, that it is expected the cities will be flooded with coins soon. No one has ever attempted to copy coins as it would take so many to make it profitable. The makeup of the metal is perfect, the design is perfect, the coins are perfect." Lou jerked his head to the side toward the counter. Carl knew his partner's little quirks, and stopped talking.

Wilma had the coffee pot in her hand and moved closer to the table having to wedge her way in as Albert had slid his chair to the end of the table for more room. "Thought you might need a little warm up. You found any more of that funny money? And since I found the first ones, do you think that I could get that five back when this is over?"

"There have been some given out in the past. On this particular one I don't know; every case is different. When did you notice the picture on the five—it was a five wasn't it?" Terri took the lead in answering.

Wilma wasn't sure she liked the new lady speaking; she had gotten used to dealing with Carl and Lou. Wilma thought that they might be able to do something, and now this little lady was spouting chapter and verse. Wilma had figured that she had given these two her best, and had stayed on their good side and all. "Well, I don't know much about what the law's going to do, I just wanted it for a souvenir. I mean that night at the end of the shift I was counting my tips—they aren't great here but it helps—and I looked at that and I showed it to Merle, and he laughed about me getting play money tips! And that pissed me off! I'm sorry! Sometimes I just think about that night and how I was concerned that he was sick or something. But if you could do something I would really appreciate it; I'd frame it and tell the story to my grand kids one day." Wilma smiled and thought that was that the little lady had horned in, and she would never see that five again.

"Anything else? We have some good apple pie, and some lemon meringue pie today."

Butch and Carl both spoke. They opted for the apple pie immediately and Terri wanted the lemon. Steve, Harold, and Lou were good. Johnny and Albert wanted pecan. Wilma smiled and wrote down the order and was gone.

"Nice kid!" Carl spoke up as soon as Wilma was out of earshot. Carl looked at Harold and nodded.

"They all had their times, just like we did when we were that age, and that's been a while ago, eh Carl?" Harold smiled at Carl.

"That it has been. Never any real trouble, just BS. And didn't you say she knew this Sam Young?" Carl was back to be an FBI agent for his comrade in arms.

"Yeah, they were a wild bunch, drinking and drag racing, and driving in the exit at the drive-in. But never any real trouble. Don't think that anyone one of them was smart enough to have copied the bills, and the coins are a real piece of work. Merle still doesn't know that we took him for an additional fifty-eight cents. That is still something to see when they are done that good." Harold tipped up his cup.

"Perfect, is what the treasury says?" Johnny had chimed in at Harold's comment.

"That's why were all here, that's why I'm here," Terri said flatly. "Wilma is the first, so I need to set up an interview ASAP." Terri looked over her coffee cup, awaiting any dissension.

They had all wondered how this had gotten as big as it had. Now with this statement, there arose a renewed wonder. All sat quietly, and thought how their asses were covered, or what might have been let go to the sideline. Coffee cups seemed to be the object of everyone's attention as Wilma came back with pie.

"Wilma, my name is Terri Joanses. I'm with the Treasury Department. Could I talk with you just a minute!" Terri's voice flat and cold; the agent was back.

"Sure." Wilma set down the pie in front of each recipient as ordered. "Right now. Or would you like to have your pie first?" Wilma wasn't smiling anymore.

"Just a second if we could." Terri was recovering her purse and getting up.

"Sure, we can go over to the waitress station. There's never anyone over there." Wilma pointed to the little area at the end of the counter.

Wilma and Terri walked across the restaurant to the small waitress area. All heads at the table turned to watch the two women move across the room. Those seated at the counter watched too; they knew these were government people. Most were local truck drivers, and they didn't like the government, just because it was the government, and they were screwing with their people. But some thought the government might know something about the waitress that they didn't know; maybe she knew something about counterfeiting that they had not been told. Little town girl, wanting to make some money. Just a little extra money. One never knew now a days, these kids got on that dope and you never knew what was screwing with their minds. Conversation was quiet now, but all had their own opinions as to what was going on in the back room, and the agents were no exception.

"Carl, what's that all about? We talked to that kid, and she has done everything we asked." Lou asked for the ashtray and lit a cigarette, his coffee and pie still on the table untouched.

"Well, I sure as Hell don't know. Johnny, what is she, who is she? I haven't got any information from Lammers." Carl asked. He had his fork poised over his pie, waiting for the answer before beginning.

"Al?" Johnny held up as well, his cup in his hand.

"Why does everything rotate around me? I just got the call that an agent was coming, Terry, not a Terri." Albert was just as much at a loss as anyone. "I'm always pegged as the one that knows what the fuck is going on. I'm just like you guys. Don't fucking believe that the bookworm knows everything."

Now everyone was at a loss; the thought of cursing coming out of Albert's lips had never been an option. Albert forked his pecan pie and began shoveling it down. They all looked at each other and began to laugh.

"Al, that was amazing! I didn't think you had those words in there anywhere." Lou tapped Al's head with his index finger.

Albert smiled and kept eating, and the rest started anew what was the latest subject, pie! Small talk around again. Those at the counter still didn't trust those government people but the laughter allowed them to go back to their conversations. They would keep watching those guys, and they would feel better when they were gone from Sandoval. But seeing them laugh allowed them to know that they were at least part human.

Wilma and Terri came back across the room and were smiling. They heard all the laughing and did not think it was about them. "Okay, about two tomorrow. At the Palace in Carl's room." Terri looked at Carl. "Carl, we're using your room tomorrow for a couple of hours."

"Okay, I don't know what you will find, but you're welcome to look. I guess that's your job, huh?" Carl began on his pie again. "You are a Treasury Department investigator, aren't you? I guess they don't trust the FBI anymore."

"That's not it and you know it. You and Lou have been in the FBI for some time now." Terri was cut short by Lou.

"Is that it, we're getting old, we're surrounded by kids. Steve or Butch here can do the investigating then!" Lou stuck his fork in the remaining pie, and held it there as if to keep it from running away.

"Now, Lou," Terri started.

"There's no 'now Lou'! Just tell me"! Lou had raised up off his seat and leaned toward Terri.

"Agent Marks. Calm yourself. I don't want to be in the field because of this BS. I have been with the Treasury for some time now. I may look quite young by your standards, but let me assure you that I'm not a baby. I have been doing this job for some time now. And every time I go to the field, and out of that Goddamn office, I catch Hell from some other agent that feels threatened. Have I made myself clear!" Terri held her fork in defense mode against any attacks that might come. Her claws had started the battle and her fork would finish it.

"It seems that we have had two revelations at this meal! Me, I'm about to have some of that pecan pie. Wilma." Harold turned his head away from the rest and looked for Wilma.

"Pecan pie, right, Harold. Wilma smiled and gave a little hand wave; she had heard it all. Wilma turned and headed for the counter again.

"Handled that nicely, didn't we!" Steve's sarcasm was showing. "How is that pie?"

Terri, seated now, knew what the conversation had been. Or at least thought what it had been.

"The department has a mode of operation; you are here to bring that out, and we will follow what you decide." Butch was venturing into the conversation slowly. "We have been chasing our tails and would appreciate any new ideas that your department might have." Butch sat quietly waiting for the next explosion. None came.

"I am paid a lot of money to do a job of a bookkeeper in our office. To get out here into the field with agents that keep the faith and make things happen is what I want to do. I would appreciate any and all help that I can get from all of you. I'm not here to undermine anything that you have already done. I am a woman, and may be able to look at the same things that you have already done differently. Then we will get together and compare notes, see if something is just a little different, anything. Okay, guys, all I want is a little help, I'm not here to take over." Terri leaned back and unbuttoned her jacket. "Lou what are you smoking?"

"Winstons." Lou handed her the opened pack.

Harold had his lighter out and working, and lit her cigarette.

Terri inhaled deeply, she exhaled. "I needed that!"

They all laughed and began eating their desserts. Wilma was back with the coffee pot and refilled all the cups. Steve shook his head no when Wilma looked at his half-full glass. The conversation was subdued. The only voice was that of Harold. "I think I can work with her, and how about you guys?" They all nodded and kept eating. And Wilma, by the waitress's door, smiled. She did well on tips that day, no funny money either.

III

Evelyn had talked to herself for the last two days. She had not come to any conclusions. She had heard her own voice aloud. That had been a little unnerving at first, then, it had began to give her someone to talk to. She had heard Sam talk to himself for some time now, in the years in the office; she had gotten used to it, she thought. Evelyn had never said anything to him about it. She smiled when she thought about Sam, and she also frowned inside. Inside, where she had always trusted her judgment. Now that wasn't a known factor anymore. She worried for Sam's mental health; she worried about what he might do to himself. "You sure helped his self-image along! Yeah, well, what was I supposed to do? I was lost! I am going to tell him that I feel that he needs to see a doctor. Boy, are you going to be a real hit there! Well, that settles it, a doctor it is, no matter what he says or does!"

"Aaaahem. Here's your mail, Evelyn. Are you alright?" The mailman George looked a little hesitant.

"Yeah, I was just discussing something. And I sometimes talk out loud to hear it clearly." Evelyn had laid her hand to her chest. George had really slipped in that time. He always crept around. Evelyn took the mail from George. "Thanks, George."

George was on his way out. *Now that girl needs help,* he thought.

"Way to go, Evelyn! Now the mailman thinks your nuts too." That's what Sam had said. That's what she had thought. Evelyn sat on the edge of her desk, as the phone began to ring. Evelyn looked at the caller ID. "I don't know you and don't intend to start finding out what you want today." Evelyn looked at her watch. It was four-thirty. Thirty minutes past time for her to leave anyway. George was late today, or he had been watching her walk about and talking to herself. She thought the latter; he was always looking anyway, always looking and creeping about. Evelyn picked up her purse and looked about the office. "Good enough. I'm the only one that sees this place anymore." She put the keys into the deadbolt and turned; she heard the bolt slide across, just as she had for years. Everything's the same, as always, but different now. Good or bad she was going to talk to Sam tonight.

Evelyn started her car, shut off the radio, checked her hair, adjusted. Readjusted the mirror, and leaned back in the seat. "Where do I start? Sam, we need to talk. No. I'm not his mother or his doctor. Just what am I? A concerned friend, that sleeps over occasionally. Not too often lately." Evelyn backed the car up, put it in drive.

George had come back from down the street to get into his Jeep, saw Evelyn and walked over. "Are you alright, Evelyn?"

"Oh, George! Yes, I'm just having one of those days—everything is a mess today." Evelyn was caught again talking to herself, and by George.

"Okay." George turned and started to the Jeep again. *I'd like to have one of your days and nights!* George thought and he smiled; he was a dirty old man and he liked it.

"Oh my Gawd! If you don't pull yourself together!" Evelyn sat quietly.

Decisions were made and she was off to the store—steaks, baked potatoes, peas and a little bottle of wine. Then whatever came of the situation, would. Evelyn back in control drove into Salem to the Wal-Mart to shop. She ran into several friends that she hadn't seen in a while. A few didn't make anything out of asking how she and Sam were doing. All of them would say, somewhere in the conversation, that they really didn't know Sam. All knew who Sam was, and what he did for a living. But none really knew Sam. A few were even forward enough to ask if he was quiet in private as he was in public; they didn't really know him he was a recluse, they heard. Evelyn wanted to tell them that he might be reclusive, but not a hermit. He sold property for a living, he was out in the public every day, not on an occasion, but every day. At least till lately, a few had asked her if she was alright, they hadn't seen her in a while. Had she been on a diet, she looked good. It had been a long trudge through the grocery. Then she ran into Mr. Morrison, of all places, the checkout. It was Friday, and the lines were slow. And Evelyn's day was going down the tubes.

"Evelyn, how are you? I know we have talked a lot lately, but I haven't seen you in a while. You made that deal so good, and all the paperwork finished, all I had to do was sign, and send a check. You should be in the sales part, and let Sam do the secretary end." He laughed.

"Thank you, Mr. Morrison. Sam's been under the weather lately and I've had to do some extra." She really disliked Morrison, and could only wish the line would move faster. But she kept on her happy face, for business, and that alone.

They exchanged lies and the line inched forward slowly. Evelyn looked at what Morrison was holding—no cart, just a box and a toothbrush. "Mr. Morrison, you can go in front of me. Looks like you're on a trip, forgot your toothbrush."

"Yes, I'm here overnight. In the morning I'm meeting with the engineers on that property. Gotta get it started if I ever intend to make any money out of it. What are you doing tonight? I am here alone tonight. Linda stayed in Decatur, something with the kids. You and I could have a drink later. I'm here at the Holiday Inn." His smile looked pasted on.

Evelyn had always thought that his smile looked like a sneer, and there it was. Evelyn didn't like the man to start with, and this engagement wasn't helping. "Well, Mr. Morrison, I am sitting with friends tonight, they aren't doing well and I really can't. Maybe some other time." She put on the best smile she could muster after that pickup line. It was finally her turn. "Here, Mr. Morrison, you get in here I've got a lot of things and I don't want to hold you up." Evelyn was still smiling.

"Thank you, Evelyn. I have to remember to tell Sam what a special lady he has working for him, very special indeed. And just remember that if you can get away I'm staying at the Holiday just down the street. And there's no need to be so formal, it's just Gary." *Hope her friend sends her away; I'd like a shot at that. Keep smiling, Gary, you can win her over.*

Gary paid for his things and walked away after acting like he was tipping his hat to Evelyn.

The cashier asked if she was okay; it had seemed that man seemed to bother her. Evelyn assured her that business kept her from spreading the truth about some people. She paid for her groceries and made her way to through the parking lot. There she stashed all the groceries, and got in and started the car. That's when she discovered she was ready. Ready for what might become the end of her and Sam. But the condemned would have a fine meal first. She smiled; it felt good and she was right.

The drive to Sam's was only about ten minutes. Had it been much longer her subconscious would have stopped her. *If I would have to drive to Sandoval, I would turn around and go home.* Evelyn thought, *At least I'm thinking and not talking aloud anymore.* At the driveway she hesitated before she made the turn. *Go for it, this is no longer just for him!* As her car pulled up behind the house she saw Sam's old car and his truck. She hadn't even thought about him not being at home; she thought that she was happy that he was there.

It was late afternoon about an hour before sunset. The light was shining in Sam's back door. Evelyn pushed the door open with her foot and set the bags down on the counter.

Evelyn looked about the kitchen. Two glasses in the sink; she smiled. Then the hair on the back of her neck stood on end.

Sam's voice was clear, not loud, but close. It had the same angry tone she had heard in her dealings with him in the office. He hadn't gotten angry yet, but close. Then the other voice, familiar voice, calm and measured. "Sam, have I come at a wrong time?" Evelyn moved down the hallway slowly, turned slightly in case she had to leave in a hurry. *Now why would you have to leave in a hurry?* she thought.

"I'm tired of this. You tell me you have a plan—what kind of a plan? I'm really beginning to believe that your only in my mind, and I'm just about to go crazy trying to get you out of there! I see nothing, I don't see you. I assume that you have a mind? I don't really know that, now do I?"

The other, familiar voice. "I will show you who I am soon. I can't yet...Of course I have a mind, I must have. Sam thought I'm thinking so I have to have a mind. That is how I have been able to plan, and make all happen that has happened." Sam was thinking when a distraction became too close.

"Sam? I will come back later. I'll just put the groceries away."

"Evelyn?" Sam.

"Evelyn?" "Sam."

"Yes, Sam. Are you alright?" Evelyn thought all her hair was standing on end now. I didn't mean to interrupt. I came to fix dinner. Evelyn couldn't leave she couldn't even move. She was scared, very scared. She felt herself getting lightheaded, she leaned against the wall. Evelyn tried to stop....

"Evelyn!" Sam took the five giant steps needed to get to Evelyn in his short hallway.

"Now see what you've done, what I've done."

"You know that I have to go now!" the voice, 'Sam,' panic, and sadness in its tone.

Sam looked over his shoulder as though he was about to see something like in normal life, but his hadn't been normal for some time now. Friend had a tone to his voice Sam had never heard, excitement, panic! "Don't go! Stay so Evie will see that I'm not nuts." Sam was sliding his hand under Evelyn's head, feeling for blood or whatever and trying to cushion between the floor and Evelyn. "Friend." "Sam." Stay, I need you to...

"You know the rules, do you not? We will have to discuss the rules at a later time." Silence.

Sam knew "Sam" was gone. He focused his attention to Evelyn. He brushed her hair to the side so he could see her face. Evelyn's eyes fluttered and came full, wide open. She looked about, then back to Sam almost as if he were a stranger, all the while her hands tried to find purchase on anything that would give her leverage to get up.

"Sam? Who was here? I didn't mean to intrude, I came to fix dinner and we could..."

Evelyn's voice trailed off as she struggled to a sitting position, with Sam's help.

Sam looked terrified in Evelyn's eyes. As with most people that have fainted she was confused and scared. Evelyn was very scared! Sam talked to her and asked all the usual questions. "Where do you hurt? Are you alright? How's your vision, can you see me?"

All Evelyn could was sit quietly. She rubbed her hip, and made a face as she did.

"Does it hurt there?" Sam would ask several times. Slowly she came to the realization of where she was.

"Sam, help me up. I've got to get off this floor." She rubbed her hip again, and made the same face again, but she got off the floor with little assistance, and stood quietly for a few seconds. Sam started her toward the living room. "No! No, let's go to the kitchen!" She didn't know what was in the living room, and didn't want to know.

"Okay, but you would be more comfortable on the couch." Sam supported her to the kitchen, pulled out a chair and eased her into it. He immediately went to the cabinet and got a glass for water. Sam saw the two glasses in the sink that had been there for a little while. He frowned. He set the glass down in front of Evelyn, and splashed some water as he did so. Sam turned for the sink to get a paper towel.

"Sam." Her voice was flat.

Sam spun on his feet bringing him back to the same spot at Evelyn's side. "What, Evie? I should get an ambulance, that's what I need." Sam spun on his heels again and was stopped by his name being called again.

"Sam. First off, sit down before you screw yourself into the floor." Her voice was lighter, had some tone to it now. "Sam, sit down here. I'm alright just took me a second or two to get my head back, I'm alright now." Evelyn took a sip from the glass, sat it back down and moved the water that Sam had spilled about with the bottom of the glass. "Sam, we have to talk. Perhaps you don't need to, but I have to!" She looked into his eyes now, and saw the fear. She wasn't sure it was fear of Evelyn hurting herself, or something more.

"Yes. Yes, I know, first things first, are you alright?" Sam's fear of Evelyn's being hurt was going away, but he had a deeper inset fear, of what was about to be discussed.

"I'm fine, haven't busted my butt in years, and it set me back a bit." Evelyn's mind raced for answer to the questions yet to be ask. "How about some supper first?" This would give her time to sound out Sam, and see what had been going on in the living room.

"Okay. Where do you want to go? We could go to Mt. Vernon, they've got a good steak house there, wait Bonanza is in Centralia, or..."

Evelyn was waving her hands back and forth in a halting motion. "I have been to the grocery store. It was an experience, and I am going to cook an in-house meal, unless your heart is set on driving to Mt. Vernon?" Evelyn got up slowly and started for the sink, moving better with each step. Evelyn saw the two glasses again; she only smiled this time.

Dinner was moving along in short order. Evelyn too was moving too, without pains now, or at least didn't acknowledge it in her facial expressions. Sam made several trips to the kitchen to check, and only asked once, as he was assured in no uncertain terms to leave her alone if he expected dinner tonight. Sam needed little encouragement to stay away. The cooking done, the table ready, only was the need for dinners. The meal was quiet. Only the weather, and school starting were really discussed. Sam ate, ravenous. Evelyn kept watching; knowing that Sam had not been eating regularly for some time now bothered her. What really bothered her was yet to come at the table, and it sure wasn't going to be dessert.

IV

Time! there was a word, that Sam had taught "Sam." The newly named "Sam" liked being named for the person he had emulated for so long. It wasn't a requirement, but then it became something that was needed, for his mind to develop in the mode that had been programmed. The Spirit had been to visit many times, but "Sam" had been able to find ways to comply, and be as his Spirit wanted. The visits had become less frequent, till he had built the shelter. Not possible, they had said. "Sam" had done the impossible; words again, not able to complete, unsuccessful after many attempts. All words that Sam had taught him the meaning of. It was simple, the difficult part was making sound into words to issue forth from his orifice, er mouth. But nothing ever went into that space, that was absolutely impossible. This "Sam" believed to be true. Many messages he had proven to be wrong, why he did not care, but wrong in Sam's words, were just, just, wrong. Language for "Sam" had been as hard as had English for Sam. Sam didn't like school; "Sam" had thought it to be very good, and he had tried to encourage his real self to work harder; he thought that he had done very, very good at that except in English. So there were spots that did not come out well. There had been times that "Sam" had felt bad about his association; he always knew what was going on with Sam. All times except the medical doctor, not medical, but a doctor phase. He prided himself on having stayed through that part, other entities had gone now, but his shelter had kept them from him. The high Spirits still did not like it now, but they too used "Sam" to learn. Their learning was slow and "Sam" knew how to keep it slow. They wanted him to become a Spirit. That had been the day he had laughed out loud, they had been amazed, and fearsome as well. It had been a terrible thing, that he could not see them. They had to have a shape in their early time, when they left here. But maybe they cannot leave here! Times have gone, and he had never thought that before. He smiled; he liked to smile, but to smile here took away power. That Evelyn lady was there now; now was the time to power again. This is going to stop soon, very soon. "Sam" turned to his shelter.

"Sam's" shelter was somewhat off center, well, not somewhat, but a lot. Mostly made of signs. The words were unrecognizable to entities here; they were annoyed to be anywhere around the shelter. The shelter said "Pepsi, Schlitz, oranges, hamburgers," all metal. Metal was an unknown, not only unknown, but feared; entities would make sure they did not touch any metal. Entities never came into contact with anything, ever. They were signed pictures, when first formed, "not to become, never to come into contact with anything!" Contact caused bright spots that made noise, and were gone as quickly as they appeared. Popping sounds that caused sensations in their energy. No entity had ever, or at least had never signed, that they had contacted any object in the human world. No one ever came to this place either! No entity exchanged signs with it, that powered here. Most thought he was a Spirit. Those that did not think that did not let any other entity know that they had ever had signs about it. It was bad; they knew bad, because they had a human of their own. The sign bad, was forever in their thought processes.

"My power problem will be repaired soon, but now there is another human." Sam has acted odd for many times. "Sam" had plans for time now, but he does not understand time as Sam knows, explanations have not been sufficient. "Sam" was to seek the spirit. His only solution, to his human problem. The spirit would have no choice but to exchange signs, that is his reason. "Sam" would simply request and they would supply assistance, as always. He was unaware of any deviation from the always, and the always is what the Spirits' place is all about.

"Sam" had never requested assistance. He felt what Sam had felt, but was unknowing of the processes. He needed to power to recondition to carry on, but he had to request now, he too had become impatient, patience and impatience were not available for entities, but through his time, he had developed these on his own. "Sam" needed answers form Spirit, but human traits could not be present to the Spirit when he requested assistance. "Sam" moved from his shelter, being careful to touch only the cloth on the covering.

Spirit....Spirit, requests to be made on understanding. "Sam's" mind was blank, like a sheet of clear paper, no noticeable edges, no writing, no pictures, nothing. Spirit...

Acceptance, and only waiting, the spirit was waiting, and would wait forever, unknowing of the question, only waiting for requests.

"Spirit, I have requests in regard to my human. My request of need of information about time, does time never end, did it ever start?"

"Time exists only for our humans, it is not of our time, or place, knowledge of time is only a fragile part of their place that is never encountered, in our place. It shall never end, because it never began, it is. Your human has had need too long. Time is short for your human, or does your human require assistance longer, something not right about your human? Energy has but to be refocused, it as time, are without being, it only exists. It has been long that time has been needed by your human. That is time in what can be determined by humans. Humans have a cycle that has been deemed to represent a determined time, days, and hours have been established as short time. Beyond that are months, and years. Humans have established time as a way to determine energy levels. Here we power, as it is signed, there the power time has never been established. Humans do not power and by their own failure to do so, become weaker, as do we. Our energy is designed to aid, as humans can not cause energy, to assist them."

"Spirit, my human experiences time by sections. My human has days, days amount to weeks, and to months, and to years. My human has thoughts of eons. I can be of no assistance without this knowledge, you are bound to supply knowledge to assist, I am bound to supply the same."

"Eons this entity, as will your entity experience, many time. Humans could experience that as well. But they do not power, to cause more time. Your human has had time. It is the process that a human must travel, as we do in our assistance to humans. But at the end of human energy, they return to energy. Humans are not meant to exist without being reprocessed. They cannot, or will not power. Our own process is the same; it is gauged by energy. Your energy will never stop, like time, it only is used for more human assistance, they then reprocess. As I will too become energy in a new entity again, my energy will always be energy, humans will have time, and again time. Nothing ends, only is. Your human uses much energy, as do all humans, but it is not done, it only moves to another form. In our place energy is, entity, not identity, just energy no other form exists here. The place you occupy will be occupied again, and again by the same energy. You have spent foolish time on the thing you surround your entity with, it causes energy that goes away, it takes energy from all that contact it. My knowledge is only to assist, I know not how it was created, but in time it will be the same, and it will continue to take energy that is for human assistance. Our place is in contact, but in a parallel place to our humans. We entities need not of food, or surrounding, humans need all things to protect energy. In our place that is not necessary. Your surrounding is of no value here, it will only remove energy that is for use, for humans. And so full compliance has been achieved as in energy it is. All energy knows only energy, energy to assist humans to become, and they too will reprocess to energy, to assist humans. All things are made from energy and will return to energy, no beginning nor no end. So time is only a human endeavor to create a belief in a time that is forever. So to your request to comply, this spirit signs that time is nothing, and at the same time every thing. As has been said, by humans, forever."

"Spirit, request assistance for my human. Spirit again awaits request. Spirit, my human is a male human, he has involvement with other humans. One of those humans is a female human. An energy, exists between these two humans, I do not understand this energy."

Spirit has no recall of the just signed request. No recall of any request has ever been mentioned to any requester. "Sam" is trying not to allow his mind to give him away; he is anxious. But he knows that he can't be, only energy, good energy.

Spirit takes the next request as given; no change, no inflection to its message of signs.

"That is a human trait that has nothing to do with what is given. Our efforts are only to prepare humans for life, prevention of catastrophes before they happen. There are times when our own power must be rekindled to allow us to continue serving the needs of the human we are responsible for. Interaction between human kind is not of our concern. It is only to cause loss of energy. This spirit will attend this request only to assist you in your challenge to move your human to a point that it is prepared. Knowledge of human interaction is only a flicker in my resource, much like the energy that is lost at the contact with your surrounding. No concern of human interaction has ever been needed in preparation. This energy will attempt to assist you. Humans require a belief, a knowledge if you will in something other than the truths that are evident. This belief is that one such as themselves will have this same mistrust, in true life. The transfer of energy is not believed. Human belief, is that once their life on the world they exist upon stops, that all is gone. This is not the transfer of energy, that is true. This interaction may cause a flaw in their ability to accept what is real; dependence upon other humans to cause a function is only a fallacy in reality. Humans are because, the reason for the because, is not of my need to function. My entity exists for signs only.

"My entity has observed humans in times that have become reprocessed. Times that have moved, to a new entity have left signs, that my entity have processed, to assist and shall pass this to you at this time. Many 'emotions' are expressed by humans that are not true. This dependence is an error. My entity does not comprehend male or female. Basic different structures have been observed as time progresses. A union creates more humans, and thus the need for entities. These structures by human entity require attention by other humans. This is not the true. This is caused by the human belief that needs must be fulfilled. Needs do not exist, therefore error in judgment is a belief as well. Most human belief is directed to a God of one design or another this is error. Supreme is not a true, it is only a belief. No entity is supreme, only caring, preparing, and re-processable. This interaction has been caused by human inability to accept the true. It exists in many forms that are not understandable. My entity's observance is of the ability to come into direct contact with other humans, for what is expressed by humans as pleasurable experiences. Touch can only cause needless loss of energy, as in the contact made with your 'shelter.' Humans do require touch; it is unexplained, only known but having no signs to define. By this joining of energy's they are losing not gaining, this is in part, to the human error that limits their existence, some improvement has been observed, by entity's in the reprocessing and have been reserved for signs, as now. Human interaction has been the downfall of humankind for times now, and before. A history if one refers to human knowledge, is a truth of what signs my entity, has become aware. This history will show truth as not being knowledge to humankind. True is energy, pure energy."

Spirit had become silent.

"Sam" inquired as to Spirit having ability to respond. Not a question, but stated as a sign only.

"Entity requirements to assist are a truth, but no fissure has ever caused a request to be delayed, for lack of sign, but the fissure now exists, and will require responses at time, not my entity, not yet aware. All energy known to this entity have been signed for request response. Awareness to request response will be at time not known." Spirit had passed signs. "Sam" was aware of the confusion, and lack of understanding. Power must be obtained to cause direction of energy, that "Sam" would require. "Sam" understood energy, needed to direction. "Sam" was then caused to return to surrounding that he knew as "shelter." "Sam" also felt an emotion, that Spirit would be forever without, Power he would have, and not, from what he was about to receive. "Sam" returned to the shelter to power, it would take much time to restore, but he would, and he knew that what ever he had gained now, would always be his, and the things yet to come would be his forever as well.

V

Bob and Paula Young were unaware of all around them, except for work, pay the bills, and have a little fun in these times. The house was about paid off, and the new electrical contracting business was going well. Paula was the chief bookkeeper, and ordered supplies as needed, and just about everything else. But she was getting it done.

Bob had just hired another young electrician, and was trying to outfit him with a truck. Bob just about had Paul talked into a good deal for a two-year-old van. Paul, a salesman at Quality GMC, knew that Bob would not buy till the price was right, and he was close to giving in. But he wanted his electrical work done basically for free on his new house that was just about to become a reality. Bob knew this too and was unsure how to approach Paula about a freebie. They would all hit a happy medium soon, and all would be happy again. But right now he had to let the kid take his truck out and he didn't like that at all. But this too, will become fact soon.

"Bob, I'm not going to make breakfast if you aren't going to eat it. I have other things that have to be done today." Paula kissed him on the top of his head and moved around the table. "Just call him and say today is the day or you'll go to Ford." Paula took a sip from her coffee and waited for a response.

"You know what he wants?" Bob looked over his cooling eggs and saw her smiling back.

"Yes I do. Sheila told me that they were starting a new house and she hoped to be in by Christmas. So that means that he wants you to come out and drink some beer and wire his house for free." Now she had a grin on her face. "I don't just sit here, I do see people on a regular basis. You go to work and come home and sleep. Myself, on the other hand have to go to the grocery store and the bank and pay utilities and do see other people on a not for hire instance."

Telephone starts to ring, Bob just gets up and smiling at Paula's answer. "Young Electricians." His smile fades away, and a serious countenance takes its place. "Oh, oh yeah, I thought that, well you know. About ten… well, I had several jobs this morning. How long? Okay, just tell me up front from know on, right. Are you coming too? Yeah, I'll tell Paula to have coffee on." Bob placed the phone back on the rest and went back to the table and sat down.

"Well, that was a shock, but it may still be more yet to come. I really have no idea what this about." Bob forks his cold eggs and turns them over. "Ben says he will be here with some other cops at ten today and he wants me here. If one of those kids has screwed me up on this business I'll have their ass."

"What other cops?" Paula too thought about that kid Mark. He appeared a little shady, but they needed another electrician. That's when they had decided to hire young guys and give them a start. "Now what did the cops want that you could not discuss on the telephone? You had Ben run a background check on Mark, didn't you?"

"Yes, I did. And don't ever say anything about that. Ben's not supposed to run checks on every Tom, Dick, and Harry for the general public! He did that 'cause we've been friends all these years and he knows I've put a lot of work into this business—we have put a lot of work into this business. When I decided to run with kids I knew that in these times I needed to be sure. So he checked both of them out before we hired them. Now this! I can't imagine, maybe it's nothing."

"If he's such a good friend how come he can't tell you who these cops are?" Paula went for another cup of coffee. She picked up Bob's cup as she walked by. Pouring coffee Paula looked over her shoulder. "Probably after me; after all, I'm the bookkeeper, probably the damn FBI!" Paula laughed, and was joined by Bob. Both laughed, but very hearty, worried as well, the business was shaky, and didn't need any problems right now.

"Well, I've got to thread some pipe, so I can do that and let Mark use my truck today, till I can get Paul off of square one." Bob kissed Paula on the right cheek and took the filled cup from her and was headed to the barn out back that had become the new "Young Electricians." Mark passed him in his rattle-trap Mustang as he walked down the driveway. Mark tapped the horn lightly as he went by.

Bob's mind was racing about the telephone call. He and Mark met at the big overhead door. Bob keyed the lock and Mark pushed it open.

"How's the boss man this morning? I'm on time this morning but it was a stretch this morning; we fished till late last night, caught some good channel cats. They were biting good and I didn't want to go home."

Bob thought, *I surely hope that's what you were doing.* "Mark, today I want you to go to the Freelys', and drill out the joists for the loom, when we start, it won't take too long to get this job done, then we have the Grinder place and that's going to be the money maker; that should be a three- or four-week job." Bob set his coffee down on the work bench and tripped the light switch that brought the shop into life. Bob took the extra key ring off the peg board and tossed them to Mark. "You'll have your own truck in a few days, so be careful with mine." Bob stressed the "mine" part.

Mark smiled and caught the keys in a backhanded motion. "I'm outta here, boss man!" Mark turned and was on his way to the newly painted white Chevy van.

"Just be careful!" Bob thought, *What if it's not Mark, and it's Larry? I mean it was important enough that you have to be here. Ben did call, of course he couldn't tell you why, that doesn't make any sense.* Bob moved to the pipe rack and started to drag out water pipe. He still had to do the plumbing at his brother's yet. High-class lawyer can't hire a plumber. He smiled.

Bob had made a lot of headway with several projects, and was surprised that there had been so much to do at the shop, when he saw the sheriff's car pull into the driveway. Closely behind were three Chevys, plain wrapped. *Cops,* Bob thought. Bob retrieved the rag he had been using, and started to clean his hands. He didn't like the looks of any of this. *Better get your hands clean, looks like there might be a lot of introductions coming his way.* Bob stood his place; they could see him in the open door. *They came to see me on my time,* He thought. *I haven't done anything wrong, have I?* Bob looked at the back door, saw it open, and out came Paula.

Paula intercepted Ben as he walked past the house and kept pace with him. "What's all this about, Ben?" Paula asked outright.

"Can't really say right now, but these gentlemen behind us will let all of us know in just a little bit, is my guess." Ben never looked at Paula, he just kept walking.

Paula knew Ben well enough to know that he was done talking, so she just walked to the barn with Ben. The two were leading a strange array of official-looking men toward her husband who didn't offer to move from the door way of the barn.

No one got in a hurry, slow steady pace to the barn, eight people formed a half circle in front of the open barn door. Paula stepped inside and wrapped her arms around Bob's right arm and stood close to Bob. "What's this all about?" Bob asked.

Ben stepped forward to take the place just like the football referees before the big game. "Bob, this is Carl Flaners and Lou Marks. They're with the FBI. They will have to do all the other introductions as I can't recall names that were just given to me, and I don't want to make any mistakes."

Paula remembered what she had thought at breakfast, and a sense of doom flowed over her. Bob shook the hands of Carl and Lou. Carl stepped forward one step, and started his portion of the ceremony.

"Mr. Young, this is Johnny Smith, Albert Kannes, Terri Joanses; they are with the Treasury Department. This is Steve Porter and Butch Kelley with the FBI . Mr. Young, we would like to ask you a few questions about your son, Sam. First off there is nothing wrong with your son. We have been in contact with the 1st Cav. and they have assured us that he is fine, and serving in Southeast Asia, Viet Nam. I'm sure you are proud of him for his service in the US Army. What we need to do is to sit down with you, as it is a long story, and I want to make sure that all the facts, as we know them, are straight in your mind before we begin. If you would like to have a lawyer present before we begin, we can make an appointment with you at a later date and time to conduct this portion of this investigation." Carl stopped at this point to allow Bob and Paula to think about what he had just said.

Bob stood for a second or two trying to absorb all that had just been said. "First off what's this about? What could be the problem, and if my son is alright, what are your questions about him, he's been in Nam for almost ten months now."

"We can arrange for a meeting room at the sheriff's office if you would like, because, as I said I want to tell you the whole story, before you commit to anything." Carl gave Bob the disclaimer again.

"If Sam is okay then we need to go to the house and sit down; I have some coffee brewing and we can get a bit more comfortable." Paula started toward the house slowly waiting to see if any of the others would follow.

"Well, I guess that is the plan." Bob stepped to the side of his wife and started the slow walk to the house. "Ben, what the Hell's this all about? I don't know anything that would interest the FBI."

Ben shrugged his shoulders. "I don't really know anything, I just brought them out here." Ben was thinking that there was more. But the story as he knew it was pretty farfetched and would need some telling. "How's the business going? I don't see all that of you much anymore."

Paula gave Ben the look that he understood—SHUT UP—it was plain and to the point.

They all walked to the back door, where Paula took over again and directed them to the living room, a larger than normal room that Bob had created by opening up two rooms some years before. "Bob, what is this all about? Who are these people? Sam is okay?"

Sam shrugged his shoulders and gave Paula the "I don't know nothing" look, and asked, "Hon, do we have enough coffee? These gentlemen need to ask some questions."

Paula looked at the half pot of coffee and moved to the counter to make a fresh pot. She looked over her shoulder at Bob and gave him the same look "what's up?" Bob only shrugged his shoulders again.

"Sam's okay." Bob patted Paula's shoulder and continued to the living room.

Bob could feel Paula's eyes boring into the back of his head as he walked toward the living room with all the strangers, and Ben.

"Bob, we will need a few chairs from the den, and I will get a fresh pot of coffee made up. Everyone drink coffee?" Paula asked as she stopped at the kitchen door frame and held onto both sides to steady her. She knew they were cops, but didn't recognize any of them, except Ben.

Steve spoke up. "Nothing for me, ma'am. I never developed the taste."

"I've got Coke, milk, or iced tea." Paula was trying her hardest to be nice to these strangers that Ben had drug in.

"Tea would be nice; I don't get much in the motel." Steve was trying to be as nice as he could be. This part of the job he just wasn't sure of yet.

"Anybody else?" Paula put on her best smile and looked about the room. She thought that the woman could help her, but thought again, that to serve was below her place in life. With the suit she had on she was probably a little funny anyway. She thought, *Motel? They have been here long enough that they have rooms at a motel.* Paula turned to the kitchen and began to get cups out of the cabinet. Her smile was gone now. She hoped she could bring it back when she was done with the coffee. Paula poured the last of the pot into the carafe and started a new pot. Her mind was clouded with thoughts of Sam. Bob had said Sam was okay. Why, did he even mention Sam, he's in Viet Nam!

"Okay, now what's this all about?" Bob sat down in his reclining chair and leaned forward, toward the strangers in his house.

"Let's wait till Paula has returned, Bob," Ben said as he took one of the chairs that Bob had brought in from the den. They all sat quietly till Paula returned and had placed coffee at their disposal and Iced tea for Steve. She went over to Bob's recliner and sat on the arm of the chair.

Carl stood up, and told everyone that he works better on his feet if they didn't mind.

All nodded in the affirmation.

"This as I have begun to know has a few twists to it. I don't really want to answer any questions till I am finished, if you don't mind." Carl looked at his audience. "Mr. and Mrs. Young, I know what you are thinking, and first off I have checked on your son, and he is doing fine. I have been called here to investigate a counterfeiting case. First off no one is being charged at this time. The individual in question gave his name as Sam Young, that's what brings us here this morning. I have been investigating this for one week, at this time. The individual that I speak of has passed forty-one dollars and fifty-eight cents in counterfeit money. I have bills I will show you when I have finished. The individual stayed at the Palace motel in Sandoval, he had several beers at JR's, he bought some items at the Country Store, and he ate at Merle's Truck Stop restaurant. We have not got a good description as yet, but will have an artist's conception in a few days. Isn't that right, Agent Joanses?" Terri nodded yes. "The man we are looking for disappeared from the Palace, almost as into thin air. The proprietor of the Palace says that the man entered the room and never came out. Now we all know better than that."

Carl went on to describe the investigation, and how it had not progressed, as no one has seen or heard from this individual since. "There has not been any more money turned up anywhere, as yet, and that is to include, anywhere in the United States, as anyone else could tell. In a week's time this investigation has gotten pretty big, nationwide, at this time." Carl told how everyone had been of great value to him, his agents, and had not held back at all, it seemed. All eyes were trained on Bob and Paula, as those present had been actively working on the case and were bored with Carl's never-ending story, and his delivery.

"There is one small part that no one else has been told, except for my partner Agent Marks. The fingerprints on the bills, and the motel room, and the car outside the motel are those of your son, Sam Young. Only one difference is that there is a scar mark, on the left thumb print. It repeats itself on all the prints taken. As I said we have spoke with the 1st Cav. in Bein Hoa, South Viet Nam, and your son is in the bush somewhere near Tahy Ninh Province. When he was fingerprinted in basic training there was no scar. My first question that I would want you to answer when I finish is does your son have a scar on his left thumb?" Carl paused, waiting for anything, a reaction, a look. None. "I have been authorized to show you the money that has been passed."

Bob and Paula passed a glance between them, a look of total loss.

Lou opened his briefcase and took out several plastic bags with bills inside and a folder; he passed that to Ben, who was sitting next to Carl. Carl had moved to the reclining chair that the Youngs now occupied. He opened the folder and took out pictures of the bills as well. "I want you to know that I am here in an official capacity of the US government to ask for your help in solving this crime. I have not assessed any wrong, on anyone's part at this time." Carl handed the plastic bags containing the reproductions of the bills and handed them to Bob.

Bob was looking at the bills and smiling. He passed each to Paula, who now stood beside the chair. "These look like money around the edge but the pictures are all blown up. I don't see how anyone could ever mistake these as real money. What in God's name is this all about! You say the fingerprints are of my son, from a week ago. I don't think so! This is really starting to bug the Hell out of me." Bob looked around his living room to the people that now occupied his home. They returned his look with no emotions noted. All businesslike appearances returned his look.

Carl handed the pictures of the same bills with circles and arrows drawn to typed explanations in the margins. Carl was still quiet and professional. The pictures had been taken to show pictures inside the bills as well. "Look at the dates that have been circled on the bills. One is 2001, one is 2003, and I believe... Carl was looking at a typed sheet with parts underlined in red. Yes, here it is... all the others were 2004. These bills are all dated thirty or more years in the future." Carl stood holding the folder and looking at the Youngs. "I know what you are thinking, I have had the same thoughts—no spacemen, no extraterrestrials. He gave the name Sam Young."

"Bob, do you have a twenty on you, or a one even?" Paula asked as she looked at the pictures with circles and arrows. Bob began digging for his wallet. She gave Carl a look of distrust.

Johnny spoke up first. "What you will see is that the photos are the same, different border and the bottom of the picture has more fancy swirls. What you can barely see, in the copy, is the numbers and dates inside the paper. Whoever copied these had some kind of knowledge of printing and paper. Some kind of knowledge that doesn't exist. At least, to our government's knowledge."

Carl had one more group of photos to show the Youngs, and he was still holding them as Johnny finished. "Here is the problem that no one can figure out." Carl handed the picture of the coins, front and back; they had circles and arrows as well.

Bob looked the coins over closely. "Coins? And you all think that our son had something to do with this! That's incredible, to even accuse our son, and he's in Viet Nam, as we speak. You said that yourself." Bob leaned back in his chair and handed the last picture of the coins to Paula. He hadn't really looked at the picture of the coins. Bob looked about the room for some sympathy, or at least something resembling care. "Why on earth would anyone counterfeit coins?"

Terri stood up and walked to the center of the group. She took the paper from Carl. "This sheet states that the quality of these reproductions is perfect. These have been replicated to exacting standards that no one but our own government has ever been able to duplicate. The coins are exact duplicates of the coins now being produced, to size, weight, and metal makeup. We have to find the person, or correctly the persons that might have been able to create the duplicates that you see before you now. No one feels that a single person has made these coins; it's far too complicated to have done in someone's garage or basement!"

Paula had turned on the dinning room overhead light and was studying the pictures and the money that Bob had produced. Paula was joined by Ben and Butch. Ben was looking as closely as Paula, and Butch stood off to the side hoping to be asked questions.

Bob looked aver his shoulder at Paula, then back to Carl, who had not moved. Bob could see the pistol on Carl's hip as he stood with his hands resting on each hip. This brought to him the reality that these were real FBI. "I ask again, do you think that Sam had anything to do with this?" Bob's head turned from side to side, from face to face.

Ben looked at Paula. "I was told to get these guys to your house. I have never seen any of this. It's quite a job to make it look that good, then put that big picture on them."

Paula stopped looking at the bills and looked at Ben Holeman. "I can't believe that you are admiring these pictures, and to be here, with these people, who are here trying to accuse my Sam! I thought you were our friend. You should have told them that there is no way that Sam could have ever been involved in such a crime! This is a crime, and you are supporting this bullshit!" Paula's voice was getting louder. "Allowing these people to come onto our house and as much as say that Sam is guilty! I would have never believed such words would come out of your mouth, Ben!" Moisture collecting in her eyes.

Butch spoke to Paula. "Ma'am, I first want to tell you that we are here to ask questions; that's all this is about right now. There are many Sam Youngs that are all being investigated right now."

"What about later! When Sam is done fighting in that damn war, does he get to come home and go to prison! Does that come later! WHEN!" Paula was crying hysterically now.

Bob had moved to Paula's side and had his arms around her. He lowered his head to hers. "Now, Paula, let's get to the bottom of this thing first. I've got a few questions to ask then we'll call Jim Nals." Bob looked back to find Butch had moved back to the group. Terri and Carl were still standing, not mentally or emotionally moved by the crying Paula Young.

Carl spoke, as no one else wanted to ask much, with the highly charged emotional state of the Youngs' living room. "Please sit down, Mrs. Young. I know you are upset, but as Agent Kelley said, we are only asking questions and looking for clues. I will be the first to tell you that I can speak with almost certainty that this was not Sam. I know where Sam is and there is no way he could have been here to have participated in this crime. But I as a professional must tell you that I cannot allow any information to go without giving it my fullest attention. This is very serious." Carl stepped aside to allow the Youngs to cross back to the reclining chair. "I understand why you are so upset. I want you to know that you may want to seek legal counsel before I go on, if you so choose." Carl paused to readjust his holster and appraise the Youngs. He knew this was going to be bad, before he had started.

Paula had a tissue to her nose and eyes. She was shaking her head "no" and waving her other hand in a hurry up fashion. Paula eased herself back to the arm of the chair.

"I must ask you to have no conversations with anyone but counsel at this point and time. We are, anyway the US Army is having Sam fingerprinted in Viet Nam, and those fingerprints will be shipped to Washington, DC, to be analyzed. We as field agents have to find the origin of these reproductions. This is very serious." Terri had her hands together in an interlocking grip; she stood quiet.

"We are here because Sam's fingerprints are all over the place. I do not in know of any way that prints can be reproduced and applied to all the articles that we have checked. From the reports that we have turned in, and investigations that are being conducted here and elsewhere there is a mountain of paper being used. But Sam is in Viet Nam! That is a fact that cannot be left out of the equation. The FBI in Washington is cross matching fingerprints in their files and looking for any matches, anything that is close. This has really confused and confounded everyone. The CID of the Army will probably speak to Sam; they will verify his location now, and during the time in question. I believe Johnny has a few questions if you will go on." Carl bowed out of the center stage.

"I have a lot of questions, but first I want to tell you the same that Carl has said. I do not see how this could have been your son. First his location. And our investigations at this point have revealed no other money. I have a lot of questions, but I will not ask many here, as the questions I have don't have anything to do with your son. Does your son have any friends that might have been corresponding with him while in Viet Nam? And if so who?"

Bob and Paula looked at each other and shook their heads. "Not too many of the boys that Sam ran with have moved away, and most are not in the Army. I think Donnie is over there too, but they are not in the same unit. Sam would have sent us news of having run into anyone over there. And we both read his letters. Most are still around I imagine. I'm not sure that I know all of them, but I could try to make a list."

"That would be helpful. Has your son ever shown a direction or interest in anything associated with copying or making anything from metal?" Carl had his personalized pen that his son had given him for Christmas making notes.

"For God's sake, haven't we told you that our son never did anything wrong? He did a little drinking, and drag racing, but this is so wrong!" Paula had the tissue at her face again, the leak had started again.

"Now, Paula, we aren't going to get this cleared up with that. We have to do what is right. If Sam were here he would do the same, right." Bob put his arm around Paula and pulled her closer.

Terri stepped up to the chair and spoke directly to Paula. "We do not want you to think that we are here to chastise your son. We have a major problem here; we have had some difficult moments with this. The people we work for have poked a lot of fun at this like we have been visited by outer space or time travelers. But at the same time we have a very serious problem in that someone has made the best copies of our currency that have ever been produced. Not only that, but the coins are perfect. That could topple an economy such as ours right now. With the war, that the two of you are very aware of, our economy is shaky at best. Had we not ran across this how long would it have been? And how many dollars would have been distributed? The Treasury Department wants to find the source of this problem and stop it, now, before it becomes a really big problem."

Paula looked up and wiped her eyes again. "I know. It's just that our son is so far away and can't even defend himself. What's he going to say when someone comes to him in the jungle in Viet Nam and wants his fingerprints?" Paula wiped her eyes again.

"In Viet Nam the person taking his fingerprints will have no idea what is going on. There will be no red lights and siren. Just a man with an ink pad and a fingerprint form. The Army uses them and no one will think anything about it." Carl had let his pad and pen drop to his side and trying to make it as easy as possible for what the was about to ask would probably start the water works again. "Having said that, I have to ask something that we have to do at the same time, if you will allow us. I will have my associates to go through anything that you might have of your son's, to check for anything that will lead us to a conclusion to this part of our case. I don't want you to think that when we leave today that all is finished; we still have an ongoing investigation that we will solve." Carl had his hands on hips again and his pistol was showing. This time Paula saw it; she stared. Carl saw the stare, and let his hands drop to cover the pistol again.

"Yes, yes, his room is downstairs. I've cleaned it but there's a lot of stuff down there. It's just like he left it. I wanted it to be just like he left it." Paula wiped her eyes again and looked at her tissue. It had about had it; she crossed to the end table and pulled another from the box. "It's this way." Paula waited for someone to follow.

Lou looked at Butch and Steve. They got up and followed Paula to the door, by the bathroom door, opened it and they started down.

Carl watched as the two new agents went to the basement with Mrs. Young. "Now, Mr. Young, does your son have an area in your shop that he might have used for…?"

"To make coins? Is that what you wanted to ask? I'll take you to the mint! Well, I can tell you that I didn't like the insinuation, but Sam had an area, a room in the barn for his hobbies and stuff. You are more than welcome to look into whatever you want to clear this stuff up. It's not even that it's the feeling of guilt, what we are doing behind Sam's back, that bothers me so."

"I know you don't want Sam to have this on his mind where he's at right now. I think he needs a clear head for what he's doing right now." Carl had the look of a father on his face as he passed the last comment; it was in reality Carl's belief.

Johnny, Terri, and Albert were left in the living room of the Youngs' with not much to do, so Albert decided to go downstairs with Butch and Steve. He stepped aside as Paula came up the stairs. She had picked up a cloth handkerchief while downstairs. She told Albert it was the only room downstairs. Albert nodded and started down the stairs.

Lou spoke to Carl about moving to the barn, and Carl thought so as well. The two FBI agents with Johnny in tow started to the back door with Bob. Terri started to pick up cups and take to the kitchen.

"No, don't do that, I'll get them." Paula moved to the table and started to clear up the cups there. "I can't imagine, and I know that you can only raise kids the best you can. Does that make any sense?" Paula looked to Terri, who still had cups in her hands too.

Terri spoke in a voice that Paula had not heard yet, a voice of caring, and concern. "I am not in the league of the FBI, nor of Johnny and Al. I'm an office desk jockey that has always wanted field work and they thought I would be all businesslike. Well, I know what we are looking for and how important it is, but I'm very new at the investigation part. I'm not sure I like this. No matter how this comes out I want you to know that if you need to talk I'm, here, somewhere." Terri took her share of the cups toward the kitchen, set them in the sink and started to take her jacket off. "I am a professional, but not an asshole. Maybe I'm not an investigator." Terri looked about the sink for something.

"It's under the sink, the soap, right?" Paula, still lost in her own emotions, but had seen that look in her kitchen; she was a neat freak and kept everything put in its place.

Terri opened the doors below the sink. All was neat and clean, not like most sink bottoms, and surely not like hers. "Thanks." Teri took out the soap and squirted some into the sink and fixed the drain to hold water and began pouring out left-over coffee into the second sink.

"You shouldn't be doing that. Here, let me do those." Paula moved in beside Terri in an attempt to move her aside.

"No, you dry, I'll wash. I don't want to look for the dish cloths too!" Terri smiled and looked into Paula's eyes. There was fear there, concern, a mother's worry.

Paula smiled back and broke into a light laugh. Terri laughed with her. Paula put her hand on Terri's shoulder and began to sob quietly.

Terri turned to Paula and wrapped her arms loosely around Paula's shoulders. "I really can't imagine what you're going through. I really don't want to know, but at the same time I do. I'm sorry. But I have this job that I have to do."

Their heads side by side in conference, they ignored Bob as he came back in the door long enough to reach up and get a ring of keys form the wooden key-shaped holder inside the doorway. He looked, hesitated, started to say something, turned and left back to the barn.

Paula broke the hug and dabbed at her eyes, and Terri shut off the water that had come close to the overflow drain. She unbuttoned her shirt cuffs and reached into the water to allow some of the excess water to drain to a usable level. Paula opened a drawer and took out a clean white cotton towel. Terri started placing cups in the sink and began washing. Conversation was over for the time being.

Bob had told the three government agents that he had forgotten the keys and would be right back. "Still smells like a barn. Had animals, once upon time here. There's still some tack on that wall. Lou pointed to some leather harness hanging and dust covered. Not too long ago I would say either."

Carl looked about the barn. "Yeah, that's probably true. Hey, what is this smell thing? You don't even get out of the city. How would you know what the hell a barn is supposed to smell like anyway?"

"I've got a dog!" Lou exclaimed.

"A dog! I've been in your house—that little thing I thought was a mouse till it started yipping." Carl laughed while looking around. His mind still running, pipe, electrical conduit, wire, lots of wire, boxes marked with names and numbers, all appeared to be fairly new, and had "Young Electricians" in black magic marker. All the stuff an electrician would need. There were four Dutch doors on the north side of the main room and three doors on the south side. One had been changed, and had a regular door put in its place. Carl thought that that would be the kid's hobby room. *Kid!* Carl thought. *He's in Nam!* Carl walked to each door and looked in. *Horses,* he thought. *Yeah, horses.* Johnny and Lou talked of dogs, and the little thing Lou considered his wife's toy dog. Carl had heard the story on how they had come about getting the little dog. So he was back into the FBI mode, as Bob came back, twirling the key ring on his finger. Johnny and Lou were laughing belly laughs about how the dog had attacked one night when he and Linda had been making love.

Then the kids came to the door and wanted to know what was the matter with Tiger, 'cause Tiger was raising hell.

"Well, what did you do then?" Johnny was forced to ask.

"Well, I looked at Linda, and I said, 'Not tonight, baby, I'm developing a headache.'"

Lou laughed. It was one of his many favorite stories.

Johnny smiled, and Carl too, as he mimed the words to Lou's story, he had heard it enough, as Bob walked into this barn.

Still spinning the keys on his finger, "Did I miss something?" Bob looked about and could see that Carl had been going through doors, and the other two were laughing, he hoped not about his little problem.

"Let me tell you…" Lou started again.

"No, Lou, I don't think that Mr. Young wants to hear about your love life." Carl gave Lou the FBI look and started to the door on the south side of the barn.

"No, no. Mr. Flanners, that's my office. Sam may have grown up but his hobby room is still in the kid's location." Bob turned to the ladder and began to climb.

Carl started to take his jacket off. Johnny and Lou followed suit as the athletic portion of the investigation began. Carl started up with Lou in close pursuit. Johnny looked, shook his head and began to climb. Dust was heavy on the ladder; no one had been up here in a while. There were bales of hay stacked against the west wall, ten feet high, neatly stacked, and baled with twine. The air was thick as they stirred up dust that had not been moved in some time. Sunlight shone through all gaps around the outside door to the hayloft and one could see the dust swirling as the foursome moved to a room that had been built against the east wall. Bob unlocked the door, not a padlock but a regular door lock, as he turned the knob to open the door more dust joined the swirls that had begun to settle toward the loft floor. Bob reached inside and found the switch, an audible click was to be heard and the very dark room came to life. The overhead fan began to turn slowly, gaining speed as the current urged the mechanism back to the living world.

The fluorescents snapped on and off, then stayed lit to show a kid's room. Airplanes, and airplanes, everywhere, and rockets suspended from the white ceiling of the room. The walls were covered with posters of all kinds; horses were prevalent, singers in various modes onstage. Two tables were stacked high with everything from carburetors to models, the room twenty feet by maybe ten feet was full of kid's stuff. In one corner was a drawing table slightly elevated at the top with finished and unfinished drawings. A couple of *Playboy* pinups were stapled to the walls; older kids had been here too. Above the drawing table was a single balsa glider with a couple of dings in the wings. It was old; it caught Carl's attention, and he walked toward the corner. All had been quiet here for some time; it was like opening of a time vault, the time of childhood lost.

"That's the first glider Sam ever had. He kept it all these years. He and his invisible friend flew it for a long time. I'll never forget his friend." Bob was standing beside Carl and looking at the motionless glider almost expecting it to begin flying about.

Carl and Bob each saw, in their own minds, gliders. Bob saw Sam running about and calling to his invisible friend, "Catch it. Boy, that time it went high!" Carl with his dad at the lake, and his plane had flown too far, and had landed in the water. They had broken one of the wings trying to get to shore, but his dad fixed it, and it flew again. Johnny and Lou looked at each other and shrugged their shoulders and laughed, maybe too loud, because Bob and Carl both looked at them hard when they turned together. Reality came back suddenly, and the gliders went away as quickly as they had come. Later Carl would think of the glider, and he would smile.

"Quite a place for a kid, I would have loved something like this when I was a kid." Johnny tried to cover up the fact that his laugh had caused Carl and Bob to startle the way that they had.

"Yeah, we used to stack hay all around this room so he could come out here in the winter; no heat but he would still come out here for hours in the coldest of weather. He would have to bring whatever he was working on into the house, because the glue wouldn't set out here. And..." Bob realized that these were FBI agents and not family and he had to get back to the main project of proving his son innocent.

"Mr. Young, I'm going to have to have this room checked for anything that might be of value to the department, They will be very careful, and everything that will be handled and listed on their investigation, will be given the utmost care. I can't see anything that would be useful to the department but that's not my call." Carl's professional side was showing.

"It's just, Bob, I am here to do all I can to help, but just, Bob. Please!" Bob was looking about the room. This had been Sam's private room, and he had not been allowed here too much. He didn't remember all this stuff; there was a bunch of it. But it still amazed him that the glider was still intact. He caught himself looking at it again.

Johnny spoke up after the trance had been broken. "Did he fly all of these? Some of the rockets are pretty large. Did they go high?" Johnny was looking at a six-foot rocket with multiple engines.

"Some of them went pretty high. Some were so fast that you couldn't see them until the chute opened. Had to use 'binos'; they should be here somewhere too." Bob had a model airplane in his hands turning it over and over. "Some took hours to build and only seconds to ruin, some beyond repair. Just like NASA, build them and scrap them. He was pretty safe, and only got his fingers burnt once in a while. Somewhere in here is the tracking device and the speed chart for seconds to speed. They would reach several hundred miles per hour in three to four seconds."

"Did he ever have accidents with these things?" Lou asked.

"Not many. A couple of the ones that they tampered with the design blew up, and there were a few fires on the launch pads. I know that this is a bunch of kid's stuff, but you will be careful with all of it, some of this is ten to fifteen years old."

"The utmost care is given to all materials that are being evaluated and inspected. Only because the FBI has an extra effort on this investigation, that they will even look at all this; this has nothing to do with this case. I see a bunch of kid's toys and stuff here." Carl almost said "junk"; he was glad that he had not. "It is necessary, the investigation dictates that all parts make a whole."

Bob watched as they nosed around in private things. Oh, it was only a cursory glance compared to what he expected, but they were looking at things that he had never seen. Sam had always been a loner, quiet, and he had always been given the respect and privacy that he had earned. And now, here, while he watched, they defiled his son's private possessions. It wasn't right, and there was nothing he could do about it, nothing! He did think that he would call Jim Nals anyway, just to be on the safe side. Bob was in a daze and didn't hear his name being called; he did feel the hand touch his shoulder. He jerked away. "What! Oh, I didn't mean to be so jumpy." Bob was still in a bit of a daze. "What did you say? I guess with all of this and all, I'm just a little nervous."

Lou thought, *Nervous, sure, you were out in la la land.* Lou had let his right hand fall to his pistol. He recovered without Bob seeing his hand release the grip. "I need you to lock this room up until the lab guys get here. They will go through all of this. We'll call in advance so you know when they will arrive. Are you alright, Bob?" Lou looked at the pasty appearance, but he had seen that with guilty people before, but he had thought this was a done case already. It will probably be tomorrow or the next day.

They all descended the ladder with ease, but Johnny's city shoes almost let him down the hard way. Johnny slipped on the dust-covered steps, but recovered without a spill. Then the slow, even-paced walk back to the house; twice they stopped and discussed the way the war was going. Carl of one mind and Lou of another, no one would have ever pegged them as full-time partners, to include Bob.

12:30 August 1, 1969. It was hot, the three government agents with their coats slung on their backs might have been anyone looking to have electrical repair, or contractors looking to hire an electrician. They had just made the shade of the old elm tree at the back of the house when the door opened, and Paula called out "Lunch!" Just like Bob had heard for years. But had not expected it, not today, not now, not with them here.

Bob smiled. "After you, gentlemen." Now they were off guard Bob thought, but then too, he didn't think that Crazy Horse had fed Custer and his troops before the Little Big Horn. They all stood their ground; they had looks of being lost and they looked back and forth. Bob turned and walked backwards toward the house, his smile in place. "Gentlemen, she will be pissed at you if don't get in here."

Carl bowed slightly at the hips and gestured the other two to go first. They smiled and walked toward the house. Carl's mind, as were the others, was thinking this is not right, no one invited the bad guys in for lunch. Of course he thought the case here was done, unless they had a sub basement or a underground building hidden somewhere. All that kid's stuff was going to give the lab guys a real smile. They would be flying the damn planes instead of checking for prints. Carl smiled. He thought about his glider.

Inside they found Butch and Steve with plates in front of them, hamburgers in hand, French fries in a large bowl and all the fixin's. "She made us sit down and eat," Steve said with his mouth full of hamburger.

"Yeah, I'll bet!" Lou looked at all the food and he was hungry. "I need to wash my hands." Lou held his hands in a pleading gesture, of those about to be handcuffed.

"The bathroom is just off the living room, you remember." Paula jerked her head in the direction of the living room and said. "Towels and washcloths are on the second shelf behind the green curtain". Paula set down a pie with a piece missing, and told Butch and Steve that there would be more fries in just a minute, and to eat those before they were cold.

As they passed into the living room they met Terri. She was smiling, her top had the two top buttons loosed, and her scarf was gone. "Lay your coats on the couch, gentlemen." She gave a short laugh as she walked toward the kitchen.

Not much was said, they washed their hands and smiled at one another, and returned to the dinning room. Extra chairs were around the table, a center leaf had placed in the middle to make the table larger. Paper plates and silverware in place. They milled about for a few seconds till Johnny spoke. "If we don't sit down soon those two are going to eat it all."

Ben came in the back door about that time, smiled and headed for the bathroom. He called over his shoulder as he passed. "Had to call dispatch and tell her I would be out for lunch!" Ben laughed as he slid into a chair against the wall.

Lunch had been put together in a few minutes by Paula, impromptu if you will, and she had worried that they would not stay, but all stayed and enjoyed the meal. Conversation was another matter. Conversation began as the usual weather, cars, discussions, but soon expanded into politics, Nixon, and finally the war. Carl was all for the war; Nixon could be the man to straighten out all the world. Bob had a son there and really didn't have an exact opinion of the whole matter. Ben was up for re-election this fall and produced several political handouts for Bob and Paula and offered fingernail files and matches to all that would have them. A few stories were told as "impossible pie" and vanilla pudding topped the meal. An uneasiness fell upon the group again as the meal came to an end.

Carl was the leader here, and it was his time to speak. Carl cleared his throat. All had almost become quiet anticipating someone having to lead. "First off, I want to thank you for this meal. Johnny, Lou, Al, and I have been eating a Merle's or Jim's for a week now. And I am sure that Steve may try to move in with all of you, if how much he ate is any indication of how much he enjoyed himself. But not to cast a pall on the friendships that have been begun here, but I still have an investigation going on here. This meal has reasserted a few things that I felt in the beginning. You are good people that work hard for a living; there is a love that cannot be denied, for each other, and for your son. I cannot say how I feel this is going to come out but I feel there have been mistakes made that have pointed us in your direction. I can't change any of the plans; we will finish our part of the investigation. When that may be, I do not know. I am awaiting the report on Sam's fingerprints form Viet Nam, and then we will have better direction on where, and what we will pursue. Bob, Paula, I will keep in touch with the two of you and will let you know when the lab guys will be here to look at Sam's hobby room. I will make sure that if I am not taken off this investigation, and I will not forget this hospitality that you have shown us. Now all the rest of you are overpaid government employees that are not doing your jobs at present, and Uncle Sam expects you to get back on the job!" With that Carl pushed himself away from the table and stood up.

The rest followed suit and started to gather their personal belongings that had been spread about the room. All thanked Paula for the lunch, and Bob was reassured that all would be found in Sam's favor. All of them had pretty much decided that when they had first seen the evidence anyway. Had they always thought that? Most wondered to themselves that question.

It had been a long lunch; it was almost two-thirty. Butch and Steve didn't want to begin canvassing businesses, as had been the obvious plan, and Ben didn't want to return to the office, and answer all the questions about the FBI; he wanted to go fishing.

Paula thought that the lunch idea had worked well. She smiled to herself as she talked to Steve about the fresh hamburgers that they had just had.

Terri thought that Paula's idea had worked. Nothing had been said about the "idea," but Terri had just known, and she knew it worked.

Johnny had thought that Paula had made a remarkable recovery from hysterics to a fine meal in less than two hours. Lou and Johnny's minds had been almost together on equal wavelengths, and Lou had added. Never have understood women, probably never will, at least not his wife! Lou had smiled at the thought of his wife.

All walked to the cars in the driveway that many had slowed as they drove past on Illinois route 37, and had wondered "Who died?" Ben's squad was first in and would be the first out of the circle drive. He was thinking that after a few reports that he would have some campaigning to do at the lake with a fishing pole.

Butch was full and belched aloud. "Excuse me. But I'm full and I didn't eat half as much as Steve. I don't know where you put all of it!"

Steve placed his hands on the side of the car, stretched his back, and smiled. "It's a talent. Can't tell you the secret, I'd have to kill you!" They both opened their doors and laughed. It had been a good day after all. And so ended August 1, 1969. At least in each of their minds.

In later years Carl and Bob would discuss that day. Carl built a new house five miles south of Bob and Paula. Bob had done the electrical work, and had refused any pay for his services. Bob had become a friend, not a fishing buddy friend, but a friend. Carl had been a pallbearer at Bob and Paula's funeral. It had been tragic, a terrible accident on Interstate 64, in a Hell of a rain storm, coming home from vacation. Sam had never had much to do with Carl; he wasn't Sam's type. He had been told of the story many times, but just didn't like Carl much; they spoke was all. And when Bob and Paula had moved to Odin, Sam had been older and was usually doing his thing when Carl had been about.

Chapter 5

I

Storms were brewing. Tornado alley, they called the strip of the Midwest that was visited by these violent storms each fall. The weather was hot, humidity was high, and the sky had taken on a greenish hue. Plumes of dust were swirled about on the roadside, and two young boys lifted their hands to wave to Sam. One boy had a fishing basket with a lot of fish in it; some still flopped about in dying efforts of hope to land in water, before they didn't have energy left. Their gills opened and closed in unison with their mouths, needing the oxygen that would not be there. Sam could not see that far but he had been those boys, and he had seen the fish many times.

Sam had grown up in Odin, and moved to Salem. He had moved back to this house; his dad had called it "his last place" on earth. And so it had been; he had not finished it, and nor had Sam! Sam waved in return, his thoughts on fishing that had consumed him in his earlier years, just like those two. He and Friend, Sam had probably sat in the same places as those two had. Sam could see rain in the distance; he could smell the moisture in the air. He also thought that he was going to have to put the deck on the back of the house, as he had planned.

Not thinking Sam got up from the chair, folded it up, and started toward the house. It was going to rain and he was under the tree out front. There would be lightning and lots of rain, no sense in tempting fate. Sam walked slowly, not like a man fearing lightning, or rain. Just a man enjoying his house, his thoughts and his slow walk. His dad had built it just before the accident, it had not been finished, and Sam was still working on that. It had been a long time now, fifteen, sixteen, not seventeen years now, they went before their time. Friend had been there then, but Sam had not thought anything then. Friend had not had a name then, Friend had only been in Sam's mind. Maybe that was what he was now, "in my mind." Sam spoke softly, and walked slowly as a few drops of rain fell onto the driveway making little tufts of dust as they hit. He spoke of the fishing, like he and Dale had done, forever, now forever gone. Same knew his lips were forming words, but his mind would not allow the words in. Sam's mind flowed like the storm clouds, moving into his world now, quick and wild, dark and angry. As he walked in the beginnings of the rain, he got wet, he thought of his now. That too, was dark and angry. Sam pushed those thoughts away, he thought of Evelyn, he felt the rain, it began to run down his back.

Evelyn had only been a person, someone he didn't know, didn't want to know at that time. Sam had remembered dancing a few times, when she had been out and their paths had crossed. He had thought then that she would be good in bed. Sam smiled. And that had been true, but only recently. It had only been a one- or two-night stand, no complications. Things had become complicated, so very complicated. Large raindrops had hit his shoulder, Sam felt them but did not hurry. Sam thought of Evelyn and smiled, that part of his life was complicated, but he liked those complications! He didn't want to hurry to the house, there were too many complications there now, inside was always where his real complications happened. Maybe he should move. But Evelyn was here, his life was here. Sam was here too. A car horn tooted twice. Sam never looked; it was Evelyn, Sam smiled. She was always good for a smile. Her little red car and Sam arrived at the back door at the same time.

II

Evelyn had jumped from the car as it settled on its suspension, ran around the front of the car and to Sam's side. "It's really raining, you want to get wetter? Let's get in the house."

Sam tossed his chair on the little porch, grabbed Evelyn and changed her direction from the porch to him. She struggled slightly, Sam wrapped her in his arms and kissed her long. The rain came, not pitter pat, but in buckets; they were drenched in a matter of seconds. They didn't really care anymore. They were warm, the rain was cold, their body heat gave off steam as the rain soaked them. Sam broke the contact between their lips.

"We're gonna get wet out here!"

They went in the door, not in a hurry; Evelyn wanted to get in from the rain. They held hands as they entered the kitchen dripping as they did. Sam got towels, and they were drying each other's hair and face. Evelyn looked at the floor and saw the water standing as in a pool at her feet. She began to unbutton her blouse unbeknownst to Sam, who was patting his legs with the towel and thinking, *Now you've caused quite a mess; you started this, and you need to clean it up, not Evelyn.* Sam turned to Evelyn and started to tell her, that he would get a mop. Much to his surprise Evelyn was stepping out of her wet pants as he turned to speak. Then he couldn't talk at all, just look.

"Get out of those things and I will wring them out and toss them into the dryer." Evelyn was back to rubbing her hair and smiling at Sam. Evelyn started picked up her wet clothes and crossed over to Sam and pulled at his shirt tail. "Come on get out of those things!" She unzipped his pants and felt the bulge, and she smiled. She knelt down on the floor, pulling at Sam's pants. She untied his shoes and pulled them away, tilted her head back to speak to Sam. Her attention was directed to the bulge as she pulled down his underwear. She looked up to Sam and smiled.

Later, the rain still coming down, the sky had become a constant grey, as it poured water from the sky. Evelyn was smoking and looking out the window of the bedroom, where their activities had moved. Sam watched too, as the lightning lit the sky with a brilliant white light. Evelyn exhaled deeply, leaned over the bedside, and put the cigarette out. Evelyn pulled the sheet up to her neck, turned toward Sam and braced her head with her hand. "Sam, tonight we talk, if it takes all night, I don't care. Tonight we get all of this out in the open, tonight!"

Sam never turned; he watched out the window, like hoping the answers to magically appear. "Yes," he said, nothing else. He lay very still. "We were going to talk three days ago, I couldn't, the words were not there. I have spent many hours listening and trying to come up with answers that didn't make me look like an absolute idiot. I haven't heard anything from my mind, or anywhere else. Well. here comes idiocy at its best." Sam took up a reflection image of Evelyn. Sam did not smile. They lay there looking at one another, no smiles now.

The lone street light on the dead-end street where Sam lived flickered twice and went out. The sun wasn't even a distant glow. Now all was dark, and the rain came down with no letup. All the house sounds that they had taken for granted stopped, and silence was upon them. Only the rain could be heard, in its never-ending goal to flood the world away.

III

The shelter had been avoided by all the entities at all costs. The static electricity caused irreparable flaws that left a mark, a spot that caused problems. It could not be seen in a physical form here. But when the entities crossed over to assist their humans there was a break in their ability to concentrate on their human entirely. This spot would act as a constant presence that entities could not deny, when with the humans they could see a darkened spot, that they could mentally locate, an ache if you would. Entities took on a form, a vague human form, ghostly in appearance, if at all. No one, not even the Spirits knew that Friend had ever been seen by his human. "Sam" knew this too; he liked to know, and especially that what the Spirit did not know. It made him happy, he had grown to know "happy"! and he liked to be happy.

Entities do not exist; some humans think of them as ghosts, a something, so that they have something to believe in, an afterlife. Some thought that they too would become a spirit, a ghost, heaven bound. Those that had seen their entity would never admit to having seen anything. Some would recall having seen a form. They would generally remember the entity, after having read a grocery store tabloid. Carried away by aliens, Raised by Spirits. Friend knew something that most humans did not; energy, that was all there ever was, but they would then lose all knowing, and start all over, just as humans. That would never do, he laughed aloud. Entities would not come near his shelter; they could not shield themselves from his signs, their signs, that came back to him, from his laughter. Fear! They would fear Friend, No, Sam! He had begun to have individual thoughts for some time now. Now he would find answers on his own, if the Spirit did not, in quick time. Friend had for times now, had a plan; his Sam had been small, hardly worth thoughts. But "Sam" had only came to his own thoughts in time. Thoughts, I will like my Sam's world.

Friend was outside the shelter now looking at what he had created, something the entities did not understand. Friend allowed his form to become opaque; here that was all he could do. His opaque form would could be seen by the entities, it would be just as the entities appeared to the humans they helped. Friend did something that even he had been fearful of before; today his energy was unstoppable. His opaque hand moved with the speed of only knowing; he ran his ghostly fingers down the Pepsi sign, sparks flew from his touch and trailed behind his unseen fingertips spraying outward, and then disappearing. It tingled, to his ghostly touch. "Sam" liked the feeling. "Sam" tried a ghostly smile, but became aware that this was still something that could only be done when he was in Sam's presence, a direct reflection of Sam. "Sam" knew there were things that could be done when he was with Sam that no entity before had ever tried or accomplished. All this show was enough, he could only stay a short time as he was he needed to power soon. But no one could know that, not the Spirit, nor Sam, no one!

Friend was inside shelter and mentally pulled the metal closure to its tightest fit. He used care to mentally only touch the cloth on the edge. All entities received the sign of what had happened, but Friend did not care; they would not come to shelter, they were afraid. Friend liked that; even Spirit could do nothing, only assist. Friend laughed again. Fear? Yes, and what else; yes, he knew from Sam, confusion. Yes, that's right, confusion.

Once the mental echo had stopped, Friend assumed his energy position. Friend could sense the energy coming back to his entity, weak energy, but coming. His entity became a slightly observable circle of light, not measurable by Sam's standards, but there, ghostly. Friend could only take energy now, no entity could change that, just as Spirit could only assist, no laws, only energy. As though awareness departed, with the energy Friend took on, a noise, that could not be heard, maybe, could not even be felt. It gave the energy a blue color, something seen, but not, without form and might be seen from the corner of Sam's eye, but when he looked all he would be left with was the sense of the hair at the nape of his neck standing out, by the little muscle attached to each hair. But only in a millisecond then the feeling was gone, all was gone, nothing to be gone, nothing there at all! Or was there?

IV

"Sam!" a voice yelled. "Where the fuck is that asshole?" Sergeant Bond wiped his forehead and put his helmet back on. The chin strap fell from under the helmet band to his bare chest. Sergeant Bond's hand went to the strap and efficiently tucked it under the band. Sweat ran down his chest where his blouse was opened to the waist. "Sam!" Sergeant Bond called again.

Musky called to Sergeant Bond, "I've got him on OP. He'll be in, in about an hour."

"Naw, get someone out there, and get his ass in here. When he's back send him to the CP."

"The CP? What the fuck is goin' on?" Musky asked but didn't get up immediately; he had his shirt off and was lying on his side, a letter in his hands. "Right now?"

"Right fuckin' now. The captain wants him, now! Don't ask, I don't know, somebody wants him and that's the end. Now get off your ass and go get him!" Bond stood in the grass about waist high, sweat continuing to run down his chest. He only wiped the sweat when it got into his eyes. Bond stood, and watched Musky for a minute. He hadn't moved, he wasn't reading his letter, he just lay in the same place. "Musky, get off your ass and get Sam—move it!"

Musky laid his letter down and looked Bond's direction. "Okay, I'm on my way. Can't get any down time to enjoy my letters, that's pretty fuckin' bad, man." Musky picked his booney hat out of the surrounding gear that was Muskey's home, today. That was all they had to call home, in the bush, home was on your back, all of it. Musky picked up his weapon and started toward the LZ. "Back in a flash, Sarge!"

Bond shook his head and smiled. He turned and started for his position so he could read the letter he had gotten today from the "world." Bond's hand swung at a flying insect with automatic movements unnoticed. Just a guarding movement, that had become part of life in the bush.

The Huey was coming back and security was a bit lax. Bond knew his job was afoot and he started to rouse all his men, he kicked their feet and woke them back up. "Log" days were always this way in the bush, sleep when you could, as the day might bring whatever; they had seen most all of it in Thay Nihn province. It had been slow and that's what bothered him. If you were shooting back everyone was busy, and awake. He made his way toward the CP as the Huey was making the last approach. Gunner was out there, and bringing the Huey in. The breeze felt good as the bird passed by not twenty meters away. There was some dude at the CP in new jungles; that was probably what this was all about. Doesn't look like a priest—was Sam Catholic? Who knew? But Bond was nosey, and wanted to know. Bond slipped into the CP and told the RTO that the bird would make one more pass, and he had hoped for ice on the last chalk, but thought they were out of luck this time. Just small talk to get comfortable, in the inner circle, to snoop.

"There's nothing wrong at home for Sam is there? I mean you've got a new guy here and all, I was just wondering, Sam being mine and all." Bond tried to act interested for Roach, the RTO.

Roach knew that Bond was just nosey. "Naw, something special for little Sammy. This guy's a cop of some sort, kind looks outa place in the bush don't he!" The New York really came out of Roach when he was in control. "Don't think much of coppers, especially the ones that come into my world. This is the last place I ever figure to see a cop!"

Bond leaned toward Roach and spoke low. "Who says he's a cop?"

"When they called the bird's ETA in they said they had a special package on board. An official investigation type they said! What do you figure Sam's into? I don't see him the druggie type, Hell he don't even drink too much. I just figure it's something from back in the 'world,' that' what I figure."

"I'm just gonna hunker down quiet, and see what the Hell Sam's into." Bond leaned back against the rucksack that was there and tried to be unseen.

"Sergeant Bond, what can I do for you?" Captain Ranger himself was looking at Bond knowing what he was there for.

"Just to let you know that Gunner says there's one more bird coming yet, and I wanted to see if it had ice on it. It's been really hot and all, and the men could use some ice, and I…" Bond was trying to sound concerned, but Captain Ranger knew better.

"Bond, you nosey bastard, I know, and you know I know why you're here. You will have to ask Corporal Young what this is all about. Now get the fuck out of my area, before I find something for you to do that you probably won't like." The captain stood with his hands on both hips in his most officer stance.

Bond grabbed his weapon and was on his way. He knew Roach had the biggest mouth in the company and everybody would know before dark anyway. *Fuck you, Ranger!* Bond thought as he walked away.

"Everybody wants to know what this is all about. And you are telling me that you don't know?" Captain Faber asked the clean jungles that was occupying space in his AO. He still held his open-footed stance, as he directed the questioning. He knew his men called him Ranger and he didn't mind that at all. One day they might even call him Ranger during his campaign when he got back to the world; "Senator Ranger" will now speak to the assembled

Congress, blaring trumpets and red carpet. Ranger smiled inside and gave off a little chuckle. "You know you might just have to spend the night with us tonight if we don't get this done pretty soon." Ranger smiled again.

Mr. Chute had met this variety before, God like, in all they perceived as their territory, and he had had about enough of them. Chute pulled his briefcase from the bag he had carried it out to the jungle for his mission, dusted it lightly, and set in front of him. Once opened, he took out the fingerprint sheet and a small inkpad, took out a tube of ink and started to prepare the pad with a small roller. "Well, Captain, You'll be right here with me till were done. And that will make me feel safe, I'm sure." Chute looked around and saw no table or any of the things he normally worked with and decided to use his briefcase as a short table. Chute looked up toward the captain and could see the sun streaming through the trees, and pushed his sunglasses from the top of his head into place on his face and smiled. This captain might bluff these men but not Chute; he held his pose till the captain turned away. *Gotcha, ya asshole!* Chute's smile never wavered.

The captain did not like this. He knew Chute wasn't an ordinary cop; they didn't send cops to the bush for jay walking, Young would answer for this, he was just as nosy as Bond, but tried to make it seem that he was concerned. His gaze turned to the LZ where the Huey was just lifting off. Someone was running across the LZ that he thought, had better be Young!

The CP all watched as the slim figure of a man came straight toward the CP. Roach knew Young and said, "That's Young, sir."

"About time!" Captain Faber said, not knowing what else to say after Chute's last remark. Chute might be important, and Faber might need him later to be on his side. *All votes count, and they all have to be silent, and just vote,* Faber thought. "Where the Hell have you been, man? We've been waiting forever!" Ranger was back.

"OP, sir. Musky just told me to get here. Something wrong?" Sam looked at the new jungles and all kinds of thoughts about home came into view. "Who? Fuck!"

Chute was on his feet in a flash, and had his hand out in front of him. Sam's hand came out to meet Chute's slowly. Chute grabbed his hand in a thumbs-up grip and shook it soundly. "First off, I'm not with the chaplain, nothing is wrong at home. Some of your records have been damaged, and I have to get a good set of fingerprints, you know in case there would be something happen,

God forbid! So if you would just sit down here, in my office, I'm waiting on new furniture, and I'll try and not get ink all over the both of us." Chute sat down Indian style in an instant.

"Thank God! I was afraid that something...well you know. "Sam squatted down in front of Chute's briefcase. *Nice briefcase, for the bush,* Sam thought.

Chute proceeded to tell Sam what he was doing and how they would do it. Small talk about how Chute thought it was awfully hot here, and he didn't know how anyone could last long out here. It took two sheets to get the fingerprints the way he wanted them.

The captain was pacing just out of sight, wondering what was really happening, and why would they send a CID out here for fingerprints. This guy had looked like a REMF when he got off the bird, but a closer look had told him no. Something bigger somewhere. And he wanted to know what!

The last bird came in, with three hundred pounds of ice and the rest of the re-supply, and Mr. Chute left on it. Sam was back in the first platoon area. And everyone wanted to know who Sam had killed, fucked, or could they borrow some money from all the loot he had stashed away in a jar at home.

"I don't recall having any knowledge of any wrongdoing, at anytime," Sam kept saying and they all laughed as they spun their beer on a block of ice to get them halfway cold. The hot Carling Black Label cans made little can-shaped depressions in the ice as they spun them. "Cold enough!" Sam said and popped the top. The beer sprayed everywhere, and he tipped it up to his lips before it all sprayed away. They all laughed again. "Didn't want a beer anyway, just a shower!" They all laughed again.

The captain would talk to Sam over the next week six times, never spoke to Sam before, and would not again, once he had decided that maybe Chute had been a REMF after all, and Young's file had really only been loused up; sometimes the truth is stranger than fiction. Most of the guys forgot about it as soon as it was over, all but Sam. He would hear the story at home and go through some uncomfortable questioning from his mom. And then there was that retired FBI agent that would ask a bunch of questions later too. But it never really made any sense to him. His mom had looked his hands over really close when he had first gotten home. And that too all ended, till the day he had cut his thumb while running the new barbed wire with his dad. It had left a scar that they had all looked at funny. After he had healed, they would all look again;

they would never really make any sense about why, but they had really looked it over. But, at the time it had only been a funny coincidence. Till later.

Sam had almost felt betrayed when Carl Flaners had showed up at the house one afternoon. His thumb had been sensitive to any real grip but was healing. Carl had brought a piece of paper, an old piece of paper. The copy sent then, was not of a quality to really make a definitive call on, as far as fingerprints, but the scar was a plain as daybreak. After they had all looked, turned the paper this way and that, Carl looked Sam in the eyes, still and dark. "I've had this for a while now, Sam, you can burn it, throw it away, whatever. I have only opened another door, a door that shows only darkness, and I don't want to look anymore." Carl had held the paper out till Sam had taken it from him. He smiled and said goodbye. Sam didn't see him again till his mom and dad's funeral.

Not till much later, much later. Sam had looked for the paper for a long time before it finally fell before his eyes out of the bottom of a box marked "BS." It was placed in a steel box, fireproof; why he didn't know. But kept it he had, like the prom schedule, and the airplane that he and Friend had flown. He had them both; why he would realize many years later..

V

Carl had become a regular at the Young household. Bob and Paula had become comfortable with him about the house. He had asked a lot of questions, the questions would never stop; it was just Carl, Paula had said on evening. But his questions had become more in line with the locals, economy, houses, shopping. He had begun to dress more casual. The investigation, at least Carl and Lou's part, had lasted for almost five months. It was on April 1st the shiny red Dodge Charger had pulled into the driveway. Not too many Chargers that color; most were black. Paula had gotten up to see if it might be a customer, someone she had never seen before, or at least the car. She was leaning into the window over the sink when she realized it was Carl. It had been three months now since she had last seen Carl, but the feeling of dread came back instantly. She was still looking out the window as Bob came in the back door.

"What you looking at so damned hard?" Bob asked as he stood behind Paula, wiping his hands and waiting for her to move so he could wash his hands.

"That's Carl!" Paula told him.

"Carl who? Can I wash my hands? The water is off at the shop till I get that new sink in and I would like to get some coffee." Bob was still wiping his hands with the red shop towel.

"Carl Flanners! And he has an older woman with him. Bob, I don't think I can put up with this BS anymore! Sam's due home any day now, and I don't need this." Paula still leaned across the sink.

"He said it was over. I don't know. But we will deal with it. Calm down, maybe it's because Sam is due home, I don't know. Now let me wash up, and you had better get some more coffee on, I'm drinking the last cup. That is, if I can get my hands washed."

Bob knew he had to make light of it; he heard the change in Paula's voice. Bob too, was worried; he had heard of cases that the FBI had had in the past that had never been solved, and they just kept coming back. Sam would be told all of the details when he arrived home, when he ETS'ed. He had never heard the story, and he and Paula had decided not to tell him till he was out of the Army. Bob busied himself with cleaning up for the FBI agents, and worrying. The doorbell rang at the front of the house. Odd, they both thought; Carl had always used the back door.

Paula brushed her blouse down her sides and pushed her hair back as she crossed the living room. When the doorbell rang she wanted to let out a little scream, but she only slowed her pace and took a few deep breaths. Paula paused at the door, her hand on the knob. She turned the knob to the right slowly.

The door opened slowly. Paula stood in the opening, and Carl started the conversation.

"Paula, how have you been? It's been a few months and I wanted to bring Joan down here to see the property that I've been trying to buy. Is Bob around? I've told Joan about all that we put you folks through, and she's a bit scared to be here with me now!" Carl chuckled.

"Carl, don't start with that FBI bullshit; you probably got this dear lady scared to death." Joan stood with Carl just to the right, and behind her; she knew it was an uncomfortable moment.

Paula stood in statue form for a few seconds. Recovering slowly she pushed the screen door open. "Come in, come in. I was just about to make a fresh pot of coffee—would you have some?" Paula took Joan's hand in hers lightly and said, "I'm Paula, and you're Joan?"

Paula was relieved, but not completely. "Bob, look who's here."

Bob had another towel in his hands, as he came through the kitchen door. "You said it was Carl. She's been watching out the kitchen window since you pulled in the drive. What can we do for you, Carl?" Bob could feel Paula's stare as she let go of Joan's hand, and turned his direction.

"Joan, I would like you to meet my husband, Bob. And that had better not be one of my good towels." Paula slipped her arm into the crook of Bob's as he continued to dry his hands. He had gotten most of the dirt and oil off but some was being transferred to the towel.

Bob stuck his right hand out to grip Joan's; his grip was gentle. Bob smiled. "This is an unofficial visit, or is your new partner now, your wife?" Bob smiled and looked at Carl; he still held Joan's hand.

Joan looked over her shoulder and looked at Carl too. "Carl?" her eyes asking as much as her voice. Bob still held her hand, almost as if for ransom.

"No, no business. I had never mixed business with pleasure till I arrived here, but there is no ulterior motive. Bob, what I would like is for you, and Paula, if she likes, to go with me to show Joan the property I had looked at down the road a bit." Carl had a sincere look to his face.

Bobs face lost the fake smile that he had been wearing, and he let Joan's hand go free.

Paula still had her doubts. She had gotten comfortable with Carl when he dropped by twice a week for those months through the winter, but this was like an old injury coming back again. Now he wanted to live nearby. She still didn't like it much, her fake smile was longer in trying to go away. She did the next best thing and turned toward the kitchen, and walked away slowly, so as to allow her to hear Carl bring up the case again, if he did; she still didn't like it.

"Paula. Where you going?" Bob looked concerned again afraid that she was right.

"I told you I was going to make coffee," she stated flatly. "Joan, you can come in here if you like. I never trust them alone, but I never want to hear what they have to say either."

Joan stepped around Bob. "Excuse me, Bob." Joan was around Bob and headed toward the kitchen door. She looked at the living room as if inspecting her new location. She too felt Paula's worry, and didn't blame her one bit. This was after all, an FBI agent seeking help from someone from an investigation, an investigation that he had been the supervisor on as well. But here they were, in these strangers' house. This might be difficult yet.

Joan stepped through the kitchen doorway and felt at ease. The kitchen was big, clean and neat, she cold see the dining area through the large doorway at the other end of the kitchen. It too looked pleasant. Joan walked across the kitchen, to Paula at the sink. She touched Paula's arm just above the left elbow gently. "Paula, you don't have to make any coffee for us, but I want you to know that this wasn't any of my idea at all. I told Carl that this might not be his best move, and to want to buy land here. It just makes me a little uncomfortable." Joan was talking at light speed now; Carl had always said she could talk the ears off a dead mule.

Paula turned to Joan, still with the untrusting in her eyes. "First off, Joan, I want to say I'm sorry how we met." Paula stuck out her hand and Joan took it. Paula squeezed it slightly and shook it twice, her smile a bit more at ease now. "Now, we're, or at least I am a little more comfortable. Carl has tried to be an asshole a few times here but, I wouldn't let him. I think it's the FBI thing." Her smile was melting into something that seemed, more true now. "Now, coffee!"

Joan was in high gear now. Paula added her comments when she could. "We have always lived in the 'burbs' as the agency always wanted their men to be part of the community, and now he wants to move into the country. Have you always been here? Do you like to live in the country?"

Joan quit, almost as suddenly as she started. "I know I talk a lot, and for that I am sorry, but he is going to move away from all I know and all the people I know. We don't have a lot of friends, because of Carl's job. And I just don't know anymore." Paula detected the same distrust and anguish in Joan's voice that she had felt when they had arrived.

The two women had been sitting on the corner of the dining room. Paula reached across the table and took Joan's hand; she gently squeezed it. Joan's other hand was covering her eyes, and her head was shaking back and forth slowly.

Meanwhile the men were doing men's things in the shop. Carl was helping Bob install the sink and they were talking about fishing and guns.

Bob almost had the last bolt tight. "Yeah, I used to hunt all the time, but Paula got tired of being left alone all the time. I worked all day and hunted or fished all weekend. She said enough is enough. I still get a license each year, but haven't shot anything but at a turkey shoot in two or three years. Let it go now; it will say in place till I get the base under it. I haven't had a chance to get this thing installed. The boys are always working on jobs, and I haven't had the heart to ask one of them to stay over. I appreciate this, Carl."

Bob was scooting out from under the sink, and sat up. "Now I have to ask, what about your case? Will all this start up again when Sam gets home? I wouldn't ask in front of Paula; she hasn't done well with all of this. When you pulled into the driveway in that shiny red beast, she didn't expect you to get out of it. And when you did, it all started over."

"When's Sam due home?" Carl asked, still holding the sink.

"In about a month. He's going to drive back form Fort Hood, Texas. I think he's ready to get on with his life." Bob turned the valve to allow water into the sink.

"Don't take this wrong, but I would like to meet him. If he has any questions of me he can ask them. I'm sure you will tell him the story, such a story that it became. I will be retired from the FBI in two months. I want to start building the house, if me and the bank can come to terms. But I'll tell you something else too! I will deny that I ever brought this up. Joan has told me all the way here this morning that she will have nothing of me carrying on business that has been closed out." Carl turned the faucet on the sink and water started spit once, twice and then settled into a steady stream. A stream that was running on the floor. Carl quickly turned the water off. "I thought..."

"We were talking and I didn't even think about the drain." Bob walked to the wall of tools and took down a squeegee and started to push water out the open door. "Well, Sam doesn't know any of it. I know that I have to tell him after he has settled in. And all I wanted to know, is it over? And if it's not where does it go from here?" Bob pushed the water out the door and leaned against the squeegee. He stared at Carl.

"The case as far as your son goes is over. I don't know how it ever came to you. The fingerprints of the person passing those bogus bills were Sam's, but the lab boys said that they had so many prints, that they ran a bunch of them through. They will swear that they are Sam's, except for the scar on the thumb. The prints in Nam do not have a scar. The once infallible system of no two prints are ever exactly the same has been proven wrong. He was in Viet Nam, in the field with ninety-three other men; never left the field. So, therefore is as innocent as new fallen snow. It was a real screw-up. There are six Sam Young's in this state. Eleven in Missouri and several in other states. All of them have been through the same investigation as you and Paula.

"I will tell you that I am personally sorry for any inconvenience that we may have put you through. You have been more than helpful, and patient, throughout the entire investigation. But it still doesn't sit well with me. One shot, and never again. The guy that made those bills would have been on easy street if he had copied the picture and not blown it up the way he did. The Treasury Department said they were perfect in every way, perfect. Now the subject is dropped as far as I am concerned. And yes, I want to meet your son. But not for this case."

Carl was squatted down at the sink front and starting to put the drain on. "Hand me some of those god-awful big pliers, Bob. The case has never been solved, and there has never been another bill or coin passed. I still keep an eye on that kind of thing. It's a matter of pride, but I guess it will follow me to the grave. You know I don't like to lose, and I had never lost before. And with only two months left at the department I will not lose again." Carl started to screw the fittings together.

The drain was a success and the men headed to the house for coffee. As they approached the sliding doors they could see the wives holding hands. Carl thought, *How nice*; Bob thought, *What now?* The women separated as the sliding door was pushed open.

They both looked as thought they had been caught with their hands in the cookie jar. Neither man said a word, as they passed to the kitchen to get coffee.

Small talk, and a hamburger lunch, then a ride to the prospective property.

Paula knew Joan's feelings and was unable to tell anyone. The ride was quiet. The men wondered what the women knew about their conversation. Bob turned down Whippoorwill Lane and drove slow as he wasn't exactly sure where the property was located. Then they all saw the realtor's sign, pretty much grown up in weeds. Carl had the key to the lock on the gate as he had made arrangements to see the property the week prior.

"This place has already grown up in weeds and it's not even summer." Joan wanted to like it, but not a whole lot. Maybe she could let Carl down easy; maybe she would start to sneeze or her eyes would water.

"That's just last years weeds greening back up. You've probably been trying to buy a real dump here, Carl." Bob laughed. Carl joined him half heartedly. the women were silent.

Carl got back in and Bob started up the lane, it turned to the right and on the left was a small lake, with geese, and a heron took to flight just as they came out of the trees. Bob stopped the car. They all looked at the lake and the surrounding woods.

"This is beautiful!" Joan said. "Let's get out and walk a bit." Joan's eyes were wide now; she was mentally recanting her earlier statements.

"I didn't even know this was here." Bob shut the car off and opened the door. He stepped back and opened Joan's door.

Carl did the same for Paula, and the foursome stood quietly and just looked about. The geese were busy moving about and dipping for small fish; they moved in unison, and put on a show for the foursome. Carl walked down the lane, by himself, toward a point with apparent intent. He was headed somewhere and the other three followed. Carl got to a point and turned sideways and put his arms out in front of him. "Here! Right here is where the house would go, set back just inside the trees. The property comes with all but that corner at the front." Carl pointed back to the gate. "Cooper family have fought on this piece of property for years, and most have died. The last two are tired of fighting and offer this for thirty-two thousand. It will cost another twenty thousand to build the house. This is better than the pictures. What do you think, sweetheart?" Carl walked over to Joan and took her hand in his; he just watched Joan.

"This is like the place in Colorado. This is beautiful. I love it!" Joan smiled, turned and looked at Paula. She gave her a toothy smile, and squinted her eye like she had not done since she had been a child.

The ladies walked away holding hands and talking a mile a minute.

Bob stuck his hand out to Carl. "You just became a hero, neighbor."

Carl took Bob's hand and shook it vigorously and his smile grew with each shake.

VI

Sam had bought a 1969 Chevelle, and was driving about Fort Hood clearing post. Two weeks early, and he felt good about getting out of Texas. He was sure that there had to be places in Texas that were nice. But this place was the asshole of the world! He had made some good friends in Nam, and most were still with him. When the 1st Cav. came home so did he. He wore a 1st Cav. patch on each shoulder; he was proud, but not proud enough to stay. His stay with Uncle Sam was about done. "Got you through that one." Sam slammed the brakes on in front of the battalion supply, gravel flew and a SFC stopped and looked at him sternly.

"Pull it up here, boy."

Sam eased the car up to the rail about another ten to twelve feet and shut it off. The sergeant first class walked to his side of the car and looked in the window at Sam.

"Do you know how to drive this thing? Have you been drinking?" The SFC stood with his hands on his hips motionless.

"I don't know what happened, I just hit the brakes too hard. I just bought the car and, I'm sorry." Sam just sat there waiting.

The SFC looked at Sam's shoulders and saw both the Cav patches. "Just back?"

"Yes, just." Sam waiting for the worst to happen.

But, instead the SFC stuck his hand in the window. "Proud of you! Welcome home! And you had better practice with this thing before you leave Hood; those cops out there are a real bad bunch when it comes to soldiers." The SFC turned and walked away.

Sam didn't want to admit to himself that the voice was in his head; he had heard it in Nam twice. Both times it had saved his ass. Now this, and he got away with it too, thought that that SFC was about to have his ass. Sam grabbed his paperwork and his duffel with all his TA-50 and headed up the walk. The checkout was easy, no shortages and he got his paperwork one step away from being done and outta here! One of Sam's boot laces was sticking out and he knelt at the side of the car to fix it and straighten out his boot blouser.

"I am still here, Sam. You are about done here, and I have to power. I will be back at a later time."

Sam looked about and saw no one. It startled him for a second, then he stood up, looked about again and got into the car. Sam spoke aloud, "What the Hell is going on?"

"I have told you I have to power now. I will be back at another time. be safe and I will return."

Sam knew it was Friend. He had known in Quan Loi, and in Cambodia as well; he hadn't talked to him, but Friend had been there. Both times he had been a help. Sam sat there, he gripped the wheel, then he spoke a loud again. "Thanks, Friend!" no answer. "I hope that you ring me or something on the way home. I don't want to wreck this thing on the way home." No answer. Sam pushed the clutch in, shifted to reverse and backed out slowly. In a few minutes and a few blocks Sam was himself again, turned the radio on and listened to the music on the way back to the barracks.

But Sam knew, he knew that there was something that was different. The doctors had pronounced him okay, mostly because he agreed that to go against them was only to continue to visit the doctors. He knew that there had been a lot of loud talk that wasn't meant for his ears. His mom and dad would stop talking when he came into the room; they would smile, and ask him if he needed anything, and wait till he left the room again.

He knew that most people did not have imaginary friends, maybe Red Skelton, or some other comedians, but not real people, and Sam was a real people, and he didn't have an imaginary friend, he was real. But Sam had other things on his mind, getting out of Texas! After Fort Hood, he would shun Texas, and the Army for that matter as well.

The barracks was its usual self, card games, sleeping and loud music. These guys were mostly fresh back to the world, and did not like the Army anymore, just biding their time till they too got out. Sam went to his locker and opened it up. Not much left; he had sent home most of the excess equipment and clothes. The necklace that he had had made from the bullet that had scratched his arm in Nam was hanging there. Just a scratch, then it had struck the tree. After the firefight he had dug it out of the tree and had had it mounted so it would fit on a chain. The first sergeant had a fit every time he wore it. But he saved it for the ride home, it was his lucky charm. Friend had yelled at him, and he had ducked in the nick of time. Just lucky! That's what he had always told everybody, Just lucky. So when Friend showed up, Sam would pay attention! Always and forever!

He never talked to anyone about Friend. They would lock him up nowadays; a kid was one thing, but he wasn't a kid anymore. But at the time he wasn't sure it had been Friend, till today and he knew the voice was the same. Something that he recognized, but couldn't put his finger on it, almost, but not quite. He was standing in front of his locker, his hand outstretched, holding his bullet, his lucky charm. Poor Boy came up and touched his shoulder. It was like an electric shock. "What!" Sam jumped to the right and banged into a bunk.

"Are you alright? It's that fuckin' bullet! You're outta here in a few days; you had better not let the lifers see you like that. They will lock you away and never let you go home!" Poor Boy looked a little scared at Sam's reaction.

"No, no, I'm alright, just, you know, thinking about getting out of here. I guess I was in a daze or something, I don't know. I'm alright." Poor Boy had caught him off guard, way off guard, and had scared him. In the milliseconds that had passed he had relived the entire firefight and all the Hell following. Shooter had been killed that day, not four feet away. They had almost cut him in half with the machine gun, and Sam only had a little scar on his upper arm. That had been his lucky day alright, and the bullet had become his lucky charm.

Barney had woken when Sam had fallen into the bunk, and he was on his side and looking up at the two of them. "You two need to go somewhere else if you're going to wrestle, I'm trying to rest, ya know. I need my beauty rest. This Army stuff takes it out of me!" Barney lay back on his bunk and smiled up at the two.

"Fuck you, Barney, you're fresh meat and haven't been anywhere yet. But we're going to make sure that you get your turn." Poor Boy didn't like Barney; he wouldn't have made it in Nam.

"I'm only here till my medical release comes through, then I'm gone, gone. You assholes can live this bullshit forever for all I care anyway. Bunch of fuckin' baby killers, anyway!" Barney was pushing, and Poor Boy was looking for a fight.

Sam stepped in front of Poor Boy. "Let go, man. He's not worth getting busted over."

"Yeah, you'd lose your precious sergeant stripes, and I would make sure of that!" Barney was about to let his mouth override his ass.

Sam turned in an instant, bent over and had his right hand on Barney's neck. "I don't have anything to lose! Shut up or I'll break your scrawny neck, and let Poor Boy have what's left over. I do most of his light work. And you would be a waste of my time, let alone his!" Sam leaned into his throat; he didn't put up any resistance. Sam stood slowly, and turned back to face Poor Boy. "Come on, let's go get a burger at the shoppette." Sam turned Poor Boy away, and pushed him forward to get him moving. Poor Boy started to say something and Sam put his index finger in front of his lips. "No, don't even start it. He's a fuckin' basket case, and they will throw him out with the trash soon enough." He pushed Poor Boy again.

Poor Boy went to his bunk to get his blouse and cap. He was buttoning his blouse and looking at Barney over Sam's shoulder. Barney had turned over to his side so as not to be facing Sam and Poor Boy. "That asshole's only been here for two weeks, and half the platoon wants him dead! I'm not too far from making that happen." Poor Boy tucked his blouse in and they started for the stairs.

"Man, you know he's only goading you on to get a rise. If you beat the shit out of him he'll find a way to make it work for him. Leave it alone!"

"Yeah! You're probably right. How long?" Poor Boy was over it now, and they were off to the shoppette for burgers. Sam would buy as usual; Poor Boy was always up to his name. Poor Boy was gone after that; Sam never heard from him again, nor most of the rest of them. They had been family in Nam, but the world was different now. Very different, especially for Nam vets!

"Two weeks! Two weeks and I'm gone! Outta here like the fuckin' tumbleweeds, but I'm never going to stop! I'm going to travel and see it all!" The two laughed as they had many times before Sometimes, just to keep from crying. It had been good, but, Sam would never really travel, just the states around him, just to make money. Their free spirits had been left in Nam, their spirits and a whole lot more, that would never come back. The darkness would follow all of them to their graves.

Part 2

Chapter 6
Friends Forever

I

16 April 1970, 12:30 p.m., Sam wrote in his steno pad. He thought, the pen poised over his pad. *I'll write something when I stop. No, something.* Pen and pad again met. The words were slow, "Out of the fucking Army." He marked through the *fucking Army*—"have said my good byes. I will miss most of these guys, someday. But right now I'm out of here. My bags are packed, I'm in civilian clothes, cars tank is full, and I begin my journey!"

Poor Boy came up to the window, tapped on it. And Sam rolled the window down.

"Broke again, and I'm not even off the fuckin' post!" Sam laughed. He saw moisture had collected in the corner of Poor Boy's eyes, Sam opened the Chevelle's door.

They stood there for what seemed an eternity, hugs in the Army were not an issue item. Poor Boy squeezed Sam so tight that he was having difficulty breathing. The two said nothing till Poor Boy broke the choke hold.

"Man, I'll miss you! You be careful on the trip home. You and that stick shift aren't the best of friends, just yet. You'll get the hang of it all right." Poor Boy made a fist and pushed Sam's shoulder, rocking Sam slightly back. Poor Boy kept his eyes turned down and wouldn't look straight at Sam. "I'll be by one of these days, if you ever get there."

Poor Boy turned and started away, his right hand went into the air in a parting shot, wave.

Sam stood quite still. He watched as Poor Boy walked away. "Be cool, my man!" Sam felt something in his eyes too! Must be this fucking Texas dust. Sam got back in the car rolled the window up and started the engine. He shifted to reverse and wiped his eyes.

Sam had to wipe his eyes several times that day. He looked at all of Fort Hood differently that day, as he left, the last time he would drive on this road. He drove slowly, and looked at the post command headquarters, and he smiled. He honked the horn loud and long as he left the post, the guards knew it was a free man. They watched drive out of the gate. They smiled, a knowing smile; they too would leave one day, they too would honk the horn, long and loud.

Ten thousand thoughts entered Sam's mind, all the things that he wanted to write down, he wrote a few when he stopped in Lake Charles, Louisiana, for the night. The drive had been a mental focus on what he had done for the past two years. He had met a lot of people, some had become friends, some brothers. They had done what few had done, they had lived together, slept together, killed together. And other than Rock, Tinker, and Poor Boy, Sam didn't even know their names; so many were just people he had passed in his quest to stay alive. *They almost got me!* Sam sat in his car outside room 23, both hands on the wheel. His eyes were leaking again; he wiped his eyes.

After unloading the car and settling in the motel, Sam looked about the room. He looked for his pad and pen. "It's in the car, or somewhere; I'll find it later."

His voice startled him. "You spoke aloud—there you've done it again!" Sam thought that this was a habit he had to change before he got home. When did it start? Couldn't remember, he hadn't always done that had he? Sam had seen a bar at the corner where the motel shared a driveway in the back. "Yeah, a beer, and a fine Louisiana girl to celebrate my first night of freedom!" *You did it again!* he thought. Sam checked his left rear pocket for his wallet, and picked up the room key, and was off.

The bar had a name that struck Sam as odd; "Harry O's" didn't make any sense to Sam, but they had cold beer, and it tasted good. Sam, never much of a beer drinker, asked himself why he was there. No answer, just cold beer. Sam had two and left Harry O's. He walked up the street and looked around, for what he didn't know, but he could do it, and put his hands in his pockets if he wanted to, and didn't have a hat on either. Sam smiled and locked his elbows in place. That made him look a little odd, but he didn't care. "You're free now, and can do anything you want!"

"What was that, mister?" a little girl asked as Sam walked past.

"What? Nothing, I'm sorry." Sam felt his face go red as he realized he was talking out loud again. Sam smiled at the little girl, eight or nine, Sam thought.

She watched as he walked back toward Harry O's. He turned about a half of a block away and she was still watching. It was then that Sam realized he was eight or ten blocks away; he didn't remember walking this far. "Oh well! She will remember you for awhile, probably thought you were drunk!" Sam took his hands out of his pockets; his elbows felt instant relief. "How long have you been walking like that?" *Aloud again. Man, this is getting bad, no wonder she looked at you! My head is alright, two beers, that was all.* He stopped at the light and waited for the walk signal. Sam looked back and saw the little girl on the sidewalk. She was still looking, but she saw Sam looking, and she turned and ran toward the house. *Weird little girl,* Sam thought, or did he say it out loud? He didn't know.

Sam made a conscious effort on the last few blocks, full strides, hands cupped inward, march, left, right, left. His mind was working overtime, on something, but he didn't want to know. Just get back to his new home, at least for tonight. Thoughts flooded in, hundreds of thoughts, home, Mom, Dad, work? What work? Sam had a whole new life ahead of him, but what, what life? Sam was rapidly approaching the motel, but turned at the last minute to Harry O's. "Why are you here?"

"What's that?" The bartender wiped the glass rings left by the former occupant of Sam's stool.

"Schlitz. On tap, right! Give me a Schlitz." Sam looked odd he knew, he felt it.

"Are you alright, bub?" The bartender had stopped wiping the bar top and was looking at Sam.

"Yeah. Yeah, just got out of the Army today! A little lost I guess." Sam felt like the little girl was there watching him.

"Just got out, huh? I remember that day too!" The bartender walked to the tap and drew up a Schlitz, set it down on the stainless drain cover, and drew another. He had been talking and being ignored by Sam. "You sure you're all right?"

"Yeah. Just a long drive, and a late start." Sam took the beer from the bartender and tipped it up. He sat the half-full glass down on the bar starting a new set of rings for the bartender to wipe later.

"Hood's a ways. I never been there, don't intend to go either." He smiled and tipped his glass. "Don't usually drink and work, but in celebration of you just getting out and all..." He held his glass out to Sam and they touched lightly with a fragile clink.

Sam had three or four beers; they tasted good tonight. He told the bartender of his little stint in Southeast Asia, and they were the best of friends. Sam couldn't pay for the beer, Steve wouldn't hear of it. It seems that Steve had bought the bar, and the name; didn't want to pay for another sign, so it was still Harry O's. Steve told Sam of Korea and vice versa. Sam smiled a lot, and he thought a lot; sometimes the smile was hard to keep going. Sam had a good buzz on and it was just getting busy with Steve's regulars.

Sam made his excuses about this drive the next day and shook Steve's hand and exited as gracefully as he could. Sam's buzz allowed him to get back to the motel and sleep like the dead. That was good. Dreamless nights were not usual for Sam. It was good.

The awakening was a new chapter in Sam's life. "Awake, where, how? Okay, now remember, you're a free man!" Sam sat up and thrust his hands over his head as though the had just won an Olympic event. His head told him he had not won, and it had been a valiant effort, but there was baggage! Sam didn't drink much, and he began to recall the evening at Harry O's. It flooded back, one drink at a time. It wasn't a bad headache, but it wasn't a very good way to start off your new life as a civilian, either. Alka Seltzer was what his grandpa had used, that's what Sam needed, now. But first it was load the car, pay the bill, and get out of here. Sam checked his watch as he went to the office to check out. It was eight thirty. *Better start today,* he thought, yeah, he thought. He made good with the office, picked up a "convenience pack" with two Alka Seltzers, a plastic cup of water, and plop, plop, fizz, fizz. Sam looked at Harry O's and kept walking to his car. The headache would go away in time he knew, but not the nagging in his stomach.

"Food!"

"What's that, sir?" the maid asked as she pulled some pillowcases form the bottom of her cart.

Sam was again asking himself when had he started this talking aloud. "Food. Where can I get some food? Sorry I didn't mean to startle you."

"You'll want breakfast, ya know sit-down style. Or some of the truck stop stuff. There's two truck stops on ninety, and a little sit-down place 'bout two blocks on the left if that's what you might like." She never stopped unloading the clean linen as she spoke.

"Thanks!" Sam tried to be jovial, but his head had not benefitted form the Alka Seltzer just yet. "Sit down, that's what I need, something clean, not too greasy, no truck stop food this morning." Sam proceeded to the local sit-down restaurant, and the Alka Seltzer had had the time to do its trick. Grandpa had been right after all!

Soon Sam was back on the road again. He drove slow, telling himself that he wanted to see all there was to see on his maiden voyage. He was free, and it felt odd. It had only been a two-year stint in the Army, but they had had him at a young age, and had caused habits, Army habits. Sam wondered what Poor Boy and the guys were doing, but he knew what they were doing. They were setting up on the top of some god-forsaken mesa and were about to test the same equipment that he had used for a year in Nam. It worked there, why keep testing it here? With those thoughts Sam was glad he was gone. But he still missed the guys. His brothers, that he had never had, friends for life. Friends, that kind of stuck in his brain as the thought passed through, friend. Sam found himself driving without seeing anything. He stopped at a local barbeque stand, "Hot Finger Licking Good," the sign had read. Hot wasn't the word for it; it burned his fingers, and then it had entered his mouth. He was even stupid enough to swallow, then it had gotten really hot, two iced teas, and a large Coke had not put the fire out.

The large black lady had laughed at Sam and said, "You northern folks have to take Cajun food careful, it's powerful!" Powerful was a mouth full, and then some!

Sam made a mental note, no more Cajun food! Sam was watching the roads; somehow he made the turn toward New Orleans. After a while Sam started to see Nam from the window of his Chevelle. The exhaust made a melodic sound that kept noise in the background. Sam pulled over at a roadside stop and sat quietly, watching, for what he did not know.

Sam's mind was doing the things that the old sarge had told all of the Nam vets, don't let the heebeey geebeeys get to you. You've been to the dark side of the moon, you ain't got no place left but the Army, just stay awhile, they'll find ya another war somewhere They had all told him he was crazy, and they really thought so, and old Sarge would just nod his head. He was nuts, and he knew it, and he liked it too! Sam had had thoughts, and they came back to the forefront. Sam put them far, far away. Sam only knew of two that he had personally killed, that hadn't been too bad, but all the carnage he had seen had pretty much made up his mind. The carnage had been on both sides, dead Americans had been a bitch. He had his nightmares, he guess they all did, but no one talked about them, no one. That would have made them less of a man, they each had thought, so thought Sam, because no one talked. The scenes played through his mind, the devastation was accepted at that time. But now he sat on a picnic table in Louisiana thinking about NVA dead! When did everyone else have their dreams, in the middle of the afternoon.

Sam tossed the RC Cola bottle in the green litter container. It said "keep Louisiana litter free and beautiful"; it made a hollow sound. The Louisiana Highway Department had been through here already this afternoon. There were swamps all around the road, a few houses here and there. Sam saw bamboo. He smelled the swamp, the damp, the air was thick, he was back, back in Nam. A car pulled in and Sam's trance was broken. He got into the Chevelle, and watched the lady in stretch pants two sizes too small take her little dog to the edge of the woods. She looked at Sam and smiled. Sam smiled back, and thought, *Wish a big old gator would come outta the swamp and snatch that little mouse!* Sam chuckled, turned the key, the Chevelle's engine roared to life and the little dog almost jumped into the lady's arms, she wasn't smiling now.

Sam goosed the Chevelle a bit and the tires found it hard to grip, they spun, and the sound made the little dog yip, Sam thought, he never looked back. On the road to New Orleans, forty or so miles now, the road became four lanes, and the traffic picked up.

Lots of out-of-state automobiles, tourists. Sam was a tourist too. He didn't like the word much, tourist.

New Orleans wasn't much for Sam, beautiful in an old-fashioned way, but too many tourists; they pushed and shoved their way into stores, onto busses, and they were loud. Sam never liked people much, and this wasn't doing him any good; he felt trapped. The bus ride ended, and Sam moved to his car with no wasted time. The tires barked again and there was no little dog to scare. Sam just wanted out of the city, he needed air.

Out of town, Sam slowed the car down. He looked for a motel. He thought that they would all be full at this hour. He saw a vacancy on a Cozy Inn. *Cozy,* he thought, *I'll bet.* It looked clean, and they were individual little cottages, private. Sam paid and moved his baggage into the little cottage. He had told the man at the desk that he might stay for a few nights. Sam's mind needed mending. Maybe Sam needed to go back to Hood and restart his life. *Restart,* he thought, *I haven't even begun, let alone need to restart. I just need to slow down and breathe deeply.* Sam walked to the restaurant that was attached to the office and had some supper. He stayed away form the Cajun surprise.

Surprise! he thought. *It'll burn you out before you know what has happened!* He knew he had thought that, he had hadn't he? Sam was trying not to talk aloud, and at times he knew he had missed a few lines, by people's reactions. They were too polite to come out and tell him that he was making a fool of himself in public.

Mr. Cozy Inn had all the bases covered, motel, restaurant, and package liquor sales, all under the same roof. Sam paid his bill and bought some Lone Star; he had had some of that in Texas, and it hadn't been too bad. He picked up some postcards and a bag of chips, and some OFF, after Mr. Cozy Inn told Sam how bad the "skeeters" were in and about the cypress trees. Sam went to his cottage, roman numeral IV, put his beer in the fridge, and sprayed himself with the OFF. He adjourned to the little porch, complete with swing.

Sam swung, and he sipped the Lone Star, and he swung, for what he seemed to be an eternity. He was going to settle down and not do anything tonight but enjoy himself. He made a trip back for more Lone Star, and Mr. Cozy Inn pointed to the "rules of the house" conveniently posted on the front of the ancient cash register. Sam nodded and said he would be as quiet as a mouse. Mr. Cozy Inn gave him a smile in return, that was almost a sneer. Mr. Cozy Inn never introduced himself, wore no name tag, and was the only one that Sam ever saw at the Cozy Inn. He must really be busy. Then Sam looked down the rock driveway, ten little cottages, four cars, and no one moving except those in the restaurant. Sam tried the TV—local programming, on both channels. "Maybe later," Sam said. The beer had began to have an effect. Sam smiled and burped long and deep. He chuckled to himself. Sam lay across the bed, and set his can of Lone Star on the night stand. Moments later he was sleeping soundly.

II

Sam was asleep, he knew he was asleep, but something, someone, was trying to wake him. Something familiar, a voice, no, no, a what? Sam pushed himself to a sitting position with much difficulty, the can of Lone Star was back in his hand. He tipped the can to his mouth and it was hot and tasted nasty. The ghostly light from the driveway filtered through the small glass on the door. The dust hung absently in the light and the thick southern night. Something else, a slight light, but not light, from the chair in the corner of the room, the one part of the room without light, a glow. Sam's mind still under the alcohol's soothing influence, didn't see anything out of the order, not yet anyway.

"Sam." A voice, inside his head, no, his ears had heard his name called, so very quiet.

Sam set the can down, shaded his eyes as though the sun had suddenly come inside to cause vision problems. "Who are you?" Sam now had both hands on the side of the bed, he gripped the edge of the firm motel mattress.

"You do not know? Come now, Sam. We have been together for time now." The glow adjusted as Sam watched, moved.

"No! It can't be." Sam felt his spine go jellified, he seemed to sink into the mattress. His grip loosened. "No. I'm drunk."

"I must admit that you do not seem to be yourself. I have received these signs before, times past. I have something for you to do, something for we two." The voice was familiar.

"Yep! I'm drunker than I thought! That Lone Star packs more of a bang than I thought! I even talk to myself when I'm asleep." But Sam didn't feel drunk. He had had a few opportunities to get loaded in the last few years, not many so he had remembered them. Sam's subconscious told him to go across the room and prove for himself that there was only a dream talking to him. After all if he could talk in his sleep he could surely walk in his sleep too. But his subconscious said, "Stay where you are!" And he did.

"Listen, I will map out a plan for we two. It will be time yet. You must do as I have planned to allow time to make possible many time for you, many things, are planned to become assessable for your time." Voice spoke, no echo, not attached.

Sam shaded his eyes for a second, then put his hand back in place at the edge of the mattress. His head felt odd, no ache, no pain, odd. It was friendly, a good feeling, and he lay back on the bed. He tucked the second pillow behind his head and looked at the glow. There were features, vaguely familiar, but Sam had decided to hear this dream out; it wasn't a nightmare, just an interesting dream. Sam made himself comfortable.

When asleep, time is of no importance, the dream will play itself out, almost, generally most wake, just before the dream has come to an understandable end. Some dreams come and go, without our conscious mind realizing that there had been a thought process. Dreams are sometimes thought processes that we would like to happen, a hope, a want.

Sam was awake, but he did not know that he was, he was on a beer-induced dream of proportions that could make a psychiatrist have nightmares to understand. And Sam knew that the dream meant nothing, and would not be remembered the next morning. Sam smiled. He listened intently, and absorbed all that the familiar voice told him. Sam looked at the bedside alarm and thought this will end anytime now. The clock marked the hour of 2:00, 2:00 a.m. *Late,* Sam thought. *Or early, no matter.*

The voice droned on and on. Sam knew he was asleep, and only thought himself tired. The glow shifted from time to time, only slight movements to emphasize a point, but never moved. The glow continued, no more, no less, features never improving, only constant. The dust in the air held steady, much the same as the glow, changing but not changing at the same time. Another glow had begun, the sun was rising, the light from the small window in the door was now diffused, to begin to show shapes in the room.

"I will require to power. I must return, I will sign again at the earliest time. Remember the time and the plan. I must power." The glow began to fade just as the room began to take form. Sam looked at the bedside clock as the glow became quiet and faded, it read 5:15. Sam yawned and closed his eyes.

III

Sam stretched and felt the sweat on his arms. His mouth felt sticky and thick. His mouth made chewing motions, the taste grew worse. Sam looked at the bedside clock and it read 2:15. Sam stretched again and sat up. He was still clothed and sweaty. He moved to his suitcase and opened it, took out his shaving kit and smiled. The small bathroom was neat, clean and had plenty of hot water. It was a natural move in the morning. It didn't even dawn on Sam till he was drying off, and really looked at the clock. He stood like a stone, stopped drying, and thought that he must have really tied one on last night, but he felt great!

When Sam arrived at the office to pay for another night, Mr. Cozy Inn actually smiled.

Sam smiled back, stuffed the receipts in his pocket and walked into the sunshine. Sam went to the his car and unlocked it. He looked to the sky and thought, *A beautiful day!*

Sam took the atlas out of his console and opened it to the marked page. He had used a grease pen to mark his route, each page held separate by paper clips. He turned back and forth till he was sure of his path to Key West, his ultimate destination. His finger followed the red grease marker line to, Key West. Something was not right about the trip now. He was homesick, and really wanted to get home and see his mom and dad. But this trip was planned since his being stationed at Fort Hood. Lie on the beach, fruity drinks, and scantily clad young women. That was his ultimate goal, women, Sam had gotten close a few times, but never "all the way." According to all his stories he had been there, but Sam knew those were just stories, the real story was yet to be told. Key West was the setting for his story to end. The beautiful white sandy beaches, the women, yeah! Women of less than Middle American morals. He was sure to score there!

"Got your route planned out, do ya! I figured you just out of the Army. Fort Hood the sticker on your windshield, I figured." Mr. Cozy Inn was making conversation.

Sam jerked to the sound of a voice; he was zoning about Key West. "Yeah, I was just checking my route. That way I don't have to screw with a map while I drive."

Mr. Cozy stuck his hand out. Sam took it and the grip was firm. The accent was southern but not deep southern, and one couldn't get too much further south in Mississippi than right here.

"Tom Spencer, I have the title to all of this glorious property here." Tom released Sam's hand and gestured around in the direction of the motel. "Planning a trip to Florida, before going home?"

"Key West! I want to go there once before I die, just to say I've been there. I guess I slept in a bit this morning and thought I would just stay another day and enjoy the southern air, and maybe go into Biloxi maybe." Sam closed his atlas and stood outside the car.

"Well, you worried me a bit, when you got the second six-pack last night. Thought there might be trouble, but not a peep. Then I looked at your sticker this morning and the license plates and figured you out, and about one last time, before going home." Tom, Mr. Cozy Inn now had a name.

"Not much of a drinker, still got most of the last pack in the fridge. Guess I was just tired, and overslept." Sam felt more at home now, a name always helped, and it didn't have an officer rank in front of it either.

"Been there once, that was my objective too. Girls wore more back then, but didn't care, Madge was still alive then, and I was in love. Those were the days." Tom set the bag of trash down and had decided on a long conversation. "I tell you'll once, though, if'n you go into Biloxi, be careful. Those people are a little different there. Lots of tourists, bunch of whores that'll pick you clean too. Just be careful. Not too rough, but just watch where you go." Tom stuck his hand out again. "Be careful, Sam."

Warning signs went up. "How did you know my name?"

"Don't get too leery just yet. You signed the register, right?" Tom smiled, bent to pick up his bag.

"Yeah! Sorry, I didn't mean to be that way." Sam's face was flushing; he could feel the heat.

"That's alright, kid, been there. I keep a close eye on my place. Not a lot of people stop here anymore, they want a Holiday Inn, or Best Western nowadays. So I keep an eye out, specially someone as young as you, don't need any trouble. Sometimes it's best I keep watch on what's mine, that way it's still mine in the morning."

Sam had a name, seems like a nice man, a little fatherly. Sam looked at the mid-afternoon sky and decided to drive around and see Tom's world. The Chevelle was, as always, ready, the engine fired into life, and Sam tapped the gas pedal just a little as Tom walked by, just to let him know he was there. The clutch was working better for Sam now and he felt a little more comfortable with the entire machine. Sam hadn't seen anything that had spurred his interest on the way into the Cozy Inn, so he thought that he might just as well head toward Biloxi. "If'n you go into Biloxi, be careful." Sam's mind thought that he was going to do just that. The sign read 22 miles to Biloxi, just a short drive. Sam had quit looking at license plates, and was only watching drivers in general. Nothing to see out here and the tourists were going like mad, got to get to the next site and enjoy all the vacation time available. The locals, on the other hand, were just going about their daily routine, the ocean smell was here, not in southern Illinois. Sam had all the windows down and was enjoying the drive.

As he neared Biloxi, Sam could see intermittent views of the ocean, he had seen the Gulf of Tonkin, and the ocean on the way to Nam, but this was at home,

America. It all looked different, better. Sam stopped at a roadside burger joint, Burgers are Us; no hot Cajun food here, at least none he was going to eat. The Whopper was a big as most plates, and Sam loaded it with goodies. Hot peppers, and catsup, but no Cajun sauce. He adjourned to a picnic table and proceeded to consume his burger and fries, the Pepsi, was in a bottle. He thought of Sally the Coke Girl, in Quan Loi. In the end, she too, was the enemy. Sam wondered if everything would be associated with Nam, for the rest of his life. A little girl with big brown eyes kept looking Sam's direction; she would laugh, and cover her eyes. Her brown hair would flip about, her mother would push her hair back from her face and continue to talk to the other lady at the table. She finished all she was going to of her meal, and got up to play. Sam too, finished his meal. He had seen on the menu, soft serve ice cream, and decided he wanted one. Sam ordered the medium cone. When money had been exchanged, and Sam had his ice cream, the little brown-eyed girl was standing there looking up at Sam.

Sam looked down at the little girl. She stared back, smiling with her front teeth missing, in a wide smile. "Do you like ice cream?" Sam smiled and asked the little girl.

She only nodded her head in an exaggerated up and down motion. Her hands were in front of her moving slowly with one another.

"What's your name?" Sam asked softly, not wanting to cause her to look away; she was cute, freckles and all.

"Paula," she replied. And her face turned to the ground.

Sam squatted down beside her. "Well Paula, that's my mom's name, and just because that I like that name, and I'm headed to see my mom. I think you need this ice cream. Don't you?" Sam held the cone out to Paula.

"Momma, can I have an ice cream?" Paula turned her upper torso toward the table where the two ladies still sat.

"Paula, what are you doing? Are you bothering that man?"

"No, Momma. He said I should have that ice cream." Paula turned back and forth, pointing with one finger out of her two clenched hands she held close to her chest. She still faced the ground, waiting.

"Paula, how many times have I told you not to bother people?" The lady with the slight auburn cast to her hair turned to face Sam and Paula. "I'm sorry if she's bothering you, mister."

"No bother, she looks like she could use an ice cream, if that's alright?" Sam still held the ice cream out to Paula.

"Well, I guess it would be alright, if you want." The lady sat looking at Sam now.

"I guess it's alright. You had better start to lick soon; it's hot out here and it won't last long." Sam held the cone in front of Paula.

Paula's little hands took the medium cone gingerly, her head tilted back, and her brown eyes met Sam's. "Thanks, mister!" Paula took to the ice cream instantly; her little tongue was expertly catching all the melting runnels of ice cream before they could reach the cone. She turned and walked back to the table, and wiggled herself onto the picnic table seat. Her concentration was directed to the cone, a large cone for her little hands. She stopped once, and looked at Sam as he turned away from the window with another cone for him. Paula smiled and said, "Thanks, mister!" Her lips were already covered by the ice cream, and shining in the Mississippi sun.

Sam sat down at his table and began working his cone over. He was turned away from Paula and her mother. The ice cream was good. Everything was good, now that Sam was away form Fort Hood, and Viet Nam. The field behind the Burgers are Us was swampy, bayou country Sam thought, probably some gators there come nightfall. Sam had finished his cone and was making an attempt to get the sticky residue form his lips with his tongue. Paula came up to him with a napkin.

"Here, mister, this'll help; my momma always has extras when we come here."

Paula stood with her hand outstretched with a wadded napkin held between her thumb and forefinger.

"Thank you, Paula. That's really thoughtful." Sam took the napkin and smiled. Most of the ice cream had dried on Sam's lips and wiping only made it worse.

"Lick it!" Paula said flatly. "That's what my momma does!"

Sam licked the napkin, and proceeded to wipe again. "That helps!" Sam smiled and saw that Paula still had the last remains of the cone in her hand. It was still in a form similar to Sam's memory from years gone by, and damp with the last of the ice cream dripping lazily from the slightly tilted remainder.

"It's good, ain't it!" Paula's smile was glistening in the sunlight from left-over ice cream. She shielded her eyes to watch Sam clean up. When he was done, still smiling, she turned and walked away.

"Look at you, Paula!" The two ladies laughed at Paula's smile. "Now, are you going to finish that thing, or wait till it completely melts in yer hands?" her mother asked, as she pulled napkins from her shorts pocket.

Paula plopped the rest of the cone in her mouth in one smooth movement. Her cheeks puffed out like a squirrel's, after finding the mother lode of nuts. As she chewed to finish the cone, vanilla-colored spittle projected form her slightly opened lips. But soon she was in control, swallowed hard, and extended her arms to her sides. "All gone!" She smiled a big toothless grin, her tongue stuck out of her mouth to prove that it was indeed all gone.

Paula's mother licked the napkin, never missing a beat or a word, and began wiping Paula's lips, and part of her face that had came too close to the ice cream earlier in the tasty treat.

Sam disposed of his napkin mess and turned to his car. He reached in through open passenger window and retrieved his map. Sam leaned over the map, and looked at his position. *Grid,* he thought. He frowned slightly. Another of those thoughts that he wondered subconsciously would ever leave. His finger tracked the red mark he had made in Fort Hood.

"Are ya lost, mister?" Paula stood beside Sam with her hand up shielding her eyes from the sun again.

"Nah, just, lookin'. I'm staying down the road at a motel, and was looking at where I wanted to go next. I'm not from around here and wanted to get an idea where to go from here." Sam looked at Paula, still in the same position.

"Whatcha going to do? Are you going fishing? I know the best spot in the whole world! Momma said my daddy usta take me there. I could show ya where!" Paula was trying to make a friend. With Sam she already had.

"Paula, I think you've worn out your welcome, by now. I'm sorry, she doesn't take to strangers too often, but when she does, she's like a leech." The auburn-haired lady walked up, and placed her hand on top of Paula's head and pulled her in close.

"Well, she was about to tell me about the best fishing spot in all the world." Sam smiled, ad he turned to meet the auburn-haired lady's blue eyes.

"Paula, we had better get going." The auburn-haired lady tilted her head to look at her daughter. "Thank you, for Paula's ice cream."

"It was my pleasure! She seemed to really enjoy it!" Sam caught a look of slight dismay in the auburn-haired lady's face.

"It's a little ways home, and we had better get started. Thanks again." The auburn-haired lady turned herself, and Paula's feet scuffed in the driveway rock. "Now, Paula, you know that we have to go now, don't do this now."

Sam watched as the two started west along the highway. The other lady had already left and was headed east. Paula was still clinging to her mother's leg in a slow walk.

Sam tossed the map in the open window, walked to the driver side and got in. He sat there with his hand on the key. Sam started the car without thinking and backed out onto the highway. He headed west.

No traffic, as he pulled up beside Paula and her mom, on the wrong side of the road. The Chevelle's engine purred, as Sam pushed the clutch pedal in to let the car roll slowly.

"How about a ride? Seems awful hot to be walking into the sun this afternoon." Sam eased out on the clutch to keep rolling forward. The engine pulsed with the clutch pressure.

"That's alright, it's only about a mile. And I saw you looking at your map, probably got things to do." The auburn-haired lady gave Sam a slight glance and looked down the road.

Paula was in front of her mom now, holding her hand and walking backwards. "Can we, Momma? It's a long way home. Can we please? You said he was a nice man." Paula's feet got tangled with one another and she sat down hard. Her hair flew up and covered her face as she came to rest.

The auburn-haired lady bent at the waist and brushed Paula's hair to one side. "Are you alright, baby?" She squatted and looked Paula over.

"I'm fine, Momma. Can we ride, huh?" Paula asked as she stood.

A car passed slowly, honking its horn as the driver took the wrong side of the road to go by.

The auburn-haired lady stood, picking Paula as she did. "My name is Sara." Sara stuck her hand out toward Sam. "We had better do something to keep you from getting yourself run over!"

Sam accepted her hand, shook it gently, and shifted to neutral. Sam leaned to the passenger side and tossed his travel bag to the back seat. He opened the door and motioned for Paula to get in while he held the driver seat forward. Paula jumped from Sara's arms, and into the back seat almost without touching the ground. She was in place and working the seat belt without a thought of being in a stranger's car. Sam and Sara stood side by side on the shoulder of the highway and looked at Paula.

"Well, you gonna get in?" Paula looked back at the two of them, for just a second and was back at the seat belt.

Sara and Sam both laughed simultaneously. "Well, that sounded like an order to me!" Sam said, as he trotted around the car and opened the passenger door. Sara followed, but much slower than Paula. She got in, and Sam closed the door. At the driver side again Paula was still working the seat belt. Sam bent and took the seat belt form Paula's hands and locked the clasp. "There ya go!" Sam looked both directions before getting into the driver seat. He pulled away slowly, back into the right lane. "Where to?" Sam asked, glancing at Sara as he did so.

"It's up the road a piece, about a mile. It's on your side, just around the curve. There's a mailbox out by the road. I'll show ya, it's kind of hard to see till you're right on it," Sara said, and returned Sam's glance with one of her own. Sara looked out the windshield and placed her hands in her lap after pulling her shorts legs down.

"What's your name, mister?" Paula asked from the back seat. "I can't see much from back here."

"Paula! He's nice enough to give us a ride, and now you're complaining. I never!" Sara looked over the seat to Paula, who just smiled back.

"I'm sorry! Not very nice of me. My name's Sam, Sam Young. And you're Paula." Sam adjusted the rearview mirror so he could see Paula. "And Sara. Now we know each other, at least names." Sam smiled; he felt good today, and even better now. It didn't take long to cover the mile to the mailbox. Sam was watching close, he spotted it before Sara told him but kept quiet, as Sara had not said a word on the short ride. Paula, on the other hand, had chattered the entire distance. She asked about what kind of a car this was, what was the color, she knew it was red, but what kind of red, and why did it have different color rugs in the back, and where was he going, and why.

Sam turned off the highway onto a rock-covered lane. He didn't see any house, as they turned. He looked around to make sure he was going the right way.

Sara spoke again. "The driveway is narrow, and it's a little bit further. Thanks for the ride, I, we, appreciate it." Sara assumed her position again.

"Well, I don't have anywhere to go, just got out of the Army, and am going to Key West before I go home. Probably won't ever get a chance again. After Fort Hood, it will all be nice; anywhere is better than there!" Sam laughed, and glanced toward Sara again.

"My husband was stationed there too." Sara spoke softly.

"Really! And when did he get out?" Sam smiled, but was a little set back at Sara's mood.

"He didn't." Sara spoke softly again.

The back seat had gotten quiet suddenly. Sam looked at Paula in the mirror. She too was quiet, and looked back at Sam. "Did I say something wrong? I'm sorry."

"Jimmy died in Nam," Sara said quietly. Her right hand went to her forehead and she looked out the window.

"Hey, I'm sorry, I didn't mean to bring up bad times. I just got back from Nam, too."

Sam saw the house, a small white clapboard-sided house with shutters, grey shutters. There was a circle drive, and Sam pulled the Chevelle up to the steps and stopped. Sam turned to Sara; he touched her shoulder. "I'm sorry, real sorry. I didn't know, and..." Sam felt bad now, all the good feeling had drained away. The three occupants sit quietly.

"You wanna go fishing, mister, I mean, Sam?" Paula had the bubbles back in her voice, the bad feeling ebbed away with her question.

"Can't hardly go fishing. Don't have any fishing poles with me. Didn't need them much, at Fort Hood, I mean in the Army." *That's right, stick your foot in your mouth deeper, asshole,* Sam thought. Sam turned to Paula and smiled, hoping the smile would make up for his blunder.

Paula smiled back. "I got poles!"

IV

The afternoon had gone well. Sam had had a ball with Paula. She had a good mother from the way it appeared, but outside attention was a real new item in her life. And she took to it well. Paula had shown Sam a few tricks that he had never seen before. Fishing was the afternoon adventure. Sam had asked what kind of bait they used, and she had chimed in with "worms." Sam looked for a shovel, but Paula had had a better idea. It only took her a minute to appear with a digging fork, with an electric cord attached. Sam had looked at this contraption really hard. Paula took his hand and led him out to the garage, told Sam to "stick it in the ground"; Sam had done so with a few questions. Paula had opened the side door and plugged in the cord. "Just you watch now!" she said. Sam watched and in a few minutes worms were eager to come to the surface, just pick them up, simplest bait shop in the world. Sam had ventured too close to the impaled fork and had gotten hold of a worm that had sent a shock up his arm. Paula had gotten a good laugh out of that and told him not to pick them too close to the fork as they were "electrical worms." Not a fan of electricity, Sam would obey that order without question.

About a half mile through the woods, the woods that looked more like a swamp the further they went, was a small boat dock. It was here that they would try their luck. It had not been too bad of luck either, smallish, but fish nonetheless. Sam would clean them before he left for the motel. That way Paula could eat her fish, the ones that she had caught. From Sam's conversations with the six-year-old girl, there wasn't too many relatives nearby, and those that did come were seldom. Their car had a bad transmission and when her mother had saved enough money she would have a car again. Sam had tried to get a word in edgewise on occasion, but had soon given up that folly. They hadn't been but two hours, and the shadows were getting long already. They had had a few minutes of solitude after they had arrived and had to get the bait, and of course, Sam was the guest and Paula had had to do all in preparation of the fishing adventure. Sam was just relaxing and enjoying the evening.

Sam may have been asleep, at least a cat nap. Sam felt the foot falls on the dock; before he knew what was happening he was on his feet, facing the danger. No danger, just Sara, with two drinks, one cream soda, and one Lone Star. Paula looked at Sam with an odd glance that went away as soon as she saw her mother. Sam tried to relax back to his sitting position without looking awkward, it didn't work. Sara looked a little uncomfortable with Sam's reaction.

"Momma, were fishermen! We've caught a whole bunch of fish! We can have a fish fry, can't we?" Paula had hooked another and lifted the fish unceremoniously from the water. Her pole waved in the air looking for a target then lay on the dock, without hitting anyone.

As Sara and Sam watched, Paula went to work. First she stepped on the fish, caught the string and was removing the hook from the fish's jaw. Sam was in awe of the little girl's ability, no fear of the fish. and total concentration at unhooking the fish.

"Well, it seems that you have a fisherman. She has had a lot of practice at it, that's for sure." Sam smiled and found his arm over Sara's shoulder.

Sara had her right hand over her mouth trying to cover her giggles that were trying to get out as she watched her daughter unhook and open the fish basket and drop the fish into the bottom with all the rest. "Sam, she's never been fishing before. Paula was two when Jimmy died. She was only a little over a year and a half when he left for Nam."

"See, Momma, I old ya that I could catch a bunch!" Paula was baiting her hook and ready to catch more; she was about to put the line back in the water.

"Paula, don't put your line back in, It's suppertime, soon to be bedtime, it's eight-thirty now. You've got to get a bath, and eat, not to mention those awful fish." Sara had reverted to the MOM, now. She stood with her hands on her hips, in anticipation of the argument. None came, much to her astonishment.

"Well, okay! But we can come back tomorrow, right, Sam! Tomorrow we can catch some big fish!" She bent to the task of wrapping her line. No more questions, no arguing.

Sara stood in the same place on the dock, her hand fell to her sides. "I can't figure you out, little miss. Sometimes I can't just can't."

Sam was busy packing the old tackle box up and wrapping his pole in silence.

"We can come back tomorrow can't we, Sam?" Paula was working at the pole but wasn't having too good of a time with it, she had never turned around. "Can we, Sam?"

Sam took two steps and knelt beside Paula and started to straighten out the knot her line had become. "Now you know what I said earlier. I mean I've had a great time, you're a natural fisherman, and it has been fun, but...."

Paula's eyes were wet with tears, a few ran down her cheek, she stood silently. She looked at the reflections on the water. Her small hands swiped at her eyes to clear them. "I know, you've gotta go to Key West. Is it a long way? Will I..."

Sam wrapped his free left arm around Paula, and pulled her against him. "Now, baby, listen just a second. I'm a total stranger, we just met at the burger joint, you don't even know me. I think that your mom might have something to say about the stranger that dropped out of the sky."

"I like you! Can't I like you now?" Paula looked into Sam's eyes. The tears were starting and her brown eyes were shimmering behind the moisture. "Will you come back?"

"I haven't even gone anywhere just yet. We've got to clean fish yet. Now let's get this line untangled, 'cause if we don't the dark's gonna catch us! Okay!" Sam rubbed her head, and restarted at the fishing line.

V

The walk back was dimly lit, the shadows had merged, and were one continuous dark; the path was lighter since no grass grew there. Closer to the house Sara directed Sam off the path, otherwise Sam would have kept skirting the water and who knows where he would have ended up. At the house Sam looked for a piece of wood and a shovel. Paula told him that she would get the worms for tomorrow. It took a few minutes to explain that tomorrow was as yet another day. The garage light had to be changed to have light in order to clean the fish. It was a slow process, as Paula had to help. She didn't cut herself; that had been the miracle part of the evening. There had been twenty-four fish, some had perhaps been a bit small, but they had been cleaned as well. Sam had shown Paula how small some of them were; she had wrinkled her nose and smiled simultaneously. Sam had laughed so loud that Sara had come outside to she what all the commotion had been. Sam was still laughing and Paula had come to realize that he was laughing at her; she had her hands firmly planted on her hips in defiance.

Sara wasn't really wanting the fish smell in the house, and Sam had put them in water and poured salt over them. "See, no smell!" Paula, not tall enough to see, had to be picked up to see the fish, and of course poke her finger once into the salt on the fish. She turned her head and smiled, she was over Sam laughing at her.

Sara had dinner ready, roast, green beans, corn, and biscuits. Sam was in heaven! "This is great. Do you know how long it's been since I had a home-cooked meal, and I don't mean one of the truck stops that says home-style cooking. It's been almost two years now!"

Sara smiled, Paula smiled and leaned over toward her mom and whispered. Sam could not hear but had his suspicions. Now it was their turn to laugh at Sam. Sam was busy filling, or at least trying to fill his face with all the food he could get shoved into it. Sam was the last to finish; most of the table had been cleaned off by the time he was done.

"Well, did you really enjoy it or just trying to humor me?" Sara sat beside Sam as Paula tore off to the bathroom. "She wants to get done before you leave. It's been a big day for her, just about as big a day as she has ever had."

Sara leaned toward Sam and touched Sam's arm. "Thanks, Sam. She has really been happy today.

Sam had thoughts of the mouse coming out of the hole in the wall to see a new chunk of cheese. Sam's suspicion of the worse had come to the surface, but he had had fun! A lot of fun and he hated to go as much as Paula hated him to leave.

"Momma! I'm clean—you wanna check?" Paula's voice was almost strained to the limit.

"You've only been in there for a few minutes, you can't be clean yet! You were filthy! I'll be right there." Sara only smiled as she got up.

"You tell her, that I will be right here. Okay!" Sam smiled in return. He watched as Sara crossed the room. She was a very attractive woman, and awfully nice to a total stranger. Had a cute little girl, too! Sam smiled to himself, nothing outward, his defenses were still in place. Sam's thoughts had only cleared his mind, then to have a six-year-old flying through the air and yelling wild Indian sounds as she did so. "Help! I'm being attacked!" Sam rolled to the floor with Paula ending up on the top, and Sam begging for mercy.

"Now listen, you two! If the cops come in here wanting to know who is killing who, I'll beat the both of you!" Sara stood with her hands placed on her hips, almost in a direct image of Paula in the garage. Her face was firm, for almost ten seconds, then she broke out into a full smile, a pretty full smile. One that Sam liked a lot.

Paula stopped tickling Sam, took his face in both of her little hands. "You know, she says things like that all the time," Paula whispered. "But she's just kiddin'."

Sam whispered back, "Are you sure? She looks pretty mean to me!"

Paula loosed her hands and was back at tickling Sam. She rolled off of Sam and took up a position beside him. They both lay quiet and looked up at Sara. "I don't think she's too mean, do you?" Paula whispered with her index finger at her pursed lips.

"I don't either, let's get her!" They sprang from the floor and the chase was on!

Sara was out the door in a flash. She stopped at the driveway, looked to the yard both directions and then ran to the other side of the car.

"Nah, Nah, Nah, Nah!" Sara waved to them in imaginary contempt. She bounced up and down. "Can't get me!"

Sam and Paula ran around the car twice, then Sam called Paula to his side and whispered in her ear. Paula ran to the front of the car, Sam to the back. Sara feigned fear, and put her hands to her face. Paula was on her in heartbeat, laughing and tickling her. Sam grabbed the both of them and pulled them to the ground. The two tickled Sara till tears ran form her eyes and she begged for mercy!

"We've got her now!" Sam yelled.

"Yeah!" Paula yelled in unison.

They all lay on the moist grass, looking skyward at the stars and the darkness around. No street lights, just the glow from the garage light that had not been turned off. Paula lay on Sam's right arm, Paula was in between the two. She wiggled once or twice, and pulled her hands up under her chin. A slight yawn could be heard, as Sam and Sara looked toward each other then to Paula.

"She'll be asleep in a moment, and I've got to get her cleaned up to get to bed now." Someone instigated a wrestling match in the wet grass! Sara looked to Sam's face. He was still watching Paula.

Sara sat up, and Sam was up with Paula in his arms. He reached for Sara with his left hand. She took his hand slowly, and increased her grip, just a little squeeze, then was standing beside Sam. She brushed Paula's hair out of her face, and slid her arm around Sam. He hand pulled back as soon as she realized what she had done. She stepped aside.

"Let me have her." Sara reached for Paula.

"She's just fine, just direct me to the right places. She don't look dirty to me." Sam held Paula, and looked her over.

"Of course she looks fine to you, you're a man. There's chiggers, and mites, and probably grass stain on her gown. This isn't Illinois; things get out early here, and then you can't get rid of them." Sara turned toward the house.

Sam watched Sara walk toward the door, then he too began to walk. Sam smiled to himself. This was nice, and he smiled, and he still felt good, real good!

VI

Sam had deposited Paula on her bed, gone outside to shut the garage light off. He was standing in the driveway and looking at the sky again. The moon was just beginning to show above the trees. Sam heard the door open and close.

He knew that Sara was coming up behind him. He didn't know what to do, he didn't like not knowing what to do. He never turned to greet her. Her hand touched the small of his back. It was electric, but he didn't move.

"Sam."

"Yeah." A long pause, without any response from either.

"Sam. I want to thank you for today. I really enjoyed myself. I haven't had any meaning for a long time. I cooked, and I, well I cook a lot, you know. It's not like I don't cook, I cook for me and Paula all the time. Oh, I just want to thank you. Paula hasn't been that happy in quite a while. She was new today. She never really had a daddy. She was so young when Jimmy was killed, she doesn't even remember him, just what I have told her. My memory has become hers. She went fishing with Jimmy when she was a baby, but she doesn't remember any of that. She was remarkable today that she could do any of that; she baited her own hook. I've never taken her fishing. I just don't know, she's a good little girl." Sara stood by Sam, her hands to her face.

Sam took her shoulders in his hands and turned her toward him. "Sara. I enjoyed today too! It was fun!" Sara pulled away from Sam's grip.

"I ...I can't, Sam. I just don't know what to do. Paula was so happy, and that makes me happy too. Now listen, I am going to make a pallet for you on the couch for tonight. You can't drive back tonight." Sara had turned away, and was not looking at Sam, her hands had fallen to her sides.

"No, I couldn't put you out that way. You don't even know who I am. I could be the friendly neighborhood serial killer. It's only thirty or so miles away, and..." Sam was cut short in his oration.

"I've already decided! That's that. I have sheets and blankets on the couch, it will only take a minute." Sara was off at a fast pace toward the house. "Come on now."

Sam looked at the moon rising. *What the Hell are you into now!* Sam's mind asked, but only once before he turned toward the house, with the yellow light falling just short of his feet, projecting, like a carpet, showing him the way. Sam took a step, and another. Into the house and whatever was supposed to happen.

Sam made the couch up as Sara finished the kitchen. The kitchen opened to the living room through a high vaulted doorway. Sam watched Sara. He knew he was smiling, but he liked to smile, it was new to him but he liked it.

Pleasantries were exchanged, somewhat withdrawn. Their happiness had been replaced with a clumsy exchange of words without meaning. Sara touched Sam on the shoulder as she said goodnight and passed toward her room. Sometime in the night after what seemed hours, Sam felt lips, ever so gently, touch his forehead, then they were gone. Sam slept well, very well, then.

Sam's sleep was gone, a fresh, clean smell, powdery, had awakened him. In an instant, he was aware of a new form beside him, warm, soft. He could now make out the origin. Paula had come to him in the night and lay curled up slightly on top, and tucked into the couch side of Sam's sleeping area. He pulled the blanket and covered Paula. She snuggled for a second and lay quietly. Sam could feel her breathing. He laid his arm over her and was back asleep himself. Later Sam woke slowly, Paula still sleeping, and he could smell something else. Light had filled the room. It was morning, no idea what time. Sam could see Sara through the archway moving about the kitchen; she turned her head as he watched to see him watching.

"You two had better get up and get dressed. Breakfast is just about ready." She turned back to the stove.

"Hi, Sam," Paula's soft voice said. Her head was turned to Sam, and she smiled. "I'm glad you're still here." Paula turned her head back into Sam's chest and lay quiet. Sam eased out from under Paula, laid her gently and covered her back up. Sam slipped into his pants and went to the bathroom. He had no shaving kit, no toothbrush, nothing.

There was a knock at the door. Sam opened the door.

"Thought you might need this." Sara smiled, and handed Sam a little Colgate toothpaste and a child's toothbrush. "It's small, but thought it would work. I have a lot of them from Paula's school. They send this stuff home with her and I keep it tucked away; you never know when you might need an itty bitty toothbrush. Towels are on the top shelf behind the door." Sara smiled and closed the door.

Sam felt foolish, brushing with the small toothbrush, but it worked, and he felt good after a shower. Everything in the bathroom was girl oriented; he felt like an invader. But he felt good, except for the slight kink in his back; couches will take their toll! He went to the car after cleaning up and found a tee shirt in the trunk, a little worn but clean. He looked around and took a deep breath. He felt good. Back in the house Paula was just rising as Sam came in the front door. She waved a small hand at him and smiled.

"Paula, you had better get cleaned up for breakfast. And you know that school starts again Monday. It's eight-thirty already, no more sleeping in then." Sara smiled and turned back to the stove.

Paula was up, no, she's down, back up and headed for the bathroom. Sam watched and tried to remember the mornings when he was that small. First grade was blurry at best. That's what Paula is this morning, blurry. Sam could only remember Friend. He remembered maybe, no, Friend had always been there he had said, but Sam could not remember seeing him, never when anyone was around. The things a kid's mind would conjure up. That was something that he still had, an invisible friend. He wondered if Paula had an imaginary friend. Sam's thoughts were moving in a direction he had not decided upon, he was "gathering wool" his grandma would say.

"Sam! Are you alright? Sam!" Sara had put the platter of eggs on the table and moved beside Sam. He was unaware of any of the goings-on of the past few minutes.

"Just....What!" Sam turned to find Sara almost in his face. Her face showing concern, and wonderment as well.

"You've been standing there for almost ten minutes. Are you alright?" Sara asked Sam again.

"Oh yeah, I was waiting for Paula to come back." Sam knew that was what he was doing. Wasn't he?

"Sam, Paula's at the table." They turned together to see Paula at her place ready to eat, just waiting for the guest to decide to join them.

"Oh yeah, I guess I didn't sleep too well, couch and all, I guess I was dozing. Just a little cat nap I guess." Sam felt this face flush, and the alarm was going off in his head.

"In the Army sometimes you sleep when you can. I guess I haven't lost all of the Army just yet! It is a little embarrassing, I mean the guys all do it, it's a Nam thing. You wait till you see me sleep with my eyes open, that'll freak you out!" Sam was trying to get out of this one as quickly as he could. "What is today? That may sound dumb, but I haven't been really keeping a good log of the days!"

"Silly! It's Friday. The last day of spring beak, I mean break. Everybody knows that!"

Paula had her hands hanging on the back of the chair and her chin planted firmly on them watching what was going on; she didn't know what it was, just one of those grownup things.

Sara took Sam's hand. "Are you sure you're alright?"

"Just fine! I guess I don't do couches too well! Maybe I'll get to sleep earlier tonight, right after the carnival!" Sam looked from Paula to Sara and back again.

"Carnival. What carnival? And you had better sit down here and eat before it's all cold. What are you talking about, Sam?" Sara directed Sam toward the table.

"I saw a big billboard about a carnival in Biloxi. And since it's the last day of spring break we should go to the carnival." Sam had changed the subject well, now they had something to talk about, not him. "If it's open?"

"You forget, this is about as far south as you can go without getting your feet in the gulf. That carnival is always open, it's open almost year round. I believe that they close in February and March." Sara, looked quite pretty, no, beautiful, this morning.

"So! I haven't been to a carnival in years! Sounds like fun to me!" Sam wanted to have fun, and he wanted to stay a little longer. "What else do you have planned?"

Paula was all smiles. "Please, Momma! I haven't been to the carnival in years either!"

"If you really want to, I guess it will be fun!" Sara was smiling, a nice smile.

"All I've got to do is call the motel and tell Tom I won't be back till late, not to throw all my stuff out. Can I use your phone?" Sam was happy now, he was as happy as he could remember, in a long time.

"I don't have a phone. Never needed one, never wanted one, sorry. We might go later, Paula." Sara looked deflated.

"No mind, they had a pay phone at the Burgers are Us. I'll just run up there and call. Now, how about some of those eggs!" Sam lifted his leg over the back of the chair nearest to Paula and sat down. Sam rubbed Paula's head, and she giggled.

Breakfast was mostly about what Paula wanted to do at the carnival. Rides and cotton candy, and Sam made it worse with each subject brought up. Paula was in heaven, and hadn't left the breakfast table yet. She wanted to know all about the carnival, and where it was, and how long it would take to get there, and then she asked how much does it cost? Sam had assured her that there was plenty of money for his best girl, she was to have it all! And they laughed. Sara had become a little withdrawn. Sara was cleaning the table while the two kids played "what if." Sam told her that she needed to get dressed, and get ready. Off like a shot, she was. Sam waited till Paula was gone from the kitchen and he went to Sara.

"What's the matter? Am I being a little too aggressive? I don't mean to come on too strong. I would understand if you told me to get lost. I dropped out of the sky, and just take over. I will leave if you want." Sam wanted to hold Sara, size her up a little closer.

"It's not that, Sam. I've got some money for the carnival and all. I... I...I don't know how to say it without coming across like some kind of a tramp! I haven't had so much fun in years. But there is something else, I....Now don't take this wrong." Sara was still facing out the window.

Sam thought, *Here comes the big drop. I'm outta here like a big herd of birds!*

"Sam, I haven't had this much fun in a long time, a long time, not since Jimmy left for Nam. That's what is, well, I ... I like you, Sam. Can you understand what I'm saying/ I just met you, and I don't want you to think that I'm a country whore. I...I don't want you to go, and I know you have to. Sara turned to face Sam, literally, as Sam was about as close as he could be without touching her. Sara immediately dropped her gaze away from Sam.

Sam put his hands on her shoulders, put his thumbs on her jaw line and tilted her head back so he could see her beautiful blue eyes. "Let me tell you something, first off. I've got nowhere to go, and a whole lot of time to get there. I've been in the Army for two years, and haven't had any fun either. A little drinking, and some carousing, but no fun. I had fun yesterday, I had a ball! Today, I'm going to have some more fun. And this is the hard part...I like you, Sara. I don't know what has happened, but I spent a whole lot of time last night thinking. I thought about a lot of stuff, places and things. But mostly I thought about you. I like you!" Sam was about to run out of words, when he was unceremoniously interrupted.

"What are you two doing? I'm already dressed and ready to go. Are you going to do the dishes, Momma, 'cause we're gonna be late if you are!" Paula was standing beside the two grownups looking sincere, and concerned.

"Look at you!" Sara squatted down to Paula, and began to adjust her shirt. "These shorts don't go with that shirt, Paula. Let's go and get you something better to wear." Sara stood. As she did, she looked deep into Sam's eyes, she gave him a little smile. There's plenty of time.

Sam stood and watched as they crossed the living room.

Paula turned back to Sam. "Aren't you gonna make a phone call?"

"I'm outta here!" Sam dug his right hand into his jeans to make sure the keys were there. He tossed them into the air, and caught them. *It's a good day!* Sam thought.

Sam checked the gas gauge; not quite three quarters a tank, good to go. He started the engine, it purred, he tapped the gas pedal twice to hear the pipes. Around the circle, he just couldn't stand not doing it, he goosed the engine just a little, he heard the rocks. He was happy, and off, another adventure lay just ahead, and adventure he looked forward to! He hadn't really started to roll and was on top of Burgers are Us. Sam looked for the business card he had picked up at the Cozy Inn, right where it was supposed to be in his wallet. He hoped he had the right amount of change. The information tag on the phone said that all local calls were ten cents. Sam kept out three dimes, just in case.

The phone rang, once, twice, again. *Don't be taking the trash out right now, Tom,* Sam thought, *I've got two ladies waiting for me, and I don't want to be late!* It started to ring again, and it stopped.

"Cozy Inn, this is Tom. How may I help you?" It was Tom in his usual Mr. Cozy Inn voice. Tom was proud of his little introduction; it was a Hell of a lot better than a damn recording.

"Hi, Tom. This is Sam, Sam Young. I won't be there today, maybe late tonight. Can you run a tab on me? All my stuff is there. I've run into a little lady and we are going to take her little girl to the carnival in Biloxi. I'm good for it and I will be there sometime tonight or in the morning. Okay?" Sam knew he was about to get the lecture.

"Nice lady, huh. I've got all your stuff. You're not in any kind of trouble are ya?" Tom almost sounded sincere.

"Nah. Met her at an ice cream stand." Sam tried his best "I'm innocent" routine. "A really nice lady, and a cute little girl. Six years old, cute as a button."

"Just be careful, kid. Don't want to be stuck with a whole bunch of Army duds. That carnival in Biloxi, be careful, I told ya about Biloxi, didn't I." Tom was trying to be sincere again.

"Yeah, Tom. I'll be careful. I got two more to watch out for today. I'll be careful for all of us today, Tom." He had run into his dad, in Mississippi!

Two more "be carefuls," and Tom hung up the phone as quick as he had picked it up. Sam stayed on the phone waiting for the dial tone to make sure had hung up. Dial tone, Sam hung up too. Sam's head was abuzz; he didn't know what to do first. It was too early to make anything out of all this, he didn't even know what it was all about. He was lost in his thoughts, but he was happy. What would his mom say! *Your mom—you don't know what is going on and you wonder what your mom might think—about what, asshole!* Sam smiled to himself. Probably just horny; he knew horny, he had been that most of his life.

My God, you've never done the dirty. What the Hell are you thinking! Yeah, she just likes you, she doesn't want to fuck you. Does she? Sam had only thought that there were lots of thoughts running around in his mind; now it was full, and he could not sort much of it out. Sam got back in the car and started it up. He revved it a couple of times, smiled and put it in first, eased it out onto the road and dropped the hammer. The car was sideways in a heartbeat, second and it was gone. Sam smiled. "Got the clutch down now, Poor Boy!" Third gear and Sam let off of it. Just cruise now, the turn is just up the road. Sam thought that was how he had got here, just up the road a piece.

VII

When Sam had returned to the house, Paula and Sara were sitting on the front porch. Sara had packed up a few snacks for Paula, Paula had packed up a few things as well. Paula wore her sunglasses, had her small white purse, and had just a bit of extra color to her cheeks. As she walked to the car with her best smile in place, Sara was behind her with her own smile, one she did not want Paula to see. She handed Sam the bag of snacks, and covered her mouth with the back of one hand trying not to laugh. Sam bowed at the waist, while opening the door, laid the front seat forward to allow room for her majesty, Miss Paula to enter. Paula tried her best to enter gracefully, short legs and all. A little assistance was required for her grace. Sam assisted with her seat belt and replaced the seat to its upright position. Sam bowed to Sara and assisted her with her seat belt as well. Sam walked with his best posture to the driver's door and got in. Once in he started the car and started to shift to first, he heard a slight throaty sound from the back seat. Sam turned to face Paula.

"Yes, Miss Paula. What would be your pleasure?" Sam had his head slightly tilted back as he spoke.

"Your seat belt, Sam. They say at school that everyone should wear a seat belt. It's safer ya know!" Paula was into a new game as soon as she had entered the car. She had paper and colors out already; her total concentration was now attached to her latest artwork.

Sam snapped his seat belt in place, he pulled and tugged to get it comfortable, he didn't really like the damn things. "Okay, new game". He looked at Sara who was outwardly laughing now. "I tried to make a silk purse out of a sows ear, and nobody appreciates it!" Sam shifted to first and started away, his newest and latest adventure.

"Do you know where you're going, Sam?" Saras' laughter had subsided now.

"Not really, but I figure something as large as a carnival, even I should be able to find. The billboard said Biloxi." Sam was still trying to get the belt adjusted.

"It's been years, but I think I can find it. There should be some signs as we get closer. That gives me some time to ask a few questions, if you don't mind?" Sara had that scowl on her face again.

"Shoot, I don't have too much to hide, I don't think". Sam prepared for the worst. Traffic was light and Sam took the opportunity to look at Sara as much as he could. She had auburn hair, a little longer than shoulder length, it was pulled back behind her ears on the sides and hung beside her face. Her face was showing nicely. It was oval, with a slightly pointed chin, dimples when she smiled. A cute little cupid's bow on her upper lip.

"Are you listening? You and Paula have the same attention span. None!" Sara had been looking out the windshield but had turned her attention to Sam now.

"Sorry, I was just in another world for a bit." *It was a nice world too,* he thought.

"I'm going to have to break you of that world, you seem to visit there a lot. Now just where are you from? That really isn't too much, I mean after all I am riding in your car, and we're off to a carnival, and God only knows what!" Sara smiled.

"Okay, you've got me, totally, I'm yours. What did you say?" Sam laughed as Sara brought back the scowl, but this time in jest. "I am from a medium-sized town, not a city, just a town, Salem. It's in south central Illinois, about sixty-five miles east of St. Louis. How am I doing now? You've got my undivided attention now!" Sam leaned over the console and smiled at Sara; this time it was just for her.

"There's a start. Parents, mom and dad, or were you hatched on a stump by frogs?"

Sara had looked at Sam too, just to Sam.

"Mom's a bookkeeper for Dad; he started an electrical business, and that was just as I went into the Army. I have been home twice since then, and it looks like a struggle for Dad, but he'll make a go of it." Sam waved to a man getting his mail out of a box alongside the road. "There's not a whole lot other than that. I grew up, had a good childhood, had great parents, liked school, got drafted and went to Nam. There it is in a nutshell. Now, how about you?" Sam smiled and didn't think that would fly.

"Sam Young, that's it in a nutshell! That didn't tell me a damn thing. Great childhood. What did you do as a kid? What did you study in school? Real stuff!" Sara was reaching, and she had turned sideways to look directly at him, awaiting answers.

"Wait just one second. I have a real question. Something I should have gotten long before now. What the Hell is your name?" Sam looked at Sara for a second as traffic was getting a little heavier. "And, one more thing. If Paula sees you without your seat belt you're in trouble!"

"She's asleep, she has always nodded off as soon as the tires turn. It's Farthing, Sara Louise Farthing. Now back to Sam Young." She had her elbows on the console and her chin cupped in her hands.

"Okay, if you're going to get that way, Louise!"

"Don't start with that, I'm surprised Paula hasn't ran about calling me Louise. She does that to change the subject, she knows I don't like it. So don't change the subject, Sam. What's your middle name?" She has a smug look on her face now.

"Alfred. They wanted me to have my grandpa's name, I never even knew him, but they said when they called me Al, I wouldn't answer. So that stopped that. Maybe you should try to ignore her when she does that." Sam looked and she still held the same pose.

"Okay, I'll tell all! I lived in a little town, Odin, when I was little and had a great time; we had bicycle races and played in the pasture. I didn't have a whole lot of friends, I knew a lot of people, but stayed to myself and a few close friends. It was still a great childhood. I did all the usual stuff, paper route, sold seeds, all the kid's stuff." Sam hoped she wouldn't pry too much; he didn't want to slip about Friend.

"What kind of seeds? You did say seeds."

"American Seeds. From the back of a comic book, you know, garden seeds, and flower seeds. I had regular customers that looked for me in the early spring. I guess that's why I was so upset when Dad moved us to Salem. All my friends were in Odin. Of course later things got a little mixed up with drugs and all. I never did any drugs, I guess that's when we pretty much broke up, and went our separate ways. I remember when I told them I had been drafted, they said 'bummer,' and took some more dope. It pretty much ended all then." Sam hadn't thought about all that in a while.

"Does it upset you to talk about it? You look a little sad." Sara had sat back in her seat.

"No, it really doesn't. It's like when you find out the Easter Bunny doesn't really exist. It is one of those days when you realize all the things you knew have just gone away. Nothing's real anymore it seems, there's always something or someone to ruin it all." Sam put his best smile on and looked at Sara. "I'm not the only one, surely."

"No. No, you're not. I lived on top of the world, till Jimmy was killed. Sometimes it just seems so long ago, and so very cruel. I was so much in love, and we had Paula, and then I had Paula, just me. It was mean. How could God do that to me, to us. No matter how much I tell her about her daddy, he will never be real to her, and he should be." Sara had occupied her usual place with her hand to her face.

"Sara, I don't know what you must have gone though. I'm sorry." Sam drove.

There were a lot of miles before a voice was heard. Sam figured he had really been stupid in his attempted revival of his life. Sam has never lost anyone close to him; his grandpa hadn't ever been close after he had grown up, there had been that pulling away as he grew, and then he was gone. Now Sam was trying his best at starting a life of his own, whatever the Hell that was going to be. He had a lot of feelings for this lady; maybe he just needed someone to pay attention to him. Maybe he was a real loser and just hadn't settled in yet, to that reality. Traffic had picked up a little as they came closer to Biloxi. Sam was paying more attention to driving, and hoping not to become a complete ass the next time he opened his mouth.

"It's the next right, Sam." Sara had been watching the road and the signs. Biloxi had become a whole lot more spread out than before, but she had seen the sign. "I want to start over, if you would consider it." Sara stuck out her hand so Sam could see it and not take his eyes from the road. "My name is Sara Louise Farthing, and your name might be?"

Sam took her hand. "My name is Sam Alfred Young. I'm new around here. Have you been to the carnival here? I hear it's a nice carnival." Sam gripped her hand snugly, not too tight. Her hand was warm, it felt good.

"I understand it's a nice one, and it's about a mile to the right. Just turn at the next corner." Sara did not try to recover her hand.

"Thank you, miss. Would you like to accompany me, and my little passenger?" Sam stuck his thumb up from his grip toward the back seat. Then he let her hand go slowly.

In no time at all they were parking and bouncing across the parking lot; not too many cars yet. Sam paid for all three, even though Sara insisted on paying her and Paula's way. Sam would not allow it. They were still early. It was just noon, most of the carnival hawkers had not started their never-ending song, as yet.

Sam sniffed the air; he had both hands and arms spread full length. "Do you smell that?" He squatted beside Paula, who had just began to wake good.

"Smell what?" She looked at Sam with a questioning face.

"I smell steak kabobs, corn dogs, and, just a second, yes, yes, funnel cakes!" Sam was back at her level looking into her big brown eyes. Those big brown eye were starting to light up.

"What's a corn dog?"

"What's a corn dog!" Sam wrapped his arms around Paula. "Poor dear has been deprived, doesn't know what a corn dog is!" Sam scooped Paula up in his arms, and swung her around and around. He stuck his hand out to Sara, and she took it. "We're about to treat this young lady to her first corn dog! Are you a mustard or catsup person?" he asked Paula.

"Catsup, I think, yes catsup." Paula was giggling.

"A CORN DOG with catsup! That's what it will be!" Sam had made a megaphone with his hand and was announcing Paula's choice.

The afternoon went flawless; anything and everything Paula wanted, Paula got. Sam couldn't hit the broad side of a barn at the baseball throw, but Sara had won the stuffed monkey that Paula had wanted. They tossed rings, bean bags, and threw darts. Sam had bought a paper grocery sack with "The Biloxi Fun Park," emblazoned on the side to carry all Paula's loot. She had everything in the sack. Political handouts, matchbooks, balloons, and stuffed toys, the bag was full, and getting quite heavy. Paula's eyes were heavy too. They were sitting on a bench, when the decision was made, it was time to go home. Paula objected weakly. As it turned out, Murphy's Law, they were about as far from the car as possible. Soon, Sam was carrying Paula and her bag of loot. They had to stop twice so Sam could shift his load from one side to the next. At the car Sam passed Paula to Sara. He got into the trunk and took out a blanket and a small airline pillow. Once he had Paula secured in the back seat, with a seat belt buckled over her as best he could, he stepped out and rubbed his back.

Sara moved his hands aside and rubbed the small of his back for him. "Better?"

"Much better. I'll be alright once I get in the car and can relax just a bit." Sam stretched long and put his arms into the air.

Sara put both her arms around Sam's neck, she was shorter than Sam by five or six inches, she pulled Sam down toward her. She kissed Sam, soft, then harder, then soft again. Sara broke the kiss, and looked into Sam's eyes. "Sam, thanks. I really mean it. That little girl has never been this happy before, in her life. She has always had to live with her hermit of a mother. I have kept her in the past, not wanting to admit that she had a life too' she lives my life, not her own. She goes to school, and comes home to me. And she lives my life, in that little house. I'm such a bitch." Sara's eyes were full of tears.

Sam had his arms hovering above Sara's back, in fear of touching her, now wrapped them around her. He kissed her tears away, then he kissed her, he kissed her long. Sam had wanted to kiss her since the beginning, he knew that now. Sam never said a word, he led Sara to the other side of the car and opened the door. Sam took Sara in his arms and kissed her gently. People walked by and giggled, they said soft things that Sam didn't hear or didn't want to hear; he didn't care. Sara got in and Sam closed the door slowly, their eyes staying on each other.

"Sam, you should get in the car." Sara said, never looking away.

"Yeah, I guess I should."

The drive back to Sara's house was long, in that all were tired, and in anticipation. Sara would rub Sam's shoulder and occasionally ask if he was alright. It wasn't late, just a long day. The ride was quiet, with Sam catching a glance to Sara when he could. The traffic had thinned the farther they drove away from Biloxi. Each time Sam would look to Sara, she was still looking back at him, they would smile, and several times they would start to say something, their lips would move, but no words came out. Sam saw the Burgers are Us sign; a few cars were out front. "Hungry?" Sara shook her head. Sam wasn't hungry either. In only a few minutes Sam turned into Sara's drive, and all his fears returned. The car seemed louder tonight. Sam came to a stop in front of the porch. When the car was shut off the silence was complete, and total.

"Momma, I gotta pee." Paula was not really awake, just had needs.

No words were spoken. Sam scooped Paula up in two tries, he had forgotten the seat belt, and blanket streaming behind, he was off to the house with his precious cargo. Sara got Paula's bag of loot and hurried to the door to open it for Sam. Sam took Paula directly to the bathroom, set her bare feet on the floor and held her till she could navigate across the room. Then he waited outside the door.

Sara came down the hall to the bathroom. "I'll get her from here."

"I'll get her shoes from the car." Sam left his post at the door. Confusion reigned—what, when, and how, was he to, do what. Sam rummaged around in the floor, the first shoe was in plain sight, after some five minutes he had the other in his grips, under the seat, but he had it. Sam chuckled to himself. "Boy, she had that one buried." Had he said that? He wasn't sure. "Don't start that BS, now." Sam raised his head to look out the window to see if anyone was out there; just the light coming out the windows. Sam gathered up his newfound prize and started for the house. Sara came outside at the same time. She leaned against the house watching as Sam walked from the car. "Found 'em, they were way up under the seat. Don't have any idea how she could have gotten them under there."

"She can do some strange things, and I just scratch my head when she does. Sam, you had not planned to go back to the motel had you? I thought that since it has been a long day that you should just stay here tonight." Sara looked at Sam and smiled.

"Well…I hadn't planned anything really, just kind a footloose right now. I do need to get a shower pretty bad, and get cleaned up. It has been a long day." It wasn't hot but Sam was sweating, really bad right now.

Sara took Paula's shoes from Sam. "You know where everything is in the bathroom. Paula is out for the count, big day for a six-year-old. Thanks again, Sam." Her hand gently slipped away from Sam's. "Go in an get your shower now. I'll make your couch up."

Sam almost ran to the bathroom, he was almost scared. Sam had developed quite a problem, one he had had in the past, but not quite this bad before. The bulge in the front of Sam's pants almost ached, he hoped Sara hadn't seen his problem; it was embarrassing. Sam undressed and it didn't go away, he looked at it like it had become a traitor, revealing his most secret of all secrets. Sam touched it and it tingled. Sam prepared the shower, and got a towel down, no change. He hoped the shower would get rid of his problem or he might have to help make it go away. The water ran down Sam's chest and dropped off the end of his private. He was unsure of whether it would ever go away.

The shower curtain opened, first Sam saw a hand, pale red fingernails, the next thing he expected was the scene from *Psycho*, then, a leg, with the same color nail polish. Sara stepped into the shower, completely naked, Sam's breath came quick. Sam knew his eyes were wide open; he was afraid to speak. Sam backed against the wall. His feet were off the mat, his hands slapped the wall groping for purchase. Sara placed her right index finger across her lips. In Sam's position his private jutted outward, he blushed, the blush traveled all over his body he knew. Sara's arms were around Sam's neck, she pulled him to her, their lips locked. Sam could feel his private between them, it felt good. The kiss broke and Sam drew in a deep breath.

"Sara, I have never…I know that sounds…." He felt her finger cross his lips. The water continued, blurring Sam's vision. Sara kissed his ear, his neck, his chest, her head disappeared, she kissed his abdomen. Sam was about to explode, his head felt hot, he knew there must be steam from the water striking him, it too felt hot! Sam didn't last for any longer, his chest caved in, he struggled for air. Sam now more embarrassed than he felt possible, his hands fell to Sara's shoulders, she was still kissing Sam's abdomen, lower with each kiss. Then she took his somewhat relaxed private in her hand, Sam's hands went back to the wall for balance. It took much longer this time, slow, and steady, it never seemed to end for Sam; he had had dreams, but none like this! When Sam could not hold back any longer, his hands fell to her shoulders and pulled her closer then, he exploded again. Sara had complete control of Sam, he could feel himself being drained away. He was unable to talk, or resist, he only gave in, completely.

Sam did not know how long he stood there; the water continued. Sara took Sam's wash cloth and soaped it and began washing him, starting with his now only slightly erect private. It began to grow again, and she moved to other parts of his body. Sam began to soap Sara, and he looked at her when she stood. She only smiled; he kissed her hard. The water began to cool, as the water in the heater began to cool. They finished and turned the water off. They stood there wrapped in each other's arms till they began to chill from the evaporation in the bathroom. Sam pulled the curtain back and they took their towels and began to dry each other. No parts were left untouched, all dry and excited again.

Sara took Sam's hand and led him to her bedroom. Sara backed Sam to the edge of the bed, pushed on his chest till he sat down on the bed, he could smell the soap and he inhaled her womanhood. Sara pushed Sam back till he lay on the bed. She walked around the room and lit candles, she pulled the door fully closed now, the weak light from the hallway night light was gone. All that was left was the flickering light from the flames atop the candles, and Sara and Sam's nakedness. Sara crawled toward Sam from the foot of the bed. She gripped Sam's growing member, took it in her mouth, her head bobbed up and down till she had it good and moist. Sara now continued to crawl toward the head of the bed, she kissed Sam, and impaled herself on Sam's throbbing member. Her hands began at the apex of their desire, by massaging both of them and then her hands moved up her flat abdomen, to her breasts, she thumbed her nipples. Her up and down motion had Sam hot, he pushed up and down with her. Her hands continued slowly to her neck and beside her face, her fingers disappeared into her hair, her arms extended up to full extension. The up and down motion became more and more frenzied, faster, and faster till she began to moan softly. Sam felt wet, as though they were back in the shower, he could feel more and more till he could hold back no more. They lay quiet, Sara still on top of Sam. He felt his member had shrank away, ever so slowly, till it was no more. Sara lay beside Sam till her breathing came back to normal. Sara opened a drawer and took out a package of cigarettes. She inhaled deeply and offered Sam a draw. He took a deep draw and coughed lightly.

"Sam, you might as well be my first, it's been four and a half years, since Jimmy died." She took another draw on her cigarette, offered to Sam, this time he didn't cough. Sara's hand found Sam's overworked limp member, her hand wrapped around Sam, she nursed it up and down, she sat up and took a deep draw of the cigarette, handed it to Sam and bent over Sam. Her hair fell over his abdomen; it tickled his legs where it fell. Sam felt a new life begin again. Sara was driving Sam wild, Sam pulled her off of him, her mouth made a popping sound as Sam pulled her away from his erect member. Sam rolled Sara and took the top position. He began kissing Sara all around her face, then her neck. Sam spent some time at Sara's breasts, as he moved down to return the same ecstasy that he had received, he saw the same auburn hair, Sam's tongue began to work, Sara's fingers directed Sam to the best spots, when she had Sam in the right place her hands went to the back of his head and drew him in, her feet found Sam's back and spurred him on. Sam had found a new desire, a like that had escaped him till now. Sam's face became wet with desire, Sara pulled him in and held him in place as his tongue worked with determination. Sara loosed Sam's head just before he thought he could breathe no more. Sam looked as though he had been in the shower and not dried his face. He crawled to the head of the bed, kissed Sara and buried his manhood, Sara's legs were around Sam.

The night was long, the desire had come and gone many times. As the sun began to light the eastern sky, they began again. It was not till Paula had knocked at the bedroom door that they realized it was time to stop, for now, just for now. It was Saturday. The day had promise, for both of them.

Paula asked more than once why Sara and Sam were so giggly. But she had told them that she liked it. They were more fun! Paula had wanted to go fishing, but groceries were much higher on the list of things to be done. Laura had come to get Sara and Paula to go to the grocery store. Sara introduced Sam and the two women had gone outside. They had laughed and whispered for ten or so minutes before Laura had left. Grocery shopping had been fun, even for Paula. Everyone had had a good time. The hardware store had been Paula's favorite; she got a bicycle. Sara had said no, but the begging and pleading from Paula and Sam, both on their knees in the middle of Coast to Coast had changed her mind. She had been in hysterics with the two. Then it had to have a basket with streamers. When Sara said, "Enough, you two. The groceries are not going to be any good if we don't get out of here." The box said "some assembly required"—Sam's next headache. Fishing was shelved in direct response to getting the bicycle together. Sam had drug out his tools; there were a few more needed. Sam and Paula were off to the garage to find more tools. That's when Sam saw the "worm getter" plugged in.

"Did you plug this in, Paula?" Sam unplugged the cord. He pulled the fork out of the ground and it was hot to the touch. "Paula, this can't be left plugged in, it might short out a fuse, and out go the lights."

"I plugged it in this morning, I forgot. We went to the grocery, and I forgot. I'm sorry, Sam. You won't tell Momma will ya?" Paula knew it had been bad, as Sam had never said a bad word to her before.

Sam scooped her up and spun her around till they were both dizzy. The "worm getter" was forgotten. It was back to the bicycle! That was the most important thing on Saturday. Paula didn't think so much of the bicycle when it became time to learn to ride. Up and down the driveway, Sam had to break after the first hour. Sara brought iced tea out to the two cyclists and watched as they began anew after tea. When Paula got the hang of it, she was off like a shot. They hadn't discussed stopping just yet! Paula went down in a classic fall, the bicycle on top, one knee got scuffed. Untangling a little girl from a bicycle was about all Sam could handle. Paula was crying, Sara was running, and Sam was untangling. Once removed from the bicycle the pain had gone. Paula was more interested in whether her bicycle was scratched than anything. After close inspection to prove that the bike was still good it was off to the house for bandaging.

"I think that's about enough bicycle for today, it will be dark in about an hour," Sara had told Paula. Paula went the six-year-old, "Oh, just a little more, Momma, I've almost got it now." About ten times through that routine, and Sam not helping on Sara's side at all she gave in. "One more hour, young lady! You didn't get a bath last night, but you will tonight." After supper it was back to the bike. This time, Sam showed Paula how to start, and stop. She was getting the hand of it by dusk, an hour and three quarters. Sara in her "Mommy' pose" on the porch, hands on hips, and tapping one foot.

"That's enough! No more bicycle today. There's tomorrow, then back to school on Monday. You have other things to do; that bicycle will not disappear. You and Sam can find a place in the garage. Then get cleaned up for bed." Sara was still in her Mommy pose.

"Okay we're just putting it away now." Sam waved to Sara. He and Paula pushed the bike to the garage. Paula insisted the door be put down. Sam pulled and pulled; he discovered one wheel off track. Paula said that she and Sam could fix it. And Sam explained that she needed to mind her mother and get inside. "I'll fix it, I promise. I won't quit till I have the door in place, shut!"

"But I can help! Momma won't care." Paula had her six-year-old pleading working again.

"No. Your momma didn't want us to get this in the beginning, now we have pushed her buttons on the time, it's almost dark now. You're too short anyway!" Sam showed Paula where the problem was and how high it was, and she agreed. Paula was off like any other six-year-old, as hard as she could go.

Sam heard her as she ran across the porch, yelling that she was on her way to the bath, and Sam was fixin' the door. Sam had the wheel loose in a jiffy. Getting it back in place was another story, He was just about to get it back in, when Sara walked up.

"What are you doing?"

It slipped, the door sagged, and the wheel fell off again. "How long has this door been busted?" Sam asked. "I promised Paula that her bike would be behind closed doors tonight." Sam had the wheel back in place and was about to pry the track out a little to get it back on track.

"Let me help." Sara took the pry bar and held it for Sam. He lined the bolts up and put them in place, tightened them down just a bit. Rolled the door back and forth, he smiled. Sara had her arms around his neck and kissed him on the back of his neck. "You're going to spoil her," Sam.

Sam wiped his hands on his pants, and took Sara in his arms. "You know, I could get used to this kind of treatment. Monday we will go get your car."

"What do you know about my car?" Sara pulled away and looked at Sam.

"Paula said the transmission was out, and you were saving money to get it fixed. Well that's Monday's adventure."

"No! Now I draw the line there! A carnival, and a bicycle is one thing, but not that bill. It's two hundred forty dollars. NO!" Sara was adamant.

"Why not?"

"Don't start with me about this! That damn old car isn't worth it anyway, it's a '64 Chevy and it needs a lot more work that just the transmission." She struck the Mommy pose.

"Where's it at anyway?"

"Sam, don't do it! I swear, I'll have a fit, and you don't want that, that I will guarantee!" The Mommy pose was still in place.

"I just thought, that I might stop and check on it when I go back to the motel. You know, just check, that's all!" Sam smiled.

"You've been around Paula too much! I said no, and that's it!" Sara was starting to get a bit upset. "Are you going tonight? Can we talk, just for a few minutes."

"I need to get some clean clothes. I have some army gear in the trunk, but no clothes. I'm going to start getting pretty rank shortly! I think Tom will hold my stuff; he said it's the off season, and business is slow." Sam was working his hands over again.

"I bought a six-pack today, why don't you go and get out of those clothes and I'll wash them. I have a pair of shorts in the bedroom you can wear while I wash yours. We started to talk, and then we stopped. there are a few things I want to say, and not here in the garage." Sara was standing all folded in, no Mommy pose now. "I want you to stay tonight. Please! Paula will love it!"

The thought of another night like last night intrigued Sam. "Okay, but I'm sure going to have a Hell of a time getting into your shorts." Sam had a lot of thoughts too. They scared him; he thought he was in love. And he knew that was stupid. He had only known Sara for a couple of days, but there was a feeling that was eating at him. It might just be love, he had heard of love at first sight!

"They're Jimmy's. That won't bother you will it? Sara looked straight at Sam, no covering her eyes when she mentioned his name." She turned to walk away. "And you can get in my shorts, anytime you want!" She blushed, and smiled that knowing smile.

Backward as Sam felt around women, and now, this woman, who had taken his "cherry," she was hot. Sam felt stirrings. He just smiled, a big cheesy smile, and he too blushed. Sam walked outside and pulled the door down. It squeaked a bit; that was a job Paula could help him with. He went in the house. Paula was almost asleep behind her big book of numbers. She looked up and said, "Sam," her eyes were almost shut.

"How about a ride to bed?"

"On my bike?" she said sleepily.

"No, your bike is in the garage. On my back!" Sam squatted down and bent over.

Paula climbed on. "Giddy up!"

Sam made horse sounds and down the short hallway they went. He squatted down again and she jumped to her bed. Sam pulled the blankets up to her neck and tucked her monkey in beside her. "Sleep tight, sweet girl."

"That's what my momma calls me sometimes. Sam, are you gonna hafta go away? I really like you." Paula had mustered all her remaining strength to ask that. Her eyes were closed, and she was asleep.

Sam had his hand on her bed, he patted it, he felt something in his eye. "I don't know, sweet girl, I don't know much of anything." Sam got up and flipped the light switch to off, closed the door. He went to the bedroom and found a pair of blue jean shorts, a little big, but they would do. He felt odd, wearing another man's clothes, and doing his wife. It wasn't just that, that was vulgar; he had made love, not the first few times, but later. Sam took a long shower; he was dirty from all the day's events. When he was done his clothes were gone, underwear and all. He put the shorts on and started for the kitchen. Paula was standing at her door. Sam grabbed the shorts to make sure they stayed in place, he squatted down to Paula. She kissed him on the cheek, turned, and got back in bed. Sam stayed where he was for a second; he felt something in his eye again. Stood and continued to the kitchen, he could see Sara through the archway; she looked fine.

She opened his Corona and asked if he wanted a glass. He declined, the bottle would be just fine.

"Sam, I feel real funny. I don't know how to explain it. From the side of the road, to now. I know I'm a bit of an odd bird to you. I live out here in the middle of nowhere, no visible means of support, and have a little girl. You must think that I am a money grubber or a whore. I fucked you to keep you!" Sara took a drink. There was a cigarette burning in the ashtray on the table.

Chapter 7
Too Many Answers, Too Many Questions

I

Friend had been making more room in his shelter. Friend had been watching Sam; there was another, more, they were effecting Sam. Friend was in an absolute rage. The metal signs banged, made noise from the human place. Entities moved and signed, all the signs were of fear; they did not know fear, but it was fear. Friend was not opaque as all entities were, he was almost the color of the human sky. Bits of energy created sparks, even when Friend did not touch the metal. His signs were of lightning, and energy the humans had never seen.

Friend signed, everyone blocked, but not well. Sound could be felt here, and it was, it was disturbing. Friend was about to show Sam sound, horrible sound! "I have the power to do anything, Absolute Power!" Shelter had become large. Friend had to control, control like Sam, the metal signs lay back beside shelter, color ebbed away, did not drain, just paled, back to nothing. "I will not be nothing, time will show, I have the power." Friend knew color was trying to come back. Control! Control! Friend had been with the sun, he had seen many signs from Sam; the Sara human had never had an entity, she was stealing what Friend' had made. The little human had an entity, Friend had to find that entity. Friend knew how, in time, it had to be now time, not now, but how did Sam say words, short time. Sam would not be happy anymore, but he had to be happy, that had already been in the plan for time. When Friend had caused Sam to fall and not lose all his energy he had been happy, but now it was a sign that signed Friend, that happy was going to cause the time to be different. That could not be, not in short time, not in energy time. Sam would time forever, no not right, live forever; Friend would take him along, they would time forever, energy time.

Spirit was about to sign Friend about his misspent energy. Lost energy was for time, energy time. One day no energy would exist if it was lost. Friend knew many signs from Sam; the metal was not to rob energy, it was energy, but not entity energy.

"Entity!" Spirit was here to sign.

Only his energy came to sign when energy had been lost. That was what Spirit thought Friend had done.

"Spirit." Friend was in control.

"Entity, sign is lost energy from your shelter. That cannot be allowed, all energy is to be controlled and be recycled in all time. Energy that is lost can never become again. Entity, why is energy lost? Is it because the pieces that make the thing you sign as shelter? How the shelter has been caused Spirit does not sign. Not in all time till this time has any entity caused to create any shelter, why must entity cause this?"

"It is my human, his ability is cause for the shelter. The need for entity to know how to assist my human is necessary for entity to assist. When the last pieces entered they had a lost charge from creation, entity's energy have not lost, all is still as it has in time, and will be in time."

"Your human requires more assistance. This human has needs for many time now. Is time for your human to return to energy arrived?"

"Entity will assist my human for time yet, not time long, but for time short. My human is in much need to carry out his mission, he has lasted to time now. My human must time short yet to complete human mission."

"Entity, your human has had need for assistance for time, time more than other entities' humans. What mission does entity sign? Is this mission create energy for humankind, more energy than time has controlled in time gone."

"Spirit, my human will create energy that we will reprocess into entities for time yet. My human has time yet to come. Spirit could assist my human and know how energy will again be gained for entities to assist in time yet to time.

All thoughts must be exact, and Friend knew that. Spirit would know a false sign if Friend did not control all the signs between the two entities. Spirit was wise, but only in direct assistance. Spirit had not assisted in many time now. He would not assist in time again, he had energized to a Spirit, they could only assist entities with answers to signs that changed as humans became more in knowledge. Friend had been an entity many time, all entities had been as energy was forever. No energy was lost here, only humans wasted energy, their energy. Here energy was not lost, only recycled, energy was in design to assist humans to create, and prosper. There were many humans now, not as in time gone. Not all humans had entities, only a random human was assisted. There had never been a selection process; an entity would never have a sign that would allow them to know.

Some humans thought of entities as God, miracles had been attributed to God, and God had only been an entity. An entity with much power, an entity that had assisted to a great degree. Those miracles had been passed to humans as time had passed. Humans did not know nor wanted to know, that they had been assisted by energy, just energy, directed assistance energy. Humans would worship entities if they were ever to find the truth. Then humans would have to control, and harness, and they would lose energy. It was not a secret, just was never signed to humans. Till Friend.

Friend had been entity before, somehow. Friend knew how time had been in time past, Friend liked to be with his human, Sam. Friend also liked what Sam could become, and with Friend at his side would become, till Friend had become human. Friend had an ability to recall all Sam's time. this made Friend able to control Sam. But Sam could only be controlled by himself. Other humans distracted Sam and some made him believe as other humans always believed. Angels, God, miracles, and luck. None existed, only energy; humans would continue to live, till they had managed to lose all energy. Someone would cause the loss, somehow, but not with Friend. Friend could control Sam, so in time he will control other humans. But Sam had had many problems, parents, doctors, Viet Nam, and now this other human. A human that Sam was happy with; she could cause Sam to not believe again. Friend needed to power, not like the other entities, but some, but Friend could not power now. When an entity powered time would pass, 'friend' could not control this time , yet. But power he needed, and crossing over took power away and left behind power to assist entities when they returned too weak to power; it was a booster to get them through the weak time. Friend had been able to see his human without crossing over, but could not converse, or sign from this side. So Friend watched. And Spirit had gone now to leave Friend to power. Friend could not power just now, in time. Friend knew that humans were weak and fragile, they required special handling. Sam had not been handled in many times.

Watch Friend would; he knew the meaning of the word, it was good. Return all the good times to Sam. As small children entity had learned fun, he had fun with Sam; entities are not to interfere, only assist. As new entities they are programmed to assist, never allow humans to know an entity was present. From human history that Sam had told entity of man had known on several occasions, miracles! Friend would show humans a miracle again; the miracle was to be him, in time.

Friend could see Sam and the other human. He did not understand the emotion that beset humans, was fun, and happy, emotion? He would ask Sam when he was in place, in time. The female human was touching Sam, it must be as Sam has a mother unit. Friend had seen them only in fleeting glances, in time past. Friend had to listen to the entities, he had to find the small human's entity. Energy was used by humans on a daily basis; there would be and energy that could be used in the human world. Friend had to find it, otherwise he would almost be without power when he returned. They created light, they propelled vehicles, cars, Sam, had called them, Sam himself had a car now, it was a color, a pleasing color, red, yes it was red. Energy, power, soon or all would be lost.

Friend knew things, he could go backward in time but not forward, this was a paradox. But Friend had not been able to find a way to go forward. Sam had been in Friend's past, he could recall signs, and he could go back, but he could not affect the time that had already gone in time. If he could go forward all would be done. But his immediate problem was now. There was small fires with Sam and the other human. Friend had sensed fire, in Sam's past, Sam and his human friends had allowed a fire to continue one night, and Friend had put the fire out while they all powered in a cloth shelter. Friend recalled it had been pleasant to mix fire and his energy. The fire had bloomed as a flower, brightened the darkness. When Friend had consumed the fire it had left Friend with a good feeling, yes it had been good. Friend had known good, Sam had been good, his parent units had told him that many times past. The ability to watch was good, but that like all other assistances took energy; it all would come back to Friend but not now. Friend would have to stop watching, and restart when time had passed and Sam would be alone. Friend closed the part that was a mind, and rested, no energy used resting.

II

Sam took a cigarette, he got a jump off of Sara's, he inhaled just a little, and took a drink from his beer. "Now, Sara, I'm going to tell you something. I didn't know how. I have been trying to tell you this since I saw you at Burgers are Us, now I'm going to try. I'm not good with words, I get all fumbled up. I don't know how you will take this."

"For God's sake tell me! Your words get fumbled up, just spit it out!" Sara was agitated, and slightly moody tonight.

"I'm trying! It has taken me days to get this far. I don't want to scare you to death. I too have a strange feeling. I have talked to me a whole bunch about this. That has only been confusing me more. I like you! I mean, I like you! I like being around you, a whole bunch." Sam took a long drink from the bottle.

Sara thought, *If you're going to tell me to get lost, just do so, don't talk me to death. Sam, I think I love you!*

Sam finished his drink and was playing with the bottle. He shifted his eyes back to Sara. "Now don't hit me or yell, okay?"

"Okay."

"Sara...Sara, I think...I think I love you! Now just a second, don't get up and walk off. I have had...well...I have had strange feelings, feelings that I have never had before. It scares me, and I ain't scared of nothing." Sam's eyes were downcast, and he was playing with his beer bottle again.

"Sam Young, I don't want you to think I'm weird or anything, but I feel the same. I feel like we were meant to be together! Jimmy is a great memory, but he is just that, a memory, I'll never forget him. Sam, I don't want you to think that I am hitting on you. I will need some time, and I don't think there is time. You have a life, and you don't need an old woman with a kid!" Sara had her hands in front of her face again, she wiped her eyes.

Sam got up and got a paper towel, thought again, and opened a drawer that he hoped had towels in it. He took out a smooth towel and handed it to Sara. Sam started to rub her shoulders. "Now listen, you are not old, I'm old. Nam did that; you have made me young again. And that kid is the greatest thing in my world. I told you the other day that I had nowhere to go and all the time in the world to get there. Sara Farthing, Sara Louise Farthing, I may have found the rest of my world. I have never felt like this in my life, and I want to feel this way for a long time. You may find out that I'm an asshole. I have been called that before. And if the truth was known, I probably am an asshole. Now I am going to go and get my stuff at the motel, and give you some time to think about what we have said to each other. I'm scared, I'm scared that you will tell me to get lost. I'm not sure what I will do. I am going to tell you that I love you, and I love Paula."

Sara started to get up and Sam held her in place.

"Let me finish. I don't know that I can say all of this again. And I know that I can't look you in the eyes right now, in just a minute. We have a lot of talking to do—where, when, how, and if you really want me. I'm not much of a catch. I love you!" Sam kept rubbing Sara's shoulders.

Sara stood, tears streaming down both cheeks; Sam wiped them. "Sam, I'm twenty-eight years old, and I have never felt this way in my life. Jimmy was good, and we were kids. But I never felt this good in my life."

Sam tilted her head back, looked into her eyes. "I love you!" And he kissed her. Soft, becoming harder, long and passionate; he had no idea what it meant before, he knew passionate now.

"You're not going to the motel tonight, you're going to stay with me tonight, please, I need you tonight."

Sam just smiled. They both looked in on Paula. They walked to the bedroom. It was a passionate night, it was not as wild as the previous night. Tonight they made love, together they made love to each other, together they became one. The night was a night to remember, two mismatched humans, that had found each other.

III

Sunday was a beautiful day. Bicycle became more and more natural. Starts were good, stops were still needing a little work. But work, she did; Paula was worn out before noon. Sara bounced about the house and cleaned. Dinner was a masterpiece as far as Sam was concerned. Sam mowed the yard, there wasn't a whole lot of yard. Mostly around the house, the cypress leaves had suppressed most of the grass growing. Sam had clean clothes, and would soon have the rest of his stuff here; that was the only planned project as of this moment. Sam had taken up residence on the porch and watching Paula on her hundredth pass. Sam saw the snake as it made its way toward the house, it looked determined. He yelled at Paula to stay back and he grabbed a shovel out of the garage.

Sam wasn't sure what kind it was, but it didn't look friendly. The snake struck at him more than once, and then he got it. Sara had come out and watched and Paula had ridden up too. They thought nothing of a snake; Paula told him that they come out of the bottoms all the time. Snakes gave Sam the woolies; never liked snakes, and especially when they are aggressive. This one had a bad idea in its mind before Sam had decided it was to be put away. He picked it up with the shovel and took it out in the woods and buried it. Thank God they didn't have a dog or it would be back in the yard before nightfall. Sam had talked to Paula, and promised her that he would be back in time to pick her up at the bus, and he would have her bicycle with him. That made her smile and giggle. Sam liked to make her giggle; there is something about a little girl's giggle that will always be special, especially this little girl.

"Is there anything you need to take with you tonight, Sam?" Sara asked as Sam was getting ready to leave.

"Nah. I have a full-sized tooth brush at the motel!" Sam laughed and Sara smiled and giggled, a lot like Paula. Paula was holding onto Sam's leg like a miniature leech. Sam squatted down beside her. "Now listen, I'll be back tomorrow, then we can go fishing, whenever you want. I think we're going to have a bunch of time together."

"No kiddin', you'll be here tomorrow. I wish you would stay all the time." Paula's eyes were downcast like her mother had done a few times in recent history; of course that was all there was, recent history.

"No kidding, I'll even let you use the 'worm getter,' okay! And you can ride till the wheels fall off!" Sam rubbed her head and stood back up. Sam turned to Sara and took her in his arms, and kissed her long and slow.

"It's about time you two made up!" Paula smiled and giggled; she shaded her eyes to watch them kiss better.

Sara pulled away, Sam pulled her back to him more. When the kiss ended they both blushed. Paula still looked on, her eyes shaded. "I liked that, do it again!" Paula said, still shading her eyes.

"Well, what are we waiting for!" Sam said, and kissed Sara again. They stopped kissing, their arms still holding each other.

"Does this mean you love him, Momma?" Paula looked still, and her smile grew broader.

Sara stood still, a little stiff against Sam. She looked at Paula. "Yes, yes it does, sweet girl." She kissed Sam again. They parted and Sara took Paula's hand and started toward the house. She turned and gave Sam a smile, and blew him a kiss; so did Paula.

Sam returned the kiss and turned to the car. Once inside the car he leaned forward to see his girls, he smiled at them, started the car and honked the horn. Sam drove slowly down the drive way, watching in the rearview mirror, till the trees blocked his view. When he got to the highway he looked both ways, didn't see anything and pulled out and dumped the clutch. He liked the feeling of fast, and he was happy the two went hand in hand. He would without a doubt, catch Hell about burning the tires, but he didn't care. As fast as Sam had driven the beautiful drive was short and he was at the driveway at the Cozy Inn. Not many more cars than the night he had shown up. Sam pulled in at the office. Tom was inside behind the desk. Sam walked in and the little bell rang overhead. Sam had not noticed that before.

"Hi, Tom! How you doing today!" Sam was going to spread cheer today, every day.

"What gives you the right to be so damn happy?" Tom had become Mr. Cozy Inn again. Tom looked up and smiled. "You seem really happy, win big at the boat?"

"Boat? I have just decided to make everyone happy! Even when they don't want to be!" Sam was smiling, and he wasn't going to allow Mr. Cozy Inn to screw up his happiness.

"Just kiddin', kid, what makes you so damn happy, anyway?" Tom clicked off the lamp and took his glasses off.

"Got some of that good iced tea, and a few minutes I'll tell you!" Sam was being exaggerated now!

"Got some tea, kid. Someone that happy has'ta be in love!" Tom turned toward the restaurant and then into the kitchen. "Come on in, kid." They walked into the neat and clean kitchen. It was bigger than the restaurant it seemed. "June, this is Sam, Sam Young, just outta the Army. He's gonna tell me the secrets of life here in a minute. Got some tea made?"

June was making pie dough, and wiped her hands on her apron. "Hi, Sam." She went to the big refrigerator an took out a pitcher, glasses and ice. The glasses were garnished with an orange when she brought them over and set them in front of Tom and Sam.

"You was gone an extra night, kid. Must be love." Tom took a long drink. "Now that hits the spot. I work so damn hard here!" Tom laughed.

Sam started to relate his story. It was a long story, and he left out the X-rated parts; he was almost to the end when the bell rang.

"Fill 'em up again, June, please. I'll be back, kid. I wanna hear the rest of this story." Tom stood and straightened his shirt, smoothed back his thinning hair. "Money calls." He put on his Mr. Cozy Inn smile, and was gone.

June filled the glasses, and Sam thanked her. June lit a cigarette and sat on one of the stools near the counter where she had been working. "You sound like Tom. Ya know, him and Madge met here years ago and just stayed." June took a deep draw on her cigarette. "Don't mean ta eavesdrop, but not much excitement here, just gossip, and listen ta Tom's BS. He's a good man. But since Madge died he's gotten hard, that fake smile he uses, usta be real."

"Till he introduced himself, the other day, I thought of him as Mr. Cozy Inn. He seems like a nice man," Sam said, and took a drink of his tea.

"You're about the first stranger he's ever asked back here ta BS. He must like somethin' about you." June stubbed her cigarette out and went back to the dough.

Tom was back in the double doors and on his chair in a flash. "Gonna have few more for dinner, June. Told 'em it all started at five."

"Good, I don't wanta see you hafta eat all these pies by yourself, round man." June laughed and began putting dough over pie pans.

"I'll have you know I'm on a diet!" Tom patted his belly.

"Yeah, and I'm gonna run for Miss Mississippi too!" June came back at Tom; they both laughed.

"Go on, kid." Tom turned back to Sam.

Sam picked up at the bicycle lessons, and ended with the snake. Sam leaned back on his chair; he would have hooked his thumbs into his suspenders had he been wearing them. Sam smiled; he liked the story whether Tom and June did or not. Sam looked at June, who was slicing potatoes now, he looked back at Tom.

"Ya know anything about the motel business, kid? I'd sell ya this place and retire, retire to Key West. You pick that girl up, an' take her to Key West with ya. Be a nice place to start. Me and Madge went there, years ago, before we were married, had a ball. Never been back. Always meant ta go back, one day. Maybe soon." Tom had a sad look pass over his face, then his smile was back, a real smile. "Loved the story, kid. Gotta get back at it. You spending the night?"

"I'll be in to settle up in a bit, got to get my things repacked, don't want Sara to think I'm a pack rat. Of course she doesn't really have too many ideas about me yet anyway!" Sam tipped his tea back and finished it. He took his and Tom's glasses over to the side board by the sink.

June nodded her thanks, and Tom was headed out the double doors. "Kid, I wish ya all the luck in the world, sounds like a fairy tale, but so was my Madge. Our story wasn't much different, so I won't bore you with it. Kind a gave me a nice feeling, ya know."

Tom spoke over his shoulder as he moved to the front office. "Another car, business is pickin' up tonight. Sure ya don't wanta buy this place, kid? It's turning inta a hot spot!"

"I'll keep you in mind, Tom. I never seen me in a motel, except with a blonde, maybe!" Sam smiled at Tom, he held the door for the older man and woman.

"Better watch him, folks, he's in love!" Tom had a real smile on now.

"How nice!" the lady said.

Sam blushed, and smiled.

"See ya at supper, kid?"

"Yes, I'll be here tonight." Sam went outside the office and looked at the sky; he twirled about in the driveway! Sam moved his car to his cottage.

IV

Sam spent the rest of the day unpacking and repacking all his stuff; he hadn't realized how much stuff he had. There was Army gear, his tape recorder, and all the tapes, he still had some eight tracks. Fort Hood paperwork; he thought he would go through that stuff later, and save the stuff he might need later. He thought it was all a bunch of military garbage anyway, but he had a DD 214 in there somewhere, that was about it. But Sam was a packrat, and he would throw away only the candy wrappers and rubber bands. Sam has at least a half dozen pair of boots and tennis shoes; some were junk. It was unseasonably warm, had been all week, and Sam had worked up a good sweat. It was shower time, and early dinner, and to bed early. Sam was about to start a new life, with the love of his life! Sam found that he smiled a lot lately; Sam had never been a big smile person, but that had all changed.

Sam had showered and was sitting on the bed. Friend came to mind, a bad thought. Sam didn't need bad thoughts now. Maybe it had always been his imagination, maybe Sam had ESP. Maybe he had a "sight" like his grandma had always talked about. Sam rubbed his hair; it was dry, not anything there to dry. He had forgot the Army; with all the Army stuff he had packed, and repacked this afternoon he hadn't really thought about the Army, or his experiences. He had tunnel vision. Maybe he should call his mom and dad and tell them; maybe he should just show up with Sara and Paula. His mom would fall in love with Paula. And of course Sara would be the hit of the house, since Sam had never really had any kind of a girlfriend. And who could not fall in love with Sara! Sam had, he had really fallen, maybe that will change in time, but he didn't think so! His mind had strayed from 'friend' he brought that thought back into focus. Maybe that was all there was to it, focus, that was what the doctors had told him years ago. "Focus," maybe that was all he need do, just focus. Whatever the Hell that meant.

Sam smiled at his interactive daydream. His daydream took him from bad to good. Sara, now that was good. Sam had wanted this day and night to screw his head on straight, maybe a day away, he had been a virgin, maybe, it was the sex. Sam smiled and looked in the mirror. He had had his last haircut three weeks ago; it was growing, and right now it had dried, not straight up, but straight everywhere. Sam laughed out loud. He stuck his thumbs in his ears and made a face at himself. Sam had decided at that moment to focus on what that he would have to decide in his immediate future. Sam had re-wet his hair and now looked human.

Sam sat outside his cottage on the steps and thought, thoughts. Much like Dorothy's scarecrow, Sam had a brain, but it really didn't seem to function lately. Sam had spent the better part of an afternoon thinking thoughts that he could not recall. Sixteen hundred, four o'clock, had to get that straight too, no longer military. Ice cream, he could go and get an ice cream before dinner. Stupid, that was at Sara's house. Everything he thought of had to do with Sara. He thought that that was alright too, but the idea had been to get his mind on other things, and people. God knows that wasn't working. If he went back tonight he could take Paula to school. He didn't even know where she went to school. And Sara would think him a weak-willed asshole, that was only after her for sex. That brought a smile; no, his original plan was to go back tomorrow. That's what he was going to do, no change in plans. He had to find a job, or he had to talk Sara into moving to Illinois. He had to do something. He had a couple of thousand dollars yet, and that would get him through, for a while. Where did Sara get her money? That was a thought. Maybe she was wealthy. Then why did she have to save to get her car fixed? More questions than answers, there were to be many conversations soon. Sam had answers, but would Sara go along with his ideas? People were going into the restaurant. Sam looked at his watch. It was five! The daydreams had taken his soul, no, Sara had done that!

"How many, sir?" Tom asked. "Come on, kid, got a nice table for one, that will let you envision your love over dinner." Tom laughed. "You sat on the step so long I thought I was gonna have ta repaint you this summer. Are you alright, Sam?"

"Don't I look alright?"

"You look great!" Tom still laughing took Sam to a small table in the back that overlooked the marshes. "Solitude, lets you contemplate all your life, before you begin to share it with the one you love!"

The girl that waited on Sam asked if he was back to stay with them again. Sam had confused her by saying that he had never left. She looked at him strangely, and continued to the rest of the evening. Tom came by and asked how the food was, Sam had told him excellent, and the girl was more confused than ever. Sam didn't figure Tom had too much to do with the restaurant customers. Tom had been a happy man that night. Sam thought he had caused that, and he was happy too! Sam left the girl a five and thought that way she too, would be happy. Tom at his usual place at the desk.

"See ya, kid!" Tom called as Sam left. Sam threw him a big wave and went out into the sticky air. The mosquitoes were swarming around the light and were bad.

Sam pulled the door closed quick to keep them out. "Got to get the OFF out of my room or these little devils will drag me off." Did he say that, or was it a thought? Sam made a concerted effort to think. *Don't start that stuff, not now!* Sam had left the door unlocked, he turned the knob and went in, turned the air conditioner and the TV on, not much but local TV, but he figured it would make him sleepy; that's what he wanted, sleep. The daydreams had not left him with much but questions, the few he could remember. Sam had been dozing and an old *Gunsmoke* had been playing but was gone now, local news, Sam tried to watch as he thought he might just become local soon.

But rest won out. Undressed and in bed by ten-thirty, now there was a record. Sleep came slowly, the day's dreams haunted him for almost an hour. Sleep was finally overtaking him and he welcomed it, without dreams, only rest.

V

Friend was watching again, he watched Sam leave Sara, but he knew he would be back. Friend had to cross over, now was the time. His plan was ruination or he would be able to speak to Sam, make him understand, times had been planning, the plan was for the both of them. Sam would understand. Friend prepared to cross into the human world, just as he had in Sam's life for time. This would be different, he was sure of that. Friend made the passage as easily as any crossing. He saw the trees, he saw Sam's car, the red car, he entered the room with Sam. Sam was resting, Friend glowed in an unusual bluish color. He left Sam. Other ideas had come into his entity; he knew the power source that he needed badly was here.

Sara had been unable to sleep for some time; her thoughts of Sam had kept her tossing and turning, but sleep came at last. Sara's final thoughts before sleep had consumed her consciousness had been of Sam, driving his red car into the driveway, and staying. Sara slept with a smile on her face. Thoughts of Sam and their life filled her subconscious as deep sleep settled into her resting mind and body. Sara never saw the bluish light that had entered her house. The light dull, but a light, round, and pulsing.

Friend had entered where the power supply entered the house, the main connection that created light. Friend's form, not human now just a dim, bluish light that moved into the house, into where the wires carried the power. The bluish orb entered the power box, just above the washing machine, the machine Sara had used for Sam's clothes. The light became more powerful as electrical energy entered into the orb that was Friend. The power never left; it stopped feeding the wires, the electricity wanted to enter Friend. All of the wires in the house now wanted to join Friend, all of the electricity came to Friend, the lines fed into Friend. Friend pulled power like a sponge fills with water. Friend liked the sensation.

Lights in the surrounding area began to dim, not like a power outage, they just became less and less till they stopped glowing. The local power station began to crackle. Some of the lines coming in fell to the earth dead, no sparks, just fell like ropes. In Sara's area lights glowed brighter than normal, some shattered. Mostly unnoticed due to the late hour, refrigerators stopped never to run again. But Sara's house glowed from the outside, it pulsed in response to the new power, power that was never to come in such quantity. The power was immeasurable, the siding that would not burn, began to smoke, the carpets exploded into flames, wall board and paneling burned for an instant then the inside of the house became an inferno!

Sara became energy, back to where she had started. Paula opened her eyes to the brightest light other than the sun. She too became energy, an orb of energy that had suddenly appeared in Paula's room was consumed as was the house.

Some told the police the next that they saw a light in the woods, after the explosion. They said they had never seen a light that bright. They also said it disappeared as suddenly as it had appeared, they also said that they could see through the trees as though they were clear as glass, and then total darkness. Fire department members had never worked a fire that was out before they got there. The house had to have been burning for hours, but Laura, who arrived before the police or fire departments, said she had visited with Sara two hours before the power outage; they had had hot tea and sat on the porch.

The fire department had had to leave to go to the power station. It too had burnt, or exploded, with an intensity that none had ever seen before, they had left one truck behind, to make sure there was no rekindling, and to help the coroner retrieve bodies, if they could be found.

Laura told a friend that Sara had been "head over heels" over… his name was Sam, but that was all she knew. The police tried to get Laura to leave, she told them she would go back to the road but refused to leave till she knew Sara and Paula's fate. The sun came up slowly as officials began the grim task of looking for remains. Laura had told them of the layout of the house, and where the bedrooms were located.

The electrical power had given Friend a sudden burst of energy. It had been a good feeling, but Friend knew it was not real power, this sudden energy would not last, not like the power from the entity Friend had taken. The entity had come to protect and assist. It had been drawn into Friend, just like the electricity. Friend consumed the entity just as the sudden fire had consumed the house. Friend had glowed bright white, a white that was without form, almost invisible, clear but so bright that when Friend crossed back, leaves in the trees turned brown and fell to the earth. The path the light took was noted, but not explained; since it could not be explained, it was soon forgotten. But not by Friend. There had to be more power, and there had to be a way to make it last. By the time Friend had returned to shelter he was in need of power and rest. He entered shelter and began to power, oblivious to what had happened. Friend would find a way. There was time now. Sam was alone again. There was time!

VI

Sam packed his toothbrush, his shaving kit, and all his toiletry items into his suitcase, and put them into the trunk. He looked up to the sky. It was a beautiful day, a new day, the beginning of his new life. Sam had had a good night's sleep, felt rested, and was hungry. He walked to the office expecting to see Tom. No one was at the desk, the restaurant was dark. Sam tapped the bell. He heard Mr. Cozy Inn, instead of Tom.

"No, I don't know what's the matter. It's been… Oh, Sam. Hey, I don't know how long it will be off." Tom had perked up a bit when he saw Sam.

"What's off?" Sam asked. "Is the power off?"

"Well, ya must be in love! Did ya shave in the dark?" Tom looked at Sam strangely.

"Nah, the sun shines in the back window. I was busy trying to turn the sun down, I didn't need any light. No breakfast, I guess." Sam was a little disappointed; he was hungry.

"Come in the kitchen. I got down an old percolator and I got coffee and some rolls. Come on in, kid. They say power's off all over. Wasn't no storm, something broke down in the night." Tom poured coffee in a cup for Sam. "There's some rolls on the counter, there." Tom pointed to the counter where June had been making pie dough the day before. Someone called out for Tom, and he went to the front. "No damn power, no damn bell. It's gonna be a Hell of a day." June came in the back door with her arms full of grocery sacks.

Sam helped June with the sacks. "Just spread 'em out, I guess people'll hafta come in here to get the rolls; no room out front." June poured the coffee into a thermos, and started a new pot of coffee. "Ya want some milk or juice?

Gotta drink it, fridge's out too; it won't last too long without power. Grocery was out too. I don't think they know where the problem's at." June spread out the packages on the counter.

Tom was back with the older couple from last night. "Get what ya want, folks. There's some cool drinks in the refrigerator. I got some ice out front in the box; you're welcome to it if it helps. Might as well use it, it ain't gonna be good long." Tom picked up his coffee and drank half a cup. "Gonna be a Hell of a day!"

"Tom, I need to get square with you and get on my merry way. Four days, right?" Sam pulled out his wallet.

Tom motioned for Sam to come out front with him. Other people were coming into the office. "Folks, there's drinks and rolls in the kitchen. Power's out. Listen, kid, Ya owe me twenty bucks for ast night. I just stored yer stuff those other days. Now if ya tell anybody I was nice, I'll hunt ya down, got it!" Tom smiled.

Sam paid Tom, shook his hand, and told him that he might be in the neighborhood for a while now, he would bring Sara to meet him. Tom smiled and told Sam that that would be his pleasure. Sam thought of what a wonderful day it seemed. No power did not matter to him, he had his own power supply! In the car and just cruising, no hurry. Paula was on her way to school and all was fine, real fine! There was only one intersection that had had a flashing yellow light; it hung above the highway, shifting with the gentle breeze, life all gone from its one time perpetual flashing. The drive was pleasant and without incident; it was just as Sam had thought, a new beginning! There were several cars parked on both sides of the highway as Sam approached Sara's driveway. *Power company,* Sam thought.

As Sam started down the driveway, there was a cop standing beside another car, with no markings. He had a cup of coffee. Sam's senses were alerted to a wrong, a terrible wrong! Sam drove into the clearing. Smoke whiffed to the sky, from what was once a house, Sara's house. Sam gunned the engine to get closer, and another policeman yelled at him to slow down. The inner part of the circle drive was occupied by a fire truck. Sam stopped on the outer part of the circle, and just looked out his windshield. Slowly, Sam opened the door. He stood still, holding onto the door, as if he needed support. The smell of the fire that had raged here hung in blue clouds, just inside the tree line.

Laura came up to Sam; she had been crying. "I didn't know where you were. I came over here about four this morning, the fire department was just behind me. Sam, Sara's gone, and that poor, innocent baby!" Laura was crying again. She leaned against Sam, then stood back up straight. "I'm sorry, Sam! They didn't have a chance!"

"How did this happen? There were no problems yesterday when I left. Are you sure she didn't get out?" Sam had started around the door to get to the house.

A police officer came up to Sam. "Sir, may I have your name?"

Sam kept moving, slow, looking at the house, or where the house had been. The officer pulled at Sam's arm to stop him. Sam pulled away.

"Sir, there is an investigation going on here. You have to stay back!" The officer gripped Sam's arm and pulled him back, back into reality!

"What? Oh, Officer, I just, I'm ...what the Hell happened? Sam stood in front of the officer and watched as he took out a pad of paper from his back pocket. It was a Mississippi state trooper. Sam saw everything in slow motion. "I just came here to ah...we... What happened, does anyone know?"

One of the firemen in his turnout gear yelled to a man on the sideline. "Harry, I've got something over here!"

The man in a short-sleeved white shit and tie walked to the edge of the ashes. He had one arm across his chest supporting his other elbow and was cupping his chin. He nodded.

Sam started to go to the man to see whatever there was to see. The trooper stopped him. "Sir, I don't think you want to go up there, not right now." The trooper had his hand on Sam's shoulder.

Sam stopped and looked back at the trooper. "What?"

"Sir, please come over to my cruiser. I think you need to sit down, then we will complete these questions, please, sir." The trooper was insistent and Sam, after a few false starts began to walk to the trooper's car.

Sam saw Laura sitting on a stump at the edge of the woods, bent over and her head in her hands; she looked to still be sobbing. Sam looked, as others were in various attire, depending on what department they belonged to. Some had coffee, some talked, some just looked at what had been Sam's new life, all gone now. The trooper got Sam a cup of water, and then started to ask questions again.

Sam started at Burger's are Us and ended with his going to the motel the previous afternoon. Sam asked a lot of questions, and the question and answer session took about an hour. The officer closed his notebook, he told Sam how sorry he was at Sam's loss, then told him that the authorities would like Sam to stay in the area for a few days. Just till all the questions have been answered; there were a lot of questions that didn't have answers. "Where you stayin', son?"

Sam hated the answer that he was about top give. The question had had an answer, the answer to most all of Sam's questions. "I don't really know. I guess I'll just have to go back to Tom's place, the Cozy Inn. I don't have anywhere else to go." Sam sat in the police cruiser, his forehead against the window.

"I understand that you've just gotten out of the Army, and I'm sorry about your losses here, but I want to thank you for your service to the country." The trooper handed Sam a business card with his name and telephone number. He shook Sam's hand and thanked him and was out of the car to speak to other people that had just arrived.

Sam watched as the trooper talked with the newcomers, at one point they turned and looked in his direction. Laura had started his way. She was red faced and slump shouldered. Sam opened the door, placed his feet on the ground, and began to cry. Laura saw that and turned away. The man in the short-sleeved white shirt came to Sam.

"Sir, my name is Harry Mandle. I understand you were a friend of Miss Farthing. I am the coroner. I know you don't really want to a talk about all of this right now, so I want to know…when would be a good time for you, sir." Harry was digging in his pockets and found a small leather case, he took out a business card with his name and number and gave it to Sam. "If you could call my office in the next few days with a time."

Sam stood up. He sidestepped the door and slammed it. "Mr., Mr. Mandle, do you think there's going to be a good time? What the Hell's wrong with right now! You got questions, I've got questions, I've got a bunch of fucking questions!" Sam was getting pretty loud; he was pointing his finger at Harry, and Harry was backing up. The trooper came running back to his car.

"Sam! Ease up, son! We know how much this grief has caused, but…"

Sam stopped the trooper with his next outburst. "You don't have any fucking idea!" Sam was sobbing now, loud, audible sobbing.

The trooper waved for one of the ambulance attendants to come to him. Laura started to the gathering, but stopped short. Several other officers from sheriff and local authorities came in the direction of Sam and the coroner.

Sam, oblivious to any of the movement, kept at Harry. The trooper stepped in between Harry and Sam. "Sam, let's not make this any worse than it already is. Calm down. I can't imagine what you are suffering right now." The ambulance attendant had moved to Sam's side. "Sam, I want you to go with this young man and let him check you out. I know you don't want to, but take it as an order, you're just outta the Army, and this is a direct order!" The attendant led Sam to his ambulance, Laura in close pursuit. The attendant, "Bo" his shirt tag said, told Sam to sit down on the cot. Sam sat down on the bench. Laura was beside him. Laura sat quietly as the attendant took Sam's pulse and blood pressure. He wanted to put him on some oxygen, but Sam refused.

"I'll be alright, Bo. Just let me sit here for a few minutes." Bo stepped past, and outside the ambulance. Laura had her hands on Sam's leg, and was patting his leg, softly.

"Sam, I'm so sorry. Sara was as happy as I have ever seen her, and Paula was so happy too. I could see that. This has been terrible for you! Yer welcome ta come and stay at my house, Sam. It's the least I could do. I can make ya comfortable there for as long as ya wanna stay." Laura's southern accent was a little hard to make the words out, that, and her crying; tears fell on Sam's leg as she continued to pat Sam's leg, in her efforts to try and comfort him.

"Thanks, Laura, but I'm just going to go to Tom's and try and make this all go away. I've been there for a few days, and am comfortable there; it's quiet. Right now I'm going to go and make some apologies, and see what I can find out about all this."

Laura and Sam went to the trooper and the coroner. Sam apologized for his actions.

VII

There were reports, questions, and few answers, Sam stayed for a week at the Cozy Inn. He and Tom had coffee in front of number IV every morning. Tom offered to sell the place only once; Sam had just looked at Tom, and that was never mentioned again. June brought Sam meals in his room, the room he hardly ever left, after a few days of his not coming to the restaurant.

Sam finally moved on. There wasn't a dry eye in the Cozy Inn when he left. Sam had changed his plans. After a few miles on the road, the day he left, Florida didn't hold any adventure for Sam anymore. He got to Panama City and turned north through Georgia, on I-65. He was going home. The drive was long and lonely. Gas and occasional food were his only stops. Sam came into Illinois at Brookport. When he crossed the bridge he stopped at a rest stop. He cried, maybe because he had finally gotten home, or for what he had left behind. Sam never told anyone his story. Most thought he was moody about being out of the Army, Viet Nam, then most quit trying to figure it all out, they quit coming by, and Sam didn't care. He worked for his dad for a while, and then took a real estate class. Sam didn't know why, he just did. He was good at selling just the right property to the right people, for a profit. Sometimes a house would make Sam remember, but he learned to put that away, most of the time.

Chapter 8
Real World

I

Young Property, Sam's business, flourished from the beginning. Sam had found a hundred acres that had been held up in court over a family fight for years. Sam had sold a few houses and had worked a t a few real estate companies, but when he found this deal he had took off. Sam had paid a hundred thousand dollars for the property, and his dad had been pissed. "That's too much for that swamp property," he had said. But Sam had had a vision, or at least a dream. "It came to me in a dream," he had told everybody. The EPA had fought Sam, the local county officials had fought him, even the local hunters had fought him, but finally almost a year later Sam took pictures of him atop the bulldozer, when he started the lake. They also took pictures of him when he buried it in the creek! Sam knew about the magazine publishers coming to town, and his sources were right, some said lucky. "How did you know?" was the usual question. Sam would just reply, "Lucky!" Sam had builders beating his door down; they wanted some luck too! Sam picked three less than reputable contractors; he had picked them individually, not together. More than once he had to mediate between them! They had made a bunch of money. They had cleaned their reputations up too! Sam scrutinized their work; not right, he made them make it right at their cost. Sam's list of friends dwindled, his list of business associates grew. Sam just so happened to own the best property for the magazine publisher too. They had insisted on their own contractors, but the right to use them had been lucrative. Sam couldn't balance his private checkbook, let alone his business; he was spending a lot of money for an outside bookkeeper. That was when he had met Evelyn. It had taken a little bit of maneuvering to make that happen, but it was for business, and that was all Sam did anymore.

Sam had taken up going to the gym. He didn't really like it there, but Evelyn went there. Evelyn was an employee of the bank. A dedicated employee, and as good as any of the accountants he had used, better, she looked great too! Sam had had to follow her around for a week or two till they had suddenly been at the same places all the time. The dating, the sleepovers, and the hiring, Evelyn was good, on all counts. She also had become a great bookkeeper, secretary, and business associate. Sam had taken to spending more time at work than anywhere else. That had split him and Evelyn, but she still worked for him. Sam had become quite successful, his efforts were paying off, but he had become quite alone, only his dreams worked in his life, they worked very well.

Friend had been quite busy. He knew Sam well; Friend could make Sam into a very wealthy man, he was well on his way. Friend had not confronted Sam in many times; he knew that there had to be a healing for humans. Friend had taken to watching lots of humans; it took energy. Energy was to serve a purpose; humans wasted energy, every day. Friend knew what he wanted now. Friend visited Sam many times at night. It was pleasant at night, Friend and his human, his human that would make him immortal!

Sam had to do many things to make that happen; he was doing all that was necessary.

Sam had taken to collecting cars. He didn't know why; it had just started. Sam had filled the barn at his dad's house with cars; his dad had a new shop and didn't need it anymore. Sam didn't know how many cars were there till his dad had told him that he and Paula were moving to Odin to retire. He had bought property near the old house in Odin, and was starting in the spring. Sam had to move his cars.

So Sam had to build a pole building for his cars, complete with an office, and 200-amp service. George Tadlon had told Sam that much electric service would never be needed, and why didn't he get his dad to do the electric for free. Sam had told George that if he didn't want Sam's money that was alright, he would find another contractor. George didn't ask questions anymore; he put the electric in, for free.

Sam seldom went there. He hired a man to do the mechanic work and take care of the place. Wes kept it all running and made money at the same time; he didn't complain either. Sam, suddenly didn't collect cars anymore, but had a fine existing collection, that included his Chevelle.

Friend liked the Chevelle, too, Sam's only red car. Sam thought it was because of the history of the Chevelle, that he always felt like someone was with him. Friend knew who was with him. Friend didn't talk aloud much for times; he just told Sam things at night! Sam thought he had dreams. Friend knew that too! Friend had dreams too!

Sam's dad was trying to build the house by himself. Paula begged Sam to come by and help. Sometimes he did, but not much. His dad didn't like Sam's associates, and Bob was not one to hold back much. There was always an argument that caused Paula to come by Sam's afterward, and the usual conversation always came up. "You know how your dad is, but he needs help. He's never going to get that house done!" And Sam would find himself in another argument about his business standards. The house was almost done, two year late. Bob and Paula had sold the house in Salem and had to move into it, not quite finished. Sam and Bob were at it again. Sam told his dad that it had been at least two years since he and his mom had even been to JR's for a beer, get the Hell out of town. "Get away from me. I need a rest, and so do you!" Sam had it all set up to have the house all finished when they got back. Paula had heard the argument and had come out to mediate. She had listened, and told Bob that the idea of getting out of town was a good one, and they had, at long last.

It had been raining on they way home from the Grand Ole Opry in Nashville. They should have stopped, but decided to get home, and get off the road. No one ever knew why Bob had lost control, but he had. Bob and Paula had died never to tell why. The fire had made Sam remember; he never told the story, but he remembered all too well!

Friend knew this too!

Sam had gone to the visitation, and met all his dad and mom's friends at the caskets. They had been closed caskets. Sam had not been to a visitation or funeral since Mississippi; there were two caskets there too, one small one! They had been closed too! Sam had had flashbacks from that. He had not left Sara's till the remains had been found. Not many were found—the fire had been too hot—nothing to identify, but the dental records had told the authorities who they had been; the same for Bob and Paula. The car had burned in the crash, it had been a terrible fire. Sam had not seen the sight of the crash, and never questioned the report.

That was when Sam had begun drinking, not a lot, not in public, but there was some drinking. Evelyn had known, but she was too loyal, it had been their secret. Much the same as Sam, and Sara, and of course Friend. Friend knew all, all too well, and that was a secret too! Energy would go on for all time, and so Friend's secret, he was not loose lipped!

Sam and Evelyn had been an off-and-on thing for a lot of years, but the time of Bob and Paula's crash had about ended all relations, private and professional. Sam had moved into the house in Odin; he didn't know why, he just did. He had tired to finish it, for many years he had tried, but something kept him from finishing. Evelyn had helped Sam furnish the finished rooms, carpet and curtains. She kept Sam going, and of course his business. Sam bought out more foreclosures; they were what he liked. Most left the property in a shambles, and that way George had work too. Buy low, sell high, that was all there was; it was business at its best. Young Property did well; no real estate, just money. Sam seldom saw a property, just dollars. Sam was doing well, and losing his sanity at the same time.

II

Friend had been watching out for Sam for some years. He had been disappointed in Sam's use of the money. Sam had always liked toys, when he had been small, in time past. Sam seldom bought clothes, food was only a necessity, he bought lots of drink. Friend had been watching, waiting for just the right time. The time was just right. Wes was being used by both Sam and Friend, and it was convenient for the both of them. Wes kept the cars running, and Friend kept Wes running. Friend visited Wes at night too!

"Sam!" Friend had used his voice. It felt good; it had been a long time. "Sam!"

The gun had alarmed Friend to no end! Sam had become as he had when he had been small, in time past. But Sam had been able to be manipulated, as in his sleep. Awake Sam had proven to be difficult. But Friend had been up for the task. Friend had not counted on Evelyn. He did not understand why Sam had gone to another human. Friend had used Sam to gain most of what had been needed, but he now needed cooperation. But Sam had been using liquid again; that had changed much. Friend had blamed his own entity as the cause, but time was still on Friend's side. Friend was to make all happen in time. Evelyn would be handled in time. Sam would again leave her as in time past, but that had not yet happened, and time was soon. Friend had had to sign Spirit, this had not been part of Friend's plan. All other parts of Friend's plan had worked so well. Now Evelyn had become a problem. Friend had caused many parts of Sam's life to become his own entity's time. But now this, he had watched for time now, but could not for long time. Friend had taken Sam to time past, to show him, the power of energy was not measurable, at least by humans. That had had its problems, but Friend had solved all those problems, except his pawn, Sam. Sam had become hard to handle. Friend had allowed Bob and Paula the time to accept Sam. Sam did not have a problem, but meddlesome parent units. That had to be solved in the time as needed, and had been. But Evelyn! A new but old problem, at the same time, time was now, energy had been solved, but Sam had to make the crossing over permanent soon! Spirit had become impatient; Spirit had power that Friend was unaware existed. The only place Friend could not go was Spirit's brain. If anyone had a brain that functioned here it would be Spirit. Shelter had saved Friend, but for how long? Even Spirit had limits to patience, and Friend had tried them, many times.

III

Evelyn had listened to the rain; she knew Sam was awake. He wasn't talking. She thought that he was afraid to look like he was being foolish, or maybe he had a problem. But she had heard something, so who should be afraid? "Sam, I know you're not asleep. We have done everything not to talk, I don't care how it sounds. Sam, I love you!" Evelyn rolled over and took up her same position, on her left side. "Sam, either you have a ventriloquist act, or someone else was here!"

Sam's face was only illuminated by the lightning, then dark, very dark. He exhaled. "Evelyn, I'm about to tell you a few stories. There are more than one, and then I will try and tie them together. I don't expect you to believe them. I will tell them, and then you can judge just how crazy I really am." Sam exhaled long.

"I have told you the story about my invisible friend, I have told you about the doctors. I will try to tie those together first. I had a friend, he was a friend. I guess I was a geek back then, I didn't need other kids, because of Friend. I met a few kids and we became friends, but none were like Friend. Friend always wanted to do what I wanted. We fished, we talked, we studied; he was always interested in whatever I was studying, he even encouraged me to study harder. He helped me in school, because he asked questions when I was ready to throw in the towel and quit! He was especially interested in English, but I was no good at it so I would not study, and I just accepted whatever grade was given me, just to get by. But Friend had me looking up all kinds of words, he always wanted to know what words meant. He would hear other people talk and have me looking up the meaning. I had a lot of words in my mind, but couldn't tell you an adverb from a noun. We would be in my room and he would hear something on the radio and I would be off to the dictionary." Sam was lit up by the lightning in flashes and spurts, in focus and out. It was like a strobe light.

"This sounds long, I'm dry. I don't want you to stop. Do you want something to drink?" Evelyn got up and Sam pulled the sheet away from her. "Sam! You aren't getting out of it this time!" Evelyn got up and walked to the kitchen; it was dark, and she felt comfortable.

Sam followed her. When she opened the refrigerator, all was dark, no expected light. She was feeling around for drinks. "Sam, I can't see a damn thing in here. You have a flashlight somewhere?"

Sam had pulled the rechargeable from the hallway receptacle, and pushed the button forward, light!

"Oh! Holy Christ, Sam! You scared me to death! What were you thinking!" Evelyn stood in the light, naked as the day she had been born. Evelyn stood with her hands on her hips.

Sam thought, like Sara's "mommy pose." He shook it off. That story had to be told too! Tonight, the pain, the hurt. Sam didn't respond, he just stood there, with a light trained on Evelyn.

"Sam! Sam!" Evelyn's voice had fear in the tone.

"Oh, I'm sorry, just taking in all your beauty!" She was pretty, especially without any outer covering. "Here, I thought you might need this." Sam handed Evelyn the flashlight.

"You scared me. It's dark in here!" Evelyn was still standing there, but now the light was on Sam. "Are you alright, Sam?"

"I'm fine. Especially with you in my kitchen, in the 'wherewithal,' nice! Do you think you could make more appearances like that?" Sam tried to hid his blank spots. There were many stories, and he didn't know if they might take Evelyn away, maybe forever.

Evelyn had turned her attention back to the dark refrigerator. "What do you want, Sam? There's Pepsi, Coke, root beer, and tea."

"I'll have a Pepsi, in a glass, please." Sam opened the lower cabinet. Cans fell out and rolled around on the kitchen floor. Evelyn shone the light over to where Sam was rummaging. "A little closer, my dear!"

"It's story time, remember." Evelyn's feet were the only part of her illuminated by the beam of light now.

"Can't blame a fella for trying can ya! Here it is!" Sam had a fat candle and serving tray. "Got the drinks, let's go." Sam patted Evelyn's butt as he turned toward the doorway.

"Don't start it!"

Sam situated the serving tray on the bed and lit the candle. The light was concentrated at the wick. It sputtered and almost went out, it flared back and the light seemed to chase the shadows to the corners of the room. Evelyn sat down, set the drinks on the serving tray. The movement of the mattress caused the light to move and take shapes, then it settled back into a steady light. It flickered a little as it burned. The changing light caused the shadows to move; shadows were not to be feared, yet! They gathered in the corners, solid, dark and foreboding.

"Refreshments have been served, now continue." Evelyn took a drink and set her Pepsi back on the tray.

Sam watched the light on Evie's breasts, the rise, and fall, as she slowly inhaled and exhaled. "I have so much to tell. I may have some difficulty, you understand, right?"

"Yes, Sam. There's nothing you can't tell me." Evie's chest rose and fell.

Sam watched as Evie's form changed with each flicker of the light. "Well, I had to go to the doctors for my therapy. Back then it was a treatment, no such thing as therapy. Now I need a therapist, and you may too—maybe we can get group rates! Even after the doctors, I still saw Friend; he didn't come around as often, and he didn't always appear, sometimes he would only talk to me, sometimes just inside my head. I did think that maybe the doctors were right. But we held conversations; he couldn't read my mind so I would have to talk aloud. That cost me a few friends, and a few embarrassing moments." Sam took a drag off of Evie's cigarette, and took a drink. "That's where the habit of talking to myself out loud came from. I thought it had gone, but then I thought Friend was gone too. Friend had told me that he was here to assist me; he saved me a half dozen or better times. Friend explained to me, he was to keep me safe, and there were times he had saved me, and I hadn't seen him for a long time. Even in high school, he had saved me. I know he did it even though I hadn't seen him, I knew he was there! In Viet Nam I should have been dead twice; I have a bullet on a necklace. That comes later."

The lights flickered, once, twice, and full glow. The lamp on the night stand suddenly showed all, leaving only a few shadows. Evelyn pulled the sheet up to cover herself. Sam got up and went to the kitchen and started to turn off lights that had been left on before the outage. When he came back the night stand light was out, and the candle still burned. Sam continued to talk about little instances that he knew Friend had been there. Sometimes, a word, a feeling. Sam had explained that at times he thought he was just lucky, and he would try and dismiss it as, only luck! But deep in his own mind he had known. Other people had thought him lucky, at times very lucky! There was a long pause in the story, Sam excused himself, and had gone to the bathroom. When he came back, he blew the candle out.

"I know it's late but we can go on for a little longer, Sam. I want to hear it all." Evelyn was calm, but sounded tired; she yawned.

"Don't take this wrong, Evie. But the light has to be out right now." Sam lay very still for a minute or so, and then began anew. "When I got out of the Army, I was headed to Key West. My new life, my adventure. I had hopes of not being a virgin after the trip to Key West! I had many thoughts of how the trip was going to come out, but I wasn't going to be a virgin anymore. I had fantasized about all the new and different women I would find, and conquer. I had envisioned the trip all through Viet Nam. I was going to buy a car and maybe never go home, sail the Keys and become a pirate!" Sam paused; he took several deep breaths.

"I've always thought it would be a place I would like to see. Was it as pretty as the brochures?" Evelyn had some cheer backing her voice, but was tired.

"I never got there." Sam sighed.

"I met a girl, well not a girl, for me an older lady, she wasn't old, just older than me." Sam hesitated.

"An older lady! Something I never knew about you." Evelyn laughed.

"It's not what you think. She had a little girl, Paula. She was an angel." Sam felt a bit of moisture in the corner of his eyes.

"Had?" Evelyn had a tone of question, a worried sound.

"Yeah, had. I fell in love. I fell hard. I wasn't a virgin after that. I solved one great part of my life, the big mystery about sex. Sara solved that problem, and I was in love."

Sam continued the story. He told each and every part of the story of his love, and his wants, and his desires, and Paula. Sam stopped his story to wipe his eyes on more than one occasion. Evelyn became quiet, her breathing became shallow, she didn't move, she didn't want to interrupt any of Sam's story. But it was a kid's story of his first love. Sam continued, only wiping his eyes. He began to cry. Evelyn could hear the sadness in Sam's voice; he was heartbroken, and Evelyn felt like she had invaded the deepest, darkest part of Sam's psyche, a part that had never been visited. Sam was having a lot of trouble telling the story. Sam sat up, and put his legs to the side the bed. His form could be seen from the street lights glow. Sam had his face buried into his hands. His crying had slowed, he took a deep breath, he exhaled and wiped his nose.

"On the day that I had decided to chuck it all and become a family man with the woman I had fallen in love with, it all went bad! I can remember it all. Every minute! I got up at the Cozy Inn, showered and shaved, and went for breakfast. I didn't even know the power had been off. I didn't look at the clock on the night stand. It was the happiest day of my life. I remember I was hungry; I could have eaten a horse! The restaurant was dark, the office was dark. I called out, and Tom called back and told me to come to the kitchen. We had rolls and coffee. When I got back there that night the power was on, but went off and on most of the night." Sam was breathing deeply, and very slowly.

"When you got back? I thought you were going to leave there?" Evelyn had slipped closer to Sam to hear, his voice had gotten so soft. She was careful not to touch him or distract him. She didn't want to hear the story anymore, but couldn't stop him now.

"I left, I left alright. When I got to Sara's there were cars everywhere. But naive me, I thought they were fixing the power. Till I came drove in to the house, where the house had been, anyway." Sam took in a deep breath, a slobbery breath, his shoulders sagged. "The fire had been really bad. No one I talked to in the next week had ever seen or worked a fire that had been that hot! They said it was only smoldering when they arrived. It had been a real blaze to have incinerated everything."

"Oh my!" Evelyn gasped as she finally knew the end of the story, the end of Sam's young love, his life.

"Yeah! I stayed till the very end. They only found some bones, and a skull, for Sara. Paula had even less, they raked all the ashes, and that was all that was left!" Sam's sobbing got worse. He tried to speak and no words came.

Evelyn had wanted Sam's story. Now she felt she had opened a chapter in Sam's life that was so dark, and so sad. Evelyn felt sad, she felt to blame. It had gotten cool following the rain. Evelyn wrapped the sheet around Sam; she felt his cool skin. He shivered. Evelyn did not know if it was from the cool air or his recollection of the fire and all that it had destroyed. Evelyn wrapped her arms around Sam's neck, and sat quiet.

"I've got to tell it all." Sam sat up and slipped his right arm around Evelyn. "No one has ever been told this story…well, I did tell Tom."

"Who was Tom, Sam?" Evelyn asked before she realized the words had come out.

"Tom, owned the Cozy Inn; he had tried to sell it to me!" Sam chuckled in a sad sort of a fashion. "Tom treated me well, and June his cook, they were good people. I often wonder if Tom ever retired to the Caribbean; that was what he wanted." Sam had regained some of his composure. "I stayed for the funeral, not many people there. I tried to pay, and was told it had all been taken care of. I didn't know much about Sara. We had never really talked about family. I don't even know whether she had one. No one at the funeral was family. There were two caskets, they were light blue and pink, two of them. Just like at Mom and Dad's, but one was very small; it was pink, a light, light pink." Sam sat for some time before he began again.

"Till Mom and Dad, I had not been to a funeral. Yeah, I know that's stupid, but I hadn't been to one! I have never told anyone but Tom, and now you." Sam paused, he wiped his eyes on the sheet. "I'm glad I told you. I'm sorry I lost it. It was really bad." Sam kissed Evelyn on her forehead. The clock bedside the bed, flashed 12:00. Sam knew it was late, but no idea how late. He wrapped his arms around Evelyn, the two lay back on the bed.

Light was coming in the window as the two lay back on the bed. They had made love. Sam had thought of the last night with Sara; it had been passionate. He and Evelyn had been passionate; it was good! Sam felt a tear escape from his eye. Evelyn pulled him close and kissed it away. Sleep came later; it was peaceful.

IV

"Sam," Friend, was watching, he didn't have a glow about him, he had learned to control that, but Sam, that was another problem, he had thought he had control of Sam. Now he could barely control his own entity! He had heard all the story, he knew the story! And he was angry, very angry, he could do it again. Sam knew about human power; he could cause both of them to become energy, just like Sara and Paula! Just like Bob and Paula!

He could feel his own power begin to surge; he had to control the power, he could not make the fire again; he needed Sam, he had plans, without Sam he was done. But Evelyn, that was another plan, in time, soon time. He would cross over and power again he did not want to crossover, Spirit had begun to sign him many time, many times that "Sam" needed to plan. A new plan had to be made now. Time was not right for this! He had to leave, he was too angry to stay! He could not control his power anymore! As Sam left to cross over, there was a loud pop! The same pop, as when a power surge causes a fuse or breaker in an electric box when it overloads.

Sam opened his eyes, saw nothing, and was back asleep. Evelyn snuggled against him till she was motionless again. They rested, peacefully, not knowing that they had had a visitor.

Friend had been ready to cross over, but he knew Spirit would be waiting to sign him. Instead he went to where Sam kept his cars. Wes was drinking liquids; the cup appeared to have the early dark fluid in it. There was a car that Sam did not recall. The cover had been raised in the front of the car, mechanical items had been Sam's study of late. There was a wire coming from the outlets on the wall. All were high powered; they had energy, usable energy. This time there would be no fire, just energy. The fire had been a good plan, even though it had only came to Sam in the last few minutes, but it had worked. It would work again; Sam would not tolerate another fire. Then the fire with his parent units had been part of the plan, the liquid had caused a short-lived fire, it had been light, but Sam had become involved, fire gave him a tingling feeling. No other source had given him a sensation of the human world; water caused him an agony. Sam shunned water, it was like crossing over, he lost power, but it was gone, not recallable. Sam watched Wes. He enjoyed his mechanical toys. They too had liquid in them; it was a wasted power. One day there would be power for all humans. Sam would be the God they would pray to, Sam would be the power!

Conversations with Wes would be necessary. He had a plan, an additional plan. Time in human terms was not understandable to Sam. It was a waste of his energy to try and sign the waste. No human ever had to power, only put food into their opening, mouth. He still needed to become better with words…the humans used words, another anomaly. Sam knew all the words Sam had told him, but some easy words did not work, they caused him to appear without knowledge, and he had knowledge. Wes would be changing to the evening liquid soon. Then he and Wes would have conversations. Wes was now an integral part of the additional plan! Sam had many thought processes at the same time, not like before his plan. Thoughts came and went. Emotions were a part he knew the word, but could not comprehend the meaning. Spirit had been of little help in the sign of their signing. Spirit had signed that emotions were of no value to an entity. It was complicated, this emotion thing; he understood anger. And Sam had signed him anger, and Evelyn was undecided as to how to remove her from Sam. He had done many time in his own study of human. Emotions were a needed part of his vocabulary now. Had Spirit signed Sam at time past he would have been done with his plan now, but entities have to learn anew, each recall, no recall time before. No human memory of time that had been. Soon there would only be time, "Sam's" time, always! With a little added assistance from Wes!

Chapter 9
Life

I

Sam was fifty-four, Evelyn was forty-two. Sam looked used up for a long time, Evelyn had always looked ten years younger. Evelyn had made Sam to begin to look his age, minus a few years. Sam had vitality, he had Evelyn! Sam brought George in to finish the house. George bitched and moaned about the fall wasn't a good time to start a house renovation. Sam told George just to put the deck on first, then move inside, the bedroom, the hallway, and the upstairs that had never even been touched. The upstairs could wait till spring, it would not be needed or used this winter coming. It was going to be Sam's den, actually a play room for an adult, one that felt more like a child, than he had when he had been a child. Sam and Evelyn were back at work, it had been almost a month that he had been closed, or a lot of people had thought so. It took Sam almost three days to come up with a deal for some old railroad property, and he was making things happen. Most thought Sam and Evelyn had run off and gotten married, then they found out they had only been shacked up. There had been a lot of talk in the business community. Sam had not been a church person, nor had Evelyn, but the talk had been a little embarrassing for Evelyn. She never tried to explain.

They had gone to Denny's for dinner one evening, and had seen a few whispering and pointing fingers. Sam had told Evelyn to ignore them, but it had become obvious that they were being watched. Sam had a business to run, and it had been starting to affect that too. The waitress had cleared their table and refilled their coffee. Sam reached across the table and took Evelyn's hand in his.

"What now, Sam?" She knew he always had an angle working and thought it was about the business.

"My lady, wouldst thou make a man of somewhat elderly age, so very happy!" Sam was in his best knight act now. He was being overly loud this time. He had never done this in public; it was probably to make the old women steam more!

"Wouldst thou marry me!"

Evelyn leaned over their hands on the table. "Sam! Stop kidding around, those old ladies are still watching!"

"My lady, I do not kiddeth around! Evie, marry me!" Everybody looked around this time.

People at the counter spun their stools around. The waitresses stopped pouring coffee and taking orders. Everyone waited. Someone said, "Marry him, Evie!" Someone else clapped their hands, people were murmuring in the background.

"Are you serious?" Evelyn asked.

"I don't usually make an ass out of myself in Denny's, but I will get on one knee!"

Sam slid to the end of the booth and was in the floor on one knee. "Evie, marry me!" He said it even louder this time.

"Yes....yes, Sam! I have loved you for years! I thought we were too old to get married!" Evelyn had tears in her eyes. She slid to the floor and hugged Sam.

"Too old!" Sam hugged her back.

Denny's would never be the same again, at least for a while. There was still talk, but it had a different flavor now. Sam, the confirmed bachelor, some had wondered about his sexual preference, but not anymore. There was clapping, and cheering, and no bill for their meal. The coffee got cold twice; they didn't really need coffee anymore. And Sam took out a small box from his jacket pocket and set it on the table. Evelyn opened it slowly. The half carat looked as big as the moon to Evelyn. Evelyn leaned across the table, and pulled Sam upright, and hugged him again. This time they spilled the coffee, both cups!

"I thought it was just a show, you had this planned! Sam, I love you!" Evelyn hugged Sam harder.

"Evie. My pants are getting coffee all over them," Sam told Evelyn calmly.

They separated, and looked at Sam's pants; where they had been against the table they were soaked. A waitress had a towel and was sopping up the coffee. "Congratulations, you two," she said as she worked to clean up their mess. Sam couldn't buy dinner that night, but he left the waitress a fifty-dollar tip. As they left all congratulated them and clapped them on the backs, and wished them good luck. Wes had swapped Sam's Dodge for the Chevelle while no one was watching. Sam opened Evelyn's door, and bowed as she got in.

Sam got in, leaned over to Evelyn and gave her a kiss. He started the car, and pumped the gas twice, and the pipes roared. A crowd had followed them outside and was cheering Sam on! Sam, backed out slowly, shifted to first, roared the engine once more, dumped the clutch, and killed it. All outside Denny's laughed at his failed attempt at being cool! Sam started the Chevelle up again. This time he was right, the smoke billowed off the back tires and they were off. The crowd cheered!

Evelyn was hitting Sam on the shoulder. "Sam! The cops are always here, you'll get a ticket!"

"I'll invite them to the wedding!" Sam pulled out onto Route 50 and tore out again.

Evelyn had her arms around Sam's neck, as he shifted to third then eased off the gas. They rode in silence, except for the exhaust sound. The air was cool, the windows were down, and the air buffeted the passengers. The ride to Odin was slow, and others had passed them. The excitement of the moment had, it seemed, been shelved for the time.

"Now you have a lot of work! I don't know anything about getting married, I only know what I want, and you have accepted! So now it's all on you to make this happen! I don't even know want to wear!" Sam was making his turn; the amber turn signal lit his face on and off.

"My job? This is supposed to be a partnership, right! You have a big part in this too!" Evelyn had her legs pulled up under her and was facing Sam, her hands on his shoulder.

"Well, I don't know who to invite, how to invite them. Do I call them and invite them over, do we do this in a church, or what? I'm not a church person. I know a few preachers, but only in a business sort of a way." Sam looked at Evelyn and smiled.

When they got to the house small talk was in place, about the wedding. Evelyn would take care of most of it, and would ask for approval when she needed it. She had worked for Sam long enough to know that he would show up for the wedding in the proper attire. He would have to have someone to get him there on time! Sam opened the door and tried to pick up Evelyn, for a trial carry over the threshold. She resisted and told him she would have to get skinny before he could do that. His reply "too old!" They laughed and went into the kitchen. There was a smell of paint, but it had improved. The house was done now, except for the upstairs, that next spring. Sam had left a light on in the living room, as a soft glow came from the hallway.

Sam started to the living room to shut the light off, as he had other plans for the evening. He stopped dead in his tracks as he turned the corner. Friend was on the couch. He looked almost human, not a kid anymore, he had aged too, not as much as Sam perhaps, but aged! He was surrounded by a soft glow, and his hollow smile. "What are you doing here, 'Sam!'" Sam said softly. "Evelyn's here!"

"Yes, I know. That's why I'm here. I have always told you that I always watched. I know you are about to get…mar..ried, yes married. I know, I saw you buy the ring, and I just knew. It's time I met the miss, that you have spent so much time with, the one that makes you happy!"

"Oh, Sam!" Evelyn had other thoughts as well. She came into the living room with her blouse unbuttoned. When she saw Friend she stopped, just behind Sam. No word came from her mouth, it just stayed open, and she pointed, as thought directing someone behind her. She knew who the ghostly specter was, she knew!

Sam turned to Evelyn. The look on his face was loss, total loss! Sam moved to his new fiancée's side; he pulled her blouse together. Evelyn regained her composure and took over the blouse from Sam.

Friend stood, a little jerky it appeared, but stood. The glow was all but gone. He appeared to be out of sequence, his movements were like watching an old Godzilla movie, but not his voice, his moves. "I want you two to sit here on the couch." Friend gestured with his hand toward the couch.

Sam and Evelyn moved together to the couch, and sat slowly; their eyes never left Friend. "Evie, I never knew anything about him being here!" Sam spoke softly. Evelyn had not given that a thought, till now! She looked at Sam in disbelief. "I haven't even seen him since I was a kid. We've talked, I told you about that, but I haven't seen him in years!"

"Sam…I'm…sorry, I thought he was a figment of your imagination! I'm sorry!" Evelyn couldn't take her eyes off of Friend.

"Whispering is no good, I hear all, and to answer your questions, I will. I have been with Sam since he was made, er, born. I still have some problems with words, as you will see, in time to come."

"What does he mean, in time to come?" Evelyn asked Sam.

"Well, Evelyn, I have been created to assist Sam. I am his assistant, no, his protector. I keep him out of trouble, in odd sort of a way. I see things as they happen, and am able to stop them before they happen, not stop them, but make Sam stop. I have a speed that I cannot explain, it just happens. I will always be with Sam. Not all humans have an entity."

"An entity? What's that?" Evelyn asked. Her nervousness was apparent in her voice.

"That's what I am. I am an entity. I am energy that assists Sam. I do not know how Sam has been picked, I only know that I am his. I help at all times, and now I have a new human to assist as well, Evelyn. I will assist you as well as Sam; it is my reason for being. I don't make the car operate, I only assist. Now I will assist you as well."

Evelyn sat beside Sam, both her arms wrapped around Sam's left arm. "So are you always ...you know...here?"

"No. I cross over to my place and power, and I watch from there. I do not watch, as humans do the picture maker." Friend pointed to the TV. "I know, in my thinking processes, I know when I am needed, my process is tuned to Sam's service, and now yours. I have been created to preserve and keep a human, in energy...life, as long as he is created for."

Evelyn watched as his movements seemed disjointed. But as time went on the movement did not seem out of place. The carpet did not crush under his weight, if there was any weight. Friend almost seemed to float. But not so you could tell. He wore, or appeared to wear, brown slacks, shoes and socks, a lighter shirt with a faint flower design. His hair was medium blond, and a slight tan. He stood, or floated in the living room, the newly painted living room. He waited, and smiled, an odd smile.

"Friend, I know we haven't seen one another for some time... why wouldn't you show yourself when I wanted you to? Evie has begun to think I'm nuts. I would have been hard to prove otherwise, and we hadn't talked about you in a while, but I know it has been on her mind." Sam grasped Evelyn's hands in his.

"You called him 'Sam'"? Evelyn was looking at Sam.

"He wanted a name, not just Friend. I told him he was like talking to myself so I called him 'Sam.'" Sam showed a weak smile to Evelyn.

"I like the name, is that alright with you, Evelyn? I do not want to make the wrong sign with you. I have always been Sam's friend, but till time recent past

I had not a name. I can still be Friend, if you would like. I have always been more of an entity than was designed by Spirit. I have had to do a lot of time, to prepare to be visible. I have not used an image in many times now, am I acceptable?" Friend spun around, in a slow-motion turn, but at an incredible speed at the same time. Their vision was to see an image, and that they did! "Your time passes in a schedule, mine does not. When I am present, time still progresses, but at a slower time. It has taken me many times to begin to understand, that is why I must power. I recall energy that is used, I do not waste power, but use it over, and over again. I can become no more than I am, but no less. I will always be the same. I have no time…age, I do not live, but exist. Exist I do, but only while Sam, and now Evelyn, are present and need my assistance."

"Were you at Denny's tonight? I don't understand."

"When Sam has a problem, when he is in danger, when he is with illness, my thought processes are aware of the changes that are about to happen, I become aware of this. I can see what has happened, I can affect what has happened, but I cannot prevent what will happen. I can take Sam to his time past to affect his time yet to happen. I am not your God," that statement did not sit well with "Sam," "I can only assist."

Sam spoke, the first time since "Sam" had started. "I tried to tell you that I had been to Sandoval, it was 1969. He did that! I told you!" Sam smiled, as smile of satisfaction.

"I did. I was not supposed to, but I had to make you know that I am, you had had trouble in our signs…talks. No one has ever caused that before, I have improved since our youth time." "Sam" smiled; the smiles were improving, or Sam and Evelyn were getting used to them. "I have decided that this time, was to allow Evelyn to be present in a sign… talk with you, and I, to know that you're are not, as you say, "nuts."" "Sam" walked, slid over to the couch, he took Evelyn's hand from Sam's grasp, he bowed at the waist, and ever so gently, kissed Evelyn's hand. "I have to power now. I cannot stay in this form for long. My time will be again." "Sam" shrank away till only a dot was present. Noiselessly it too disappeared, leaving Sam and Evelyn in total darkness.

Evelyn had been inspecting her hand, expecting something, she didn't know what, then the darkness surrounded all that had been light. Only a slight glow from the kitchen night light. As her eyes adjusted to the light she realized that her hand was still there, and she still held it in front of her; it had a ring on it now!

Evelyn laid her hand back on her lap, the kiss had a tingle to it, not a touch, like a feather had passed over her skin, and only touched her in passing. It had been, but it had not been, as well.

"Well?" Sam spoke softly.

"Well, what? I mean I had had some thoughts about you in the past. But now, I just am in total amazement. I don't know what to say." Evelyn moved her fingers to make sure they were still attached, and did not leave with "Sam."

"The doctors, my mom and dad, and whoever, they all thought I had a few screws loose. And now in all my fifty-four years, I have been exonerated! I'm not nuts after all. Does this change all your thoughts about me?" Sam hung his head and grasped Evelyn's remaining hand a little harder.

"Not at all!" Evelyn put her arms around Sam's neck and pulled him to her. "I think you're even neater that I thought before. You've got a...a...a Friend, another you! I have two Sams now. That might be more than I can handle!" Evelyn kissed Sam softy.

Sam kissed her in return, he pulled her to him. When the kiss was broken, Sam said, "I love you, Evelyn Sanders!"

Evelyn had not intended to become engaged, she had not intended to meet "Sam," but all of those things had made her more intense. The sun was coming up as they finished making love; it had been more than either had ever experienced in their lives. Both were exhausted, sticky from sweat, the blankets seemed too hot. They collapsed into sleep. Hours passed as they rested in the other's embrace.

II

"Sam" was proud of the fadeaway. It looked good, and the looks on Sam's and Evelyn's faces had been worth his practice. "Sam" had gotten tired of watching the physical contact, and had returned to shelter. The thought of powering had been planted in their minds, and they had gone on into emotional embraces. "Sam" still did not understand what the need was, but it existed. Now, he had Evelyn on his side; he could come and go as needed. Now Sam would become more adaptable. This had been a last-minute plan. It would work now, "Sam" was confident in his goals now. Sam would do anything asked, Evelyn would make sure of that, in time yet to come. "Sam" had times that he might have done this before, but all had not been as ready as now. Time was approaching that "Sam" would become the power; he would make all available for Evelyn and Sam, but they would not stop him now. They would become powerful in a human sense of the word. Power! Spirit would sign him in time yet to come!

"Entity, we must sign. I have had many signs in time, but in recent time I have had energy lost. Small humans have passed from time, their entities have gone to recall, or should have; the energy from these entities, has passed to another form. It has been wasted, or at least moved from our energy to another energy. I am signed that you have been in attendance of your human many time; you have not powered as in time past. Are you aware of any problems with humans, or entities?"

"Spirit I have been in use of power as in all time. My human has required much assistance, and I have been in shelter to power many times. The loss of energy is grave in our place, have the entities stayed too long with humans, and not had power to return?"

"That cannot happen. Weak power is a reason, for return, assistance cannot be fulfilled without energy. They would have returned to power, the most powerful Spirit would have seen this and returned them to power. As entity in past time you have been returned to power when you had not passed over in time. Your recall has been done in time past."

"Sam" had not been aware of any Spirit but his Spirit, nor was he aware of a recall because of weakness. "Entity may have encountered a power of human kind that has prevented their return."

"Entity, that is not possible, no such power exists. I feel a sign from entity that had not been signed. Does entity have any signs for Spirit? Has entity sign from a new power source?"

Thoughts had almost given "Sam" away. "I am only concerned about loss of energy. Energy lost will make our assistance more difficult. Energy cannot be lost."

"Entity's sign was of distress, in my time of distress I sign, and my own recall has been less than it has been in time past. It may be time for this entity to be recalled as well. My time has been many here."

"Sam" was in shelter as soon as Spirit had signed no more. He would power, it would cause him calm. How did Spirit find that there had been missing entities? "Sam" had many signs to ponder now, a plan had to be created, to leave time here soon. Power had begun; a slight bluish haze came over "Sam" as he became only energy again. No noise, a feeling of POWER!

III

Evelyn was up, had a breakfast, dinner meal prepared as Sam came out of the bathroom. He walked slowly into the kitchen. Sam walked up behind Evelyn at the counter and kissed her on the neck. "Good morning! I love you!" Sam slipped his arms around her.

Evelyn turned in his arms and kissed his nose. "Well, I think we missed morning, I'm not sure about the afternoon, but I love you, too! It's kinda hard to realize that I went from the girl Friday to the future Mrs. Young in an evening dinner, and we have gained a ghostly guardian, all in the same time frame. I wonder what the local paper would say about a picture of the three of us."

Sam's fear level just went up.

"'Sam' is never going to do, he's got to come up with something different. I can't have my legs in the air and shout out 'OH Sam' and have him appear!" Evelyn laughed, Sam did not.

"Evie, you can't say anything about 'Sam,' I mean Friend. You can't ever say anything to anyone, ever! They would have us under a microscope, he would never show up, and you would be called a loony tune! I know, you have no idea how long it took me to get up the courage to tell you. And last night you found out more than I have ever known. He would never answer any questions for me. I have wondered just how much he has done for me, when and where? I really don't know. Last night I had forgotten all about Friend. I didn't propose to you to bring you into a strange family of ghosts and ghouls. I proposed to you in the place that we met, years ago. And I wanted to catch you completely off guard, and it took me a while to finally do it. I don't want last night to be the night that you met Friend! I want it to be the night I finally did something that I wanted to do, something I needed, and I hope you won't regret, and I hope you will remember it as wonderful as I have. I love you!" Sam had a serious look and held Evelyn close. He hugged her and stepped away. "Don't hate me for what I just said, but I have been a loner all my life, partly because of Friend. He has been great, but you never know when he will show up. I mean he caught you a bit off guard last night, right." Sam struck a pose with his shirt open.

"I would never tell anyone about Friend. And last night will last forever! Because we will last forever! I was never so excited as last night. Now eat something. I'm gonna fuck your brains out, Mr. Young! You're going to need your strength! And if 'it' shows up, he only gets to watch!" Evelyn let her gown fall open.

Sam felt a growing begin. He ate fast, watching Evelyn's breasts rise and fall while she ate too. When Sam stood the growth had become quite large. He tried to hide it, a man his age, acting like a kid.

Evelyn stood when Sam did, she stepped over to Sam, slipped her hand down the front of his pajama bottoms and grasped Sam. "Come with me, Mr. Young, you ain't seen nothin' yet!" Evelyn led the compliant Sam down the hallway. She turned to Sam as they went through the bedroom door; she still had her grip. Evelyn pushed the door closed to prevent any intruders.

IV
Northern Lights

"Sam" had his spot picked out. He had traced the power coming into Odin, the facility was north of Sandoval and Odin, about halfway between the two towns. They were small towns that were used to power outages in the summer, but fall had arrived, and power was usually stable in the fall and winter—no air conditioners. But with October came cool nights and warm days; everyone had the windows open and were enjoying the fall. The colors were not going to be great due to the dry summer, but some colors were apparent. Midday on the twenty-second was a major break in service. The power went out at six in the morning. Without electricity all of modern man stops. No school, now the working parents have a babysitting problem; no electric, the factory doesn't work, the can opener doesn't work, everyone looks for the hand crank model that hasn't been used since the last outage. Only half the telephones work. No power, refrigerator and freezers start to thaw. Panic strikes the towns affected. Such was the twenty-second.

"Sam" had a different view, he hadn't expected it to be so far reaching. It was energy, testing energy, an odd combination. "Sam" had visited the substation, and tried out a little taste. Eight hundred eighty amps stretched into wires, boosters at various locations to continue to step up power to all the shelters. "Sam" had placed his entity between two incoming transformers; the sensation had been good! He had feeling, a feeling of raw power, not like powering, not a recall of used energy returning, but outside power! This power was actually better than the power "Sam" had gotten from the two entities. New, additional power, power that had come from a new supply source. "Sam" had done well, but he had gotten greedy. He had started to draw power from the source, pulling in more and more. That's when the transformers had caught fire, still not enough. The fire always made him feel tingly, a feeling he had grown to like. He stayed, the transformers could not handle the power, they had already blown and were burning, they passed from being broken to unmanageable. "Sam" left the power station as red cars with red lights began to arrive, large red cars with men attached to the outside.

The fire went out by itself, no power, no flammable source, no fire. The firemen from both Odin and Sandoval had never seen a fire that melted the chain-link fence enclosure. A few posts remained in a twisted, bent position. Nothing was left of the power substation. Only a few metal parts, not recognizable by their shape and ashes. The fireproof terminals and the metal buildings reduced to ash. The firemen sprayed water to make sure the fire was out. The metal was only warm, what little that remained, melted into a form that only resembled metal. It had been so hot, it was brittle. Illinois Power was the last to arrive at the site. They only walked around and talked to themselves and their superiors on cell phones. Wires leading into and out of the substation were gone, ashes had fallen in nearby fields, for miles around no wire existed! The local fire marshal arrived, he sifted through the same ashes that the power company had been through, he checked for witnesses, he checked firemen, firemen that had been firemen for some years. It was told to the locals that somehow a switch had been thrown, and fed power into the substation from three different directions. The short created by this amount of power had caused an electrical energy that had caused millions of amps of electricity to arrive at the substation, at the same time. The devastation had been complete, nothing was left. Some bought the explanation, some didn't. Illinois Power didn't! Parts arrived from all directions, they acquired additional land half a mile away. Some rebuilt the new substation, some investigated the old site, those building had more production, than those investigating. Illinois Power finally gave up on a real explanation. They began to accept the switch theory themselves. All thought no failed systems were ever found, parts changed, and switches removed and discarded. Prevention was only a coverup for lack of knowledge of what had happened. The rates went up—someone had to pay for the new safety measures! The sweep of details continued, under any rug available. No one wanted to accept the truth, no one knew the truth, it was soon forgotten.

Illinois Power did not want to accept that a space alien had caused the decimation to a substation, and refused to talk with the "crackpots" that arrived a week later. "No comment" was how the paper read. It was of course on page seven, section D of the local newspaper, seventy-three words. When the government arrived with the same questions, a different story was told.

"Mr. Watts." Shermer smiled.

"Do you find my name to be funny, or do you just want to admit that there's something to some of the allegations?" Mr. Watts had had his name used in many parts of the United States as funny. He had tired of the jokes some time back. It wasn't the way to start an investigation.

"I'm sure you can see the irony in this investigation, that's what I'm smiling about. I can assure you, that when the government is concerned, I want to cooperate fully! There is no reason the government should be investigating this accident!" Shermer had thought out most of his answers before Watts had arrived. But the Department of Natural Resources, and a name like Watts, he had to smile.

"I can assume that all pictures and samples from the site are still in our company's possession. I will need whatever clearances are required to further evaluate and perhaps to take with me for further analysis. I do not want you to think that this is a cheap shot at your company, but when you refused to see me, I had to pursue it a bit further." Mr. Watts sat calmly looking at his opened briefcase. He leaned forward as he took out an order from the FBI, to allow him access to any and all investigation findings. He handed the order to Shermer.

Shermer looked the document over carefully. "Mr. Watts, you must understand that when we were accosted by the idiots out front..." Shermer thumbed over his shoulder toward the window. "When they arrived and presented me with a request for access to my records, that they were looking for a landing site for men for Mars, or somewhere. There are some real cases out there, and I guess I had never thought of aliens. I run a power company, not a zoo! And I must admit, when they told me Mr. Watts from the government was requesting access, well I... You do understand, don't you?" Shermer was beginning to squirm.

"I try to understand each time my name is the brunt of yet another joke. Resources is my business, and yours as well. Cooperation on your part will be appreciated, and demanded. The government is interested in what might happen next if an accident of this magnitude is allowed to happen again, not in the middle of nowhere, but say Seattle, or St. Louis, or maybe New York. The population per square mile in such a location would be devastating. You must see that. If not, then perhaps you should go back to the beginning of electrical power and see the mistakes, the fatalities. Now we have electricity everywhere, and we can't have this sort of a mistake."

"I understand completely! I can also assure you that there has been no end to the efforts to find and prevent anything like this from ever happening again. Julia, could you take Mr. Watts to the investigating record department." Shermer had a bead of sweat on his forehead, just one. He could feel it, and he hoped that Watts didn't see it.

Watts closed his briefcase and stood. He still had his coat on. He felt like he was being "bum's rushed"; he would know in a few minutes. "Thank you, Mr. Shermer." Watts turned to see a very pretty brunette. *Probably don't even know how to operate the computer on her desk; she was here for other delights,* Watts thought as Julia gave Shermer a smile, one that did not appear all business. Watts was indignant to these people. His department had been called by the people out front, the ones with the signs that read "Alien landing covered up by power company." Watts smiled inside; nothing on the outside for Shermer, or Julia.

"Mr. Watts, here is our record department. We have a gentleman here to help you with your search. John, this is Mr. Watts." Julia turned and was gone in an instant. She did have a nice wiggle to her. Shermer was brighter than what he had first thought.

Mr. Watts told John that he had a simple job this morning, he wanted all samples and reports in front of the building ASAP. Not to leave out or lose a single document, he would know. And so went the day at Illinois Power.

Shermer was going crazy with all the publicity. No one ever saw all the late hours, or all the improvements, the charities they donated to. Just spacemen! John told Shermer that Mr. Watts had taken all the records. "Good!" was all Shermer had said.

It was November fifteenth when the local paper ran a back-page article about the possible alien landing that had caused three days of lost power in southern Illinois. Sam read the paper only by parts—the want ads, the funnies, the sports, and the etchings on the back of the newspaper. He never read the headlines; they were always about Iraq, and he didn't like the way that was headed. It was like revisiting Viet Nam. He smiled when he saw the pictures of the picketers outside Illinois Power. He thought he would read how the crazies had done with the power company. Sam had had some bad times trying to get power to a couple of his subdivisions, in years past. The hair started to stand up on Sam's neck as he read the account of the fire; he remembered the power outage, but had not given it a thought.

The fire had to have been so hot to melt the chain link fence, metal had been burnt, not melted, but burnt to only leave ashes. No witnesses had seen the fire due to the remote area. The "Interstellar Watchers" had immediately petitioned Illinois Power for the records to the investigation. No reply from Illinois Power at press time. A government agency, the Department of Natural Resources, could not be reached for comment, pertaining to an ongoing investigation about the site of the fire.

The article went on to interview the secretary of the Interstellar Watchers to say that a major coverup was in the process of pulling the wool over the American public's eyes. It had burnt the metal, not melted it. Mississippi, the fire had been so hot to melt all the metal in the house, the water heater, the electric box, even the sink had been burnt. Sam was shaking inside, and on the outside, he was unaware of it, his eyes went blank as his mind turned back thirty-seven years.

Evelyn was sitting at the other end of the kitchen table, looking at invitations. She had most of the details of their upcoming spring wedding planned. The little details were maddening, as far as Sam was concerned. "Sam, do you like this one?" Evelyn held up a sample of an invitation. When Sam did not respond she looked up to see the paper shaking. Evelyn dropped what she had in her hands, she bumped the table as she hurried to Sam. When she bumped the table Sam came back from Mississippi. "Sam! Are you alright?" Evelyn had pulled the paper from Sam's death grip and threw it aside.

"Oh! What? Yes, yes, I'm fine." Sam felt ill. He had a nasty smell of burning in his mind; it would never leave, it had been gone, but it was back.

"You're so pale. You were shaking." Evelyn was squatting in front of Sam. "I'm going to call Doc!"

"No, no, I'm alright." Sam still had a piece of the *Sentinel* in his hands. When Evelyn had pulled a piece had torn away.

"Bullshit! You are still pale, you look like you've seen a ghost! Doc Martin will have a fit if I don't call...if something would happen. I can't lose you! Sam?" Evelyn had tears in her eyes.

Sam bent over Evelyn and put his forearms on her shoulders. He felt weak. "I'm alright, Evie. I just read something that surprised me. Something from my past. Something from a long time past." Sam sat back in his chair. The story had drained him.

Sam had finished the paper. He had read all he wanted, but he tore the alien part away and folded it neatly and put it in his pocket. Evelyn watched and wondered. She was afraid to ask, for fear of causing a relapse. She would call Doc and ask if he thought it had been serious, and if Sam should see Doc. Evelyn knew there was going to be trouble over this; Sam was never sick.

Friend had been watching too, not Sam and Evelyn, as promised, but a power station. The last one had gone bad. "Sam" had gotten greedy. It felt good, and he had let it go bad, no one would ever know that he had caused it; he didn't care. But this power station was bigger, they made the electricity there. "Clinton" the sign said at the edge of town. This power was created from other power. "Sam" did not understand nuclear, the word had no meaning, but it looked strong! "Sam" would not cause the same problems this time; he knew how far he could go now! His Sam sense was going wild, the bother, but he had a use for Sam, Sam was still a big part of his plan. His move from Clinton to Sam but a flick, faster than sunlight, instant! Sam was in his eating room, Evelyn had dropped a paper, and was moving to Sam. Friend saw everything in a motion that his thought process could dissect. Sam was sitting, information in his hands, body functions correct. Not a lot of color, moving. conversing with Evelyn. He had better make an appearance, had to make sure they were healthy, for now.

"Sam! Sam, are you in distress?"

Evelyn shrieked. Sam had sat up and almost gone over backwards as Friend, "Sam," had suddenly appeared in the kitchen. Evelyn sat on the floor hard and her hands had gone to her face to cover them from whatever had suddenly come into her kitchen!

"Sam" was all Sam could muster. He was better, or at least getting better before "Sam" had popped in. Sam got control over his chair and bent to Evelyn. "This is how it happens. Are you alright?"

Evelyn got to her knees with some difficulty. Her eyes had never left "Sam." "I…I'm alright. I was checking on you. And now this!" Evelyn was trying to regain her feet; it wasn't going well. Sam picked her off the floor.

"Are you alright, Sam?" "Sam" asked again. "I felt you were in distress."

"Yeah, I'm fine." Sam thought of aliens. "I don't know what's going on here—you're here, and Evie's all in an uproar. I don't know what's going on myself!"

"If you could have seen what you looked like, just a second ago, and now 'Sam's' here too. I'm calling Doc Martin." Evelyn was looking for the cell phone on Sam's belt.

"It's not there, it's in the bedroom on the stand, and I am alright! We don't need to bother Doc."

"I think Evelyn is correct, Sam. I have come directly from powering to you. I do not cause my entity additional crossing over unless there is a reason."

"See! It's not just me!" Evelyn was ignoring the fact that with "Sam's" sudden appearance she had just lost ten years of her life in the scare. Now she had sided with "Sam."

Alien, the thought wouldn't go away. *I'm glad he can't tell what I'm thinking.* Sam's mind was a whirl with "what if's."

"Sam" had his thinking processes in full operating control. I wish I could tell what Sam is thinking. "Yes, you must visit the medical professional! I would not be here if I had not thought so. I cannot save your life, I can only assist. I need you to visit your Doctor…Martan…no…Martin, yes Martin."

"Now this is all I need, a fairy god entity! I'll call." Sam's mind was speeding, it was canceling thoughts that Sam had never, believed, ghosts, aliens, fire. What had caused the fire, what was "Sam," Friend had been his own, now what was going on.

"Are you alright, Sam? You still don't look good." Evelyn had only been aware and now "Sam" so fast. "I think 'Sam' has your health in mind. He was here in a blink of an eye."

Sam was looking at "Sam." He had never shown himself to anyone, ever; now Evelyn was in his care too. What was he? Was he an alien? Did the fires happen the same way? So many thoughts were invading his mind, too much, too many! "I'll go!" Sam snapped. His response even caused "Sam" to jerk to the sound of his voice.

"Sam! We only want you to be alright!" Evelyn was more worried at his tone than anything. She was glad "Sam" was there to back her up. Sam knew what had happened to him and was unwilling to share with her and "Sam."

Evelyn got Sam a glass of water. "Drink this. You're all hot to touch." Evelyn went to the bathroom for a cloth.

"Evelyn is right, I cannot predict any long-time repairs. I know how your body works, but cannot understand all that it does. A medical professional of your human kind must be consulted."

"Sam" was not moving his lips anymore; words still came into Sam's head, but not from sound. The "alien" thoughts would not go away. The fire would not go away. "'Sam,' do you follow any of the news when you are here? TV or newspapers?" Evelyn was back with a cool washcloth. Sam took it and wiped his neck; it felt good. Evelyn squatted beside Sam.

"Sam" stood. He turned toward Sam and Evelyn. "I have watched for you and your dealings in the past. I have on occasion had time to read some of the paper. I have a lot of problems with words, you are aware of that. But not much in what you call news. I find most of it as of no value."

"I had just wondered; your speech has improved so much as to what it had been." Sam did not like the answer much.

"I have tried to improve my speech in time. I do try and be as normal as I can be when assisting you. I appreciate that you have noticed my speech."

"Sam's" lips were moving almost with his words now. Evelyn was back in the room too. Questions were never made over something as simple as lips moving, but now Sam was suspect of everything.

"Sam" left as quickly as he had arrived. Dr. Martin was called and an appointment made as had been agreed with; everyone was happy. Sam's mind had become full of thoughts and ideas. He had to decide how to find out information about the fire now. Both fires perhaps. Evelyn had accepted "Sam" as a member of Sam's extended family; she had to listen to reason. Thoughts also crossed Sam's mind that perhaps it was all just a coincidence; fires happen, sometimes no one ever knows why, and of course everyone has a fairy god entity! One that just pops in and out like the crew of the *Enterprise* on *Star Trek*; they at least formed in front of your eyes. "Sam's" sudden appearance in front of Evelyn had made Sam know that he wasn't nuts; that thought had weighed heavily on his mind. But now he knew he was sane, he was going to marry the girl of his dreams, well, he wasn't sure dreams, but she had been there when Sam had needed her. He had stalked her till he had maneuvered her into his life, but that had been as a secretary. Sam's grandpa had told him, "If you think about something too much, it'll drive you crazy!" So was he back to being crazy?

It was cool outside. Evelyn was wearing a light jacket and was pulling the dead flowers off of the mums. Sam approached her on the deck. She stood and smiled. "Feeling better now? I came out here to give you some room and let you relax. I didn't mean to make you angry, I'm just concerned." Evelyn kissed Sam on the cheek.

"I didn't mean to sound mad. I have just had a lot on my mind today." Sam took out the newspaper clipping he had torn from the morning paper. "Read this, Evie." Sam held it out to her.

Evelyn put her flower clipping in the bag she had been using, wiped her hands on her hips and took the paper. She read it slowly. She had sat at the table and lit a cigarette. "I remember this, just before your birthday, right after that wonderful night at Denny's. You remember the power outage. Nothing worked, no power for two, or three days."

"Well, I don't know, something set me off this morning. I'm not sick." Sam took the paper back from Evelyn. He ran his finger down the article till he found the sentence. "Listen to this part, 'the metal had been burnt, not melted.' That's what set me off. That might sound crazy, and I'm beginning to think that more, every day I live, but Sara's house, when it burned down, nothing was left. The water heater, the doorknobs, the washing machine, it all burned. Nothing left, it was all gone." Sam held the paper out in front of him, as a lawyer would with evidence.

"Sam, that was a very tragic, heart-wrenching time of your life. It was a long time ago. It is only coincidence, unless you are starting to believe in spacemen." As Evelyn let the words fly from her mouth, she thought of "Sam." Some of the color that Mother Nature had caused on the blustery day, paled. "You don't think 'Sam's' a spaceman?"

"I have never questioned 'Sam' till today. It was a simple question, he answered it, but did he really answer it, or take it for granted that I would believe him. You have heard him say that he's always been there. I spoke to him at Fort Hood, and didn't for a long time afterward. If he's always around, why didn't he show when I needed him in Mississippi? I needed someone then, desperately! Where was he then?"

"Sam, I'm sure I don't know. You will have to ask him, I'm sure he'll tell you." Evelyn had leaned forward and was almost inspecting Sam for any of the morning's signs of whatever it had been.

"You have just accepted that I, we, have a fairy god entity! Didn't you think it a bit odd when he showed up! He had not shown himself, and I have asked him to, in forever, since I was a kid! Isn't that a little hard to swallow?"

"Calm down now, Sam. I accepted him because he was there. For the first few minutes I had wondered if you had a magic act that you had never told me about. He popped in today and liked to scared the bejesus out of me. I don't think I will ever be comfortable with 'Sam' popping in and out. But if he is part of you, and going to be part of us, I would accept it, that you were a vampire! I love you! I don't care what you have hidden under the bed, if it is part of you, then so be it! He says he only comes when he's needed. I wonder if he hides behind the closet door. I don't like it one bit, but if he comes with you, I will get used to him. I think that the fire here and the one in Mississippi are only a coincidence. Get on the computer and check strange fires. It has everything else on it."

Sam rubbed his jaw and looked at Evelyn. She made sense. "Okay, you're probably right. Do I still have to go see Doc?" Sam had his pleading face on now.

"Yes, you're fifty-five now. It's been forever since you've been to a doctor, you need a checkup. You have a honeymoon to go to in a few months, and I want you healthy! Now what do you want for supper?" Evelyn was up and rolling her sack down so nothing would escape.

Dinner at Denny's, not much else around, so it was off to the shower and get ready to go out. But, Sam had mentally admitted that Evelyn had made sense, but it still stuck in his mind; "the metal had burned, not melted." What planet would "Sam" be from? The crazy thoughts were coming back. Sam scrubbed his back and hoped Evelyn would join him, but he knew better. She was the girl of his dreams, it had only taken a few years for her to become a reality. Sara had been just a stepping stone on life's highway, a spot that had become a memory. Sam smiled as he dried himself after his shower. His life had changed in Mississippi, and it had changed in Illinois. Why did it take so damned long?

Sam was still smiling when he walked into the bed room. Evelyn had just closed the closet.

"You look better now!" Evelyn said as she looked at her hair in the mirror one last time.

"I feel better, just needed a shower. Presto change-o, all better. Was 'Sam; behind the closet door?" Sam laughed. But it didn't feel like a laugh. He kept his smile up.

Evelyn had tried her best to be a supporter of "Sam," since he had evidently always been with Sam. But deep down she had some doubts of her own. These doubts were overshadowed, by maybe Sam has a medical problem. That was incentive enough to make her befriend "Sam," at least till Sam had a good checkup, and Doc Martin said so. Evelyn had just planned to be an old maid and had never planned to be married; the thought had just never been on her list of things that had to be done. But that had all changed in the last six months. Right now he was the most important item on her list. He was the only item! A lot of things had happened in the last six months, and to an outsider, "Sam" might loom as a real show stopper, but no matter; Sam was her most important item, and she would do anything to protect Sam from all comers. "Sam" was a bit odd, and he really scared Evelyn, but he too, had been a protector of Sam, so he had become an ally, and no matter how it seemed, no one could shoo him off. Might as well be a friend to him; as an enemy he could not be defeated. He would make a good ally; he would make a much worse enemy than Evelyn could imagine, power that could not be discounted. They were driving her car, and her aimless mental wanderings had been somewhere else, then she heard the rock and roll, it was loud!

"I hear it, Sam! You don't have to play it for everyone else too. I'm going to have Doc check your hearing too! Any man your age shouldn't play music that loud!" Evelyn turned the radio down.

"It's 'Thunderstruck'! It's got to be played loud. And I thought it might bring you around. We're almost there, and you've been somewhere else. I'm beginning to think that it's you that needs to see Doc, your hearing must be bad too!" Sam laughed and rolled his window up.

"I'll be deaf if you play that stuff any louder!" Evelyn had some fine elevator music playing softly now.

"Sam" listened to the music as the car drove along Route 50. He had to agree with Evelyn about going deaf! He didn't have the same ear canals, and the complicated human systems. "Sam" would smile if they could see him, but it took energy to make the artificial countenance make facial expressions.

Unacceptable, that is what Spirit would sign. This trip was of no value to "Sam"; he would blink out and be back at shelter. It no longer took power away; that too had been mastered. His mastery of many parts of the human world were toys, to be used when he wanted, but physical touch still had to be through a human. Energy was a natural movement, moving himself, and with a little effort the movement of things was easier now, but physical touch evaded him. When he had kissed Evelyn's hand it had been a complicated mental maneuver. He still could not feel anything except energy, and of course fire, he liked that sensation. He was always out of control with fire, that too felt good! Hot, tingling, good feeling, he almost liked the feeling; it made all his energy seem secondary!

As soon as "Sam" had crossed over, Spirit was signing.

"Entity, you have been at human assistance for time. I will allow you time to power, but I have a sign. If you have energy to sign."

"Sam" kept his energy in check. "Spirit, I await sign."

"Entities have signed Spirit that power is not being recalled to your entity. I have signs that might fear for your energy."

"Fear not, Spirit. I have to energy soon, I am at a low energy level now but I have needed to assist my human much. I fear his energy is not being used efficiently; he may have recall in time soon. I too will recall at time too. I have been assisting in direction of my human; his time is not right. I sign you if you will allow."

"No, entity. I will leave you to power. I am only in hopes that your human will manage his energy to his own assistance. We as entities are limited by the human's own weakness to ignore his needs. I will receive sign in time if your human progresses." Spirit was gone as suddenly as he had became.

Time is soon, Spirit, "Sam" thought. *Time is past when I, and other entities would grovel in Spirit's presence.* Time is soon when Spirit will sign "Sam" for guidance in matters of need, assistance, will be only a game played with humans. Humans will be in debt for the power that will preserve them, as long as "Sam" felt it necessary. His thought process smiled. "Sam" would teach his entity to smile always; in human form he would be trusted, worshipped! Their prayers would be to his entity, his only, no longer those that had been written of in their Bible! "Sam" would power to prevent his thought process from being detected by Spirit. His thought processes now signed without his telling them to do so. His thought process had to be held in check. Times had been when he had to use energy to send mental signs to Sam; now it was instant. His form had to become more presentable to humans. He was aware of his inability to cause facial movements in sequence with his mental signs. It had improved in short time, it was done for Evelyn to impress the human, it had worked well. Human minds were weak and could not sign in return without the use of air in their complex systems; air escaped from the mouth as they spoke. "Sam" could speak forever with only minute use of energy; the trick was moving his facial appointments, his lips. But the power was not strong; it was of no value to "Sam." He slipped away, to his latest point of interest, Clinton. The place interested "Sam." Just a sample would do no harm. There were enormous substations. He would only sample the power. No color, no form, just energy, his form enclosed a transformer. The power was good here, more than before, he could feel the heat. Energy would have no heat, till the source was interrupted and it started to short.

"Sam" enveloped another transformer, and another, and unconsciously another and another. "Sam's" ability to control his mind was forgotten; no Spirit here. The tingling was good. He had become the recipient of all the power the station could put out. Alarms could be heard, systems would fail, the automatic shutdown of the power was too far away to be controlled by "Sam." He didn't have any worry, he was happy, as happy as an entity had been, ever!

A blue arc of electricity could be seen a hundred miles away. Workers shut down all power, all turbines. They would not respond; all turbines continued to operate as though they had another source of command. The blue arc grew in size, to cover the sky. Witnesses would say it lasted for hours. It only lasted for two minutes, the workers at the Clinton reactor said. It looked like a movie. The sky was lit by blue lightning, and the odd part was that the lightning was all straight, not the usual lightning, irregular bolts, but all had straight lines and ninety-degree bends. The nuclear plant closed for two weeks to check all the reactors. Conventional power was switched in place of the reactor produced electricity.

The local population was up in arms about the nighttime light display. The power plant had been fought from the beginning, and this was just one more strike against it. The government played it down. The power company played it down as only a safety glitch that had already been taken care of; it was safe power and the automatic shutdown proved it. It hit the local papers but not much more, some shots of the crowd and the protesters; most was cut from the national news, for more from Iraq. The situation had stabilized but it was still a hot market, a power outage wasn't.

V

Sam wasn't too good with the computer yet, but he managed to find the outage, no fire, no one hurt. He clicked off, and continued on. Nowhere in the world had any fire of the sort happened. Lots of fires, and death. Some of the pictures were awesome, some were gross. Images that haunted Sam. Then he thought of the Interstellar Watchers. They had a large web site and had all kinds of spacecraft sightings, and people who had been abducted, and a mention to the fire in southern Illinois. The terminology was beyond his understanding, but the burned metal and the intense heat had caught his eye, just like in Mississippi. No mention of Mississippi anywhere in the web site. Sam typed in a question about fires, burned metals and Mississippi; he submitted his questions. Interstellar Watchers was in Arizona. Sam had it planned to not receive any info from them.

Wes had constructed a chair. He didn't know why, but he had. It had electrical capabilities, not like an execution chair, it had only one circuit the entire chair. Metal lining to all parts, the metal was supported from the wooden chair by glass insulators to keep the electricity from contacting the wood. He wasn't quite sure what it would do, but it was a fine chair. Wes moved it to the back room. Sam never came here anymore, it would be fine there, closer to the electricity, he thought. Wes would never see it used.

Wes had had a rough two weeks. The mornings had been a real bear, his drinking had been under control, but only glass control was being used lately. He had taken off work lately without anyone knowing, then he would always wake up hung over. He had even begun to worry.

"One more and I'm callin' it quits." Shelly came to the end of the bar. She took Wes's glass and walked to the little sink behind the bar.

"Go home, Wes. You've had enough for tonight." Shelly had began to wonder what had happened to Wes, lately. He had never been on the wagon but he had been able to hold his liquor, but not lately. "Wes, go home, sleep it off, you've been hittin' it pretty hard lately. Everything alright?"

"Yes, it's all fine, just one more an' I'll be outta here!" Wes was swaying on his bar stool.

"Will ya go home then?" Shelly rinsed the glass she had just washed.

"Yep! One for the road." He smiled and tried to focus on Shelly.

Shelly knew that Wes just lived around the block and he generally walked in, so she didn't think it would hurt. He might fall down, but maybe that would sober him up. "One more Walker's and seltzer, this is the last one!" Shelly got a fresh glass and mixed Wes's drink.

Wes played with the glass, turning it on the bar, finally he tipped it up and downed it. "Whata I owe ya, Shelly? I'm goin' home now." Wes was digging for his wallet.

"Tomorrow, Wes. Tomorrow when you're sober and know how much you spent tonight on liquor. Now get outta here!" Shelly ran a bar, but hated to see people abuse it to this point. She should have run him off hours ago. But her business sense told her that two dollars a glass helped to pay the bills. She watched Wes stagger out the door and disappear when he turned right. She picked his glass up and back to the sink. She thought that her conscience was getting in the way of her business; she was going to have to quit that.

Wes had had DT's many years ago, but that had been before the "treatment." He thought that his new friend was a little better than bugs. The bugs had been awful. That's why he kept his house a neat as a pin. No bugs here! Wes had some difficulty with the front door lock, till he remembered that he hadn't locked it. He smiled to himself and pushed the door open. "Frien'! How ya doin', bud! I wish you would go ta Shelly's with me. You need ta get out and see people." Wes sat down hard on the rocker. It groaned as his weight fell onto the old chair.

Friend sat on the couch. He smiled. The glow slipped out a bit as he tried to hold himself in check. "I saw the chair. It is just what I wanted. It will do nicely. Time is coming when I will need use of it." Friend smiled. "Let's go to Shelly's and have a liquid refreshment."

"Nah, Shelly told me I had ta leave, she thinks I've had too much. I might have had a little too much tonight, she might be right." Wes was swaying in his rocker and smiling. A smile of way too much liquor.

"Well, let's go somewhere else then. There's that place in Mt. Vernon, the one by the large road. You will have to drive, I'm afraid I have become dependent on you for very much."

Wes swayed back and forth a bit. He held on to the rocker for balance. "Tonight? It's kinda late ain't it?"

"If you don't want to go I will understand. I haven't consumed much liquid today, but thought it might be a way to celebrate the finish of my chair."

"If you put it that way, let's go,.Shelly don't know how much I've had! Ya know years ago I usta drink more'n this. and would go to work, and never have any problems. Gotta fine my keys." Wes stood and took a second to get his bearing.

"I believe your keys are there by your chair." Friend pointed to the end table by Wes's rocker. He smiled, he glowed a bit. He was anticipating the plan. He had to be careful, he didn't want to ruin it now, he was so close.

"Okey we're ready ta go now!" Friend was out the door as Wes held it and bowed. "After you, Friend!" Wes followed to the car. "You sure ya wanna go?"

"I'm quite sure."

Wes got in and looked to the passenger seat. Friend was already there. He hadn't heard the door. No matter. Wes started the gold Lincoln up; it purred. "This thing'll run, don't dare do it in town, the cops here are real bad about drinkin' and drivin'. I normally walk ta Shelly's. The tickets have gotten expensive. The mayor hasta have his cut ya know. I'll take ya for a ride one-a these days." Wes patted the dash and smiled.

The drive out of town was a little slow. Wes smiled a lot and drove with absolute attention to the controls; his Lincoln was under control. They went south to Walnut Hill Road, turned left and started the drive to Mt. Vernon. Wes was driving sensibly enough, a few jerks, got a possum and finished him as he stared into the headlights. Wes laughed.

"How fast will this car run?" Friend ask nonchalantly.

"It's been bored and got a hot cam, the carburetor is gonna be changed next. I'm gonna put fuel injection on it when I get the money. But it'll still run!" Wes was speeding up as he talked about how fast his car would run. The tires screeched as they maneuvered around a curve. He eased it back to the right side as the curve ended.

"There is a railroad tracks up ahead. How fast can you maneuver over them?" Friend smiled, and the glow was around his lips.

"Years ago I took them at about seventy. I kept it on the road, but that was in an old junker. I could probably take them faster in this, better suspension." Wes pushed down on the accelerator, and the car lunged ahead. The last curve was straightened out by the Lincoln as it headed into Walnut Hill. Wes began to laugh. "Hey, it won't slow down!" Wes laughed.

Friend laughed. "You can make it go faster, right, Wes!" Friend laughed again. Friend's laughter scared Wes.

Under the hood the accelerator spring lay on the intake manifold. The engine revolutions increased, the car sped up, it passed eighty miles per hour. Friend laughed. Wes pushed his foot up and down on the pedal; it lay against the floor. Wes reached for the keys.

"Do not turn the key, Wes. Just drive the car and take us to the bar."

"Okay." Wes concentrated on the road. They were to the tracks. The car became airborne, it hit hard, and Wes fought the wheel to keep the car running straight. It was under control.

The car rocketed ahead, the headlights shone on the two black arrows on a yellow rectangular sign. Wes pushed on the brake, and the pin holding the pedal in place fell to the floor. Wes may have seen it, maybe not. The car crashed through the sign, the poles holding the sign broke away, and the sign banged against the roof. At the same time the sign broke away from the bolts holding it to the poles, the front of the car came in contact with the large oak tree, three feet behind the sign. The front of the car came into contact with the same tree that had been struck many times. It caused the collapse of the front of the car. The engine was next to contact the tree. The fan stopped, the engine buckled, the transmission casing broke into many pieces, as the tree made it bend into a shape the metal would not allow. The hood folded and bent, the car's forward progress had stopped. The bent metal and broken glass had not all stopped when Wes looked at Friend. Wes had been impaled by broken pieces of the steering wheel. Wes still gripped the wheel with his broken and deformed hands and arms. A piece of the pole that had been holding the sign was sticking out of the right side of Wes's face. His legs were pinned beneath the dashboard, his smile still in place. Wes looked at Friend, who was also bent and twisted. But still smiling. Metal was settling into new formed shapes. Sounds of water, and oil, and pieces falling inside and outside the car continued.

"What's happened?" Wes looked at Friend.

Friend melted from the car and became whole on the passenger side of the smoking wreck. "Thanks, Wes." Friend became a glow and shrank to a pinpoint. There was an audible pop. Even Friend knew that Wes had heard the pop. He had made the sound just for Wes.

Wes never saw anything else; he was still smiling.

Lights came on in all the houses surrounding the accident scene. People came out in night clothes, some ran, others walked slowly. They had seen the same accident many times before; the tree had absorbed many accidents.

Wes's heart pumped furiously, it pumped blood into vessels, and toward their assigned body parts, most were not intact any longer, but his heart still pumped till there was no blood to pump; it was pushed to the left side, it fibrillated for a few seconds, the pump was intact, but that was all. Wes was killed on impact, the coroner would say in his report. But the coroner mentioned to several following the inquest, that he had never seen a man with a smile like that before.

Friend never bothered to put the spring or the brake lever pin back in place; he had never been a mechanical entity. Inside his orb of energy Friend smiled. If he had still retained human form, he would be smiling; he had gotten better at smiling. He had done it for those special occasions, like now, and for Evelyn. Emotional states would exist for humans now. Friend still did not understand emotions, but he was beginning to!

Lights and sirens could be heard as police and ambulances rushed to try and salvage the remains of a hapless driver. The local fire department only two blocks away brought out a fire truck to wash the antifreeze, oil, and blood away. No fire, nothing left to save, they radioed the police and ambulance, "Back off, this one's done." The sirens quieted, the light bars still flashed as they came into the little town, people moved aside to allow them access. It was going to take a while to get him out. The fire department made and delivered coffee to all the EMS personnel. Quiet laughter could be hear after a while, as all the onlookers became glazed to the gruesome sight and took time to talk to all their friends and the EMS people, as Wes was slowly cut from the car, his eyes still open, he had a surprised look on his face, a smile some said. Everyone thought it was the accident. Friend knew better.

Sam called Jimmy and told him, he was sad, but wouldn't go to the funeral. He would have to go to the garage and see what was there. He might be better than he had been, but not that good just yet. He planned the next funeral he went to, was to be his.

Evelyn knew Wes, but not well. When she asked about arrangements, Sam did not know, and didn't sound as though he cared. Sam was at the desk and had accessed his computer. Sam had a return from the Interstellar Watchers. It was a newsletter, it rambled about the many sightings that were never reported, and the government coverup. Sam scrolled down to the end. There was his answer, there had been three sites where the metal had burned. Sam typed in the next question, April 8, 1969, had there ever been a fire that was unexplained, and were there records, he pushed Send.

Chapter 10
Trusting Who?

I

Evelyn was in the kitchen finishing cleaning the mess from lunch on a cool but sunny November afternoon. She had just finished putting away the dishes and was about to tackle the pots and pans. And who should show up, but "Sam"! Evelyn's hands went to her face, she eked out a squeal, and backed up till the counter stopped her retreat.

"Did I frighten you? I am sorry, Evelyn. But I do not have another way to be here. I can't open doors, so I just become. I will try and be a little better about my appearances. Sam has gotten used to my coming and going. I am a little hard to get used to." "Sam" smiled inside his mental process.

"No, I'm alright! It will take a while to get used to your appearances!" Evelyn's breath was returning to normal now. "Sam's not here; he has gone to the garage. Wes was in an accident a few days ago, and Sam has not been to the garage in a long time. He refused to go to the funeral." Evelyn was a little uncomfortable with "Sam" suddenly showing up, and her Sam not here to greet him. "Can I get you anything?"

"No, I do not require any kind of refreshment. I consume energy only. I power on regular times; it is a necessity that I must endure. Humans can go for long periods of time and not require power. I would like in time to have a source of power in your human world. But that is not in my time to consider. That would be for Spirit to devise, and I will have been recycled for many time by then."

"I have heard you mention Spirit in our conversations before. Who or what is Spirit?" Evelyn wanted more information, and what better a time than now.

"Spirit is a complex entity. His time is to sign to questions in regard to entity's assistance to each human. Spirit makes sign for all to proceed in assistance. My entity has had to sign Spirit many time; Sam has been a special human. My special human." "Sam" was winning her over. She was concerned; he could hear it in her voice tones.

"Do you have to report to Spirit? And does he get angry?" Evelyn was trying to make "Sam" feel comfortable with her. If she was going to have to deal with a pop-in, she might as well know more about him. Trust was not something she thought she could give just yet, but he must never know that.

"No. Entities do not report, entities have been programmed to assist, when created. Spirit does not get angry, entities do not get angry. Anger is a human trait that has been part of humankind. Spirit only signs assistance to help entity to assist. Some special problems do arise and require Spirits sign."

"Where do you, live—I mean, where, do you go to when you leave here?" This one she really wanted to hear.

"I do not know how to tell you this, I do not know where I go to. I just do, when I am not here, or how I get there. It is not like going to Mt. Vernon. I could not find that populated area either. I only go where Sam is located."

"But Sam's not here today, he's miles away, looking at his toys!" Evelyn had him backpedaling now. And she thought this was going to be difficult.

"Sam still has toys? I was unaware of this. My entity has never seen Sam with a toy since he was a small human." "Sam" had changed his facial makeup now; his look was of disbelief.

"Sam's toys are his cars. Haven't you ever been with Sam at his garage? I've never been there, but he keeps his red Chevelle, and a bunch of others he says are classics, there! That's why I was surprised you came here, without Sam being present."

"No, no, I have never been to the garage. My entity has heard Sam speak of his cars. My entity has been in his red car, and likes the color. Is not your car red as well? And I came here, because my entity is for your assistance as well. Sam and you are my entity's human project now and forever. I just thought that we could get to know one another better."

"So, Sam has been told of our wedding coming up soon? As soon as I set a date, that is. Will you have to be programmed for my... ah...assistance too?" Evelyn was rolling and proud of herself. She smiled sheepishly.

"My entity has informed Spirit of my decision to take on an additional assistance. Spirit has not been happy with my decision. My assistance will be to you and Sam, equals in assistance and dedication. My entity is a good entity, and has helped Sam many times. He is not aware of the assistance my entity has provided in time past, nor will he ever become aware of these assistances. That is not my entity's purpose; my entity only assists when needed."

"You can keep him from falling, or cutting himself, or just what can you do?" Evelyn projected a look of concern. She was afraid to make "Sam" angry, or not able to help with whatever it was he did.

"My entity will not tell of time past, and my entity cannot prevent those things you speak of from happening, only advise Sam to prevent them himself. My entity intervenes before something happens. It is my design to make Sam aware of a mistake or accident that will happen, in time soon, and allow him time to react, before time is late."

"Are you going to visit my life before I met Sam? I mean there has to be a limit in what you need to know about me, isn't there?" Evelyn was on the defensive now.

"No. My entity only has decided to assist you and Sam together, in recent time. My entity needs not to know your past time. My entity is now and forever, in yours and Sam's assistance. Should my entity visit your time past? Is there a time that will affect your now? Tell entity, and visit your time past, my entity will." "Sam's" thought process was attempting to play a human game, chess, or a game like it, Sam had never liked the game so "Sam" had not either, but this encounter was being played in the same design. "Sam" needed to know this human's thoughts, and that he could not, this caused "Sam" distress. But Evelyn could not know that.

"No! My past, is just that, my past. It is private! Don't go there, please. I don't want anything to screw up Sam's and my life. I have waited a long time for this, and I didn't think it would ever happen to me, and I don't want you going in my past and messing it up!" Evelyn didn't like the direction of the conversation, it had been fun, but fun time was over.

"My entity will not." It was time for "Sam" to attack now; Evelyn had given him a direction. "Evelyn, may my entity ask you a question, or possibly, three?"

"Do I have to answer?" Evelyn was fearful now.

"No, you do not. May my entity ask them and you may decide then?"

"If I don't have to answer till I hear the question, go ahead." Worry was on Evelyn's mind now!

"Why do you and Sam have your hands and arms around each other, many time? Sam had never asked, there was no need before. "Sam" had helped Sam obtain Evelyn, and had been regretful many time since.

"You mean a hug! You don't know what a hug is? Let me show you! Evelyn started to move toward "Sam"

"NO! You cannot touch the entity!" "Sam" glowed, and moved backward; he glided, he did not step. Just slid backwards.

"I'm sorry! I didn't mean to scare you, I was just going to give you a hug. You've never had a hug? That place where you go must be very cold." Evelyn wasn't sure how to take this, this move that "Sam" had made, physically, and mentally.

"My entity, only ask why, not to demonstrate a human trait!"

"Well, it is a human trait. When two people love each other, they like to touch, they like to be hugged by the person that loves them. Sometimes we will hold each other and dance, for the intimacy of the mood. It makes us feel like we are one. We hold hands, we kiss. I'm sorry that you have never had another entity to hug you; that's a shame." Evelyn was on the top again. She liked the conversation, but knew she had better get out of this soon.

"Sam" had hugged an entity, and the entity had no longer existed; he had consumed him completely, energy, and identity! "My entity also would like to know what the kiss is for? You and Sam do a lot of kisses. Is there a reason for all of the kisses?"

"You kissed my hand the other night, did you not know what it was for?" Evelyn was a little confused about the line of questions now.

"My entity had watched Sam do the same to others, in time past, and thought it would be appropriate for our first encounter. My entity wanted you to feel comfortable with my presence."

"You can touch me, but I cannot touch you? What kind of gibberish is that?" Evelyn wanted this answer.

"My entity is made of pure energy. My entity can control energy, in my touch, but not for you to touch my entity."

"Okay. I can believe that." She couldn't, but she had reacted naturally earlier, and had not taken that into consideration, she would be more careful in the future. "And you said you had three questions."

"The answers received from the first two have answered the third. It will not be necessary."

"Well I would like to know the question." Evelyn was on the attack again.

"Entities do not waste energy for any reason. That is why humans have to be reclaimed in time so soon."

"Reclaimed! What is reclaimed?" Evelyn had alarms going off now.

"Humans are returned to energy, they will be energy again. All power is energy. Humans are energy, and will be reclaimed for energy, in time yet to happen, future energy. Energy is all there is, in my entity's time and in yours and Sam's time."

"Like reincarnation?" Evelyn was getting somewhere, where she had no idea.

"My entity does not understand reincarnation. Please explain."

"Live again, come back as another human in years to come." Crude explanation, but all she could think of to answer.

"Yes."

"So after we go to heaven, or wherever, we come back?" Evelyn was not terribly religious, but if "Sam" had all he answers, why not learn them too!

"There is no heaven, nor is there a hell, only energy. My entity is energy, you are energy, we are in different forms, but we are still energy, all life forms, are energy."

"So you are alive too?"

"My entity is an energy that has been designed to assist humans. My entity requires recharging with power, entities function as energy forms for assistance."

"Spirit is energy too, or what?" Evelyn was gaining ground!

Sam honked the horn on the Chevelle as he pulled into the driveway. Conversation ended. "Sam" was happy with the arrival of his human, the other human had become a bore, and was asking questions that an entity was not programmed to tell, or even discuss, but "Sam" knew he was to make the rules soon! His entity would not be asked such questions again.. She had answered many questions, and would answer more in time future soon.

Sam came into the kitchen. He saw the pots and pans stacked on counter, and he saw "Sam." "What are you doing here?" He looked at "Sam." "How long has he been here?" Sam crossed to Evelyn, and kissed her on the cheek, and slipped his arm around Evelyn's waist. Sam smiled for "Sam," but it wasn't a real smile, just a necessity.

"We've had quite a talk. Want something to drink?" Evelyn had turned to see Sam's face, and watch his reaction to "Sam." "'Sam' has come to see you about Wes' passing, just to check and see how you were doing. I told him you wouldn't go to the funeral."

"Didn't you know where I was at, 'Sam'? I thought you always knew where I was." Sam had a bit of jealousy noted in his voice.

"My entity knew you were doing well with your friend's ending time. Evelyn is now with you and has made your life richer, and my entity was sure that having Evelyn present helped you in your sad time. My entity has used the time to acquaint with Evelyn. Now my entity has taken the additional assistance of Evelyn, as well, my thought processes, believed my entity should do so. I had many times with you."

"Your entity has never found it necessary to acquaint itself with me, and God only knows how many times I have tried to get you to talk to me. I can expect you to be alone with my fiancée more? Or is this a one time only?" Sam had become defensive in the few short minutes that he had been home.

"Sam, my entity has angered you. For that my entity will apologize to you. My entity thought you would like for it to be done so. This will not be so in time yet to come, except at a time of assistance. For that my entity will be needed, and only then. My entity apologizes again, time is not now for my entity, power is needed." "Sam" was gone in the blink of an eye.

Sam and Evelyn looked at one another as the room glowed and was gone as quick as a light, from a switch.

"What the Hell was that all about?" Sam stepped away from Evelyn and had his hands on his hips.

"You're jealous of 'Sam.' I've heard it all now! No one comes around this house, except your favorite spook, and you're jealous!" Evelyn had both hands to her face with the dishtowel, she laughed. She bent at the waist and kept laughing.

"It's not funny!" Sam still stood there.

"Yes it is! He's an entity, whatever the Hell that is! I asked him a bunch of questions, some of those he could not answer. He says he's pure energy, he cannot be touched, but he can touch. I'm not sure what all that means."

"Like what?" Sam had dropped his hands to his sides.

"Well he doesn't know where he comes from, or where he goes, he has no idea what physical contact has to do with love. And I don't think he has any idea what love is either. He is sad, he thinks everything is power, or energy, or both. I was going to give him a hug, and he about went off the deep end!" Evelyn wiped her eyes, as the laughter subsided.

"You were going to hug him? What is the meaning of that?" Sam's hands were back on his hips.

"I thought that I should become friends with him, if he's always going to be here, and he slithered away like I had the plague! He says he can touch me, but I can't touch him. And his boss, Spirit, I don't believe he knows anything about me. I believe 'Sam' has taken that step by himself. I thought you would want me to become friends with 'Sam.' After all he's got a cute name." Evelyn poked at Sam's belly.

"What do you mean slithered away?" Sam opened the cabinet looking for a glass. "I guess I have to fend for myself now; you're too busy making fun of me." Sam smiled and set the glass down.

"I think he has to make up the image that we see. I don't know what form he normally takes, but it's not what we see. And something else, he seems so very familiar, do you know why?" Evelyn took out the iced tea pitcher and filed Sam's glass.

"No. I don't. Tell me, Miss Sherlock, why does he look familiar?" Sam tilted his glass and took a long drink.

"He is you! Twenty years ago, that was you. He sort of changes at times while you watch, his features are all smooth, but he is you. You've got some old pictures here somewhere, let's look at them and you will see too!" Evelyn had her hands on her hips now. "He's secret about a lot of stuff he doesn't want us to know. Maybe he's from Mars. I just don't know. I'm not sure I really trust him." Evelyn got a can of Coke and a glass and started toward the table. "We need to talk."

Sam began by telling Evelyn that he had not seen "Sam" since he was a kid, eight or nine; that was when the doctors had all begun. He had tried to get "Sam" to show himself lately, and he wouldn't. He had only shown himself after Evelyn had been a house partner.

Evelyn told Sam of the apparent nervousness, and the hesitation to tell all that she had asked. She retold about the attempted hug and how "Sam" had become almost enraged, and how too he had told that entities never got angry. "He almost went against the story he had just told me about. He had three questions, he asked about hugs, and about kisses. He didn't ask his third question. Sam, I think he watches us in bed! He's some kind of a spook voyeur!"

Sam listened carefully; he did not interrupt. Then he told about the internet and the fires. "I just don't know. He has always been there, well it seems that

I have been pretty lucky in a couple of adventures; he never tells me anything that he has done for me. Except in Nam, you know about the bullet, he was there! I have never heard about anything like 'Sam.' You see it in the magazines at the grocery store. But I have never heard of anything like him. I think he could be a force to be reckoned with if he wanted to be." Sam drank the last of his iced tea. He didn't want another, and motioned for Evelyn to sit still. "The outer space part is maybe a little far-fetched, but I have a lot of questions now too. This group that picketed Illinois Power are a little bit off the deep end, but some of the questions I have had are questions they have always had! I'll show you what they have sent so far. I've saved their web site and all our correspondence."

Evelyn had a serious look on her face as the questions and answers had all came to the forefront. "I don't know what to do. I don't think he's going to go away. He is kind of handsome. I wonder if he could rake the back yard, 'cause I'm sure not getting it done today." *Now he's looking into outer space visitors—what next!* Evelyn thought.

"I'll tackle the backyard. I don't think you need to be started at that, you've still got dishes to do! I'll print out all I've got form the Interstellar Watchers so you won't have to sit in that terrible chair; I've got to get another chair for the computer desk." Sam was out the door and ready to start raking. It was a brisk day, harboring on a cold day. Sam's mind in overdrive; he needed the time to think about all the events of the last few months. Now he finds his bride-to-be involved in a lengthy conversation, with what Sam had decided to be a untrustworthy friend, Friend indeed. Sam raked and put himself into the backyard, but could not shake the impending doom feeling.

Evelyn washed and dried the pots and pans. She looked outside the kitchen to see Sam raking like he was mad at the leaves. He was using a lot of energy, perhaps wasting energy, as "Sam" had said. But she knew why—he felt betrayed, his ghostly friend had fashioned himself after Sam; his voice was a bit mechanical, but the tone was there. The internet had been Evelyn's idea, that too may be adding to Sam's frustration, to try and find the reasons for Sara's death, and her little girl. Sam had become very attached to that young girl, Paula had been Sam's little girl, by proxy perhaps, but his nonetheless. And now the upcoming marriage—that was a big event by itself, and now all the other distractions as well. Sam needed to see Dr. Martin, and he wasn't getting out of it this time! "Sam" had become a reality, a reality that could not be; it was impossible. But Evelyn herself had seen him, talked with him; he was very real. Evelyn didn't trust him, not one little bit! But like Sam and she had discussed, that they didn't think he was going away!

Evelyn brought hot chocolate to the deck. "It won't stay hot long—you had better come drink it now!" Evelyn told Sam. She zipped her jacket to the top. Sam laid the rake by the deck stairs. "I thought it might be a good warm-up, and it is getting cold out here. Why don't you come in for today?"

"I've been fighting the damned wind more than anything!" Sam kissed Evelyn on the cheek and sat down beside her. He picked up his cup and blew on the chocolate. "I haven't had hot chocolate in years. We used to take it duck hunting all the time. Dad even got to drinking it after a while. He preferred coffee, then everybody started to bring hot chocolate." Sam took a drink, it was still hot, and he set it back down on the table.

"I never really knew your dad. I met your mom at the beauty shop; we talked but that was about it. You know I don't know a whole lot about you. I know I love you! But you could be an axe murderer for all I know. Tell me something about you." Evelyn drank from her hot chocolate.

"What do you want to know?" Sam was a little leery of more conversations today.

"What did you do as a kid, school? You know, all about the man I'm about to marry!" Evelyn wasn't digging, just asking.

"Well, now that's a tall order. I used to have a pat answer for that question. Let me see, I don't want to scare you away with all the stories of my imaginary friend! Oops! That may have already been let out of the bag. See that tree out there?" Sam pointed to the large soft maple in the front yard. "That's where I met Friend, now known as "Sam"! I was maybe five or six, maybe younger; the age isn't what matters. He was a strange kid, that I remember. I wasn't sure what he was. I remember asking if he was a spaceman. But we hit it off, and were the best of friends, till he became the 'bad thing' in my life. The doctor never called him a bad thing; he said it was healthy for a little kid to have imaginary friends. At least till he was eight or ten, and then those things went away. I didn't see Friend till three weeks ago, in the living room. That was forty-three years."

Sam looked at Evelyn to see a concerned look on her face and he knew he needed to change the subject. "I had a great childhood. Dale, Bobby, Daryl, and I conquered the world! We fought the World Wars, and Korea too. We flew, we explored, we were great. Then we grew up. It wasn't as much fun. I still see them occasionally. I went to school here, and high school in Salem. Then I was drafted and went to Viet Nam. There's a pretty glossed-over childhood. But it was great! I wouldn't trade any of my memories for anything."

Sam tipped his chocolate up, and Evelyn was right, it cooled quick. He looked at Evelyn over the rim of his cup. "I was pretty much a loner after grade school. We moved to Salem and I ran around in Sandoval. We had a great time, drinking, drag racing, trying not to get caught at whatever we were into, nothing bad, just kids' stuff. I know you don't want to hear it, but 'Sam' was always around. I never saw him, but I knew he was there! I got into the usual trouble, as did all the other guys and girls, but he kept me out of the bad stuff. I was the only one to get drafted, drugs started about that time, and I was gone. Probably the best, I was a loner but needed friends. After the Army, I didn't need friends anymore, and they all went away. I became a businessman, and made money. Money, now there's a story I will have to tell you one day. But that's for another time. I've still got all of it."

"Got all of what?" Evelyn had finished her chocolate and was picking up her cup. "Want some more? And don't change the subject. I'll be right back!" Evelyn was off to the kitchen and more hot chocolate.

Sam and "Sam" knew all the answers to all of the questions. But it wasn't till thirty-six years later that Sam had known. It had never been discussed between the two. It had been hard to find out all the details, and most were still not answered, but Sam knew, and so did "Sam." That was where the distrust had begun. It was small at first, but it had grown in the last few months; "Sam" has changed. Sam hoped that "Sam" had not gained the ability to read Sam's mind yet; he had grown, grown into something that Sam could not understand. Maybe he was just an adult now. Kids think they can fly, and if not for the logic of adults, probably could. As Sam and all his childhood friends had grown older, reality had taken its toll. "Thanks, Evie," Sam said as Evelyn set a fresh cup of hot chocolate in front of Sam.

"You look...forlorn, that's the only word that fits your look," Evelyn said as she scooted her chair closer to Sam.

"Forlorn! Now there's a word! Doom, death, despair, agony on me!" Sam thought of the song from *Hee Haw*. "I was thinking about your question. It is to ponder some to recall your own life. I guess I had thought about it, many times, but was too busy with work to give it any real thought. I am afraid of 'Sam.' I don't know why, but I am. He has only done me good, and I guess I'm ungrateful. I don't know. And yes I was jealous when I got here today! I didn't want him moving in on my girl, the only girl in my life! I have been to bed with a few, over the years, but that beat the Hell out of the next best thing. Yes, I was jealous, he had been out of my life so long, and comes back when I fall in love! I was jealous, and pissed off." Sam grabbed for his hot chocolate and spilled some on the glass table top.

"See what being pissed off does for you! I have been jealous a few times, it had gotten bad a few times and ruined a good relationship or two. I was a little bit scared when 'Sam' popped in today, I was hoping you wouldn't be long today; I wanted you here." Evelyn wiped the spill with her napkin. "You have had this…thing that has followed you around all your life. I get here and feel that you have a secret life. I know you tried to tell me. But the story was a bit far-fetched, until he showed up! I knew something was going on, the time I fainted in the hall. I thought about that for a long time. I never saw anything, but it was like you were talking to yourself in two different voices!" Evelyn leaned against Sam, and snuggled her head into his shoulder. "You're cold, we should go in."

"It is chilly out here. I'll put the rake up and come in." Sam tipped his cup all the way back, and held it to get all the chocolate. When he set it down he had a chocolate mustache.

Evelyn laughed and pointed. Sam licked his lips. "You ought to see what else I can do with this thing!" Sam stuck out his tongue again, and wiggled it about.

Evelyn grabbed up Sam's cup and turned away. "I'll just check that out later, Mr. Young."

Sam smiled; he smiled a lot lately. The "Sam" part had been difficult. Sam knew that it had been "Sam's" influence that had brought him to where he was today. Sam had not been smart in money matters. He knew how to spend money, back then, and he had gotten pretty good at making it. In the last thirty years, Sam had become pretty shrewd; he had made a lot of money, he had made a lot of enemies. Sam had a way to turn a buck. His ways had gone against all his ways, he had gotten to the point of being a Scrooge, anything for the dollar. He bought and sold lots of people's futures; he had made some unscrupulous friends. They too had made a lot of money. Sam had brought their standards to a higher level. He could not have their unscrupulous deals in the past be labeled to "Sam." But even they took to watching. "Sam" was going to take a little watching, and probably intervention. That was the hard part, and how vindictive could he, or whatever it was, be to Sam. Sam owed him, not the other way around; it was like turning on your own mother!

Sam stood and looked to the west, the sun would set in two hours, or earlier, he had no idea what time it was. The trees were almost bare, they had only a few days and it would be cold. He stretched, and felt his back tell him about the raking. But he was going to be happy now; Evelyn made him smile. It was good to be Sam!

II

"Sam" was irritated. Energy was not a good thing to irritate; it started to show on the outside, if "Sam" had an outside. "Sam" had made the crossover in an instant, totally conscious, not like the old time now, it was "Sam's" time. He arrived at shelter to find Spirit in attendance. He sparkled as his energy came to shelter.

"Entity, I have sign with you!" Spirit sounded as never before.

"Yes, Spirit." Not time to sparkle, that was a sign to ward off other entities; Spirit was not to be taken in by illusion.

"Sign is that your entity has been in need of assistance for many time now. Much more time than is possible for entities. Sign has been given to my entity. Spirit would sign why?"

"Sam" had never in all time been asked. His entity had asked, but Spirit was only to answer, Spirit had all questions before an entity could sign. This was not to be a good sign.

"Spirit, my entity has found a power that is in agreement with needs. My entity needs not cross over as often as in time past. The power is produced by humans. My entity has begun to use this power, for energy."

"Folly! No power is in agreement with entity's needs! Energy is given as energy is needed. Power is not in energy; energy has been created for assistance in humans. Not humans' assistance for entities. It has been decreed that energy is to recycle to entity, the same energy that entity has at creation. Your human has had many time to become without need. But still you assist.

Spirit has need now, of your human's need. Why has time caused your entity to power for many time? The power, where the sign is required is without your question. Only compliance is now allowed. Time is no more for your entity. Answer, the power, or your human will be without assistance! This cannot go on in time!"

"Spirit, your entity is the power. No time has my entity not assisted human, for human kind. My entity has many time to cause my human to create and expand. To this day my human has created energy for use and not waste. Energy has been created to allow entities to become a human assistance, without having the need to power."

"Entity, no power exists beyond here. All energy is concentrated by power. Power is only a moniker for the power. You are but an entity, not to be concerned with making entities more powerful! Only to assist. Prevention of human mistakes is assistance; immortality is only power. Power has created energy. Your time has been spent in pursuit of energy for your entity. This is not assistance. This is not acceptable! Energy will sign with your entity!"

"Spirit, you are Energy!" "Sam" had let the ego of his time in the human world eke out in a slight spark. This spark whirled about "Sam" as a mosquito in a human world. The spark encircled "Sam." It did not fade, its color from a tan spark, to a blue comet, to a red miniature fireball. "Sam" could not cause it to slow. It would not stop, and was joined by yet another. "Sam's" energy was strong, and it showed, much to "Sam's" chagrin.

"Entity! This is what I sign, the display of energy wasted is not only signed, but observable by Spirit! Energy has been tainted! The energy you waste is not of our recall, it has been produced from infected sources! The use of infected energy can, and has caused many entity problems! This will not be tolerated!"

"Sam" feared for his entity. What had he done to allow Spirit to know abut the outside power? Questions that "Sam" did not believe would stop here. Power was Energy, Energy was Power! Spirit spoke as to another entity, some entity that "Sam" was not aware of. His thought processes would not fail him at this point, too many plans!

"Spirit. The Power you sign, is it not energy? Power and energy are both the same, are they not?" "Sam" tried to be a humble as he thought was necessary in the situation he found himself in now.

"Entity! You have used energy to your benefit. Not for your human. This is evident by the entity I now sign. The energy I sign is another entity that provides all knowing and direction. Your entity has been too busy providing power for your entity, to realize what you have created. You have gone where only a few entities have in all time. The time is now past for you to be beneficial to energy. Energy is an all-knowing, and forgiving entity. Even as we sign there are decisions to be made about your future as an entity. I am not sure recall can be performed, and prevent infection of the pure energy that has been used for all time!"

Spirit's language had suddenly improved to the point that "Sam" thought he had crossed over to the human side again. The two glowing orbs had been joined by two more, the orbs moved in different elliptical orbits around his energy. "Sam" had become the nucleus of his own energy. He appeared, as did the signs, at the Clinton nuclear plant. "Spirit. What must be done, I have created a mistake, I have only tried to be of value to entities."

"Thought processes have taken place of the assistance needs, that were originally programmed for your assistance to humans. You have caused a paradox that will be dealt with by energy. Entity, my entity should have realized what you had created. I will return. Await my sign."

Spirit had vanished as would the dark from the night as the sun rises. "Sam's" thought processes were working in high gear. All his plans were about to vanish, as quickly as did Spirit. The chair had not been tried yet, but "Sam" knew it would work, and now Spirit and energy, whatever energy was, would take it all away. "Sam" would not allow it! His plans were so very close to being realized, he would not allow his energy to be taken. "Sam" crossed over. Energy and power had been all one and the same till now. Power was what "Sam" needed. Energy was what power produced, so his entity had thought! Now it seemed that energy and power were not interchangeable, and might cause the end to all plans. All "Sam's" plans! And that would not be!

III

"Sam" had begun to like the human world. He had liked the toys, he had become used to the hustle and change that had become normal in the human world. He wanted these for himself, and would have them. "Sam" did not know if Spirit could follow him to the human world. All the things that "Sam" had, been known, and were all part of his plans. Now those were not known, his thought processes had failed him, not failed but he had developed an ego, and a knowledge, both had failed. What else would fail now? Had he become too human in his own entity? He had had many questions. Spirit had not signed him clearly, now his thought process knew why. Somehow Spirit had known, but how much was he in knowing? Could Spirit stop his plan? "Sam" was aware of the night stars, he was aware of Sam and Evelyn resting in the house, the Clinton power plant was operational again. All "Sam" had been involved with came flooding into his thought process at once. Sam as a child, the woman, and child by the water, Sam's parental units, Evelyn. Evelyn had become the problem to "Sam's" plan. Her arrival had begun the changes in Sam, that had caused him to speed up his plan. Evelyn must be eliminated. But signs appeared in "Sam's" thought process, "SLOW, CALM!" Sam would not assist in "Sam's" change, if Evelyn was destroyed too soon! Even Sam, in his human, emotional state would understand later. Sam had accepted all in time past, and he would accept, the loss of Evelyn. In time Sam would not be needed, he did not want to lose Sam; he had been the way, the direction. In the end Sam would accept his new God, or he would have to be removed, just like Evelyn. Humans were predictable, this was a problem, but not much of one.

"Sam" had arrived at the garage, the garage that Wes had unwittingly shown "Sam" many mechanical problems and solutions. The learning had been easy once Wes had been controlled by the power of suggestion. Wes had followed direction all the way to the end! "Sam" had so wanted fire—fire had become an enjoyment! There would be more fires! "Sam's" thought process had developed a memory of all things. An emotional state that he could not admit, a like, fire, the like of taking energy from others. Wes had been weak, as all humans were, he had allowed his energy to slip away, and "Sam" had taken it, just like he had taken Bob and Paula's energy. That had not been his first human energy; it had been exciting, not his first, and not his last. His thought process would not let "Sam" slip away he thought on, if he had been in human image, he would have smiled, but he was only energy now!

The rain had been heavy, it had made his energy stronger. The car was a problem, but the rubber line had finally come loose, and there was no way to stop the car after the fluid had leaked from the rubber brake line. "Sam" had started to take energy before the car hit the tree. They had shrieked—that had been good! He had taken all their energy before the fire. He had only stayed for the heat from the flames—that had been so good! There will be more!

"Sam" had developed dreams, the past had begun to pass in review when he would power.

There was only one star, in the sky, the sun. "Sam" had been away. His thought process was almost, not controllable, but the thoughts presented had been good. Now the chair, that had been what he had came for, he sensed no other entity, no Spirit!

Wes had dutifully moved the chair into the storage room and had locked it away. "Sam" looked the chair over again. He was sure the chair was finished; he had overseen its production. But his plans had been upset, as of recent time, he checked it.

The large roll-up door made the usual sounds. Sam pushed it all the way open. The cold light of late November flooded into the darkened garage. The sound startled "Sam"! It was time to deal with Sam as his latest plan had been started, perhaps a little early, but just the same, it was time. As "Sam's" attention was suddenly diverted, he sensed another human, not Evelyn, it was George. He was not ready yet, he would have to wait till Sam was alone. "Sam" moved out into the open air. Evelyn was too early to deal with as well, he would tap a local power source just for a "snack," a human word: a light meal; yes, his thought process signed!

IV

"Man, you're sure all this is yours?" George asked Sam.

"Yeah. I bought all these tools and supplies. Wes kept all his tools at his house. If there are any that are his they will probably be marked. He had no family that I ever knew of, so it doesn't make a lot of difference. When I hire a new mechanic they will be here for them to use too." Sam's old Dodge was parked in the place where the Chevelle normally sat. All but the '62 Ford pickup were covered. Sam had forgotten how many cars were here. He thought about swapping the Chevelle for his Dodge, but decided not to. The Chevelle had not been out in a while, and he liked driving it. But he would get it put back in the garage before the winter arrived.

"It all looks in pretty good condition. How long have you had this place? No one would ever see it here tucked back in the trees the way it is." George was looking about at all the tools and equipment that was virtually new. "Did he do any work here at all? This place isn't even dirty!"

"I told him that he was to keep all the cars running and keep it clean. He followed orders well." Sam was amazed at how clean the place was. Sam went to the office and found paperwork on the latest purchases. Wes had a new motor for the Fiero, and the order to have the transaxle rebuilt. The keys were lined up on hooks above the desk. Sam took the keys for the '58 Olds. "Let's see if it all works now." Sam went back to the garage and pulled the cover off the Olds, opened the door and got in. It's a little stuffy, he found the ignition, and inserted the key. The car cranked well, and on the second try it started. It ran a little rough for a minute or so and smoothed out. Sam turned the key and the car stopped. He smiled.

"What's in the back room?" George wanted to see it all.

"That's parts and more tools. This place has everything needed to keep these cars running. Some parts that are hard to find, and there are spares." Sam dropped the key back in the office and went to the storeroom. The door was locked. Sam went back to the office but could not find a door key. "That's odd; there was always a key to the storeroom in there."

"Maybe he had it on him when he crashed. There's a lot of neat old cars here. That's a Mustang, and that's an old one, I have no idea what it is." George patted the cover to the '49 Chevy.

"I don't really know much anymore. I'll have to come out here and look at all this stuff one of these days, kind of inventory all that's here. All but the Fiero runs, and the pickup isn't done yet, it needs painted too!" Sam looked around and wondered why he hadn't come out here more than he had. I'll get the storeroom opened and you can look in there one of these days. But it all looks pretty good to me. Heat's on and the walls are still in place. I just wanted you to see it all, and where it was located, just in case you needed to work on the building."

"I can find it, but it all looks in order to me. You'll need to come and check it out in the winter to make sure the heat stays on." George had hoped for some work. Sam's wheeling and dealing had slowed since he had become engaged. No work here, maybe a little cleanup outside, but it was getting to cold for that now, that was a springtime job.

The two left by the front door that had been standing open their entire visit. The furnace would work for another five minutes before cycling back when the temperature reached seventy degrees. George in his truck, and Sam in the Chevelle, George started his truck and left. Sam looked at the leaves blowing in the wind and he wondered why someone like Wes would basically kill himself in a car crash. The coroner had said alcohol, but he had been doing better for several years now. Sam turned the car around and drove down the blacktop. The leaves blew across the road in defiance of his forward motion.

"Sam" had moved up the road a few miles, and was helping himself to a little free power. He didn't need energy; he was gaining power. Spirit had not pursued him. Maybe he couldn't; "Sam" was still unsure. So many things had become unsure. His entity had told him to calm down, take measure in all that he had planned, and start anew. He had been at the substation for about an hour. He had settled on just two transformers. He was just taking what made him feel good. Blue orbs of electricity had begun to surround the transformers. "Sam" pulled himself away. He returned to the garage. The chair was as it had been before Wes' untimely disaster. Sam almost chuckled; if he had been in his human form, he would have. Sam reformed into his human "Sam." He needed more practice as "Sam," not his own lovable self but Sam! "Sam" sat in the chair. It was comfortable, he assumed, he only knew the word. He only knew fire, and electricity; those even his entity could feel, and he liked that feeling. He made an effort to get up, not appear, but get up. He was still a little jerky, Evelyn had said; he would work on that. He checked the chair's electric outlets. Six outlets, six plugs, six separate pieces of metal in the chair, each had its own 220-volt circuit. He was going to get a charge out of this!

As Sam drove home, thoughts haunted him, thoughts tore through his brain like the wind. They were there and gone! So many questions. There had to be a confrontation. "Sam" and he had to talk, it had to be Sam's conversation. "Sam" had to answer. Sam was scared that his life as he had begun to plan it, was in peril! There seemed to be a connection between Evelyn and "Sam," but what? "Sam" had never shown himself till Evelyn had been around; now he didn't know if "Sam" was spying on them. Sam had lived in his world, his design, his world! Now he wasn't sure if he had planned it or not. The Interstellar Watchers had to answer questions; their answers would help him. Then he could talk to "Sam"! It was all a bunch of "bunk" anyway. He just needed to relax and let things go their own way. It would all work out. Sam missed his turn. Another block, and he would correct his direction. "Now you not only talk to yourself out loud, you've lost the ability to know where you're located too! Evelyn will be back from the office soon, and she will have you visiting the shrink soon." The Doc Martin visit had come out well; healthy as a man in his fifties could be! One obstacle out of the way, now he could concentrate on the latest problem! He knew what his problem had been, it hadn't gone away, it didn't surprise him anymore, it was getting to be an everyday occurrence! Now he had to hire a new mechanic. Wes' death had just been one more little thing, all at the wrong time. He would run an add in the paper. This one had to be on the wagon; of course, he had thought Wes had been. Sam had driven through town without any knowledge as to where he was. He turned into his drive way on autopilot. There was Evelyn out back, by the pit. She had a fire going. "What the Hell is she doing?"

Evelyn waved. Sam tooted the horn. Evelyn ran to the driveway; she had a heavy coat on, and gloves. She exhaled, and the cold caused vapors to cloud before her red face. "There's plenty of parking just there beside the garage, M'Lord." Evelyn pointed to the garage. "Its roast beast ala cart!" Evelyn now pointed to the fire; she had seats and food on the little table.

"It's what?"

"It's a weenie roast! I thought I was going to have to cut more wood, you've been gone so long. Did you find a lot wrong at the garage?" Evelyn leaned into the car. "It's warm in there! Go and park and get over by the fire, the coals are just about right." Evelyn turned away from the car and ran back to the fire.

Sam just smiled and shook his head. He eased the clutch out and the car moved forward; the exhaust sounded good. Sam liked this car, always had. Couldn't remember the guy he bought it off in Texas; didn't matter, he had it now. Sam pulled into his usual spot and rolled the window shut. He hoped his light jacket was enough, he didn't even known where his winter coat was located. Sam looked to the sky. The sun was about to set. It had been high in the sky when he and George had left the garage. New problem! Now he was wandering aimlessly, no idea where he had been. But he thought "Sam" knew. He walked slowly toward the fire.

"Hurry up! You need to keep me warm! It's getting cold out here!" Evelyn hopped up and down, her hands recessed into the sleeves of her gray coat. The smoke would float upward and then get caught by the light breeze; it would be pulled upward and disappear, just like "Sam," Evelyn had thought.

Sam picked up his pace, then began to trot toward Evelyn. Evelyn ran to the chairs, and got Sam's old field jacket, with the liner in place, and held it out to him as an incentive to hurry. She held it like a matador and swirled around. Sam began to shed his jacket as he got closer.

"Thought you might need this!" Evelyn took his jacket and handed his coat, his winter coat, to him in a relay fashion.

"It is getting cold! I was wondering where this old coat was. I don't know where anything is anymore." Sam zipped the field jacket up, and snapped the storm flap. "I suppose you know where my good winter coat is located too."

"But of course! That's why you keep me around! That and to build fires, M'Lord!" Evelyn giggled, and bowed at the waist, then trailed her hand toward the glowing embers. "But you had better hurry, or there won't be any fire left!"

The weenie roast had been good. It took Sam's mind from his latest problem. Hot dogs were consumed with mustard and relish, till they were both full. Marshmallows followed, and Sam built the fire up. They had adjusted to the cold; that, and the wind had all but stopped. Sam and Evelyn were huddled together as close as the two chairs would allow, touching at the knees, with hands and arms intertwined.

Conversation had begun on how much fun it was, all the weenie roasts as a kid, and how cold it was getting. No mention of "Sam," nor of any of their recent past. It had been fun, it had been a long time since fun. The weenie forks were lying in the fire burning off; they glowed red. The hot metal was a thought to both their minds, but not spoken. Ghostly shadows moved and shaped new shadows as the fire waxed and waned.

Sam poked his hand out of the coat; he looked at his watch. "It's ten-thirty, or almost! Let's get this inside, and go get warm!" Sam waited for a response, none came. "Evie, are you there?"

"I heard you. I'm comfortable." She snuggled against Sam.

"Well, there are parts of me that may never work again! Let's get going." Sam sat up and stretched. "Can you get the food, or what's left? And I'll get a bucket of water and douse the fire."

Nothing was said, they took to their tasks and began to move quicker as the cold again attached itself to their previously warm limbs. Sam went to the garage and got a bucket for water. Evelyn passed Sam with her tray of weenie roast leftovers. Sam filled the bucket and started for the fire.

"Sam" had been watching. Once and again, the touching. No understanding. But the fire he understood! "Sam" allowed his entity to touch the fire. The embers fed on him at first then the other way around as they began to dim. "Sam" was enjoying the fire, even a little fire was good to sense.

Sam came to the fire. He noticed how it had died away quickly, but he took the bucket by the bail and its bottom, he threw the water from the bucket, shaking it to get all the embers at once.

An awful shriek filled Sam's ears. He took two steps backward and spun around to see where it had come from. He didn't notice the black form as it took to the sky, fast, then faster, then gone. Sam stood motionless, him and his bucket; the bucket swung back and forth gently. Sam looked from left to right, nothing.

"Are you alright, Sam?" Evelyn had her head sticking out the back door, looking in the Sam's direction.

"Yeah, damn cats." Sam upended the bucket and watched the fire. It looked as though one bucket was enough. He turned toward the house with his bucket, still swaying gently.

"What?"

"Damned cats! That's why I don't like the damned things. Don't think you'll have a cat here!" Sam dropped the bucket at the garage and turned toward the house. *Sure was loud!* Sam thought. "You had better get yourself in the house; it's cold out here." Sam opened the back door and slipped his arm into Evelyn's. "Thanks, that was fun!"

V

"Sam," on the other hand, had had a bad experience! His entity had never felt pain! This had to have been pain! It ran thorough his energy like nothing he had ever experienced! It had caused panic. His entity had bolted from the fire, parts of his energy throbbed, a lot like when his entity absorbed energy from other entities. An agony of pain was felt by the entities; "Sam" sensed it, but had never felt it. Humans had a similar pain, but it was so minimal that "Sam" had ignored it. His entity felt their pain, but enjoyed it! Now he had a part of him that was not working. It felt as when his entity had to strain to move things. There was a weariness, but this lingered, it would not go away. His entity could feel the element of H_2O; he knew water, but not like this! If this was pain, his entity never wanted to suffer it again! He would go to the substation and cause it to evaporate. "Sam" moved, but not with the ease of all time in the past. His entity drug the water-infected part of his energy with him. The transformer crackled and blue sparks flew. Humans came out of their shelters and watched. They used their communication devices to talk with others. "Sam" thought it was to tell others of the display. Humans liked objects in the night sky.

Soon a truck with the Illinois Power emblem on the side pulled onto the rocks surrounding the substation. It was time for "Sam" to leave, or to consume the human as he approached, unknowing what "Sam" could do. "Sam" still had lingering pain. Most of the water had been evaporated. "Sam" would try out the chair, and try to cause the energy to make all the pain to leave. Not a full charge, just a little. He wasn't sure if Spirit could find him yet, and an energy source might draw attention, and surely give his location away. His entity wasn't ready for Spirit yet! But would be, soon, in human time, soon!

"Sam's" concentration was not all gathered back on his ability to plug in the chair. His entity's thought process was still thinking about the pain. After a few attempts one plug was in, the chair crackled. "Sam" occupied the chair. His entity could feel the energy, not much yet but it soothed his pain. "Sam" went to his recycle place. His energy became bluish, a light hum came from the chair, and its contact with a true energy; it too wanted more. Dreams came again.

The only window of the garage opened to the woods in back. Only the deer noticed a slight glow, a glow that pulsed, gently, as though it were a harmless light display. So wrong, so very wrong! The animals moved away.

Sam had gone to work early. His routine had become normal, it had taken a few months to get back to norm. Most of the people that knew Sam had attributed his odd weeks, as a culmination of his love, and it had pretty much ended when he had proposed at Denny's. Many thought that the proposal at Denny's was way out of line for Sam. Few people really knew Sam, few wanted to now Sam. He was a businessman that had made it himself and was out of touch with real life. But he had fallen in love, and for those few weeks he had been like all the others, like them. And most that had any dealings with Sam, never thought of him as "normal." The bell rang as someone entered the front office. Sam got up and walked to the front office. "George. What brings you here so early?" The mail was always late at Young Property.

"I'm runnin' my route backwards to be home early. There won't be any deliveries it being Thanksgiving this week. And I can get home a little earlier if I run it this way. If those assholes at the office would sort a little earlier I'd be done by one. But they are slowern' Hell!" George was rummaging through his bag and brought out a bundle of mail for Sam.

Sam took the mail, removed the rubber bands off of the assorted papers and envelopes. "How you been, George? Don't get to see much of you anymore."

"Been just fine. Getting too old for the weather around here. Told the wife that she needs to pick out an island down south, and we could move there; kids are all gone nowadays. Hear you're getting married! To your secretary they say, up an' proposed in Denny's! I'd like to of seen that!" George fumbled with his bag. "Good to see you, Sam."

"It was quite a night! It was a little out for character for me they say. They got a good show. They can't wait for my next show." Sam pulled out a flyer from Interstellar Watchers. His alarm was ringing again. "Take care, George. Happy Thanksgiving." Sam turned and was back in his office before George could move.

George shook his head and thought, *High and mighty, that's what he thinks!* George pulled his coat together, and was back to his truck.

Sam's interest was to the headlines of the flyer. It showed a picture of the substation north of Sandoval, and below that was the picture that had caused Sam's alarm! A picture of Sara's house, or at least the remains of her house. "Is there a connection?" the article was titled. "From a source that cannot be revealed at this time," the article continued. More that a third of a century later the same intense heat produced melted stone and metal. The pictures showed rock at both sites that had become a large mass when cleanup had begun; concrete and driveway rock had been fused together. It showed pictures of metal burned away like paper. The pictures from Sara's house were grainy, and blurred. Sam didn't need the pictures to show him what the fire had left behind. Sam had not gone back when the cleanup had begun; he had been on his way home by then. The driveway rock at the substation had to be broken up to be moved; it had fused most of the driveway into a single unit. Government coverup suspected. Illinois Power sources not responding to this author. A picture of James Holly was beside each of the larger pictures. It had been the same man at both sites, thirty-five years later. *He had been a little off for some time now!* Sam thought. *Or maybe he was right and no one had paid any attention. Then!*

Sam needed something; coffee would be a start. He went to the outer office, and began rummaging for the coffee filters and coffee. He was on his hands and knees as Evelyn came in. "Sam, what the devil are you doing?"

"Coffee! I need coffee, and I don't know where anything is at around here anymore." Sam opened the last drawer of the filing cabinet. There was the plastic container of coffee, filters, and sweetener. "Here it is!" Sam stood up with his newly acquired booty. "Make coffee, please. I've got something to show you! Let me check and see what else I got in the mail first, see if there's anything else!" Sam was moving with a purpose. Evelyn just didn't know what purpose.

Evelyn took her coat and gloves off, and set to making coffee. It was a Bunn, and it was quick, but not as quick as Sam.

"I knew it! I saw the first piece, I knew there was more!" Sam was shouting.

"Coffee's not ready yet." Evelyn posed herself on the door facing, and struck a seductive pose. "I haven't seen you this excited since our first outing, sugar!"

Sam only glanced toward Evelyn, and was back reading a letter. "Here is the release form. I knew they were asking for a lot the other night, but I filled it out anyway. I figure what the Hell. Maybe I could get some real answers that way. And it really gave more than I thought it would!" Sam passed the letter to Evelyn.

Evelyn started reading the form letter before she looked at the heading. "This is a release form. What's it for?" Evelyn's eyes scanned to the heading, "Interstellar Watchers." "Sam, this is a bunch of weirdos from I don't know where. I told you about what you might get into, with this buggda boo stuff!" Evelyn looked up from the form letter to see Sam standing in front of her with the flyer from Interstellar Watchers.

Evelyn took the paper and began to read, "From a source that cannot be revealed at this time..." Evelyn first scanned the pictures, then went back over them more closely. She sat down on the chair across from Sam. Evelyn looked at Sam. He looked like a kid at Christmas, he was nothing but a great big smile. "Sam, is this the house in Mississippi?"

"Yes! Yes it is. The picture is old, but I remember it like it was yesterday! There's more to this than even they think!" Sam's demeanor changed. "We have to keep this quiet."

"It won't be quiet if you sign this form letter. These people will be camped out in the front yard. It'll look like a damned circus!" Evelyn continued to read.

"Not from them, from him." Sam sat back in his seat and looked around the room.

Evelyn did the same. They had both begun to think "Sam" was everywhere. Evelyn folded the form letter neatly, and let it settle in her hands to her lap. "What can we do?" Evelyn whispered.

Sam leaned across the desk and whispered back. "I don't think whispering will help! If he knows, then it is out. I think he would have known that I have been on the internet, and I don't know if he can understand that or not."

"If he's a damn spaceman, he sure as the devil knows more than we do already. Maybe he crash landed here, or something. I had been trying to humor you, till I saw him and talked to him. It's not hysteria, I have had conversations with 'Sam.' He scared me in the beginning, but now I think I'm even more scared!" Evelyn laid the form letter and the flyer back on the desk. "What are we going to do, Sam?"

"I don't know. I'm thinking. I don't have any idea what to do. I, we, have to talk to 'Sam.' There's not much else we can do. He has always been a help, he's never tried to hurt me, and now us. You heard him say that he's here for us now, not just me! You and me, kid! We're, in this together, now. Think!"

"Sam Alfred Young! Never in all my years did I ever think anything like this would ever happen to me. And now, now, I just don't know. What if he won't talk? If he decides to hurt us, what then?" Evelyn had lost most of the color from her normally rosy cheeks; she was almost pasty in color.

"I'm going to set up a meeting with this James Holly. I want to know what he knows, first. Then we can confront 'Sam.' I've got a lot to do! Did you know that tomorrow's Thanksgiving?" Sam was back to a somewhat normal state.

"Didn't you see the turkey in the refrigerator? You just thought it was a big chicken, right?" Evelyn stood. She had no idea where she was going or what she was going to do when she got there.

"Sam" was just waking, or at least coming back to life. The plug-in popped free and fell to the floor of the storage room in the garage. Sam could recall the past time, if he knew it needed to be recalled. Energy does not need to stretch, or have morning coffee; it is ready to go, just like a light switch, just flip it on! But "Sam" was slow, not in being ready, but in trying to sense any unknown energy, Spirit! His entity did not know what to look for, what to sense, his entity did not know fear, but he was fearful. His entity felt better this afternoon. The goings-on at Young Property had been hours before, a time that "Sam" still did not understand. His entity felt the affected part of his energy; it was better, no pain now. But it had left a mark on his energy. "Sam's" thought process thought it would improve, and go away with more time yet to come. But his thought process could not gauge time; his thought process tried to understand but was unable to adjust for time. He could only recall dreams, from his power time. Time was not a necessary element in assistance, only immediate, that was not time, that was now! Now he had to find or detect Spirit. His entity was unsure Spirit could cross over. So many questions that came up now, and they came up immediately, all the nows. "Sam" did not like the thought process to be occupied with its own agenda. His entity had a thought process that he had developed, he had made it work, but now, immediate, it had its own process, a conscious thought process. It disabled his line of thought processes by coming forward when it wanted to! This was a new process that his entity would have to overcome! "Sam" changed to his human form. He needed not to adjust himself in front of a mirror, as did humans; he knew what he had created. He adjusted his hair color to be lighter, gray, gray was the word, lighter his thought process signed. GRAYER! Small orbs of energy began to encircle his human form. His thought process strained to stop them. It took time, two boxes crashed to the floor. "Sam" ignored them.

Time and time yet to come his entity would practice till it was right. "Sam" walked, heel toe, heel toe. The infected energy gave his right leg a little drag, step, drag step. More time, his entity had time, it had always had time. "Sam" could feel himself getting better at the transformation, each time was quicker, and more efficient. The energy was more complete, it seemed more compact, more available. His only problem was to keep his composure calm, control. Spirit had not made his appearance as "Sam" had thought. That was an ever-present worry. Worry, that was now an new word that he had known the meaning but now understood. Understanding was a new sense that he was realizing, some he did not want to understand, but his present status caused his entity to have to understand. Words, so many words, so many meanings. And Spirit had signed false; it was not what he had expected from Spirit. Sign, and the human meaning of truth, it all seemed so wrong, he had thought only his signs had had hidden meanings. "Sam" felt betrayed; he knew that word, too. He would be the one to cause pain, pain to an entity that he had felt was all knowing! Now Spirit had proven to be false; false as many humans have been, over the times, to each other. "Sam" had directed Sam to mislead many humans to accrue his funds, the funds seemed to make humans more powerful. "Sam" had caused many of the funds to be diverted to secret accounts. Sam did not know of these accounts. One time "Sam" would have to direct the use of funds for the plans.

VI

Spirit was in as much of a rage as his entity could develop. Rage was not understood, nor was the response to Spirit's sign for the entity to remain till Spirit had returned. No entity had ever disobeyed; that was not programmed into an entity at creation! Spirit had signed energy, the all-powerful entity had told Spirit to remain calm, find the entity, and bring his entity here for sign to his entity's response. Now no entity remained to sign, only the shelter he had constructed for whatever purpose. And now outside energy had been used, it would infect all entities if not handled properly! Spirit signed to the shelter. It folded, it shrieked, it allowed sparks to form as the metal folded and became smaller. Size was not a knowledge of entities, but Spirit was not just an entity! Shelter became smaller, and smaller, becoming nothing, all became nothing, shelter disappeared, a slight pop was heard. All of the sound that had been from shelter. As it become nothing. Entities again became aware of their surroundings and silence. Signs were passed. No signs to Spirit. Spirit had become a color, a red color, a constant, bright color! Colors had never been, time now, there was color! The color moved, it pulsed, it became intense!

"SPIRIT!" No entity had received sign as this in all time! Signs stopped, the color became a constant color. Red!

"Yes, energy."

"Sign is necessary. NOW!" Only silence!

Color disappeared instantly. Spirit was gone!

Entities signed with only questions, no answers. Entities thought, they thought for the first time, no reactions, thoughts! Only no one was here to answer all the questions, no Spirit! Entities began to cross over; entities began their assistance, as before. But thoughts muddled their thought processes, unsure in all assistances. Thought processes were programmed, and now they had other thoughts, which were right; had assistance been right? Entities had developed a doubt, an imperfection! Spirit's entity would return, would it not?

Entities know time; time is all they have, assistance, and time. Humans never know either; it is only life, measured in hours, days, weeks, and years. Most entities do not understand any of the increments. Night and day, are of no concept to an entity. Humans revert to energy, a wasted energy. Entities are energy, an unnamed energy. Entities are not electric, they are not fuel, they are not bought, and sold, they just are. They have not individuality, they have not name. They exist so that humans may begin to become self-sufficient. Milliseconds are time as well, and milliseconds became the only time to begin to develop into beings.

Chapter 11
Shapes of Things Yet to Come

I

Sam and Evelyn became one. The two minds read and made decisions, and discussed in one uniform operation, as they looked at the computer screen. The Interstellar Watchers, as it turned out, was not a fly-by-night operation. They had offices in ten different countries; about half had government subsidies; of those supported by governments disavowed any knowledge of such a group. There were times that funding for projects would mysteriously appear in bank accounts from sources that were never questioned, and surely never discussed. Some lab tests were performed in locations that were only whispered about in small groups. The Watchers were amateur star gazers that had found a liking to a different drum cadence.

II

James Holly was an archeology student at USC. He had a leaning toward astronomy, and a minor. James knew that his life's endeavor had to have a direction, and could not be drawn two ways at once. James had been approached by professionals at the infamous Area 51. Government officials of somewhat dubious nature. How professional he was not sure. They interviewed him at a time in the United States history that was a little dark. Viet Nam overshadowed any other projects; it was any student's way to protest government standards and direction. Many students went on to become spokesmen and women for the cause of the people! James Holly had been to many of the rallies, and even a few protests, just because. It was there that he was first confronted by the professionals. James thought he was to be arrested; his parents would surely pull any and all funding for his school. He was only along for the fun of it, and tried to explain that to the professionals. He had thought it odd that scientists should feel it necessary to carry guns. James had been whisked away to a cheap motel, and a group of real professionals that asked questions about the heavens, and stars. He had explained that his interest was in archeology, not astronomy. They had only slowed their questions for a deep breath before continuing. He had liked the possibility of working at what was a hobby, and being well paid for it at the same time. Vacations had become his archeology time, the degree had become a license to poke and prod old sites for new discoveries. His lifestyle had become finding new discoveries about old, new ideas, the stuff comic books had been written for. His additional training had been secret facts that the government had kept from their own population. He thought that a full disclosure was the only right thing to do. Once he had seen how many secrets, and what they were, and how they might cause widespread panic in the world population he decided his government was wise to keep the possibilities from the public, until all could be explained in a mature, reasonable, and government-controlled manner.

James had been off on a hunt for fossilized remains of what was thought to be a man of unknown age. A tooth had been found that had to be ten thousand years old, or so it was thought. His computer lab had been running down all the internet inquires, as to the meaning of life, the usual crackpots, that claimed to have been abducted by aliens. In actuality they had found three over the years that had been captives for unknown amounts of time. But most were only crackpots. His lab had found the match for computer files that James had personally stored. These had been unexplained accounts, that James had mapped and investigated before Interstellar Watchers had come to be. The computer cross matched sightings, locations, and any correlation to make a match, then an individual would recheck the computer findings and rehash any and all data. From there, the evidence was matched and filed till they could be examined by James, or his handpicked crew of freaks; they too had been approached by professionals. Freaks was a pet name of the group, created and perpetuated by themselves. James had been talked into a *Star Trek* convention in Germany. Later it was found that a bright student, that had fallen from graces with her own country, the United States, was to be approached by professionals. James found his holiday was to be a working holiday, for the company, or as they had become to be known, the Interstellar Watchers.

Nicole was not a known scholar in her field of endeavor, archeology, but had written many papers about the inhabitation of the Earth by interstellar visitors, million of years before modern man crawled out on a rock for a sunbathing session. James had been the one to interrogate Nicole. It had been difficult for Nicole to decide on what the professionals wanted, and she had been removed from the Trek sight, on a slightly less than amicable fashion. The interrogation began with filthy language that would have shamed most sailors. Several hours following had proved to have been civilized; the professionals untied her. James had apologized for the methods used, and proceeded to explain the government's need of her specialty. Her theory's had been a direct correlation to expressed views of those that had passed on, or were just too old and frustrated in their study. It was not a career, but a fantasy. Nicole had promised to listen, and had become enthralled with the idea of accepting her citizenship again, and money from the same people she had protested against. It had a been a serious protest that had gone wide of its mark; two people had been killed. She swore her innocence, both before leaving the United States, and in Germany. The government wanted a head on a platter, and it was hers, but now she was to be aligned with the government, instead of against them. Nicole only slept with James for the sex, not a relationship; emotions evolved for twelve years.

Their passion for archeology, still existed, their dislike for mosquitoes, helped persuade them to come back to the "shop" to see the computer's findings. Thirty-six years from the first finding, James had freelanced, the original, now the government had found another. His ability to admonish or approve an incident to be investigated was not doubted by government, or computer. Computer files were checked and rechecked by the two on the flight home. James was impressed by the computer's ability to find and confirm the information. Nicole told him to lay off the computer; it was after all only a new device that needed time to prove itself. James slept with his mind refreshing the time of the original fire; his waking only made him more impatient to meet this Sam Young. His name had been stored for future reference many years before; now not only the same findings but the same personage to have made inquires in the validity of the government's findings.

III

"Mr. Young?" The game began. "This is James Holly. I represent the Interstellar Watchers. We are always looking for the existence of proof of life from another galaxy. I had had your emails forwarded to my site for further evaluation. Most people dread the disclaimer, and I am obliged to make certain that you are aware of your rights. I am privy to numerous items that have your name on them form thirty-six years prior. But before we begin, I need you to know that you may not use the Interstellar Watchers name in any correspondence at any time, for any reason. We are an independent organization that classifies, collates, and investigates sightings of possible interplanetary vehicles, or personnel, as well as site that may have been used as a landing, or staging area for later use by same said beings. All evidence will be examined, and returned at a later date, if you agree to allow us to progress. We are not affiliated with, nor collaborate with any government agency, foreign or domestic. That all said, I want to thank you for contacting our organization, and I need to ask you a few questions, if I may?"

Sam had been on the cordless phone when the call arrived. He had immediately gone to the kitchen to a hard line, and had shut the cordless phone off. Mr. Holly had read the disclaimer in what had seemed a single breath. Government this, and that, had started Sam's alarm system. "Go right ahead, Mr. Holly."

"James, if you would. I am not one of those people that need a Mr. in front of my name for my own self-satisfaction, and I find it a little stuffy. We may indeed become quite involved with this incident, and I would like to start off on a friendly note." James was trying his best to get on Young's good side before all the professionals started.

"Yes, James. I have been involved with only one of the incidents but am in the same general area of the second time. I probably wouldn't have even noticed if it hadn't been right here in my neighborhood." Sam sat quietly waiting. Sam was taken aback by a female voice.

"Mr. Young, my name is Nicole. I am an associate of James and here at a Interstellar Watchers and I was wondering how you came by the information about each site. Did you see the sites, or hear about them?"

James voice was back, but was speaking to Nicole. "I was getting to that if you would just wait."

"Well, you had him hanging on the other end and I just thought that I could ask a few pertinent questions in regard to what we have done before. I'm only trying to assist, James!"

"Mr. Young, I do not mean for all of this to confuse and perhaps distract you. We are very interested in what you have to add to our files, what you have has been of my interest for some time now." James was talking calmly with Sam, while at the same time shooing Nicole away from the other line.

Sam had held the telephone away from his ear as the confrontation had a taken place. He placed the receiver back to his ear now. "I could call back later, if that would be better. Maybe, a better time for you, as well." Sam thought of what Evelyn had told him, a bunch of crazies! Sam paused waiting for another outburst.

"No. Now is only to make initial contact to make sure that you want to go through with the interview. Myself and my associates will come to your location, and make further tests. We will make our time with you at your convenience. I do not want you to become alarmed with any of the questions over a telephone call. I deal with individuals on a one-on-one basis. I do not want you to think we're a bunch of crazies. This is on the up and up, no tabloid news, we are a scientific group that studies the arrival and departure sites for extraterrestrials. They are here, they have been for longer than we have and we gather all the information needed to complete our study. I have to make a few arrangements here. I will fly into St. Louis on...Nicole, when is our flight? Yes, we will be into St. Louis on Thursday late. I'll arrange for transportation, and we will see you on Friday afternoon. If that fits into your schedule." James still shooing Nicole away, and listening to the silence on the telephone.

Sam had begun to wonder what he had gotten into. But he wanted answers. "Mr. Holly..."

"James, please!"

"James, I will be here. You have my cell phone number I believe. I can be reached at that number at any time. Is there anything I need to do on this end, I mean is there anything that I need to get or have ready?"

"Nothing. I will possibly need you to do some things after our arrival, but I would not know what they were, till after we have had time to talk. Any equipment needed will be transported by my people, or will be brought along with them." James asked several questions, directions to the site and to Sam's house. Businesslike, in all aspects following the initial outburst. "I want to thank you in advance. There will be a lot of questions, and I like to make sure you are ready to be bombarded, before I arrive. We get a lot of crackpots that want to see their names in the local newspaper and on the racks at the grocery store. I want to assure you, that will not happen. Newspapers are sensationalists, and want to sell their little rags for profit. I am not in this business for profit. I am a scientist, and hope to come up with the proof that other life forms exist. Any other questions, Mr. Young?" James had come to the end of his conversation; it was evident in his voice tone.

"No. No questions. I am sure there will be a lot of questions after you arrive." Sam was unsure of what kind of Pandora's box he had opened. The phone went dead as Sam sat at his desk, in his new chair. Sam looked to the computer screen; he had the web site for Interstellar Watchers showing. Sam clicked it off.

"Evie! We've got to talk!" Sam sat with his new chair turned toward the door, his hand still on the mouse. No answer. Sam began to shut down the computer, but thought against it. He left it running, his screen saver, Stonehenge, showing.

Sam walked into the kitchen. Evelyn was finishing up their sandwiches. Sam moved in behind her and wrapped his arms around her waist. He held her as she continued closing the potato chip bag. "Well, I've done it."

"What's that, Sam?" Evelyn turned inside Sam's grip, kissed him on the nose. "You said a light supper, and here it is. What do you want to drink? You've done what?"

"I'll have a Corona. I called the Interstellar Watchers." Sam released his grip so Evelyn could finish, and go to the refrigerator. "They will be here Friday."

Evelyn stopped with the door to the refrigerator open. "They will be here? Friday?"

"Yeah, Friday. The man that runs it, or at least the one that's coming here, said that he would contact me Thursday late, or Friday. I don't know how many. But there will be a few, a few more than I thought." Sam watched Evelyn's slow-motion movements. She was still operating, but there were thoughts, thoughts that she was trying to formulate into questions. And Sam might regret informing her about this one!

Evelyn got a Pepsi from the refrigerator and opened it. She carried Sam's plate to the table. "Here? I never would have thought they would come here.

What are they looking for?" Evelyn still had that look on her face and her actions were still slow.

Sam knew questions were coming. He started to eat his sandwich.

"Here?" Evelyn had picked up her sandwich. "Are we entertaining?"

"I don't believe. This man, James he wants to be called, says he has a lot of questions, and he is bringing equipment with him as well. I don' know what for, but you remember when you said I should investigate, and pursue this a bit further. Well, I think I have just about gone to the limit!" Sam took a bite from his sandwich. Sam wasn't sure just what Evelyn was going to say or do about his little episode.

"What do I say?"

"Well, that's what I wanted to talk about." The door was opened and Sam knew where he was going now. "We don't talk about 'Sam,' no mention of him just yet. This might be the answer that we've been looking for. If it comes to a point that I could expose him, I may, I don't know. But I really don't want to come off like a crackpot!"

"Now wait just a minute! You the crackpot! These people that you have invited in, they are the crackpots! You don't know anything about them!" Evelyn still held her sandwich in mid air.

"Listen, first off, eat your dinner. Next, I feel that these people are not just who they present themselves, I don't know what. But we will see. I have lived with an entity. I have always accepted him. Fuck, I don't know what to do, I think I am at the last door before I come into the light, the light may be a big-assed train! But we can't talk about 'Sam,' not yet! And if 'Sam' pops in we are to deal with him as normal. As normal as we can deal with his likes. He might be just as he says, but I've had a feeling." Sam now held his sandwich as though he knew not what to do with it. He wasn't really hungry anymore, and he laid it back to his plate.

Evelyn whispered, "What if he's watching?"

"I don't know, if he's really what he says he is, he will be understanding, and on our side. If not, he will show us that too. I have done all I can do. I have decided to find an answer that I have looked for, for a long time. I still have questions, from years ago. If 'Sam' is my protector, where was he when I needed him? Where was he when my life ended? And now, my life has begun as I never expected, and suddenly he's back. Why?" Sam rested his elbows on the table.

Evelyn took a bite from her sandwich. She looked to Sam. He only sat quietly. Evelyn laid her sandwich back to the plate and touched Sam's arm. "I'm with you till the end comes, whatever that might be." Evelyn took her hand away and started to clear the table; there would be no more eating tonight. The shadows grew long as the winter sky grew dark, early.

The week, short as it was, seemed long. The days were full of many answers. All bad.

But in this time of uncertainty, Sam had committed himself and was determined to finish what he had started. Sam's life had begun anew and he had to have answers to the unasked questions. Sam only hoped that answers would come. And come they did!

"Hello, Mr. Young?" James asked as the voice came over his cell phone. Talk.

"Yes, this is Sam Young. How can I help you?" Sam had been anticipating this call, but it came as do all others.

"Mr. Young, this is James, James Holly. I am in Odin. I picked up a map, and arrived about a half hour ago. Where can I find you?" James stood at the counter of the local restaurant, talking on his cell phone.

Liz set the glass of iced tea in front of James and Nicole. "Mr. Young? Sam Young? I can tell you how to get to his place, home or work?"

"No thank you. He's coming here to meet us." James tipped his drink and looked around the small restaurant. Locals looking and talking.

"Should I send the crew to the site?" Nicole asked James while they were sitting at the counter. "They have the grid."

"Not yet. I want to talk to Sam Young first. I don't want to walk into this thing with any preconceived ideas." James tipped his glass again.

"Preconceived? You have a report on this thing already. You know it was like a back feed on the lines, the rock just got hot. That's the only reason we're here, to test the rock, nothing else is left. By the time we found out it was too late!" Nicole played with her glass of tea.

Liz returned with a pitcher and filled James's glass. Nicole hadn't drank much and waved the waitress off. A white van pulled into the driveway, closely followed by another. James got up to look out the window. He hadn't been sure on who they had sent on this investigation, but he saw Darryl and Jerry. They jumped out and quickly donned their coats and headed for the restaurant door.

James greeted the men as they came in. "Hi, boys. How do you like the Midwestern fall?"

"Fall? This is Siberia. I'm going to quit this damn job if they don't start sending me to Hawaii!" Jerry was his usual happy self.

"You guys going to get something to eat first?" James looked them over; they knew the routine.

"Yeah, what did ya'll have?" Darryl asked.

"We just had some drinks. We will talk to Mr. Young and perhaps be out later. Where is the rest of the crew?" James looked out the window again.

"The happy boys aren't too far back, obeying the law and all that you know. I'm starved, let's find a table." Jerry moved into the main part of the restaurant, a little larger than most living rooms.

"Isn't Charlie and Bill coming in?" James looked to the driveway again.

"They got a bunch of snacks and sodas; they're probably good for another two days. And they were bitchin' about the weather worse than us." Jerry motioned toward Darryl as he made the comment. "Now, the happy boys don't care; you could send them to the dark side of the moon and it wouldn't bother them! Why can't we get somebody decent to work with? Those guys give me the creeps."

A blue Ford Crown Victoria pulled in beside the vans. The car stopped and no one exited; they never did. An old Dodge pulled into the driveway; it had been kept up, but it showed the miles. A man got out, stood and looked about the driveway, then started for the door. The bell jingled as he opened the door.

"Hi, Sam. How's your future doing? I've never met her. You're going to have to bring her by and introduce her. There's a bunch of people here waiting for you." Liz grabbed two menus and headed for Jerry and Darryl's table.

James stepped up and stuck his hand out to Sam. "James Holly. You must be Sam Young."

Sam took his hand, firm grip. "Yes. Yes I am. This place is pretty crowded for this time in the afternoon." Sam looked about the room. A few of the regulars had coffee cups in front of them, some nodded as Sam caught their eye. They had been wondering what all the strangers were here for, but now they knew it was some kind of a business deal, with Sam there. They went back to their coffee and conversation. "Are you eating? What, I had planned on going to my place to get out of the public eye." Sam was as nervous as the night he had proposed to Evelyn.

A brunette lady slipped off her stool and stepped up to the two men. "I'm Nicole White. My partner never introduces me." Nicole stuck her hand out and shook Sam's.

Nicole's grip was as firm as James's. "If you will just follow me, I'm in the old Dodge." Sam gestured toward the driveway.

"You don't have any appointments that require you to be somewhere else do you?" James knew all about Sam Young. He knew about some of the shady business deals, and how Sam had come to be quite a businessman, but not too many close friends here in his hometown. A loner, a man who liked his money, and privacy. He also knew Sam had cleared his books for the afternoon. Busiest shopping weekend of the year, Thanksgiving just over. Nicole and James followed Sam out to the parking lot, and followed as he started across the highway. The blue Crown Vic followed too.

Sam was paranoid when he left the office, and now his alarm was going off. He watched in the outside rearview mirror, James, and Nicole, and a blue car. Not with them, surely, but it made all the corners, and even the last into the driveway. Sam sped up to get to the back of the house first. He was out and watching as the rental unit, and the blue car pulled into the back of his house. The blue Crown Vic just parked; no one got out. Nicole and James were walking up to the deck where Sam stood, and Evelyn opened the back door. Clouds of hot air on cold billowed just outside, as the door stood open. Evelyn gave Sam a quick kiss on his cheek, her hand on his shoulder, she could feel the tenseness in Sam's body. He smiled quick, and it went away.

Sam made introductions and invited James and Nicole in. "What about your friends?"

"I will introduce them later, they're not needed now." James ushered Nicole in before him. "This is good, dead-end street and not much traffic I would imagine. Would have to fill in the pond before they could ever make it a through street."

Sam looked at James after he said that. James never looked up. Nicole and Evelyn smiled at one another. Neither had been a homemaker; Evelyn had taken to the job well, Nicole didn't intend to.

"What would be the best, here or in the living room, and can I get you something to drink?" Evelyn was a little nervous as well.

"Coffee. I smelled the coffee as we came in, that would be nice." Nicole spoke up.

"That would be nice, Evie. How long will this take, Mr. Holly?" Sam asked.

"James, please! How long? That is entirely up to you, Sam. We want to hear all the details to each episode. Like I told you, I'm not a reporter, I want to hear it all, every detail."

Evelyn stood with the cabinet open, listening. She dreaded this day. Now it was here, she even dreaded it more! Sam caught the glance she gave him. He saw her eyes go to the back door. She too, wondered about the men in the car outside. Sam led James and Nicole to the living room. It was going to be a long afternoon.

IV

Time is a constant, it moves along at a determined rate, a scale predetermined. Spirit knew of time, his entity did not try and measure time. It need not be measured, but in his now time, it was slowly moving on, very slowly! Spirit had only to measure time in anticipation; energy had been a given, a knowledge of a supreme entity. Energy measured time in eons, not in human reality. Spirit now began to understand time. A fear, a dread, a fright, and a feeling of relief, the relief became a knowledge as time moved in slow steady progression toward Spirit's time to sign. Nothing seemed important anymore. A time to sign for assistance was upon Spirit, a time his entity had not sign to recall. Pictures, of places long forgotten, signed to Spirit. Times past that could only be lived by humans, Spirit could only receive. The light that surrounded the signs was brilliant, a light long time past, forgotten. Spirit felt, his thought process, recalled, he was light in burden, no burden, no sign for assistance, only freedom!

"Sam" on or about the same time, was having trouble trying to affect time. His entity had become unmanageable, his power, his energy, his entity, had come to need of direction. "Sam's" plan needed attention. His entity needed to recharge, but his thought process had arranged for energy, his energy! "Sam" thought; it was an obligation to think, it was not automatic. His entity became human form. It was a good form, his entity thought of Sam, and his form slipped, the glow began, his thought process took the glow away. His entity's thought process scanned his surroundings. "Sam" was in the garage, the shapes moved, the thought process stopped the movement. "Power, I must power!" A thought. Yes a thought. And, another. "Sam" saw his human hand form. He moved it, the fingers moved in his thought process, and the image of the hand moved. Not a thought, a reaction to his thought. This might take time to master, but time he had, now!

No sign from Spirit. No entity was sensed, no problems, just power! "Sam" moved to the storage room; shapes moved. Did his thought process see them, or was it sensed, or was it all the same. His entity was still in the garage. His thought process moved his entity to the storage room, movement, chair, movement! Shapes moved as his progress to the chair became more evident. His entity was before the chair. "Sit down!" the thought process commanded his entity to occupy the chair, and it was so.

V

The foursome, of somewhat dubious nature, had occupied chairs, and were sitting quietly. There was an air of uncomfortable surroundings; this was mostly from Sam and Evelyn. James Holly had opened his briefcase and taken out a small tape recorder and many papers; the papers were in a definite disarray. Nicole began to sort thorough the papers, and James was moving papers as well. In all appearances, they were quite unprepared for whatever was about to take place. Before James could begin, a man appeared at the hallway.

"Mr. Holly, I have received a message that assistance is required at the site." The man stood poker straight.

"Yes, Robert, we will not need you for now. Take all necessary paperwork with you. Do not cause any problems. We can take care of that later if needed." James sorted papers, and never looked up.

"I will report at my first convenience." Robert turned and started away.

"Do be careful—we don't need an incident," James called to Robert as he left.

Sam and Evelyn heard the work "assistance." They looked at one another at the same time. That word meant something that made them wonder just what Mr. Holly and Nicole White knew, and where they had found out. And even who have they invited into their house! The eyes tell much, it is said. Between Sam and Evelyn the eyes said to wait, don't tell, follow the plan. Sam took Evelyn's hand, and gave her a half-hearted smile. They might be crackpots, but Robert was carrying a gun, Sam would bet. What assistance? What site? They both hoped that enlightenment was about to happen!

"First off, I want the two of you to relax! You have invited us into your home, and we do not want you to be uncomfortable! That is a little difficult, I know, but we do this on a regular basis. I want you to know that this interview is not being recorded for anyone but our company. I have three forms that I must ask you to sign. One is a form stating just what I have said. It has a lot of legal jargon to make it stand up in the legal offices that we have to put up with in this day and age. The next is to prevent you from using our names or the name of Interstellar Watchers in any documents that might be produced by you for profit or fame. That too has a lot of legal jargon to accompany the short statement I just told you about. And three, which is heavy with legal jargon, makes anything you give us, or tell us to be used in our investigation, our exclusive use, and maybe returned at a later date, as our investigation is concluded." James gave the paperwork to Nicole, she in turn crossed the room, and handed the papers to Sam and Evelyn.

"I want to tell you a little about Interstellar Watchers. I started to work for them about thirty years ago, shortly after the incident in Mississippi. I do not recall ever seeing you, Sam, at that site. I took lots of pictures of the site. I really didn't know what I was looking for, at the time. I have been on the payroll of Watchers since shortly after that. I went to government agencies, that pretty much threw me out. They thought I was some kind of a nut!" James paused to take a deep breath; his shy outer shell hid an exhibitionist at heart.

Crackpot, Evelyn thought, *I wonder how they came to that conclusion!*

Sam thought about the word "assistance."

"I have been all over the world looking, and sorting, and interviewing many people since. I spent a lot of time in our lab examining evidence. I do not know whether you have any physical findings for either site, and I will get to that later. I want you to be assured that I am not a crackpot; we are very serious about our work, and the existence of 'aliens,' if you will. We take our business to heart. No matter what you tell us, it will not be taken lighthearted. We are very serious. We are believers in visitors; they do visit on a regular basis. They might not all be from the same place, wherever that might be, they have an evident superior mind, and we want to learn from them. Our many attempts are history now. We use past experiences to guide us on toward the next encounter. We do not and will not scoff at anything you might tell us. Nicole and I have been together for twelve years. We have had some experiences in our travels, most have been good, some have been nightmares. So do not hold anything back, please!" James took a drink of coffee. "That hits the spot!" James pushed the button on his recorder. "Now, let's hear your account of the fire in Mississippi."

Sam was still uncomfortable. He fidgeted on the couch. He started three times; he kept going back and restarting. The story began at Fort Hood. Sam closed his eyes. He watched the story as it unfolded; sometimes he smiled. He opened his eyes as the account came easier. He told his feelings, not in words, but interwoven into his voice, and his body gestures. Sam got to the fire's aftermath; he excused himself and went to the bathroom. There he washed his face. What he saw in the mirror, was a man of advancing age, a scared man. Sam looked at his hands as he dried his face with the towel; his hands shook.

Sam's imagination created a mirror image of himself. It stood behind him. He turned—nothing, nothing but nerves and fear. What had he allowed himself to cause? Evelyn was now his responsibility; he was putting her into jeopardy. Sam looked at himself, he just looked. A knock at the door brought him back to reality.

"Sam? Are you alright?" Evelyn was outside the door. The handle turned, but the lock held it tight. "Sam!" Her voice had taken on a tone of urgency"

"Just a minute. I'm fine." Sam's tone was flat. The doorknob relaxed. He heard Evelyn walk away slowly. "Let's go, asshole!" Sam re-hung the towel, straightened it, and unlocked the door. Sam retraced his steps to the living room, and paused at the arched doorway. "Sorry. This part of my life has been a closed book, till recently. I told this to Evelyn, a short time ago. It was very traumatic. This is difficult." Sam walked to the couch where Evelyn was standing. They sat down together.

Nicole and James were here to get the facts, no sympathy here, they were patient. The recorder's red led light was still aglow. Sam took a deep breath, and started again. Tears fell unnoticed from Sam's eyes as he told the end, the part he had left out when he told Evelyn. There were not enough bones left to fill a grocery sack. The skulls were horribly disfigured; they had to be handled with asbestos gloves. The bones, they were still hot. One small skull, and a few bone pieces. Sara, there was more of her bones left; they were smoking, and black in color. Sam sobbed, he felt Evelyn's arm around his shoulders, and she patted him gently.

"I'm so sorry, Sam. I never knew." Evelyn pulled him closer.

Nicole broke the silence. "Sam, I am sorry if this brings back a bad memory. This was not our intention."

James spoke softly. "Sam, maybe we could finish this at a later date."

"NO! Today is the day! I will be alright, I'm sorry for my emotional state. I will be alright. I guess when the day came that I was going to have to tell the story, the whole story, this would happen. It was a long time ago. I have tried to not think about it. Till this thing at the power station. I have entered into this, and will finish. I have questions of you as well. I will have them answered tonight, as well. This might take a lot longer than tonight, but I have to know answers to questions that have haunted me for years."

James spoke, after a few minutes. "You need to tell me about the substation site, then we will play with questions. The answers might be discussed for a while and I want to link the two sites together first. If you wouldn't mind." James drank from his coffee.

"You are going to answer, if you can, not some off-the-wall answer just to get me to shut up, right?" Sam tipped his cup up. It was cold; he hated cold coffee.

"I will answer all the questions that I have answers for. And I will discuss all that I don't know too. I will tell you up front, I don't have all the answers. That is why we are here, to find answers. I have no doubt in my mind that we are visited, most likely today. Somewhere, they get sloppy, they make mistakes; if they didn't we would still be scared of shadows. Now if you would please tell me about the latest site." James sits back and becomes relaxed, as though he's about to hear about a fairy tale.

"I don't know a whole lot about it. I have called up all of the sites on the internet, and I went out to the substation. By the time I got there, there was a big hole in the ground. They dug it all out except for a few rocks; I've got some of those. The ones I got were unimportant. They broke all of the big rock up and took it somewhere else. The paper took a lot of pictures from a ways off. The cordon was large; no one could get within a half of a mile of the substation. The pictures are from outside the cordon. It was a couple of weeks after that, I was there." Sam picked up his coffee cup and walked to the kitchen.

James raised his voice so Sam could hear from the kitchen. "Why did you wait so long?"

"Well, I didn't really wait. I didn't know anything about it." Sam was coming back to the living room with the half pot of hot coffee. "Evie told me about it. I remember the power outage; it was two or three days. But I didn't think about it. After I had told Evie about the fire in Mississippi, she told me to look on the internet. That's when we started to email back and forth. That's when I went out there." Sam poured coffee for all present. Sams' thoughts went to "Sam." Where the Hell was he, it, whatever? "Sam" never drank coffee, he never drank anything, didn't eat, sleep, or anything. *Should I tell this man about "Sam"?*

"Thanks. It wasn't till after the fact that you called us. You see, like I told you I was in Mississippi; we already knew about the substation. It was your involvement that brought me here. I would have looked you up in Mississippi had I been as aware of all I am now. That is what brought me here, Sam. I think we are close to something, and I intend to find it. I don't even have any idea what I have dredged up in your past. I am sorry for that, but you invited me in, and now I want more. That might sound selfish, but I feel we are close to something, I'm not sure what, but something." James has leaned forward. He looks like the kid waiting for Santa to bring him an electric train. He drinks from his coffee. "I am a businessman, like yourself. I deal in facts. Those facts are my money, I take it to the bank." James sat quietly, looking at Sam.

Sam got up and went to the kitchen again. They heard a door close and heard his footfalls as Sam returned. In his hands were three rocks, two large, about five inches in diameter, one small, three inches in diameter. Sam set the rocks on the floor in front of James. Sam returned to the couch with Evelyn. "I thought that the construction crew had gotten sloppy; these three were the only ones I found. I don't think they were supposed to leave any behind. but nothing larger was there."

Nicole picked up the largest of the rocks and examined it with knowing eyes. She turned it over slowly, only stopping on special looking spots. Nicole exchanged the rock for another, she examined it closely as well.

James gave the rocks a cursory glance; his attention was Sam. "What else did you see there? What did you feel?" James was into the story; now he wanted more.

The conversation went on for hours. The questions had not started, at least not Sam's. It was early in the morning. Evelyn yawned.

"It's late, or early I should say. We have to make arrangements for a room for the night, what's left of it anyway!" James started to pick up his paperwork and put it in his briefcase.

"You don't have rooms?" Evelyn asked.

"We thought it would not take as long as it has. There's a motel in Salem. A couple of them I think," Nicole said as she helped James straighten up his paperwork.

Evelyn looked at Sam, and back to Nicole. "We have a spare room, but there's only one bed."

James looked at Sam; he nodded. "We only need one bed."

"Yes, we have been together for twelve years. He wants to get married, I'm not sure just yet." Nicole smiled.

Evelyn took Nicole to the extra bedroom. They chatted, but only conversation.

Sam still on the couch, watched as James closed his briefcase. "James, is this the same thing?"

"I won't lie to you, I'm not sure, but I think so."

The ladies returned and the foursome split into two. The twosomes went to opposite rooms, no conversation, just looks and smiles.

VI

Spirit was existing. His duty to his entities was not being accomplished, his energy was wasting away, only time was not worried about the outcome. Spirit was! In all time his entity had never been called to sign with energy. Worry was something that an entity was not aware of, was not part of an entity's programming, but Spirit was worried. His entity had always followed the teachings, his entity had always believed in energy, but to sign with the entity signed as, Energy was worrisome! Spirit felt a power from his own energy that was cause for fear, worry, and elation! Spirit was compelled to do something. He did not understand this sign!

Spirit knew his energy was being directed, his entity was moving, his thought process did not understand! The blank whiteness of the surroundings, began to move, to form, to become something his entity had not experienced, ever! The whiteness became rounded billows, gold-rimmed clouds. They moved, moved with slow stately grace. Spirit's entity became aware, aware of many things, that had not been seen in many times, times past when his entity had been in assistance, and servitude to a small human, Sandy. Sandy had been his only human, before his entity had become Energy's Spirit! Spirit's thought process recalled, thoughts, not a reaction, not a processed sign! A thought, Spirit's thought!

The billowy clouds began to move, upward. Blue sky was greeted by Spirit's thought process, blue, yes blue. Colors flooded into the processed signs, the colors were recognized, the breeze, cool upon Spirit's energy. His energy felt, it felt! Spirit could not feel, he was energy! He was in a false place, a place of infected energy! Panic was this his entity's payment for allowing one of his entities to have strayed from belief. Thought process was overloaded, it could not take any more of the falsehood! His entity tried to cause sign to return. He could not!

Beneath his energy, rough feelings. NO! His thought process was directed to discover what this feeling might be. His process saw through limited sight, rocks, fine rocks, a path. Children could be heard, not felt but heard, feet were running on the fine rocks. Spirt looked, feet! Children ran before Spirit. His sight assaulted his thought process. He began to assimilate his surroundings, his entity. A hand passed across his sight. He saw with eyes, his eyes, the sight of a hand, his hand!

Spirit had never been surprised; his entity had never been happy. Satisfaction had eluded him because of his one failure. He has felt a sense of satisfaction for the direction, and signs he had passed to entities to cause assistance, to move forward. His hand touched his face, his cheek, his nose. Spirit had a sudden sense of awe, total awe. This was a manufactured dementia from an outside source. His fear was as fearful as awe, what deviant could have caused this? His hands found one another, the grip! Spirit's thought process was no more. He felt his muscles respond to thoughts, he felt movement, he felt the breeze again, he felt the cloth that covered his body move with the breeze. He felt wonderful! He began to walk on the path of fine rocks. He felt the rocks, as his feet took steps, his steps, the irregular feeling as they compressed beneath his weight. His toes gripped the rocks as he walked. There were people, humans, people! What was going on? What power had caused this? Surely his sight was that of another, but who?

VII

Spirit's discoveries were being matched by "Sam's" discoveries! "Sam's" were not of fascination, but of frustration. His entity had lost the power that it once possessed. He was forced to manually manipulate things around him. The power was there; he could feel its pulse inside his being. It was strong, but could not be directed. He had been stopped by a door. His entity could begin to penetrate the solid door, but could not transport him to the other side. There was pain, pain as it began to penetrate the door. He had to manipulate the door as a human. In his anger he had become a dark blue, force, a force of energy;

he had slammed against the door, the walls, the ceiling. He moved with speed, great speed, but the manmade objects would not give; they exhausted his energy as they repelled his attempts. "Calm, slow!" He had heard the voice, the voice he used with Sam. He could feel, too, only it was not a good feeling. His energy would not last having to physically perform. He could not control his physical efforts without expending excessive amounts of thought processes as well; it was exhausting. "Sam" was tired. His entity had not been tired, ever. His efforts had not been in vain. The door had been opened. The metal fixtures that allowed it to swing open had been damaged. The door made contact with the floor and caused "Sam" to become enraged again. The fire had only been small. He had received a good feeling when his energy had suffocated the flames. "Sam" allowed himself to become energy again. The physical form had been a good form, but it was tiring. As an entity he felt refreshed, but he also felt a need for energy. He would have to power more than his thought process had planned. Plans were meant to be changed to make the end result! The voice, this too he would have to control. The sunlight fell upon his energy as he sat on the chair; it felt good. His entity would have to power now. Mental processes caused the plug to be attached to the small grooves in the receptacle. The electricity hummed at first. He found the pulsing sensation uncomfortable as it began, then it became more natural. The energy began to pulse through his entity. It was good. He could always feel the power; he liked the power! Even though he had to be in his human form to receive the power.

The outside light flickered almost off, then on, then finally off, as the electric sensor decided there was enough light, and the light above the roll-up door became dark. The sun came up. Shadows formed and disappeared as quickly as they had arrived. Small animals resumed their forage for winter food stuffs. The deer were silent already, always alert, but lying in wait for the evening, many hours away. The wind was cold, blowing out of the north, but the garage was in a slight depression, and wind seldom found its form. The form inside was not aware of anything but the electricity. The furnace came on; a forced air fell upon the form in the chair. It felt nothing of its surroundings. It felt thought processes as they made signs to "Sam," signs that his entity would not recall. Signs that he would like to remember, the signs that would cause his plan to be recalled! But his thought process would not recall, could not recall. A flaw in a plan, perhaps! And an ache, it was a cold feeling, the furnace was off, his mental processes turned it to the highest number. The mechanical wind, it was warm. His entity relaxed into the chair, into the power.

VIII

Evelyn was as most women with guests in the house, she was up in time to see the sunlight begin to make shadows, and make them go away. Coffee was brewing. She wished she had woken Sam, and then they could talk before Nicole and James arose. Evelyn busied herself with preparations for breakfast.

Footfalls on the hardwood of the hall. Sam, Evelyn thought. But it was James that appeared around the door facing. "Good morning!" Evelyn said in a bit of a surprised voice.

"Morning," James replied. Could I get a cup of that coffee?

"Of course." Evelyn hoped her voice didn't give away her disappointment that her first had not been Sam. "Let me get you a cup."

"Just point me in the right direction, you're busy. I hope that all that's not for us. I didn't intend to make you go thorough all of this trouble for us." Evelyn told him which cabinet, and James had produced a cup of large proportions. "Cup for you?" as James poured himself a cup of coffee.

"Please. I just made it so it should be good and hot!" Evelyn was arranging rolls from a frozen package. "Hope you like heat-and-serve stuff. I'm only opening some quick rolls for breakfast."

"Anything's fine with me. I'm a light eater in the morning." James sipped at the steaming coffee. "Plenty hot!" He moved to the kitchen table and took a seat.

It was quiet, Evelyn moving about making breakfast, and James even quieter. Occasional sounds from the pans, and glass as Evelyn mixed, and set the table. James retrieved another cup of coffee. James stood by the counter and looked to Evelyn.

"How long have you and Sam been together?" James sipped at his coffee.

"I've worked for Sam for five or six years steady, but we've been together only for six or eight months now." Evelyn set the last of the silverware she carried. "I am happy now, but all of this scares me."

"There's nothing here to scare you. This is only a daft crackpot looking for a space alien or two." James saw something, he didn't know what; he had been a detective too long to pry, just yet.

Evelyn was alarmed to think she was here, with this man alone, and she wanted to tell, tell him about "Sam." That was not her place, not till she thought that it would help Sam. And that was not yet.

"Last night was the first, that you had heard all of the story. I thought that from your expression." James looked out the window over the sink.. He sipped his coffee.

"Yes. It was the first time. I knew part of it but not all, till last night. That must have been a very tragic time in Sam's life. His life has been devoted to business since then. Make money, and take his mind away, I guess." Evelyn took up her cup of coffee and drank. "What else are you looking for, James?"

"What do you mean? I'm just the little old alien hunter." James turned to his cup.

"Those two thugs, the ones from last night. They work for the government." Evelyn looked confident at her question.

"We all work for the government sometime in our life. And they just make sure we aren't bothered by the local papers and all. Sometimes we have a little assistance from the government. They too want to know more." James set his cup down and looked out the window more intently, but not seeing the small snowflakes begin to fly around the backyard. "I'm not a monster; that is rather evident. You invited myself and Nicole to spend the night in your home. I can't help what I don't know about. What can I help you with?" James looked out the window, but not seeing anything.

"Morning." Sam walked into the kitchen and headed for the cabinet for a coffee cup.

"There's cups on the table." Evelyn stopped what she was doing and went to Sam. She gave him a quick hug and a peck on the cheek. "Breakfast in about twenty minutes." Evelyn moved back to the counter where she had been working.

"Morning, James. Been up long?" Sam moved to the coffee pot. He took notice on how much was left in the pot and poured his cup full. "Anyone else for coffee? This one's about done. I'll make some more." James held his cup out to Sam, and nodded to Sam in thanks for filling his cup. Sam sat down at the table, and James followed suit.

"James, how much of this is of any value to you? I have kept most of this harbored inside for years. I didn't think anyone else would ever want to know any of it. I just put it away, but the substation started my mind to working, and

I saw several similarities. That's when I contacted the Watchers. Is this just a figment of my imagination?" Sam leaned back and looked hard at James.

"Well, I really don't know. Years ago I would have jumped on this and run with whatever findings that I would have picked up at the site. Nowadays, it's all different. We are a scientific group, nothing is left to chance. Something happened at the site last night. That's why Robert went away. I did not see his car in the driveway, so he must be there for security. Robert is a special agent that works for me, but is employed by our government. A very special group." James drank from his fresh cup of coffee.

"You just said a mouthful, and didn't tell me anything." Sam looked at James.

"I was on vacation. Nicole and I are archeologists, we were at a site in China when we got the details. Nicole brushed it off. I came here because of what the report said; it had already compared the two sites. That's how we come to be here in your kitchen drinking your coffee. I want to know something out of this too. Mississippi was my first, that's what got me going on the outer space deal. I do believe, and yes the two sites are connected. How, I don't know. But I will find out. What I find may not be what you're looking for. I find a lot of information about a lot of things, but the Mississippi incident and here are a separate group. The rocks you had in the living room last night, that's why I'm here. Those rocks got hot, damn hot. Too hot for electricity to have back feed into the substation and melted them together. I expect that the tests will reveal that something else caused that kind of heat. There are too many safeties involved to have allowed that kind of accident! Just like in Mississippi. There was no way that the electricity caused that fire. I will be around for a week or so, at least. I just imagine that Illinois Power doesn't want us poking around. But, that too will be dealt with. Once again, Robert and his pal will insure that no one stops our experiments. People want us to fail; they believe in God, but not space men, visitors from somewhere that isn't on our road maps. Not yet!" James smiled and looked at Sam, who had been joined by Evelyn.

"So where do we go from here?" Evelyn asked as she slid into a chair beside Sam.

"I don't mean to sound like I'm talking down to you, but this is the way it goes. We did not find a spacecraft, we did not find any aliens, and we don't expect them to come back for anything left behind. So what we have here is a clue, evidence, evidence that will be checked, and re-checked, then if it is valuable it will be stored for future reference. I told you that the answers that we find might not answer your questions. I came to talk to you, Sam. I need to ask many questions about the Mississippi site. Not much was ever looked at, or sampled; it was just a fire. I didn't think so then, and I don't think so now. But I've been back there; no one is still alive to tell me anything else. Most everyone that had anything to do with the fire is either dead or so old their memories fail them. That was a long time ago, and you were there, and you are here. That's why I'm here!" James felt good about his oration, he sat back and waited.

"This is off the wall, but do you think that whatever this is, is following me? That's spooky!" Sam's mind was moving at light speed. He didn't want to give any outward response, but "Sam" had been following him for years. "Sam," the ever-present ghost, not a space man, that's what he had said. Evelyn's mind was running a close second to Sam's, and they were so close together that their minds might have been linked. Evelyn too had the same thought.

"Evelyn, could I take a shower? I really need to get my hair washed. James, are you telling horror stories to these fine people? They will think we're a bunch of freaks!"

"I'll show you where everything's at." Evelyn crossed the kitchen to take Nicole to the hall bathroom.

"I have not told the three-headed alien story!" James laughed. He laughed alone; Nicole wasn't yet awake, and Sam and Evelyn had other thoughts.

The two women started down the short hallway.

"So the jury is still out on how nuts I am yet!" Sam said and crossed the kitchen to get a fresh cup of coffee. He filled his cup and looked out the window. He saw the light, wind-driven snow; it was picking up now. "It's snowing."

"Snowing? That might hamper what the crew is doing out there." James looked to the window but could not see anything from where he sat. "Sam, there's something… something else. I can't imagine what it might be. But I want you to know that any and all that is found here will never go beyond my team." James walked to the counter to freshen his coffee. He still had plenty, but the closer he got the more he could see in Sam's reactions.

Sam stood motionless at the window, his cup still held halfway to his mouth. He noticed James poured a small amount of coffee and take up a position to see Sam's reactions. Sam had been selling himself too long to miss James's move. "There is something, yes there is, but I will wait till you have made your determination as to how much off the wall all of this is, first." Sam never moved again, till Evelyn came back to the kitchen.

"James, if you like, there is another shower in our room. You're more than welcome to use it." Evelyn looked at Sam; she knew he was pensive.

"Yes, that would be good. Where might I find a towel?" James tipped his coffee and drank long. He set the cup down, almost empty.

Sam spoke first, still unmoving. "The slim door in the hall, all you need."

James turned to the hall, smiled at Evelyn and left the kitchen.

"What's going on, Sam?" Evelyn asked as she stood beside Sam. She entwined both her arms with Sam's right arm.

"'Sam'!" Sam said quietly.

"Did you tell him?"

"No. Of course not, but I want to. I want to take the burden away, if 'Sam' is a burden; I don't know anymore." Sam finished his coffee, turned to Evelyn and hugged her long.

The pair held onto what they knew, each other, what else, was unknown. They stood and watched the snow begin to accumulate around the posts on her fence by the garage. The brown grass began to highlight by the fine, white snowflakes as it continued. Evelyn opened the oven, took out the rolls and turned the stove off and took the sausages from the skillet. Evelyn placed the rolls on a platter and the sausage on a plate, set the orange juice on the table. All was still silent in the kitchen.

IX

A voice, it was gentle, he could not hear it yet, but knew it was coming. A sense, his entity sense. If that still existed. Spirit had been able to sense when something was about to happen, many times ago. He had forgotten the time when he had assisted, too many times ago, but now, he could remember now. Spirit remembered the colors now, long times ago! He remembered his marvel when he first assisted, his thought process had been bombarded with the awe of the human world. Now too he marveled, marveled at time past, time that consumed his entity. It was dizzying, the colors, the shapes, the people, the sound. Spirit walked. He heard the sound of the fine rocks under his feet, he changed directions to walk in the grass, to feel the softness, the uneven surface. His vision changed as his head turned, the marvel of it all. But deep seated were his worries, but they too seemed to have no real significance, not here, not now.

"Spirit. Sit with me."

The voice, the voice he knew was coming, it was here, now. Spirit looked down to a man sitting on a bench. Spirit never hesitated. He looked to the man. His features were worn, not worn, but had knowledge expressed, some wrinkles in the skin, but they had seen many things, and Spirit wanted to know too. Spirit looked upon the man, the human, he saw many things that his thought process could not correlate, thoughts moved in and out, Spirit felt his own skin move, it smiled, he touched the face of the man for some reason he had become, he touched "his" face to make sure he, indeed was real. He felt the skin of the man, and he felt his own skin. He could not fathom the feeling; it was real, he too was real. Spirit laughed! His newfound hands had feeling, not sense, but feeling!

X

"Sam" knew of breakfast, he knew of needs, but not his needs, they were incessant, he felt more energy, as his entity became aware of its surroundings, the garage, his chair, the sound of the human world, the wind outside, the feel of the furnace's manmade wind. The electricity, the energy, his thought process could stay in the chair. He could live here. Live? What was that! He did not live, he was life! He was the power! "Sam" willed his entity to a standing position. He could feel his energy. It was good! His thought process disconnected the power source. It stayed connected to the receptacle. His thought process worked again, harder, more power, the electric cord moved, and back, it moved again and fell to the floor. "Sam" moved to the door. He did not walk, but his human-formed legs went into the motion of walking; no contact with the floor, he forced his form to make contact. Sparkles of energy at first contact, then nothing. "Sam" willed the human-formed arm to push the door open. He felt the coarse form against his hand. It opened, it made scraping sounds as it dragged on the concrete floor. He had to make it happen in his thought process, and make it actually happen. "I can do this." He heard Sam's voice, no not Sam's, but his. Did his thought process feel the voice? No! the voice was his, his entity had sound, it had motion. "Sam" willed his human-formed hand through the door, it moved slightly as contact was made, he could feel the texture of the inside of the door. It pricked at his hand. His hand went further. He felt the wood slide on his arm. It was pain, his thought process decided, but not much, nothing like the liquid had been. That too was present, but not a process of his entity, only a time past, to remember.

"Sam" began to experiment with his new energy. It was his, it would grow, it would become. "Having been separated from Spirit was good for my entity. I should have done this many time ago." The voice had been loud. He would master it too! He would master all that was in the human world, soon! The time was soon, and the quicker the time the more "Sam" would like it! But there were still matters to be mastered! "Sam's" entity moved to the office. He picked a key, a key with the GM emblem on it. It took several attempts to grasp it; it fell, and it fell again. It passed through his fingers, it passed without his control; each time he gained more control. Not of the key, but of his rage. His anger was without end! Papers flew, a glass cracked in the window. "Sam" tried again and again. Once the key fell behind the desk, and his rage threw the desk away as a paper is whisked by the wind! "Sam" picked up the key without knowing. It was hot in his human-formed hand, he looked to it as it fell through his hand. This time he remained calm. Calm! That's right, calm. His newfound voice was calmer as well. "Sam" looked to the desk, lying on its end. His thought process reversed the move that had pushed it away. Slowly it came back to upright, the legs banged as the desk became into normal position again. It scraped and shrieked as he pulled it back to the exact position as before, not close, but exact! "Sam" smiled. He knew it was a smile, he felt the human skin pull his facial features, unpleasant at first, but this feeling went away, only the liquid mark remained. "Sam" bent at the waist and picked up the key again; it stay in his hand. He noticed the smile, but only small time. He paused at the storage room. His thought process began. The door moved, it made sounds, it hung again to the rightful place. Small pieces remained on the floor, splinters, insignificant splinters. The door moved slightly as his thought process stopped reforming the door. "Sam's" smile was broad now. He liked this feeling, not as good a fire, that was a feeling, he would feel that again soon, he liked fire!

"Sam" felt for the key. It was still in his hand! His entity walked, his feet against the floor, to the Chevelle.

"Sam" uncovered the car with little energy expended. The door was his next problem. The handle would not give. His entity pulled, but it too slipped through his hands, the key fell to the floor. Calm! "Sam" levitated above the floor, his legs disappeared, his arms became transparent, his energy grasped for the door. "No good! You have to have human form!" "Sam" formed the body parts again. His attempts began, but he halted at the door handle. A button, what was the button. His entity touched the button, resistance. He pushed harder, the button recessed into the door, then returned to its original position. Calm "Sam's" rage was upon him again. He levitated again, relaxed, allowed his energy to return to a controllable level. Control "Sam" pushed the button again, the button came to stop against something again, and again, little to no resistance now. His concentration allowed his hand to enter the metal, it drug against his false skin, sparks flew. "Sam" withdrew his arm and hand. His human eye examined the door more carefully. A brightly colored post stood out against the black interior, it had a square on the top of the post with recessed dots fashioned in designs on each of its flat surfaces, three dots, four dots, five, "Sam" concentrated and inserted his hand through the glass. Only two of his fingers appeared, he needed the thumb, it appeared shimmering, then constant, his forefinger, and thumb closed around the square and pulled up. The lock clicked as the post pulled upward. "Sam" thought his hand back to the outside of the door. His energy reshaped into a arm, and hand. He pushed on the button again, the door opened a little, he pulled on the handle, his hand melted through the handle. "Calm," he tried again the door. The door moved in and out but held fast. "The button, you idiot!" The voice made his energy look around. Going to have to get used to that! "Sam" pushed against the button and pulled at the same time; the door swung open. Elated he rose above the car and floated about the garage. He could feel the heat at the top of the garage ceiling. Odd, he thought! The car stood open and a light inside too. "Sam" looked at the car with the door standing open as he floated about the room. He liked the red color and would like to pilot it as Sam had done for many years. He would have to watch his outbursts; Spirit would surely have entities looking and watching for anything odd. His plan was near time now; he could not make any mistakes. "Calm, control!" He heard his voice, just as he had heard Sam; it did make him calmer. He had caused Sam to realize these words over and over till he could accomplish anything he wanted to accomplish, now he had to pay heed to the same words.

"Sam" would have to power again soon. The human power was a little self-limiting, it was created for light bulbs, not for him, but he knew how to cause more! He allowed his entity to re-form as a human, as Sam. He looked about; the eyes would take a little time to learn to control as well. His entity took up the driver's place. He allowed his human form to contact the seat, the key, he still had the key, no! Calm. He looked about the garage. The key had fallen to the floor and had bounced under the car. He recovered it after a few tries; it fell through his hand twice inside the car. His entity was learning quickly to remain calm and finally got the key to the silver slot on the steering post. It had been long, trying to get this far. He turned the key, the engine made noises. The car lurched forward and stopped. It rocked back and forth. He could feel his entity in the seat moving with the car. It stopped, and only bells could be heard, lights flashed on the dash. "Sam" tried to remove the key; it held fast. He turned it back toward his entity and tried again. The key came out and fell through his fingers to the floor by the shifter. This might be more difficult than his entity's thought process had first determined. His human hand slapped at the shifter and it passed through his hand. His human eyes had seen, but his entity knew, what? He left the car as wind passes through tall grass, his entity levitated in a bluish color outside the car. Waves of vapor rose from the seat. The seat was cracked and was giving off heat. His entity had caused damage to the seat, when he had unconsciously formed back to his true form of energy. This was a new problem. He had changed without his thought process knowing. He had become comfortable with his form and its changes, but now the adaptation that was going to have to be closely checked, if his plan was to survive! He was aware that the change of the seasons would keep Sam away from the garage. He would have time to perfect his change; his plan would prevail. His thought process was behind his movement;, his skills as a human needed honing. Time was an afterthought to an entity; now it became a reality, a needed ally.

"Sam" forced himself back into human form. He walked, he paced, he tried to get the swing of his arms in unison to his walk, that was going to take time! He had time, time enough, he had hopes, he had never had hopes before, but his thought process thought these were hopes! Spirit had become the enemy! His enemy was strong, stronger than "Sam" had considered. His triumph would be to see Spirit without energy, and come to "Sam" for help, not for assistance but help, only the help would not be from "Sam"; that would be the end for Spirit, and a new beginning. "My beginning." The voice was becoming less and less alarming. He began to talk more; a control was necessary to not cause the windows to rattle. He had caused the cracked window to break away, and the cold had caused a vapor to enter the office area. It had been difficult, but worthwhile to place a piece of paper over the window; the tape had been the hard part, everything was mechanical. "Sam" had became better at the manual parts of the human world, soon to be his world! His human transformation was almost complete, not as planned, but almost as planned.

"Sam" had not tried the red car again—too many pedals and too many complications—maybe in another time, but not this time. The red was such a pretty color, it reminded him of fire—he liked fire! He had found the blue Mustang. It only had two pedals and a seemingly easy shifter arrangement on a floor shifter that only went back and forth. It had been trial and error, but he got it to move, small moves at first, then more, then outside.

The garage was still as it had been, secluded. The driveway was small but caused "Sam's" driving skills to become honed. The Mustang was able to move in the small space without problems. The starts and stops had been just start and stop. It was more difficult to become more in control of the human form than the car. Control had been his biggest issue, and not with the car.

XI

James and Nicole had become house guests. They had come and gone to the site for almost a week. Robert had had his work cut out for him in the last few days. Reporters had become a regular at the site. The power company had not wanted to reveal the site where most of the damaged equipment had been stored, nor the site for the rock. The rock had been buried. It had first been run through a crusher, but damage to the crusher had caused them to just dig a big hole at a remote facility near Carlyle and bury it. They had exhumed the remains and sampled the rock. The rock had become another form. It had become as hard a granite, but not a brittle. It had been almost impossible to remove. The original measurements had a piece of rock forty-one feet by thirty-five feet at the largest piece. It had been broken into smaller pieces with the track hoe. It had to be broken up. They could have gotten a permit and taken it, but Illinois Power Company thought they had had enough publicity on this thing anyway. The hole had been deep and wide. Diamond saws had been used up trying to cut a piece off for study. The government had come and picked up all the rest of the rock. The site had been sanitized and all particles had been removed. The power company was glad to be rid of it! But worried of the outcome, as well. No radioactivity noted, only a big blue tarp lashed and tied to keep prying eyes away during the trip cross country to Arizona. A whole zoo of people were gathering to see this new compound. Was it a rock, or metal, or a new form that had never been seen before? So many questions.

James and Nicole were deep into reports every evening. They would stop and answer questions when asked, but would immediately go back to the paperwork. They explained the paperwork as best they could. Most was marked "secret" and was so secret that the sender had no idea about what they were talking about, so it got the usual treatment, "secret." Paperwork was piling up at a phenomenal rate; boxes were being filled as they pored over mountains of paperwork. But it began to run out after a week and a half.

They had all gathered in the living room like James had asked in the morning. It was now six in the evening. "Sam, I wanted you here to try and explain all of this paperwork. I have seen a lot of paperwork on a few other sites, but this one crosses over more than one area. A possible landing site for an alien spacecraft has almost been shelved. The findings from the rock has become a major project in itself. As far as the original idea, that is what we came here for, it seems to be just like most, we don't know. I have spent the last thirty years working at the same project. I thought this might have been a new and an old project. You, Mississippi, and me. Now I am at the same threshold, I'm on the same step, on the same ladder, and I've gone full circle." James folded his hands in his lap, and looked about the room.

"So you have no more answers than we had before you came." Sam looked dejectedly into his glass of Pepsi.

"We have gained a lot of questions, questions that we were not looking for. We are a secondary part of the equation now," Nicole stated flatly. "We don't even have access to most of the data now. This has been marked so top secret that we can't even access our own material!"

Sam and Evelyn had held their own meetings while the two Watchers had been reading. They had decided to tell them the basics of "Sam." They hadn't seen "Sam" in weeks now. Bad feelings had come with the arrival of James and Nicole. Feelings that now felt as though there was an answer, an answer they were afraid of.

"James, first do you need a refill? This just might take a little while." Sam looked at James; never blinked an eye, just looked.

Nicole reached for James's glass and walked toward the kitchen. She too, knew another side had not been told. Evelyn took her and Sam's glasses and followed Nicole.

"Sometimes, just sometimes, I'm afraid of what I might hear. Sometimes I think that I really don't want the answer. But I've done this so long that when I have discovered a bone at a dig I find myself thinking, Do you really want an answer? I shake it off and go on. Here I am, go on." James looked back at Sam in the same manner. Sam had not moved.

The girls returned, set drinks back on the little stone coasters, and sat back close to their respective men.

"A long time ago, in a place not far from here, a little boy found a friend. To him it was a friend as none other, none other that he would ever encounter in fifty-five years of life. A friend that was always there. When trouble was close so was he, it. That's what we're about to find out." Sam went into detail of his childhood that he had never told Evelyn, the long nights of study to help his friend understand words, and the hours of play, play that was without prodigious. Sam and Friend were the best of buddies. Sam went into the bedroom and got his necklace, and laid it on the coffee table in front of Nicole and James. The hours began to pass, as so did the story, a story of a child that had been loved so much that no matter the expense, his parents tried to help. And of a child that so loved his parents that he tried to change, but Friend told him that he would always be there for him, and the Army, and Mississippi. Sam stood and walked from the room. No one followed; they sat quietly and waited. No one spoke, no one looked about, they just sat quietly.

"I'm going to retell the story of Mississippi. I will not leave out a single detail, not one. I will ask some questions then, maybe, you will have some answers then."

Sam went on to recount the night in the Cozy Inn and how he had been sure that Friend had been there. The singsong pattern of the voice that he had not been able to figure out why it sounded so familiar. Evelyn had told him a few months ago, after she had met Friend, that it was Sam's voice he used, a younger Sam, but still Sam's voice.

The voice that had haunted Sam for years. It had not always been a haunting, as a child it had been reassuring, it had been comforting, it had been his friend. Sam told of the carnival, of the nights with Sara, he told it all. All but, Sam had been uncomfortable during parts of the story. The power outage, the funeral. Sam never faltered in his story, even when the tears rolled down his cheeks.

"Sam, we didn't come to make your life more miserable. You had said the first time, and the first person you ever told abut the fire in Mississippi was Evelyn. Now you have told us again with more detail than my mind would be able to recall. This has been trying at the least. I may be missing the point here, but an invisible friend, and childhood memories of that Friend, and your lost love, where are we going?" James had a way about not beating around the bush when he wanted something.

Evelyn chimed in. "It's about 'Sam,' I mean Friend—he is still here!"

Sam held his hand up like a traffic cop. "That's what I have been telling. This is my history with Friend. I told him one night that he was so much like me that I would call him 'Sam'! This isn't psychosomatic, it's not an imaginary friend. He's real! I have lived with him for years. I think the fire at Sara's, and this power station is all the same. I don't know how to link it together, that's why I called you! I haven't said anything till now to keep you from running away from the crazy man. And lately I've thought I'm fuckin' nuts!" Sam sat back in his chair, Evelyn put her arm on his shoulder. Sam looked at James, his face was pleading for help!

James moved to the edge of the couch and rested his elbows on his knees. "Sam, you're telling me that you have an 'invisible friend' that visits here; he talks to you just like when you were a kid?"

"Yeah. But he's not a kid anymore, he looks like me!"

James slid back in his seat. He stroked his chin. "I thought that we had been excluded from all the goings-on in Arizona. This is... well, I don't know what to say. I'm a little skeptical. Tell me more."

"That's what I'm trying to do. I guess the childhood memories are a little hard to swallow, but he has been with me since. He was in Nam. That's what I asked before, if you thought that something was following me. It wasn't tongue in cheek, I was serious, very serious."

"I am sorry, I was mistaken about all of this tonight. I really was not sure just where we were going. I have to stop you here and ask a few questions, if you don't mind?" James had his proverbial pad of paper out, and was looking for a clean sheet. "This thing, this being, you call him 'Sam'? That's a bit confusing, I'll refer to him as Friend. He still appears to you?" James wrote on his pad.

"Until six or eight months ago that's what I referred to him as, Friend. He has always been my Friend. But I had not seen him in thirty years... no, that's not right, I haven't seen him till this year. After all the doctors he just never came around, but he was always near. All through school, I would have dreams, and he has aged too, as I aged so did he." Sam was using his hands to talk, he was telling more yet, of a life that had been whose?

"You had not seen him in years? And he suddenly reappeared?" Nicole asked.

"Sometimes I would see something out of the corner of my eye, it was always gone. Everyone sees that, I never gave it a single thought. But he has shown himself to me lately, and to Evelyn. I found him in the kitchen with her one day, having quite a conversation!" Sam paused. James did not allow pauses, but it was Nicole who jumped into the conversation first.

"You've seen Friend too, Evelyn?"

"Yes, several times. I heard him one night. I slipped in the back door and heard conversations. I thought Sam had company, or business, or whatever, but no one was parked outside." Evelyn sighed and sat back against chair where she and Sam sat.

"Evelyn, where was Sam?" James leaned forward again not wanting to miss anything.

"Okay, wait just a minute! I have not conjured up a ghost for Evelyn to see. It took me forever to tell her about 'Sam.'" Sam was on his feet now. He paced across the living room and back. All heads turned to watch him, and await another tale.

"No! I didn't mean that to come across... what I meant was, both of you have had conversations, together, with...Friend?" James was fidgeting now.

Nicole stood and began to pace in smaller circles, her arms across her chest, her chin supported in her right hand. She stopped and gestured with her right hand, still supported by her left arm. "Not separate conversations, but together, and interactive talk, like now?" Nicole continued her small circles.

"Yes!" Sam pivoted in front of the fireplace.

"This is awesome!" James wrote quickly.

"Now let me tell you two something. I will deny I have ever told you anything if this ever gets out. If there is something about your work involved in this, it's yours. I don't want anyone coming here to interview me, us! I will make you out to be the crackpots that most think you are. I had my thoughts in that direction. It won't take too much to make all of the locals think that too! I will not be examined, evaluated, poked, or prodded by a bunch of your associates!" Sam stood with his hands on his hips. His look was stern.

"No! No, that won't happen. What kind of tests? I wouldn't have any idea what that might be anyway!" James looked to Nicole for a little help. She was still pacing.

"Psychiatrists! That's what I'm talking about! I'm not fuckin' nuts! Evelyn can tell you the same about 'Sam.' I didn't want to tell you this, I figured you to think me a fool! But I had to, if 'Sam' is a Friend, he will still be. But if he has caused all of this, I'll be rid of him, somehow. That's where you come in!" Sam looked from James to Nicole. Nicole stopped pacing.

"Wait a minute, we're not an exorcist! And we have to talk about what this is, this being. What does he, it do? Can you call him up, and make an appointment, or does he just happen by? You're talking like we can just take him away, like Ghost Busters! I'm looking for an alien, and you're trying to pawn one off on me. I am excited, I want to meet this Friend, I want him first, before the government screws it up!" James was talking fast. He wanted to get up and pace too, but there wasn't room!

"Let me tell you all I have, first, I have your attention now!" Sam looked at the dark of the night through the window. Only the street light showed a ring of vision available, like his story, outside the ring of light, only faith remained!

Sam began with his arrival at home following the Army. Sam had never really had a direction, he never prepared for a life, only Key West, and that had gone tits up. His interest in real estate had just come to him. He didn't really like the idea of how it worked, but it beat electrical contracting. Sam couldn't even change flashlight batteries without getting shocked! He had worked with Lester, fixing and repairing the houses he had for sale. From there it only seemed natural to begin to sell. He never took the course till he had already opened his own business, Young Property. "I just had a natural instinct for real estate, that, and I found a couple of properties that we subdivided and made into reasonable buys for working people. It always just came to me. I had been home abut two years, and Mom and Dad wanted to talk to me. They never interfered with anything, a little advice, but no interference.

"I came in that evening, and Mom and Dad had a visitor, or a business venture, I didn't know. Carl Flaners was his name. Carl was a retired FBI agent. I didn't know what it was all about. FBI was spooky to me! But they said retired, so what the Hell! Then they laid it all out, and I started to piece it together." Sam got up and handed James a piece of paper with copies of money pictured on it. He handed one to Evelyn and Nicole as well. They all looked at their copy, and studied them carefully.

Nicole asked first, as she had the coin print. "What's this got to do with an alien?"

"Look at the dates on the bills and the coins." Sam leaned against the fireplace.

"Sam, I still don't see anything wrong here." James held the paper out and looked at Sam like there was a question, a question that he didn't know.

"Look at the dates on the bills again, look at the date on the print." Sam moved to the couch with Evelyn.

Evelyn looked. The print was difficult to read, but it had been circled to make finding it easier. When the date registered to her mind, her mouth fell open. She looked to James and Nicole; they too had realized the implications.

"Friend gave these to you?" Evelyn asked.

"No. Remember when I told you about Sandoval? I spent that money in Sandoval, in 1969, the same time I was in Viet Nam. I told you I went there. There was a big investigation into the money, especially the coins. I spent money, and saw people that were twenty years old and I was fifty-four, my friends, my stomping ground! I was given those by Mr. Flaners, the retired FBI agent. In 1971. He never solved the case. And I didn't know the end of it till I was fifty-four, last year. I started to get weird then too." Sam took a drink, leaned into the couch, and waited for the questions to begin.

XII

"Sam" had began to control his image. His human self had become more perfect each time he "became," his becoming was soon. He had mastered his new form, he had been able to cause his entity to be affected by surroundings. He could become what he had planned for so many times.

"Experimentation" was the human word. "Sam" experimented many ways in his time at the garage. Walking had been difficult in the beginning, but it had been simple after a few times. Driving had been the easiest. Physical control had been the most difficult part. Talking and carrying on conversations had been the most difficult part. Obtaining fuel for the vehicle had been difficult. He understood more than anyone knew, Sam, or Spirit, or Evelyn. He had gone to the only full-service station in Centralia. He did not remember the name but could negotiate the roads, and find it again if needed. He was becoming independent in a short matter of human time. The pay he did not understand, but the human had smiled when "Sam" had given enough paper bills to him. He had visited several stores and had not been looked at twice. His presence here had not been of any consequence to anyone. The stores had music in the air, and red decorations everywhere. It was cold. "Sam" had never experienced cold; it was bothersome in the beginning, and had only gotten worse. The car had a heating mechanism that he had learned to use, it was like fire, but no destruction. He had also found that when in distress his control was inefficient. His human hand had passed through the heating control several times before being able to grip and cause it to work properly. This frustration had caused "Sam" to damage the car somewhat; the flat shelf, dash had been recipient of a bad dent in the center after his heater control problem. Later at the garage he had been able cause it to return to normal, except the covering, the material would not stay complete, a crack stayed in place, accompanied by a crease in the metal of the dash. All still functioned properly; a small dent could be repaired by Sam at a later date. Sam would find another to do Wes's work; his cars would be renewed.

"Sam" had expected Sam to show up at the garage. But his absence had made it easier for "Sam" to learn control of his human form. Only during recharging was he forced to return to his real form. He had taken on many human abilities. He had begun to note on paper his schedule, his plan. He had become aware of times, human times. The calendar had become to be noted. He used his energy to cause the paper to turn black over each numbered day. Today he marked the day by causing his human finger to become hot and only blacken the number 22, it had bled over to the outside of the number slightly; the paper was hard to control once it became hot. His earlier tries had caused holes in the calendar. But now he had control over everything but his own energy. He needed more energy, he knew where he would get it as well, but not yet. His visits to Sam's house were not as they had been in the past. Sam had visitors, the visitors were ever present. "Sam" had not been able to make himself a part of Sam and Evelyn's lives as had been his plan. Soon a new plan might have to be sought to end his hiding, and his new life was to become, soon.

"Sam" began to cause a new plan, an alternate if you will. He made several plans; it was not what he wanted. "Sam" would allow this to go on for a short time. He busied himself learning. The television had become his ally in his new plan; it told much of what was happening, and what had happened in the evolution of this world. No mention of entities, only of God. Foolish humans, they still praised God, even on the television! They would cause many people to sit and watch other humans, some in human clothes of the now time, and many were clothed in the wear of ancient humans. "Sam" found himself laughing out loud at the ministers. The ministers had many humans happy, just by talking to them, they offered no assistance, only talk. These ministers only talked, to many, not with a few, but many. Assistance had to be one entity to one human! There was assistance being done to many humans, and these ministers were unaware of all of it! "Sam" visited Sam many time in the past weeks, but had not appeared to Sam because of the visitors. Today was another visit, he was not going to wait much longer!

Chapter 12
The New World of Spirit

I

Spirit had been in total amazement or the world he found himself involved in. He had been able to feel, see, smell, and to even enjoy. Enjoyment was not an entity's place, only to assist, but here no assistance was required. All the humans here required no assistance. Had the human world evolved to the point that assistance was no longer required? His new acquaintance had only begun to talk. He was able to speak of things only Spirits knew, programming that was not for entities. He was in amazement of the surroundings; he only talked. His voice was soft. Gently, he gestured with his hands and he smiled most all the time. Spirit was enthralled with the conversation; he could sit here forever! He was sitting; to his knowledge he had never sat anywhere. And this man could talk. Everything was soft, everything was knowledge. Spirit was excited to learn! He was after all energy, resting was not needed, he only existed.

"Wait one time, if you would." Spirit felt odd to beg for forgiveness of a human. But he felt it necessary.

"Wait I will. But might I ask for what do we wait?" the human form asked, as gently as all of his tones had been during their conversations.

"I would have sign, I require assistance, if you would?" Spirit again had been set at an awkward disadvantage.

"Yes, ask your questions. I am sure you have many." The human form sat quietly.

"My entity has only been required to request sign once in my time. I have sign." The word "question" came to his thought process. "Question, that would be more in your understanding, yes, question." Spirit found his thought process to be confused, unsure; that was not to his thought process's liking. But onward he would go; he had business that must be completed. "By what are you called?"

"Forgive me! I have been out of my normal manners. What would you call me?" The human form sat and looked at Spirit.

"I have been assistance to entities for many time, but I have not a thought in my process to have any idea what to call you. I came here to see Energy, I have been signed to make this appearance for assistance, or for what my entity is fearsome of, for recycle." Spirit's thought process wanted to pass over to the entity, Energy, and receive what it was to be. "I have to make my entity available for Energy. Times are not of my entity's decision, and I must go to Energy. I must not stay here any longer!" Spirit's new form stood.

"Energy I will be. That seems a little odd, in this world, but if you like I will be Energy, for now." The human gestured for Spirit to sit back beside him.

"No, I must visit Energy. I am fearful that his entity will be unhappy with my assistance to an entity in my charge." Spirit had looked with his eyes for a sign, a direction; none seemed to direct him. His thought process was still amazed with the surroundings.

"What would you be called?" the human asked.

"I am Spirit," Spirit replied as his eyes scanned the new and beautiful world. Beautiful, a new word had suddenly emerged into his thought process. Spirit's thought process was being bombarded with many new thoughts, sights, and feelings.

"Spirit! That is a word I like. There are many names here. After a while you will make discoveries of another name for yourself. Now sit, Spirit. I am Energy. I knew of your coming, and decided to meet you on your arrival. This is a new world to many and I try to make the transition as easy as possible."

Spirit sat beside the human. He was compelled to sit. He was fearful; his entity had never been as fearful! Energy had taken an approach that had not been foreseen!

II

James and Nicole had spent many hours with Sam and Evelyn since their arrival. James and Nicole had met many types in their Interstellar Watchers investigations. Tonight they were leaving for yet another airplane flight back to Arizona. Many times they had left with a bitter taste in their mouths. So many years, so many times they had thought they were close, so many times disappointment. This evening had started that way as well. It had been time to tell Sam and Evelyn goodbye, the usual, "don't call us, we'll call you, if any of the tests come out in your favor." None ever had. Sometimes it had been difficult to get back at the job knowing that you were not going to find any evidence of visitors from another galaxy. The usual thoughts from those that had contacted the Watchers. Tonight had started the same, but now was different, that excitement was back! That want to know more, to find more, to really do their jobs.

The copies of the money had caught their eye, but not until the dates had been brought out. Now there is something. Not maybe, unless they had been duped by the best. They had been duped in the past, but this was really interesting, unbelievable to a normal mind. They were not normal; they chased spaceships—normal people they were not! It was the twelfth of December, and most minds were dedicated to Christmas, gifts, parties, and families. James and Nicole didn't really have any of those to speak of, and so they were content to chase this final story to the end!

"So following the money I want you to look at one more thing." Sam showed his scarred left thumb. He walked about the living room like a model on the runway.

James thought that this was out in left field, unless it was the key to open the craft Sam had hidden in the garage. But he had been caught off guard only an hour or so ago too, so he listened. Possibly to check with the FBI; had this all really happened to Sam in his past, and not a total fabrication!

"This scar came from stringing barbed wire with my dad. About two or three months after I got home from Nam. The Army sent a man out to the field to fingerprint me in Nam. They told me that my paperwork had been fouled up and they were reconstructing my 201 file. As I found out later, it was to compare my fingerprints with the man who passed the bogus bills in Sandoval. I was exonerated because I did not have a scar. Carl Flaners gave me this after my hand had healed." Sam gave the fingerprint copy from Viet Nam to James. There was no scar, the attached report said the prints were of Sam Young, currently serving in Viet Nam with the 1st Cavalry Division. The prints had been taken by a man called Chute, agent Chute, CIA. The copy was one Carl had made for his own file. He had never not solved this case and this one he took unsolved to his grave.

"There were depositions taken from my captain and parts of my platoon as to my exact location in Viet Nam. I didn't understand why at the time, until I visited Sandoval earlier this year. Sandoval in 1969. I have had these copies for years in my box of BS. I never throw anything away, but only recently did I start to put two and two together." Sam returned to the couch. Evelyn took his hand and looked at the scar. "I did pass those bogus bills, but they were legal tender in 2005."

"This isn't possible, we have had a lot of cases, but no time traveling. This is something else. You've heard about out-of-body experiences haven't you!" Nicole stated. Her head shook from side to side without her knowledge.

Sam had made extra copies of all the sheets and produced them. He laid them on the coffee table in front of himself and Evelyn. James looked as Sam laid the papers on the table.

"What's that? More paperwork from the past?" James asked Sam.

"Most are copies of what I have shown you. One is my paid receipt form the Palace Motel in Sandoval. You can have all of this, I don't want any of it anymore. You can have the paper tested for age. I figure you have the ability to have that done in your labs too. Now, just how nuts am I!" Sam rubbed his neck. He was tired but relieved that the story, most of it, was out. "I have just a bit more to tell, then you will have a few questions, I'm sure."

Nods were all about the room. No one wanted to say or ask anything at this juncture. James and Nicole wanted more, to find out how true it all was, or how fake it all had been—the jury was still out on that decision! Evelyn was worried about where this might leave her and Sam. She had never seen Sam this emotional. Sara had been his first love! And she had given Sam a new direction. That direction had been burned with all of his wishes, desires, and hopes.

James looked to Nicole, neither saying a word, but both knowing this man might be stark raving mad! He could also be the key to the object of their direction, and at times meaningless direction. James had become quite soured at the alien chasing for the last few years, and had considered his training as an anthropologist for some time. He didn't want to become one of those he had replaced those many years ago. Old, single minded, and pursuing an endless dream, with no reality to ever emerge from his life's work. And then of course there were the never-ending trials and tribulations with Nicole. They were too old to start a family, at least he was, wasn't he? Nicole had been his love for many years and he knew she understood that, although he had never really professed it! Not in so many words. James's mind came back to Sam, and his sanity, his story—was it just a story? If he had all the answers, where would that take him? James's face frowned; it had become a natural reaction to his mental picture of his life. James looked to Sam. "Go on."

Nicole had thoughts of what was going through Sam's mind. He was unsure, he didn't want to be the idiot, but he had a story to tell. Was it real? She would have to talk to Evelyn, then she would know. Nicole heard James say go on. "Yes, let's. I want to see the end. I will have my questions, the same ones I arrived with. But let's go on."

Sam was arranging his life before the strangers. They were, after all, strangers—did they believe them? Was Sam as good a salesman in ghosts as he was at property? Some of this was strictly Sam bemoaning his life, as though he had not accomplished anything without "Sam." If that were the case where was he now? Was he invisible, hiding under the couch and taking notes! Where was that, that...entity, when you needed him! He was supposed to be here for Sam, and now for her, too! She didn't like "Sam," but she wanted him to appear now! Pop in! Help!

"And so you see, I have come to the point in my life where I have begun to question everything in my life that I thought was real! I don't know anymore, but my life story was due to be told. Now I wonder if 'Sam' will allow me to continue to live, what he has created!" Sam slipped his arm around Evelyn and pulled her closer. "I have a life now. I don't want anything to change. If I have to start over, then that's what I will do. Me and Evie!" Sam kissed Evelyn on the cheek.

Nicole was first in the chute. "Let me see if I have this right? You think that 'Sam' has influenced all of your life, he has somehow directed all you have done. You, as Mr. Samuel Young, have done nothing on your own!"

"Well, I have done some things, it's not been entirely run by 'Sam.' I have a mind of my own, I think. But you see where I'm coming from. 'Sam' has been a part of my life for so long, even when I didn't know it!" Sam looked at Nicole in a pathetic fashion. He started to continue his answer, but Nicole stopped him.

"Evelyn, what were you doing when 'Sam' appeared?" Nicole looked to Evelyn, who was a little taken aback.

"I...I was getting ready to clean up after lunch. And all of a sudden he was here." Evelyn was still not sure what she had to do with Sam's story.

"What did he look like?" Nicole was pen in hand, paper on her knee.

"What do you mean?"

"What did he look like? What was he wearing?"

"That's when I knew he was Sam." Evelyn was trying not to mar Sam's story with her impressions.

"He was Sam?" Nicole scratched something on her paper.

"Yes, his hair was darker. Sam has light hair anyway, but not as much gray!" Evelyn ran her fingers through Sam's hair, looked at him and smiled. "His voice was Sam's, younger, but definitely Sam's. He stood by the counter, or at least tried, I really think he floated, just off the floor. I couldn't really tell, but his movements were slow, like in a Godzilla movie, the mouth and the voice were off, disjointed! When he moved it was like he had thought it out but was slow in making it happen, out of step with himself! His voice was soft and mechanical. But not…not natural." Evelyn was trying to keep the place where she was now not influence her memory, tell it like it had just happened.

Nicole started to ask a question, and Evelyn cut her short.

"Something else, I remember that I was trying to explain touching to 'Sam.' He really wanted to know about human emotions, and kisses, and hugs. I was going to hug him and show him what a hug was. He moved so quickly that I only saw him in a new position. I never recalled seeing him move, now or then he moved, just being moved to a new place. He told me that I could not touch him! He was adamant about that! He was energy only and could not be touched! And he was very vague about the guy that runs his world, er…Spirit! Yes, that's it, Spirit! Spirit is his leader, his boss. He asks everything of Spirit!"

"Anything else you can remember?" Nicole had been taking note as fast as Evelyn spoke. James had been taking his own as well. Nicole had been watching James; they would compare and argue the notes later.

"Well…I understand most that he said. I get the feeling that he wanted to ask more, but was unsure how to ask. I also developed my own feelings. I was afraid of him, I am afraid of him! I don't trust him! I think he has a plan for Sam, and it doesn't include me!" Evelyn felt Sam's hand relax around her waist. "And one more thing! Then I'm done! I have sat and watched Sam put himself through the agony of what he has told you, the telling of the fire, his feelings for Sara." Evelyn paused and wiped her eyes; they were glistening with a light covering of moisture. "I have heard in Sam's voice, that had the fire not happened in Mississippi, I would not be here now! I think that 'Sam' caused that to happen, and I don't know what he has planned for me, but it won't be nice! I am afraid! Sam was so happy! And...." Sobs took over where her voice had been. Sam pulled her into his side and wiped her eyes.

Nicole stopped writing; James picked his up, at faster pace. James and Nicole looked at one another. James's hand took Nicole's and squeezed it slightly. She smiled at James. She wanted to do more, but this wasn't the time.

Evelyn's sobs slowed. She apologized for her outburst, wiped her eyes again. "I can't think of anything else. I have seen 'Sam' three times, is all. He is a being to be reckoned with!" Evelyn wiped her eyes and put her arm around Sam's shoulder.

James released Nicole's hand, laid his pad down. "Well, we had planned to leave, but if you two are willing I would like to ask a few more questions, and spend one more night here. I think it might be another long night! I know where most everything is located here, how about some coffee?" James stood slowly.

All nodded in the affirmative, and James was off to the kitchen. Nicole excused herself and was off to the bathroom. Evelyn and Sam sat quietly. After a few minutes that seemed like hours, Sam turned to Evelyn, put his hand under her chin and tilted her head back, so he could see her eyes.

"Evie, are you really afraid?" Sam's hand was still holding her chin. Evelyn tried to pull away, but Sam held her close.

"Yes! Yes I am." Tears began to run down her cheeks again.

"So am I. We'll move. We'll go far, far away, I won't let him hurt you!" Sam looked into Evelyn's eyes. He had not looked at her like this in a while. James and Nicole had taken away a lot of private moments, but they had brought out a lot of feelings too, good and bad!

"Sam! Listen to yourself! You just told your life's story! 'Sam' has followed you to Viet Nam and back, do you think Colorado or Maine will keep him from following us! You can't look away, this won't disappear like 'Sam' does! I'm afraid for me, and for you! I don't know what his plan is, but we have to do something! And I have no idea what!" Tears streamed down Evelyn's cheeks. Sam tried to stop the flow, but there were too many.

Sam pulled Evelyn closer and held her tighter. He didn't know what to do, and his ace in the hole, James, more than likely didn't know either! Sam watched as first Nicole returned and sat quietly, followed by James with coffee for all. James returned the coffee pot to the kitchen and returned. The living room had been quiet the entire time. Evelyn and Nicole looked about the room as though in a doctor's office, uncomfortable, and not likely to get much better in the near future.

Sam finished up a few points about his business, how ideas had come to him in his sleep, and how he had never questioned any thoughts till the substation fire. The fire had set more machinery in motion than just fire trucks! "I have an opinion. Like assholes, everyone's got one, and here's mine. I keep most of my money tied up in government bonds, why I don't know, but most is not easily accessible. I don't know why, I just do. It's not easily accessible, if 'Sam' needs money, I can't imagine why. Just a thought! When 'Sam' showed himself I was surprised, to Evelyn anyway. I imagined he would have to sooner or later. But when he came to Evie by himself I became suspicious. We were a little cool here for a few days. But 'Sam' had told me that he was only mine. He was here for me, always. I was glad he finally showed himself to someone, especially the one I love, and I truly believe she had begun to think I was a little off of it! 'Sam' was always there for me, not showing up, but there. He hasn't shown up since you have been here. That's not unusual, he hadn't shown to anyone in fifty-five years. But when I was alone, when I had personal problems he would be there. I have had a lot of problems lately. No 'Sam.' Why, I don't know. Some of his remarks have been allowed to be analyzed of late. 'Sam' has told me that I will never be aware of how many times he has helped me, nor will I ever. I remember as a child he was never satisfied with my performance, always pushing. I remember seeing a glow in my room at night, not 'Sam,' just a glow. Some kids have the closet monsters, I had a glow. I was never afraid of the dark. I can remember accepting that glow. I knew it was good, even when I began to doubt myself. But I always kept a low key, I was never an outgoing person. I do not attempt to have any idea where this conversation is going, I wanted to tell you of it and the knowledge I have in my subconscious mind. But all of those years, and now he's back. He's here for a reason, I don't know what. But if you have been looking all of these years, I think I've found your alien, 'Sam.' He's here to do something."

"What! He has never been bad, has he? He has never done you any harm?" James asked.

"No, but I remember a glow in the motel room, and I slept very late. I never saw him for years—the fire, Sara, my life, my business, Evelyn. He showed himself to Evelyn, so she would be comfortable with him. So she would not shy away. We cannot touch him, he is energy. But he can touch us, he kissed

Evelyn's hand. If he is energy, why couldn't he have damaged the substation? Incredible energy, the paper said, incredible energy the firemen said, incredible energy, James said. Incredible energy could fuse rock into an new form, something that we have never seen. I'm not telling you anything, you told me. I am not bright enough to have thought of it. You are, you can help us, help us get away. 'Ghost Busters,' God I hope so!" Sam paused and looked about the room. It was full dark outside now. "It's going to happen soon. I can feel it!"

III

James and Nicole stayed for two additional days, questions, and a few answers, not many. The questions were generally how to get "Sam" to show up! Show up was not like turning a light switch to the on position. When no one was around Sam called "Sam" and Friend out loud; he felt foolish afterward, especially when James caught him in the garage calling out loud. James and Nicole had begun to doubt Sam's sanity. Nicole even tried to ask about psychiatric help. That had not gone well! Sam had all but ordered them out of his house. It had taken the better part of the last day to cool down. Goodbyes were exchanged, and James and Nicole were back to Arizona for the holidays. Sam felt an impending doom settle on his shoulders as they drove away. There was snow on the ground, just three inches, but it was cold.

Evelyn and Nicole had been shopping, Christmas shopping. Evelyn and Nicole had had many conversations, about Sam and "Sam." Evelyn had been very put off in the beginning at the suggestion of shopping. The conversations about Sam and "Sam" had consumed most of the time when not picking out sweaters and stocking stuffers. Evelyn had bought a large artificial tree and brought it home on the next to last day of Nicole's stay. They had all put it together that night, had a few drinks, and had fun. The conversations had been about their individual lives. It had been grand.

While cleaning up the dishes, Nicole had asked a question of Evelyn, a question that didn't register till later, after they had gone. "Do you know what Sam's getting you for Christmas? I believe I saw him out today. First Christmas...I hope to have a real first Christmas one day. James is so absorbed in all his work..." The conversation went on; the business of why James and Nicole were there became secondary. Evelyn had not seen Sam out shopping, ever, but she too forgot the question as idle prattle. But in the evening Sam was making a fire in the fireplace, the tree up now, standing to the right of the fireplace. Packages had been wrapped, seven or eight, and he was caught by Evelyn as she brought drinks to the living room.

"No peeking! Unless, of course, I get to peek!" Evelyn set the drinks on the coffee table.

"Well, I'll have to give you a rain check on that! You don't have any yet! I'm going to go tomorrow. The men folk stayed here and had a séance while you two were out on the town. We tried to call up the spirit of 'Sam' past!" Sam directed his attention to the meager fire he had started, and began to add some small pieces.

"Nicole said she thought she had seen you in Centralia yesterday. She said in a blue car." Evelyn had a feeling but it went away; Nicole couldn't very well see Sam if he had been here.

"I'm not sure the old Dodge would make it that far. I'm going to have to hire a mechanic, get that Dodge worked on, or bury it. I think it is about to die on me. I need to get out to the garage and check on the heat too. Maybe I'll get the Chevelle out." Sam knew better than that, there was snow on the ground, but he could get something else out, and drive for a while. Maybe the blue Mustang.

Evelyn thought, the blue Mustang, what Nicole had said was "blue car"! Evelyn put a Christmas CD in the stereo and forgot about it. She too had a few more gifts to buy, she needed to go to Penny's and pick up that big sweater she and Nicole had looked at. "Silver Bells" began to play and she began to mouth the words, very quietly, and she began to forget about the blue car, and Sam.

IV

Christmas! A joyous time, bells, and songs and friends, and shopping! Evelyn liked shopping, but not at Christmas. The crowds, the cars, the cold. And it was cold. Five days before Christmas, Evelyn had been in Mt. Vernon, and had looked at Penny's for a sweater for Sam. None to be had, so it was one more stop, but she had to go to Centralia. A bit out of the way, but she was done then, and she did so want the sweater. Evelyn was singing, humming along with the CD not really knowing what was being played, the old favorites that were in her mind, she was happy. She had taken the interstate, and had driven up Route 51 to Centralia. Lights shone everywhere, a light snow had fallen, and the lights were pretty, decorations in the yards, and happy people inside. Evelyn could remember the odors of Christmas, cookies, and pies. Her house had been like a bakery just before Christmas. She wished she had been better in the kitchen. But she had made up for a lot of it, and had bought fresh-baked bread and cookies for Sam. It might not have been her cooking, but it smelled good.

Her car was almost like home! She always went around the downtown area, but wanted to see the decorations in town. She was in the left lane to jockey for the turn to the shopping center when she saw Sam, he was at the Standard station getting gas. Evelyn honked her horn and waved. Sam was getting into his car, the blue Mustang. Evelyn turned a block before her intended turn and thought she would catch up with Sam and they would have coffee somewhere, then she could go and get his sweater. Traffic was horrible, and she turned down the alleyway to cut a half block off her pursuit. It was one way, and she was heading the wrong direction. She turned into a parking lot to cut over to Elm Street. Caught by traffic again, she watched as Sam pulled out of the Standard station. Evelyn honked and waved. People looked at her and smiled; they didn't let her into traffic, but they smiled. Sam drove away. Evelyn, in aggravation hit her horn again. The lady in the car in front of her lost her smile, her mouth moved to the sound of "Oh Santa Claus." Evelyn didn't think she was singing! The blue Mustang disappeared past the buildings. Evelyn knew it was a lost cause, she would never catch him now. She waited for traffic to clear, turned left and back on track for the shopping center. The CD started over.

Evelyn's mind listened to "Jingle Bells" as she made her turn into the shopping center. He said he was going to have to get another car, the old Dodge had just about had it. Nicole had seen Sam in a blue car, the day they had been shopping, the Dodge was blue, but it was a grayish blue. She had just been mistaken! Evelyn had to park in the outer limits of the shopping center; it was going to be a madhouse in Penny's! Evelyn shut everything down in the car, took a deep breath, exhaled, put on her best smile and was off to the Christmas rush!

"Sam" drove out of Centralia. He was thinking about how to approach Sam. The traffic was heavy. All his skills were necessary to keep from driving over people as they moved about. They needed to have more skills before being allowed to drive automobiles. They pulled out into the road in front of him. He had hit the brakes hard once or twice. He had fueled the car and would be good on fuel for some time now. "Sam" drove out 161 till the Bell Club road and turned north. The car slew around as he made his turn; he had been going too fast. Back under control his thought process told him to be more careful, cars didn't do well when striking trees. His thought process recalled Wes' accident, but he had not been in control, "Sam" was, he had been then too. A smile formed on his human countenance. He chuckled. *This is going to be easier than I had planned!* "Sam" thought, as he navigated through traffic, someone going home from shopping. It's a God thing, he only knew that humans worshiped a "God," just one. It would be so much easier than having many religions, there were a few. A few that he was going to change. Maybe not, maybe they could keep their religion, but they would worship him, "Sam," a nice name; he had gotten used to it and he liked it! He honked the horn as he passed and waved! The lady smiled and waved back. "Sam" kept the smile on his face; he was beginning to like it too!

V

Spirit didn't like the attitude of this man who had decided to call himself Energy. But at the same time he had been nice, quiet, and he had the information that Spirit needed to find Energy. They sat quietly for what seemed many time. He could not judge time, but he knew time was not a thing to squander in the human world. "I must ask, I do not mean to be impertinent, but I do need to meet with Energy. That is why I was summoned, to meet Energy." Spirit felt good here with this human that had assumed the name of his search.

"Spirit, I need to show you more. You have been in service of me for many years. Are you comfortable with years, or time?" the human asked in matter-of-fact fashion.

"You know of time? You have sign to understand?" Spirit ask.

"Yes, I know of time. Time is all there is, anymore. When humans come here time goes on. They do not gauge time as you and I. Perhaps there is no need to count days, years, time. It will never end; it, time will go on forever. Forever, a reward for a true life, a life in me. Come with me, I have something to show you." Energy stood and held his hand outstretched to Spirit.

Spirit stood, an unconscious move, no thought process involved, he stood. He felt his face move, his hand touched it. It was a smile, another unconscious move. As he felt the smile, it grew wider. He chuckled, aloud!

Energy chuckled as well. "It is different, isn't it! Feeling, sound, all of this!" Energy spread his arms and turned completely around, his head tilted back. He too had a wide smile. "I too find all of this quite to my liking. I created the surroundings, but not alone. You have been in service far too long. This is your future." Energy walked, his footfalls caused sound, each footfall.

The wind was gentle, the leaves moved, they touched one another causing sound. As they walked, Spirit could hear both of their feet in the rock. The sky had clouds, white and billowy, the sky was a beautiful blue. Children played and chased one another, they sounded...happy! The path was lined with trees, all green, some dark, some light, and all colors in between. The air was full of smells, trees, grass, the air, the beauty of all the human world, in one place. Ahead in their path was an opening, the trees fell away to small shrubs; they were neatly trimmed, as was the grass. A placid lake was before them. People young and old were sitting on the banks fishing. One small boat glided lazily on the surface. A man slowly rowed the boat, it was almost silent, only the oars made a slight sound as they entered the water for the next stroke. Swifts skimmed the water and took up the insects that hovered there. A small girl caught a fish. She giggled and held it up by the line. An elderly gentleman removed the fish and laid it back in the water gently.

"What does this have to do with my being summoned to meet with Energy?" Spirit asked the stranger; he couldn't bring himself to call him Energy. Himself, he had never thought of his entity as "himself"!

"As I told you, Spirit, I am Energy! Maybe I'm not as colossal as you might have thought, and no, you're not going to be recalled. Not in the sense that you are thinking. Recall is going to happen, but it will be your recall, your life before here. Yes, you had a life. You too were human once, you died! That's how you came to be in my service as an entity. You don't remember the early years, your early years, as an entity. You were not always, Spirit. A history, your history, it will take a wee short bit of a time, but you will remember. It is a matter of fact, we do deal with fact here, most do not dawdle on fact. That is, as you say, time past." Energy walked toward the water and gestured with his left hand. Look, see what troubles you!

Spirit paused in his time, his time, he had never had time, for his entity, at least. The sun was bright, warm, and the day was a wonder. Spirit looked about the clearing. He had become, totally, part of this world. Spirit had not uttered a word. He stepped forward and looked at the water. Birds sang, a fish broke water, and the boat moved silently.

VI

Evelyn had just finished wrapping Sam's sweater and had headed for the kitchen to check on the pot pies, as Sam came in the back door. "Sammie, I tried to catch up with you today so we could have coffee or something." Evelyn looked about the back window as she rinsed the mashed potato pan. The Dodge was sitting in the driveway, in the back. Evelyn felt like someone walked on her grave! "Didn't you go to the garage and get the Mustang, the blue Mustang? It's an old one isn't it?"

"Yeah! It a 1967 classic, fastback, with white racing stripes. I don't want to drive it in this weather. I'm thinking about a Jeep, or something like that. I…."

Evelyn cut him short. "You haven't been driving it?"

"No, I told you that I don't want to drive it in this weather! What's the matter?" Sam froze while his shedding of his coat. "Are you alright?"

"I have only seen pictures of the Mustang. It's about medium blue, fastback, and has two stripes from front to back. Am I right?" Evelyn stood with her hand holding the oven door partly opened.

"What's going on, are you alright?" Sam finished taking his coat off and stood holding it like a school boy just in from play.

"Sam, I swear to God, I saw you in Centralia today at the Standard station. I know it was you, and I couldn't get turned around to catch you!" Her thoughts were not on the oven. The heat began to build up on her arm as she stood holding the door slightly open. She let it go and it slammed shut. The noise brought them both back to reality.

"You were mistaken. I never left Salem today. I haven't been to Centralia in a couple of days." Sam resumed his slow walk to Evelyn, he put his arm around her, and drew her close. "What's going on, Evie?"

"Sam, I swear it was you, you had on that coat! Blue pants, and…and…I know it was you!" Evelyn laid her head against Sam's chest. "It was you, Sam."

"You know we have all been through a lot in the last few weeks. All because of some stupid idea that I've lived with for years, now I know the truth. Well, at least all they will tell me. When the holidays are over we will see if there is anything else that they have found. Then we will just live our lives, together. Just you and me!" Sam was trying to sound confident, but Evelyn's demeanor had thrown him off. He was racing his mind to all the known causes of Evelyn's upset. But all signs pointed to "Sam." Sam didn't want to say his name. He was afraid, he was getting more afraid.

Evelyn pushed away from Sam and turned back to the oven. "I think they are done now!" Evelyn pulled the rack out. The pot pies were a little more than golden brown, but still edible.

Dinner was quiet, neither wanted to mention "Sam," and at the same time they both knew where the conversation was headed. Sam helped Evelyn to clean the table and the few dishes that the dinner had taken. Sam put on a pot of coffee; they would both need it. Evelyn closed the cabinet and turned toward Sam.

"Can he drive?"

"Who?"

"Don't play dumb, you know who."

"He's ridden with me, but the only thing I have ever seen him even hold, or try to hold was my airplane, when we were kids." Sam thought abut his own statement as he said it, When we were kids. They had been kids together, well at least he had been a kid, and "Sam" had been there too; he was the same height as Sam. They had done the same things. He hadn't ridden a bike, he only rode on the handlebars. He had no weight, the bike pedaled the same with or without him, and Sam had never touched him. Only been a kid with him. Now "Sam" was all grown up too! Just like Sam. Just like Sam. Sam I am, I am "Sam."

"Did he take any particular attention to you while you drove? Did he ask any questions? What did he do?" Evelyn was trying to answer questions that Sam looked confused about.

"I don't know. He never asked any questions, he just sat there, well floated. His hair didn't blow, I don't think. I really don't know. I got used to him and just accepted him!" Sam rubbed his chin and shook his head. "I just accepted him. But I never really saw him! I never really had him in the car, that I know. But now, now I know he was there!"

"You just accepted him? He's a fucking ghost, and he rides around with you like one of the boys! How can you just accept him? You don't even remember him being in the car? But now, now you remember it! How?" Evelyn's voice had risen slightly and was a little strained. She waved her arms around, and the dishtowel swirled in front of her.

Sam caught the dishtowel. Evelyn held fast the other end, and Sam pulled her into his arms.

"I've got to think about all of the last few weeks, and I've got to come up with some answers of my own. We might just have a 'good fairy'!" Sam kissed Evelyn's forehead, he then rested his forehead against hers. "I had not wanted to talk about this before Christmas, but, here we are. Coffee?"

"Coffee?"

"Yeah, it might be quite a conversation." Sam opened the cabinet and took out two cups, filled both. "Here, or the living room?"

"Living room. Yes, I need some Christmas spirit!" Evelyn preceded Sam and plugged in all the lights.

Sam carried both cups of coffee, which he had overfilled, into the living room slowly, and set them on the coffee table. He straightened up and looked at all the Christmas lights; they twinkled and flashed. The garland and lights on the mantle warmed up and began to flash too, tiny white lights tucked into the fake pine needles and draped across the mantle, stockings had been hung with care! The tree was perfect. Of course it should be, it was a fake tree, but it looked magnificent. Sam had not had a Christmas tree since his parents had been killed. There were angels on the mantle, his mom's angels; he hadn't seen those in years. Sam walked to the mantle. He touched each of the figurines, looking close to see every detail. It had been a lot of years. Now, his life would be real, again, he and Evelyn! Sam smiled. He touched his face and felt the smile; it hadn't been real in some time!

Evelyn stepped up to Sam and held a piece of mistletoe over him. "I found a lot of stuff in the attic. I thought it might be nice, I hope you don't mind."

Sam kissed Evelyn long and gentle. He pulled her tight against him. "It's all beautiful! Next year we'll have a real tree! I haven't had a Christmas in years, just at business parties, and that's all about money. You, me, here in our house, our first Christmas. You have made this place look great! I love you!" Sam kissed Evelyn again; he still held her tight.

Evelyn wiggled away. "Not tonight, till we talk. This is really bothering me. Do you think 'Sam' could be driving your car?" Evelyn crossed to the couch, sat down and took up her coffee. "I know you don't want to talk about all of this, and quite frankly I don't either. But I have a few things I have to ask you. There has been a lot of things that have come out in the last few months. I am not comfortable with all of them, you might be! Make me comfortable with them too, please!" Evelyn looked over the rim of her cup. Vapors swirled around her head from the coffee. "Please, Sam!"

Sam was in pacing mode. He tried to look like he was deep into decorations and continued to touch and examine. Sam's fingers stroked the angel wings. "Evelyn. Evie, I too am bothered by what all has gone on, not bothered, scared! I have seen things brought out of the dark, and into the light, so to speak. I have always known that I had an angel, a whatever "Sam" is—I don't know how to tell you. I knew that he would get me out of whatever I got into. When a person knows that nothing is going to happen to him, no matter what he does, he kind of lets it all hang out! I've done some stuff in my life that has proved that. The bullet is my remembrance of one time in particular. I knew I hadn't seen him in years, but I knew he was there. Every time that I would almost forget about him, something would show me that he was still there!" Sam still caressed the angel wings. He stepped away from the fireplace and looked into the fire. The blaze was hot; it caused shadows to dance about all the decorations, dark to light. Combined with the Christmas lights it was a sight to warm Sam's heart. But his thoughts didn't get far away from the subject at hand, "Sam." "Ask what you will. I hope I can make it clearer than James and Nicole did while they were here."

Evelyn was full of questions, but didn't want Sam to think that she was prying into another part of his life that might still remain untold. "Has 'Sam' ever tried to hurt you? I don't mean that, but you know, has he ever made any move that wasn't...right? I know what I want to know, but don't know how to ask it, I guess."

"'Sam' has never done anything to steer me wrong, or anything like that. He has always been there for me, and now for you! But— I don't know what, but I've had a bad feeling. Yeah, I was a little jealous when I came in and found you and 'Sam' having a conversation. I forgot that he's like... like... I guess you're right, a ghost! I thought that he was cutting in on my girl! The love of my life! But I have not seen him in years, and now, until you said it, he does look like me! I'm not sure I understand it, but he does look like me. The way I would like to look now, ten years younger. And I have been searching my brain. Somewhere inside it seems to have shook something loose. I remember him in my Chevelle, on several occasions, but I didn't see him!"

"The man I saw today was a spitting image of you. You today! Not ten years ago! I only saw him across the street, and there was a lot of traffic, and I was in the left lane. I might have been mistaken, but...." Evelyn tapered her question off, and her voice trailed away at the same time.

"You know they say that everyone has a double. I've never seen mine, and I feel sorry for him if he looks like me, but it had to have been someone else." Sam sat down by Evelyn, he patted her leg. Sam thought that after the holidays they would go away for a while, and get all of this straight. If that was possible, he was beginning to doubt his own story, lately.

"But what about the car?"

"Well, they made a lot of them. I'm just lucky to have one of them, that and Wes made it alright again. It wasn't in the best of shape when I bought it." Sam tried to change the subject. He wanted to answer all of her questions, but he didn't have the answers. "I'll go to the garage tomorrow and check it out. Okay!" Sam had hoped that would make all the questions go away, at least till he found out where the Mustang was, or wasn't.

"I'll go with you!"

"I've got to do some Christmas shopping and will just stop off there; it's on the way. My cars are alright. I do need to get a new mechanic to keep them running. Maybe I'll run an ad tomorrow too!" Sam didn't want her along, if "Sam" was there he had some questions of his own.

VII

Holiday spirit was alive and well in more places than most would ever have suspected! "Sam" was playing the radio, and of course Christmas music was played on most all stations, and "Sam" liked the music, not that hard music that Sam listened to.

He swayed as he moved about the room. He could hear his feet touch down on the floor, he could feel them touch. He had gotten much better. He could open doors, and drive, and talk. Mostly without his thought process making it happen, it had become "natural." He was almost human, as much as he needed. His skin was natural; the color was a little light, but he was to be a white man, he was to be Sam. The real Sam. He would become, he would not have to be fake anymore. He had been watching Sam. He did not understand who those people were. He could not let Sam know he was present. Sam generally knew when he was there, and he did not want him to have any indication that he was around. The time was close, he would reveal himself soon, but first the last of his plan was about to take place. "Sam" continued to keep time with the music. He bumped into a car, his clothes became loose as his form shrank to allow his real self to absorb the impact, his pants fell to his thighs. He stopped and adjusted his clothing, his hand passed through his belted pants, again, his hands grasped again and pulled his pants back into place. His legs had been opaque, not colored well, but humans always wore clothes, and no one would see his legs, except maybe one.

"Sam's" thought process was working on the pants and the music. He had not heard the car outside, nor the side door open. His clothing adjusted, he swayed again to the music.

"What the Hell's going on here?" Sam almost yelled. He didn't want to anger the man he saw before him. It was him, he was looking back at himself, same coat, same hair, same everything!

"Sam! I have not seen you in many time! I tied to visit, but you had other humans there, and I could not come into your house! Others might not understand." "Sam" stood behind the blue Mustang. His thought process was making decisions, immediate decisions. This would be the test, the real test. "Sam" stepped from behind the car to expose his entity, his Sam. His feet made sound as he did so, his clothes were now real clothes, and they moved as they should. He placed his hands on his hips and looked back at his new image, his real image, Sam! "Well, how do you like the new me, or should I say you? I have always liked being your entity, and now I am you. I will do so many things for you. I will be with you always."

"What have you been doing here? Have you been driving?" Sam saw mud splashes on the Mustang's paint. "What's going on, 'Sam'?" Sam stepped into the garage and walked in an arc around "Sam." "I haven't seen you in a few weeks, I thought you had gone."

"I will never leave you. I am yours." "Sam" turned to keep his eyes on Sam. "I have emulated you to better do my work." "Sam" concentrated to ensure all was "normal."

"Your work! What have you done! What work! I thought you were here for me and Evie." Sam paced back toward the door in a reverse arc.

"Sam" closed the door, he closed it hard. The door locked with an audible click as the metal made movements inside the mechanism. No gestures, just energy! "Let's go into my office. We can talk there." "Sam" gestured toward the garage office.

"I'm not sure I want to go anywhere, at least till you do some explaining! What kind of work are you doing?" Sam wanted to bolt for the door, but he had heard the lock; as hard as the door had slammed he wasn't sure it would open anyway. He gestured for "Sam" to go ahead of him. Sam looked about the room. Papers with writing were pinned to the walls, everywhere. "What's all this on the walls? It looks like a school room!"

"I did not think of it as that. It is a school room though, my school room. Not like your school rooms in time past, but enough for me. I have been learning the ways of humans. I can write now." "Sam" opened the door. Sam could feel the heat, it was incredibly hot in the garage.

"Sam" entered the office, stood by the door waiting on Sam. He bowed slightly at the waist, and gestured with his right hand for Sam to enter. "Please, come in. I have seen on the television many courtesies. This is correct, I believe." "Sam" gestured again.

Sam was still looking about the room. The Mustang had been moved; the cover was folded neatly and lay on the shelf. The Chevelle was uncovered; it had dust on the finish. It had been uncovered for some time now. All the other covers were in place, but had been moved, and the tie-downs were loose, some were not in the proper positions.

"Sam! Come into the office, now!"

The voice was not in his head, it was loud! Sam thought about the door again, hesitated, then turned toward the office. "Sam" had a look of…of rage! That melted into a smile that was natural, no blurring, a natural facial expression. Then a smile, a smile that was hiding many secrets. Sam wasn't sure he wanted to know those secrets, not anymore! He walked hesitantly into the office. It was hot!

"I don't know what your job is, but it must be in real need of heat. It's hotter than Hell in here! I can't hardly breathe in here!" The heat was almost overwhelming in the office.

"I can adjust it somewhat for you." The thermostat moved to sixty-eight, and heat moved cross the room to "Sam." "Sam" held his arms away form his body and the heat entered into his entity; he was still smiling. "Better now?"

The room had gone from ninety-plus to sixty-eight degrees in a matter of a split second. It was now comfortable again. Papers were on all the walls. Here they had legible writing on them. Sam read what was on the papers. It was his signature, it was milk, orange juice, Chevrolet, GM, Ford, Chocolate. Sam scanned the other papers that were tacked to the walls. With each sheet the writing improved, each had a number, the one he looked at had 564 at the top.

"Sit!"

Sam pulled the desk chair out from the desk. It set somewhat askew. He sat down. It was loose. He leaned back and forth, and the chair wobbled.

"Sam" watched Sam. "I will try and fix the chair again. I do not need the chair, and have not tried to fix it again. But I will, because it is your chair." "Sam's" thought registered the thought and filed it away. "I have learned to control that anger. I have fixed most all faults. I will fix all in the end." "Sam" took up a seat on the wooden stool by the book rack. "Now what do you need to know?" "Sam" asked. His lips moved in unison to his voice, no more Godzilla movie.

"Okay. First off, are you driving?" Sam wanted to look about the room more, but he wanted to watch "Sam" even more.

"Yes."

"The blue Mustang?"

"Yes."

"Were you in Centralia?" Sam started to stand up, but could not.

Sam struggled, trying to stand. He quit as he realized it was a lost cause. "Where else have you been?"

"Do not struggle, Sam. You and I have signs, conversation to hold now. I will let you stand later. I have been to most stores in Centralia—that is the town west of here, right?" "Sam" pointed east.

"Why are you like me?" Sam pushed slightly, and his back was pushed to the back of the chair; now that too would not move.

"I am not like you. I am you. I have all of your details, most of your gestures, and have only to refine a few minor little details. Has my voice improved? I do hope so. I have used much energy to make my entity to be your exact double!" Sam kicked the bookcase hard. Books and magazines fell to the floor. Then they leaped back to their original placement on the bookcase. "Sam" smiled.

"So are you becoming a magician? That was a neat trick." Sam watched the bookcase to see if the magazines would fall again.

"I use no magic, only energy. I have had time to improve my skills. I have improved many things. You will help me with others. My vocabulary has expanded. I still do not understand a few things, but I am sure I can receive assistance from you. I have assisted you for many times now, it would only seem natural, that you would assist my entity, Sam." "Sam" shifted his form on the stool. His position was not good. Had he really been human, he was sitting on less of the stool than would be necessary, he should fall. But he did not. He sat quietly, not a care of his perilous position.

Sam just watched and waited. As "Sam" shifted his position, he exposed his leg just above his right sock. Sam could see through it, not clear but almost. The sock was pulled tight, no wrinkles, perfectly smooth. "Where did you get your clothes?"

"J.C. Penny's. That is one of the places I have visited. Do you like my choices in garments?" "Sam" opened his coat, stood and turned around. He was wearing a turtleneck shirt and brown trousers, all matched in color and were worn and moved as anyone's clothes would. He looked human. His pant leg had fallen back into the proper position and no longer exposed his transparent leg. "Sam's" apparel almost matched Sam's.

"The shirt is a little lightweight for the cold, don't you think? Is that why the heat was so high in here?" Sam looked for a false answer. None came.

"Yes, I have found that the cold affects me now that I have been using manmade power." Sam sat back on the stool in the right position. The stool made a slight sliding sound as he sat down. The screech was like chalk on a board! "I did have a few problems in the beginning of my change. Driving was exciting. You must show me how the shifter works in the red car. I was unable to cause it to work properly. The blue car is much easier to operate, but I do so like the red car. We rode many miles in that car, when you escaped from the Army."

"I didn't escape. I got out. Have you driven other cars? And how did you pay for the clothes?" Sam wiggled again. Each time he moved he could move less and less.

"I got money, money from your bank. I have seen you many times use the small card. I made myself one, and have unlimited access to money." "Sam" was confident now. This conversation was simple, no questions that he could not answer now. "Ask me more, it has been a long time since we have had the time to talk. I am yours, and I do not get to talk much since Evelyn has come into your life, I guess I should say 'our lives.'"

"I don't want you around Evelyn! You leave her out of this! She's scared to death! She doesn't know what you can do, I have not told her very much!" Sam thought that he might be able to get something that resembled logic out of "Sam." He had changed much since they had last met.

"I will care for Evelyn, just as I have cared for you. In the beginning I was afraid she would have to be removed. But I have decided that she has made you happy. And she can stay." "Sam's" reply was as matter-of-fact as anyone could answer.

"What do you mean, removed!" Sam struggled to get out of the chair. All he could do now was wiggle. His hands were glued to the chair arms now too!

"Sometimes you have been difficult on yourself with choices. I have directed you to do the right thing. I have directed you to certain people and places, like George, and Wes. I have...."

Sam cut "Sam's" oration short. "What do you mean, removed!" Sam struggled against invisible bonds, they only held tighter.

"Sam! I am limited in what I can do! If you continue to struggle, you will cause yourself to fall to the floor! I cannot restrain you and catch you at the same time! I have limits! Even an entity of my power has limits! I will correct that soon enough! Now sit still. I will release you soon enough. My entity did not want you to harm yourself. Now sit still!" "Sam" had an expression on his face that meant business.

Sam quit struggling and he felt the tightness of his invisible bonds relax. He swallowed, his throat had become very dry. "All I ask, what do you mean by removed?"

"Such as in Wes... he was consuming liquids at an alarming rate, he was not completing any of your work, he had others in this garage. The liquid was going to ruin him in the long time yet to come. I made it easy for him to make his own decision." "Sam" leaned against the bookcase. He rested his head in his hand, but his elbow was not touching the bookcase.

"So you killed Wes, and you would kill Evelyn?"

"I told you that I had decided she could stay. You will have many times together. You are to be married? Yes? But Wes should have been finished with my project many times faster. He has not started on your small car. You will find a new mechanic, and I will help you if you like." "Sam" smiled.

"You killed Wes? What the Hell is in that head you now have? Why did you kill him?"

Sam struggled again and found himself held tight.

"I did not kill him, I only directed him to pilot his car into a large tree. That accomplished what was needed. There will be others that will need to be directed, just as Wes. He did finish my project; I will show you that later." "Sam" relaxed in the same position, and was still unaware of his position, he remained unchanged as he spoke.

"Sam" was not a new acquaintance in Sam's life, but his present state of visibility was being watched closer by Sam. The position of his elbow was unnerving; it was what Sam's attention was focused on now, and he could not take it anymore. "Your elbow. It does not touch the bookcase. Can you fix that?"

"I am sorry. The television calls it multitasking, sometimes I have too much happening in my thought process and make mistakes. Do forgive me." "Sam" placed his elbow against the bookcase. "I have many plans for you, and for Evelyn too, if you like. You will be my spokesperson. I will have much use of you in the beginning. Later you will be able to live as you do now. You will have no need for money any longer. You will be able to relax, and take time for yourself, and for Evelyn. I think she was a good choice. I have made a few decisions that I have regretted, but not many. I only hope that in time yet to come, you will see that I have only your best interests in mind. I will protect you and Evelyn forever, that is my task. You have helped me to make myself part of your world. For that my entity and the people of this place will be grateful." "Sam" was as relaxed as an old tomcat. His smug smile had been seen on many a politician's face.

"I can't believe that you have killed Wes, and had thoughts of killing Evelyn. That is not something that I can accept. That is not what you were sent here for. That goes against all that you have told me in the past." Sam no longer struggled; it was a waste of energy. "What is it you intend me to do!"

"When I am the God, that is to be worshipped, you will instruct those that are of doubt, that mine is a true cause. I will provide power and leadership that will direct humans to a new goal, a new life, a life of joy. No longer will man have to waste power to live. They will recycle, they will become more powerful in their lives. In the beginning lives will be somewhat shortened, but once mastered they will live and survive." "Sam" was on a roll. He would do well in Congress at the yearly filibuster time; they would love this being.

"Wait just a minute! What are you talking about! It sounds like you're setting yourself up as a god! A king, a ruler of all this country!" Sam felt the bonds loosen just a bit; "Sam" was relaxing and he had to take advantage of it, but he could not allow "Sam" to know. Sam wasn't sure what he was going to do, but he had to do something, just get away, then he could think, decide, run. But he had one more question, one he didn't want to ask, but he had to ask it, and he had to now. "I have one more question."

"Surely you can see where my entity is the only way for the people of this planet. Yes, ask your question, you do agree with me, right, Sam?" "Sam" was as calm as Sam had ever seen him, not a care in the world, literally.

"Did you kill Sara and Paula?" There it was ask, flat, and to the point.

"As my entity has always told you, I have never killed anyone, I have arranged for powers in this world to happen to benefit you. I have only done these things to keep you on the right path. Had I..."

"WAIT! You haven't answered a damned thing! Answer me!"

"I caused the fire that ended the lives of two people that would have caused you to have been drawn away from the life you now lead. My entity has..."

Sam was up from the chair. Limited struggle had him up and moving. Once started the chair fell away, it landed on its side, and one of the arms broke free. Sam moved across the small office at blinding speed, all thoughts of escape were gone, only rage remained. He wanted to damage "Sam"—he didn't know how, that would come when he had made contact. That was his mistake.

"Sam" never moved. His facial expressions had not changed. His thought process had planned for such an outburst. His energy had been fully charged. He only made a sign in his mind what he wanted to happen, and it did.

Sam found himself halfway across the small office, head down, arms outstretched, running hard, driving. All his energy had been reversed—he was airborne! Sam like the drowning man saw his life, he saw the charred remains of his first love, and an adorable small girl, and the opposite wall! Sam hit hard. He could feel the shelves give way as his body forced itself against them. He felt what must be his ribs give way at the same time. The pain was intense. Books and models exploded from the shelves; they all traveled in a starburst from where his body struck. All the shelved items were moving at an extreme speed, while Sam felt himself in slow motion, till his body could not compress any further. Then he fell, he fell onto all the broken shelves, and the items that had reached the floor before him. Sam looked across the room. "Sam" had not changed his position; his face was no different than before Sam's assault. Sam lay on the floor, in pain, amid all of his books and pieces; he too was in pieces. Before unconsciousness overtook him, he saw "Sam"; he was smiling, his lips moved, but Sam did not hear.

Chapter 13
From Where He Came

I

James and Nicole were having Christmas in James's apartment. The tree was small, and there were only a few presents, but they were equal in numbers, size etcetera, etcetera. They were not a holiday couple. Those that knew them could not even come up with an idea why they were still together. But that had been everyone's assumption in the beginning, so it wasn't a new judgment. Just a fact. They had the same wants, needs, and desires, but for some reason they didn't do any of it together. The same was true today. Christmas was two days away, and the only Christmas spirit was on the radio. Nicole came in and tossed her jacket on the couch.

Nicole crossed the living room and looked over James's shoulder. "Still on that stuff." She kissed James on the cheek and headed to the kitchen. "Salad for dinner, or we go out, nothing else here." James heard the refrigerator door shut. "There's pizza in here too! Pizza and a salad?"

"That's the choices?" James never looked up.

"That's what I said. Pizza, and a salad, or we go out—what's it going to be?" Nicole walked back to the living room door and leaned against the door facing. "I really liked those people too, but enough is enough, get out of it. He should try writing a book, he tells a good story. But that's enough." Nicole had moved to the chair by the door and flopped down.

"This close to Santa day, we would have to have reservations, or stand in line, and I hate lines. Pizza and salad! Didn't think I heard you, did you!" James looked up and back to his paperwork. "I've got something new here. I'm not sure what it is, but it's something new."

"That's so I won't harp anymore. Well, I would like to find the elusive alien too. But let me tell you something. James, I'm serious this time, I've had it with going out and making people think we care. For God's sake we have spent twelve years together chasing the 'aliens.' We're no closer now than then. I've almost stopped telling people what I do for a living! 'Hi, my name's Nicole. I work for the 'Interstellar Watchers.' 'What's that?' they ask. And what I want to tell them is that I'm a crackpot from Area 51, and I turn into a werewolf when the fuckin' moon's full!" Nicole leaned back in the chair and let her arms fall to the chair.

"Are you going to put the pizza in the oven? Or do you want me to?" James looked sideways to see Nicole.

"That's just what I mean! You don't even take me serious anymore! How am I supposed to be happy to chase aliens, when you don't care either!" Nicole threw the pillow from the chair at James. It hit the table and scattered papers everywhere.

"Now, now, violence doesn't fix a problem. Now look what you've done. I want to show you something that works on the same line you were just talking about. Of course I have to find it now! Are you going to put the pizza in the oven?" James still sat on the couch and surveyed the paperwork mess.

"On my way, master! You want dressing on your salad?" Nicole turned the oven to 350 degrees and opened the freezer.

"We got any French? That was good."

Nicole held the frozen pizza in hand and opened the refrigerator. "There's a little."

"Okay, that'll do." James was squatting in the living room picking up and sorting papers.

"I have something that you will understand, but I may have to explain a few parts. I have dug through all the research and have made a determination that others might not like."

"Well, you still have your face buried in the papers, so I have already taken a bit of a stand myself. I think you're making mountains out of molehills, and I will take a little convincing. Make that a lot of convincing!" Nicole came back in the living room and sat beside James. "Okay! Show me!"

"Remember when I dug up all of those old rocks and had them analyzed. I had a lot of tests run to see how hot the fire had gotten, how it could consume metal and fuse rocks that had been formed by time and pressure. Well, here are the new reports. This is the site in Illinois, these are the reports on the rocks in Mississippi." James held them out to Nicole.

"First off, the pizza takes thirty-five to forty minutes. If I am not convinced by then, you had better give up." Nicole took the reports and scanned them. "This has nothing to do with me. I am a school-trained, part-time rock hound that doesn't have any idea what electricity has to do with aliens! Start explaining!" Nicole took the reports and laid them on the table. She scooted closer to James.

"Look here." James pointed to a line of figures. "The fusing of rocks was done by the molecular realignment of the components of basic limestone and whatever strata that was mined at the time. Alternating current would not have caused the realignment. Therefore it is an impossibility to have fused into a new formation during realignment. The rocks would have burned at five hundred degrees Kelvin, but not realigned. The limestone would have disappeared, but not fused; the other rock origins are undeterminable after the heat. On the other hand direct current will cause realignment in molecular structure. Direct current would produce more heat, at a higher unregulated amperage, as in this test shows what would happen and has." James placed another sheet of figures in front of Nicole.

"So, what does that mean?"

"That the current from these lines, first off, could not continue to energize the fire. The fire would have burnt the wires free, instantly, but the heat involved here was not a form of oxidation. This was a heat that is unknown to man. That kind of heat is only found on the surface of the Sun! Something pulled the electrical current into the fire. It fed…it fed on something not of this world! A source that multiplied the current to change it into a controlled heat, a flash, like lightning. Like a giant magnet—power was out for miles! I'm not sure how far the electricity was out in Mississippi, but in Illinois it was out for a total circumference of fifty-eight miles. Substations that had no connections to this site were affected. The power was pulled like metal filings around the end of a magnet! The circle on a map was almost perfect!" James locked his fingers behind his head and leaned back on the couch.

"Well, Mr. Wizard, I have been fascinated with this little class on the uses and abuses of electricity. I still have no idea what the Hell you're talking about! Gotta turn the pizza, otherwise this oven will burn the part at the back. Maybe you could fix this thing—it's electric you know." Nicole laughed as she walked to the kitchen. "Go on, I can hear you from here." Nicole opened the oven, donned her oven mitt and turned the pizza.

"What I am saying is that nothing manmade could have caused either of these fires. It's like spontaneous combustion. A flash fire created by something that we do not know." James still sat in the same position. Like the Cheshire Cat, his smile would not go away. "But Sam may know a source."

"This isn't the first thing that has been found that has not been answered, Mr. Wizard! You want to clear a spot for food. I already know this is going on into the night!" Nicole set plates and forks in front of James.

James continued with his oration. "The power of the Sun, like a giant magnifying glass that became and ended in a millisecond. Like a firecracker without any dispersion. An implosion, the heat was created and controlled, to only become, on that one spot, for that one second. The power of the Sun, two million, seven hundred thousand, that's one Kelvin, for one brief time. Had it lasted it would have vaporized everything for thousands of miles, the heat would have not stopped, everything flammable would have instantly been ablaze, the earth would have become another Sun. Only for a few seconds, as the atmosphere would only have sustained it for a few seconds. Now that's some kind of heat. That's what caused the rocks to burn, fuse, and recreate what we have known, up till now." James held his pose. The smile on James's face was irremovable.

"So, where do you go from here? Can you reproduce the heat? How can you show the government that this is a real substantial lead?" Nicole asked questions and set the salads on the table. "What's next? What do you want to drink?"

"Is there any tea left?"

"Are we off to Illinois after the holidays?"

"I don't know why, but yes." James stacked papers to make room for the pizza. He gathered all the papers from the floor and placed them in his briefcase.

II

The lake was mirror finished. The trees reflected their image upon the surface. Only small ripples from the boat caused slight distortion in the picture. The placid view began to change. Ever so slowly an image foreign to Spirit came to the water's surface. Two humans came into view. They were talking in normal voices, voices inside Spirit's head. Spirit looked about to see other forms, but none spoke to him, or Energy. The voices remained to Spirit, they seemed to be absent to Energy.

"One human is your little problem, one is his human, they two have confounded you for many years now. One is old, in human years, one is as always, energy. But he wants to become more, so very much more. He would become a god! He will cause many to have loss of faith. He will become a human want, a human need. But he will no longer be your problem."

Spirit watched the two humans. They slowly became the trees and clouds again. The gentle ripples of the boat had gone, the ducks landed in the water, erasing the picture. The colors danced on the water as it shimmered in all directions at once. Spirit watched till the water was still again. The clouds in the sky were as beautiful in reflection as in the sky. Voices again. Spirit's attention was drawn to the beauty of the pool. Spirit looked away to address Energy, he had gone. Spirit, now confused again, not anew, but still. He had been confused since being compelled to make his journey, but he looked about. "This is good!" But still he had signs that the problem was his!

III

Sam awoke to strange surroundings. At first strange—he had not been in the parts storage room for some time. He had not been here since the building had been completed. He and Wes had been in here. It had been empty at that time. The odor of oil came to his brain as a question. A question he soon resolved as his memory came back to him. He remembered the pain, he expected it now, but it did not return. Sam tried to raise his arm. He remembered "Sam" had him bound, but not here! Sam turned to look at his surroundings and discovered that only his head could move. He looked at his arms, his legs, silver! The realization of what held him now came swimming into his somewhat clouded brain—duct tape. He had been duct taped to a chair. He wiggled trying to find a loose limb—none. He was held fast by duct tape!

"Sam" floated into the room. His legs moved, but made no contact with the floor, no sound from his entrance. "Back among the living! Are you comfortable? I do hope so. I had to use the tape to keep from hurting you, Sam. I tried to warn you, didn't I. You had me excited for a moment, and I am afraid

I hurt you. Several of your ribs were fractured, but I have repaired you. I can repair most anything. I cannot repair the dent in the dash of the Mustang, but later you will have someone fix that. I understand how most things work, but cannot make some forms return to original. You are me, and I am now you. I do not have the same fragile structures as you, but I know what the structures are, and you have been repaired. I did not mean to hurt you. I am… 'sorry' is the correct word. Yes, sorry. You are my human that has needed assistance for many time now. I would be wrong to hurt anyone that has brought me to my destiny. The heat will remain on to keep you from becoming uncomfortable. I too require heat now. I understand the need for heat. I am afraid that you will not be able to have any food for a few times now. I will return after I have held conversations with Evelyn. I think you will be far more receptive to my conversation after Evelyn and my entity have held conversations too." "Sam" had a smug look on his face, Sam's face, his smile was repugnant.

"What conversation! You stay away from Evelyn! I'll get you!" Sam struggled only to find the tape held fast and seemed to become tighter, especially around his neck! The adhesive bit into his skin and pulled against his neck. He stopped struggling; he looked at "Sam." "Evie has nothing to do with you and me. Don't involve her in any of this. I'll do whatever you ask! Leave her alone!"

"My entity will not harm Evelyn. In time she will know me well, she will accept me just as you do now. I am real, and I am about to become more real. Now I want you to listen to me, without interruption I hope. I will have you announce my entity to the local paper. We, you and I, will travel much in our quest to show humans my power." "Sam" smiled as he spoke. He was quite happy with himself! "I will be known as you. You will become my entity so to speak. You will tell humans of my plan."

"What plan is that!" Sam replied. He could feel the tape pull against his skin as he spoke.

"I will make humans a more powerful race, they will become reenergized as they learn of my power, they will learn of recycling, how their power will increase, and return to them instead of dying. They will become more like me in every way. But they will not have to power. My entity will power them; my entity will recycle them into better humans. Don't you think this place you live could use improvement? Don't you think that human lives could use some renewing?" "Sam" smiled with a glee that was almost frightening.

"You have told me all I need to know! You were the reason for Sara and Paula's deaths, now you're going after Evelyn! I'll not stand for it! I'll find a way to end your little charade, and be rid of you! Don't you go near Evelyn!" Sam's struggles, and his anger had caused him to be bound tighter. His throat was restricted, breathing was difficult.

"Sam! Hold still! If you fight it, it will only get worse! I am not going to harm Evelyn! I am only going to have a conversation, a conversation that will reassure her of my intent. She will probably be quite understanding, not as you are now. I need you, Sam. You are as much a part of this plan as I am. You will live on to see the benefit of what I have planned. It will benefit your world, now my world. I will always be yours, and now Evelyn's too. Do not make this more difficult. Evelyn and I have to hold a conversation, a conversation that had been originally been planned to be the three of us. But alas, I must make time to encourage Evelyn, and you need to make time for yourself, and for Evelyn. This might not be what you want to happen, but the next plan is more difficult, and it does not include you, or Evelyn. I'm sure you will in time see what I am doing is for the betterment of your world. And the lives you so love, together." "Sam" had gone from being frightening to having a sincere look about him.

Sam had seen the error of his struggling and had relaxed. His lungs filled with oxygen; he was breathing again. "Please! Don't hurt Evie. She isn't part of this, this is me and you. I'll do whatever you ask."

"That's much better, Sam. You know we have a history of many times. There are many times yet to enjoy, you and Evelyn, and my entity. We will rule the world in a manner that has never been seen here. It will be orderly and beneficial to all who live now, and those in the time yet to become. I will be a gentleman. Evelyn and I have many plans to discuss. I will return following our conversation. You will sit quietly and think of plans of how to introduce my entity to your world! We will continue later." "Sam" turned and floated away.

Sam heard the Mustang start and the overhead door open. He could hear the engine noise fade away and the door close. The only sound was the furnace running, and running. The room immediately began to get hot. The door to the storeroom was left open and the heat rolled into the small area. Sam began to get hot. He still had his coat on and it was still zipped. It was going to be a long wait!

Evelyn was not unsuspecting, she was very suspicious of any and all details. Sam had made many statements in the last few weeks. Was he still in love with the dead woman, and her little girl? Since Evelyn had known Sam he had always been a loner when she met him, and he didn't have a very large ring of friends at all. They had both been loners, and friends had never gotten in the way. Now it was different, she had a friend, Sam, and she was worried about him. She was in traffic headed to the IGA to pick up her pies for Christmas. The radio had promised snow, not maybe, but a promise. It was small fluffs of white passing the car at speed, her speed. The radio was playing music again, and she smiled. Everything was going to be just fine, a white Christmas, and a happy New Year!

Evelyn passed the office on her way to Salem, the business had been left idle of late. That too was a problem, but nothing that Sam couldn't fix. He had a way with business, she thought. Unless "Sam" had been telling the truth, and he had influenced Sam's decisions. No matter, Sam had plenty of money; after all, she was Sam's secretary, bookkeeper, and soon-to-be wife. April Fool's Day, that would be a great wedding day. She smiled, forgot about the business, and watched the snow.

"Sam" drove out of the wooded area that had a few houses and the garage. "Sam" waved to a man as he retrieved his mail. Snow was beginning to fall again. Not many cars out today. The weather affected the humans so. There wasn't anything "Sam" could do about the weather, not yet anyway. As he pulled out onto the highway the car drifted to one side, "Sam" steered into the slide and it came back into alignment. He chuckled. Driving had become one of the joys. He could drive better than most he had encountered, and he was new at it. He chuckled again! The blue car was fast and he liked fast! But he realized the snow had made the road slippery, so he kept the speed low. He had plenty of time to get to Sam and Evelyn's, plenty of time. Sam was going nowhere, and he was a human of reason. Sam knew that Evelyn's existence depended on it! At the intersection he turned left, toward Odin.

Evelyn picked up her pies and a few other Christmas goodies. Everyone was happy; after all, it was almost Christmas. Music and a light snow had turned into a fresh white blanket of snow to cover the blackened slush that had been plowed into piles around each light pole in the parking lot of the IGA. The fresh white blanket brought back everyone's spirits, even though they all knew they would have to dig out in the morning. The snow was light and very slick. Cars were spinning their tires trying to get out of the store. An orange state dump truck went by with its bed tilted up, and the spreader on the back was spreading salt as it went by. Evelyn hoped the drive home wasn't too slick. Her little red Mustang wasn't very good on the snow. Evelyn packed her purchases in the trunk and wiped the snow off her windows. As quick as she removed the snow it was back. They had been promised a white Christmas, and it wasn't a joke this time. Santa surely wouldn't have any trouble with his sled this year.

Evelyn pulled out of the IGA and slipped and slid her way through town. She thought it was a good night for Kentucky Fried Chicken. She eased her way into KFC and slipped to a stop. She had thought about the drive through, and was glad she hadn't as two cars slowly came together; no damage but her nerves couldn't take it today. She stood in line at the counter.

"I'll have ten pieces, mix it up, and I want one cole slaw, and three mashed potato and gravy. No, I won't need drinks I'm going home." That sounded good, "going home"! It had been a maddening whirlwind dream these last few months. Sam's proposal at Denny's, all the happy days since! She was happy, she hadn't been really happy in many years; she had figured herself a spinster living alone till the end. It was almost as though this was meant to be, something had kept her single for all those years, nothing serious. Now she had Sam, and he had her! It was going to be few years, but they would be great years.

The girl brought Evelyn's order and she paid, dropped coins in the jar for someone's surgery, and was off. It was going to be a great night, she could feel it. She overheard a conversation as she left KFC.

"You're a friend of…."

Evelyn never heard anything else, just Friend! That brought her mood to a dark spot, the light seemed to go away, the snow didn't make her heart light anymore. Evelyn unlocked the passenger door and set her order on the seat. She stood, looking at nothing, just staring, and watching nothing. An elderly gentleman asked if she were alright; he asked again. "Yes, yes, I'm fine, just thinking about Christmas, and the snow, and all. Thank you for asking. I guess I look a little odd here… Merry Christmas!" Evelyn moved to the driver door, unlocked it and sat down. Evelyn started the car and drew her coat up tighter around her. It had gotten cold, no longer than she had been inside. A chill overtook her. She started the car, let it idle and got back out and cleaned the windows again. The snow had taken on a serious look about it, the flakes were larger, and the wind had picked up, it was driving the snow almost horizontal! It was pretty and ominous as it made a pecking noise when it struck the car, ice had joined the fray! Evelyn stomped her feet and clapped her hands together to rid herself of as much snow as she could before getting in. She shifted to reverse, and slowly backed out of the parking space. Once again she slipped and slid out of the parking lot and pulled onto Route 50. The car gained speed to forty-five mph—that was fast enough, she thought! Off to home! The thought came to her mind again, she was going home! Sam would be there by now. He would have a fire and the Christmas lights on. Evelyn smiled!

"Sam" had not thought his driving skills were to be questioned, but he had begun to question them in the last few miles. The blue car was sideways more than once. He wasn't going very fast. A big orange truck had passed, it had honked its loud horn many times till it had passed him. Then it had thrown rocks all over the blue car. Strange that it would be allowed to throw rocks that way and make for harder driving on this snow. Another car had passed "Sam." It too had honked its horn, and the lights had come on and off as it passed. "Sam" remembered the lights on the blue car, he pulled the silver knob out; it took two tries to get his hand to make the knob come out. His lights were on now, he didn't need them, but humans did, he thought. Other cars passed. He looked at his mph gauge; it read fifteen, fast enough for "Sam." He didn't like the car sideways, it taxed his driving ability, he didn't like that either! The lights of other cars behind him became annoying, the mirror reflected them into his human eyes, they were distracting his driving. Cars moved around "Sam" in a steady line and they all honked their horns; that was beginning to annoy "Sam" as well. The snow wasn't heavy yet but it was slick. The other cars had cleared a slight path, and the driving had become easier. "Sam" kept his mph gauge between fifteen and twenty-five. He didn't see any cars close to him in the mirror.

"Sam" could see Sam, not well, but he was still sitting in the chair, with shiny tape. His entity could not see Evelyn. His entity didn't know why. His thought process had tuned Evelyn in, and had been able to see her as well as Sam, but not now. It was the snow, "Sam's" thought process decided, "Yes, the snow." "Sam" spoke aloud, he hadn't processed the thought. "That's alright, humans do that many times. Sam does, and I am 'Sam'!" His entity's thought process had not made that decision, it had been an automatic response. "I'm going to like being human!" The car skidded to the right, "Sam" steered it back right. The clock on the dash read 2:25, early in the human day, but everyone seems in such a hurry! "Sam" would figure the humans out soon, or they would figure his entity out. They would be happy! "Sam" saw the large rise in the road ahead, the bridge over the railroad was at the edge of Odin. His entity would be happy to be off the road.

Sam had wiggled himself into a real bind. Not only had the tape seemed to have shrunk and gotten tighter, the adhesive had balled against his skin and was pulling and biting with every movement. He had watched a movie about a kid and a vampire, and the kid had been an aficionado of Houdini. Sam had not had the advantage of swelling up and making the tape loose in the beginning, but he had tried to rotate his arms slowly, and try to loosen the tape. *Well, asshole, the kid had ropes, not duct tape, and he had been young, and it had been a story. This is real, and you're in trouble!* Sam's air came slowly if he relaxed, but it was hard to relax when the woman you love is about to meet her end. Sam was sure that "Sam" intended to burn the house down, or burn Evelyn, or both! And here he sat taped to some kind of a throne! His right arm was looser, but every time he moved the tape around his neck got tighter! It was insufferably hot in here; the furnace hadn't shut off since "Sam" had left. Sam was sweating, his coat was completely drenched. Sam worked his hand. He twisted back and forth. The wet coat allowed his right hand to become free. He lifted it off the chair arm, up and down. The tape on his throat tightened. He held his breath. Sweat ran into his eyes and off his nose. Sam stopped his movement and took a few slow deep breaths. Sam worked on his left arm. It freed up in the coat, and cut off his air when he raised it up and down. The left arm seemed more free than the right, but he had to stop to breathe.

After a few moments of breathing Sam renewed his efforts on his left arm. He flexed his left hand up and down. The tape had a small tear, the way it was overlapped if he could just get it started. Sam thought of the movie, it had been a book, *Salem's Lot*—the kid had been slow, very slow. Sam slowed his efforts, slowed and concentrated on the small tear; it gave a little. Minutes seemed like an eternity. He had to stop, it was useless. But he had a lot at stake here, and Evelyn was worth all his efforts. He began again.

The pizza burnt at the back of the oven again, James said he liked it crispy, and took the worst piece. As James broke away the worse of the blackened crust, Nicole looked on, she smiled, and set a bowl of salad in front of James along with the last of the French dressing by his plate. Nicole tossed the pillow on the floor beside the coffee table and plopped down on it.

"I think there's a little pizza in the freezer, want me to toss it in the oven?" Nicole watched as James poured the French dressing on his salad.

"No, I'm good here. I think I need to call Sam and Evelyn as soon as I can. Everything else shows as true, both incidents are related. I know it's a little hard to believe, but his spaceman just might be—what did he call it?" James speared his first bite of salad. "I have thought about this, this, entity thing. Sam said it's been with him forever, childhood dreams, an invisible friend, but he's not a kid anymore. He seems a little too sincere for it to be an act, and Evelyn substantiates all he said. I can't see him as a hypnotist. I can't see any elaborate ruse to make himself famous. Fifteen minutes of fame doesn't fit."

"I had some time with Evelyn too, I don't find her the type to make up, nor to go along with some kind of rouse. She's scared of this thing they call 'Sam.' She's scared for herself, and for Sam. They seem a little old to be madly in love, but they are." Nicole took a bite of the good side of the pizza. "But, just what are you planning? Do you have a plan? No you don't!"

"Not yet! But I will. If this critter does exist, I need to meet him, it, whatever! I'm not sure how to make that happen. Sam says he comes around whenever he wants, but he also said that he comes around when Sam is in trouble. Trouble might be the answer now! I'm not sure what kind of trouble, but I'm thinking." Sam picked at the pizza, found a not so bad piece and popped it into his mouth. He smiled at Nicole. She didn't smile back.

"It would have to be something he didn't know about, he would have to think he was really in dire straights. You're diabolical! You can think on burnt food!" Now Nicole smiled.

"Sam" arrived at Sam's house. He had acquired the keys. They weren't needed, but his entity would damage the door if he didn't use the keys. "Sam" really meant no harm to Sam, or Evelyn. Evelyn was an extra, but she made Sam happy. Sam would only be needed for a few human times, but later he would be left alone to live his life with Evelyn and do whatever humans did when work was no longer required. Sam had been very angry to have found out that "Sam" had disposed of Sara and her small child. It was going to take a while to smooth that time out of Sam's mind. Now he had Evelyn, that should make him easier to deal with. He would cooperate for fear for Evelyn's life. He had not liked to anger Sam, but it had been necessary, it had become part of the plan. The original plan had not included Evelyn. Changes had been made, and still on schedule. A schedule was something that Spirit had never understood, but even Spirit would know of "Sam's" power, he could not interfere anymore. It was too late to cause any interference.

"Sam" parked the blue car and got out. His hand had passed through the handle twice. His thought process had made it work, but too slowly. "Sam" walked to the back door and unlocked it, then turned the knob, first try and entered the house. It was quiet, no one home. No matter, Evelyn would be home soon. "Sam" walked into the living room. Most everything happened in this room. It had green and red decorations everywhere. They must be planning a party or something. No matter, the plan was set now, no turning back.

Spirit was watching the picture fade from the water's surface and return to the reflection of the trees and the sky. Energy, or whoever he really was, had gone, gone where he wasn't sure, and the questions were mounting, every time more, and more. The man who had been rowing the boat was walking away, after he had tied the boat to a tree. He walked with no intent or purpose, just a casual walk. The children played endlessly. The giggles and laughter were pleasant to Spirit's ears. "John! What was that?" Spirit searched the trees and the path, no Energy. He began to walk. The sound from his feet was still a bit unnerving, but pleasant at the same time. As he walked he saw many things, houses, people, dogs, birds, and hidden thoughts of John. Not of John, just John. His mind became a kaleidoscope of thoughts, none ending, before others began. They ran together like the ripples of the lake, changing, forming, and re-forming into something new. John. Not as surprising now, but just John, entered and exited his mind as he walked. People waved and smiled at him. People, he had seen people, but it had many times past, they were happy! Happy made Spirit, John, feel happy too! John!

Evelyn was on her drive home. There was a minor fender bender at the Wal-Mart turn and she had to wait. The snow kept getting deeper; it was building up on her hood. So as not to sit and worry, she turned into the Wal-Mart parking lot, parked and went in. There were always bargains to be had just before Christmas, and she liked bargains. The lot had been plowed, but in a few hours you would not be able to tell. Just a quick pass through Wal-Mart, and off to home. She would have to reheat the chicken, but what the heck, she at least wasn't one of the poor souls in the accident. Her spirits were elevated as she walked into the store. Christmas music and Santa!

"Sam" practiced as he waited. Waiting was not a problem to "Sam"; his entity had waited to make plans happen for many human times! The plan was to happen now. There might have to be a few adjustments, there had in past time, but only minor changes. "Sam" sat on the couch. The couch compressed with the weight of a human of one hundred eighty pounds. He rose to a standing position, he walked and made sure the footfalls made a slight sound on the carpet. Practice made perfect, Sam's mother would tell him, and "Sam" had taken the same knowledge in his entity's thought process. Sam had not taken many of the stories and old sayings to heart, but "Sam" had. His plan had begun many times ago, it was of course unknown to his entity at the time. Destiny had a way of fulfilling itself, without an entity's being aware of what they were doing or headed toward. Youth, as a human or as an entity, was all the same—learn, do, become. Become was all "Sam" had to do now, all the rest would take place as his entity had designed. As "Sam's" thought process wandered so did its influence on his human traits. His feet stopped making contact with the floor, no sound, and he had that giveaway glow to him. Lights flashed across the living room wall. "Sam" came back from his dreams of grandeur, and knew Evelyn was home. The test was to see if his human form could fool Evelyn! That would be the real test, the first human test. His human form would not be needed much longer, but now it was important!

Evelyn saw the blue Mustang in the driveway out back. She smiled and worried at the same time. No lights were on. Not a good sign. Evelyn opened her door and looked at the snow, about four inches. She got out of the car and her feet were covered by the snow. As she walked through the snow, Evelyn noticed that hers were the only prints; Sam must have been here for some time now. He had fallen asleep on the couch, watching the television! She hoped! She was sure! She would sneak in and wake him in a special way! She turned the knob. Good, he hadn't locked it! She pushed the door to the point she knew it would squeak, carried her bags in, and returned for dinner. The kitchen had cooled from the door being left open and she closed it quietly. Took her snow-covered shoes off, laid her coat and gloves on the table, and tiptoed to the living room.

"Sam" always knew Evelyn was coming and stood by the tree—an odd place for one, he would learn the customs later. He waited.

The lights were off and Evelyn crept quietly to the couch, no Sam. She stood slowly.

"Hi, Evie!" Right voice inflection, right tone. "Where you been?"

"For God's sake, Sam! You scared the devil out of me!" Evelyn clicked the lamp on. Light filled the room, and there was "Sam," but not her Sam! "So you have been driving the Mustang! Where's Sam?" Evelyn stood. She tried to put on a good front.

"I…I came to talk to you," "Sam" began.

"I don't want to talk to you, not without Sam here! He should be here anytime now." Evelyn crossed her arms on her chest.

"We could talk till he gets here. If it is as you say and he will be here in short time." "Sam" was cool and calm. She would cooperate; that, too, was part of the plan.

"I've got some things to do. You can wait if you like." Evelyn went to the tree, making sure she had plenty of room between her and "Sam." She stepped on the light switch and the tree sprang to life.

"Sam" backed away as the tree lit up.

Evelyn went to the fireplace and switched the light on. She had seen "Sam" move when the tree lit, and she pushed the musical switch on the fireplace lights. The music began in time to the flashing lights. Evelyn turned and headed for the kitchen.

"Sam" followed, after making sure his feet touched the floor and made the appropriate sounds. The sound of his steps preceded him to the kitchen. "Sam" walked in with his hands in his front pockets and he leaned against the door frame. "This Christmas, what is it exactly? I am not privy to a lot of your customs."

"How long have you been here? And you don't know about Christmas?" Evelyn leaned against the counter and looked at "Sam." "I thought you were really something in the beginning. You want to talk, we're going to talk. I don't say a lot, and am very supportive in Sam's life, I have worked for him for many years. But you have planted doubts in his mind, you have caused him a horrible heartache. You have no idea what that is, do you?" Evelyn stared at "Sam."

"That's the reason I wanted to talk to you, just you and my entity. I do not know what a heartache is. Is not that what he visited the doctor for?" "Sam" had his inquisitive look on now.

"No, it's not! You killed those people in Mississippi didn't you? You caused Sam a loss that I can't imagine. He was in love with that girl and her daughter, and you killed them didn't you!" Evelyn's voice had risen with each syllable of each word.

"Sam" was no longer leaning against the door frame. He stood and looked a Evelyn. "It was not on purpose. My entity was looking in on them, curiosity was all it was, and a fire began, there was no way to stop it. My entity tried and only made the fire worse. It was a very bad fire." "Sam's" hands were still in his pockets. He stood quietly.

"There have been many things that you have told Sam, that have made him think back to that day. I think he questions his love for me now. The fire was bad, Sam was young, and it left a scar on his mind and heart. You try to be Sam. I even gave you his name—that was wrong. I have caused him many problems too, and now you seem to be after his own self—look at you!" Evelyn had tears in her eyes, but she had decided she would not cry!

"Evelyn, we need to talk; we need to talk about Sam." "Sam" spoke quietly.

Back at the garage, Houdini he wasn't, but progress had been made. His left hand was almost free to the elbow. His breathing had not been affected in his last hour of trying to dislodge his arm. The tape had stretched and allowed him some room. He had always believed in the powers of duct tape, so he had only bought the best, and it had been good. He was about to roast from the heat! It must have been ninety-nine in the garage! But that too had helped; his arms and his coat had been soaked with sweat, and the moisture had assisted him in getting this far. His mind only thought about the tape. He strained against the bond again and again. His upper arm had only a few wraps of tape. Suddenly came free, he fell forward and choked himself against the tape on his throat. He leaned back to get air. It came in rushes, it burned his throat on the inside as it rushed to get in! Sam sat still, and enjoyed the air flow into his lungs. His left hand went to his throat and pulled; it only made breathing worse, and he sat back again. His mind returned to Evelyn, and his own monster, the monster he had called Friend for so many years, and now was named after him! He was close. Sam returned to the tape. Suddenly he remembered the pocket knife in his pants. He felt for it; it was gone. He felt his pockets and they had been emptied, but the asshole had left his coat on. Sam began to pick at the tape with his left hand. Little by little he started the tear the tape away.

"Well, when do you want to go back to Sam's?" Nicole picked the pizza pan up and tipped the two pieces of picked-over pizza into the trash can.

"I've already called Ivan and told him what I wanted to do. Anyway I told him there were things to look into. He asked what, and I gave the story of more samples." James set the salad bowls on the counter. "He didn't believe a word of it!"

"I don't imagine! You could start a driveway with what we've got already. What the devil did that cost to fly back here?" Nicole started to run water in the sink to do up the few dishes from supper. "You were a little overzealous with your collecting this time!"

"That was my first. Mississippi was how I got into the watchers society. Did you know that it was originally called a society! You think we have some freaks now, you should have seen it then! Nothing happened anywhere else, just the Southwest! Flying saucers didn't fly anywhere else. UFO's and whatever, only landed in the desert. They were a group. I didn't do a good job of collecting then, and there's no way in Hell that anyone would ever admit to anything being covered up back then. You ask too many questions and you just disappeared! The locals were scared and thought it was a big government coverup. Bobby Jonston was the honcho then, and he wasn't exactly a normal one. But he was there trying to collect samples, and I met him then. I went to work for him a short time later. Bobby would comb his hair in the morning and would look like Igor by noon, and his glasses made it worse."

"I never met him." Nicole listened mostly as she washed the dishes.

"No, Bobby blew his head off one night—no note, just one shot. Nobody found him for days. Not much left, out in the desert. His glasses and part of his billfold were all they identified him with. Nowadays they would have to have DNA to have buried him. Coyotes and whatever else out there had eaten the most of him." James poured the last of the iced tea into a clean glass.

"You couldn't have used the same glass!"

"It was already in the sink. We leave Christmas Eve day, seven something in the evening, I'll have to check." James picked up his glass and started to the living room.

"Christmas! What did Sam have to say about that?" Nicole turned her upper body in James's direction, her hands held just over the dish water.

"Can't reach him yet, but I will. It'll be alright. His cell just rings and rings; he doesn't have a message thing-a-ma-gig on his phone. But he'll see my name and number; I've called all afternoon." James walked into the living room.

"That's one day! For God's sake, James! It is Christmas! We have a party tonight, remember?" Nicole was finishing up quick. She wanted to see James talk his way out of this one! Nicole dried her hands and moved to the living room. She stood in front of the coffee table and looked at James, her hands on her hips.

"Can't go. Got to clean up that mess of papers someone tossed about!" He looked back at Nicole without a smile.

"I'll clean up that mess with a match!" Nicole stood, glaring at James.

"I'm going! Just, kidding!" James smiled at Nicole.

Nicole jumped the coffee table and was beating James with a pillow.

"Wait! Don't kill me, I haven't done that much!" James spilled his tea on the couch and grabbed Nicole around the waist and rolled onto the couch. He laughed and she quit fighting after a few seconds. James pinned her arms and kissed her gently. "I do love you! And I wish you would marry me!" James kissed Nicole again. He released her hands, and they went around his neck, locking her fingers together.

Nicole looked deep into James's eyes. Their eyes stayed locked on each other. "Ask me when this is over and done."

"You got a deal!" James kissed her again.

Spirit felt something he had never felt before, his legs were weak, he needed to sit down, he thought he was... was... tired! He had never been tired! He saw a bench at the turn in the path. He slowly trudged to the bench. As he sat down he exhaled long. He looked to his front. It was the lake; the light was dim, the ducks swam slowly. They must be tired too. The voice came from him; it was strange, no signs, sounds. The ducks quacked quietly, almost as if to say, be quiet we're tired, time to sleep. John. The name, again, nothing else, just the name. Spirit was tired, his shoulders slumped and he leaned against the bench, he lay his arms on the back of the bench, he felt something, someone. Energy was sitting beside him. "Where have you been?" he asked slightly sharp.

"Tired, are you, John?" Energy smiled and leaned forward on with his elbows on his knees, cupping his chin.

"John, why do you call me that?"

"It will take a little time, but that is your name. No questions, that is your name. Have you had any strange thoughts today?" Energy looked at the lake, and the ducks, the light grew dimmer and the shadows lengthened.

They sat quietly and watched as the last of the colors dimmed and blended together. The shadows began to lengthen to a dark carpet that overtook the path, and slowly took in their two forms as well. Lightning bugs flew about, making small beacons in the distant woods. Stars twinkled in the sky, and reflected on the lake, a breeze so gently caressed their forms as they enjoyed the beginnings of night.

"Spirit," John spoke first. "I have had many thoughts in my walk, I have walked many steps today, only to return to the same place I began. Tell me things, stories. How did I come here?" John had turned to Energy.

"In time I will answer all your questions, that you do not come upon yourself. Many things, as you say, will come to you. Stories will be for your telling, not mine. You will have many. They too will come, soon. As an entity you have seen many things that will become part of your memory, happy, and sad. This place is for you. It has all aspects of your life, your times, it is your home. It will be a place of wonder, it will be a place of memory, and your life yet to happen." Energy had turned and was facing John.

"How did I come to this place?" David asked.

"Not tonight, my friend." Energy stood, and motioned for John to do the same. When he had stood Energy placed his arm over John's shoulders, and they began to walk. "I have a place for you to rest, and we will talk tomorrow, or the next day, whenever you like."

John stopped and turned to Energy. "I have a problem. I have an entity that has crossed over. I do not think it is good!"

"That too will be taken care of. That is human business. They aren't as helpless as they appear. We will talk of this too. Come now." They began walking again, John did not seem as tired.

Sam had his arms loose. He was absolutely worn out, his clothes were soaked, there were stains on the floor from sweat that had fallen, dried in place as the temperature had continued to rise since "Sam" had left. Sam had no idea how much time had elapsed since his escape had begun. "Escape, you're not out yet!" Sam looked at what remained. His torso and legs were silver from all the wraps of tape. Sam began tearing and picking at his chest; it was going to be some time yet. He had relaxed long enough. He let his mind wander to Evelyn and "Sam." What the Hell was he doing? Had he already done it? What? Sam was doing no good with the tape. He was panicked, and was thinking, but not about getting free. "Slow, calm." Sam voiced the words that had been taught to him. Who taught him? He didn't know anymore! "Slow, calm." Sam began at the tape. The tape had been weakened by his sweat; it had helped him, but now, his chest was slimy underneath his clothes, the sweat had not come to the surface. His clothes were like a sponge and had all the moisture trapped, the heat that had escaped through his clothes had only made the tape stick tighter. His arms were free from the elbow to his fingertips, not much leverage. He began to methodically tear one wrap of tape at a time.

Sam slowed his efforts to make them more effective. His mind was on another subject, Evelyn. Sam pushed Evelyn out of his mind, and it only went to Mississippi. He was a prisoner of the tape and his mind. Panic tried to rule, Sam pushed it back. He thought of Sara, he thought of Evelyn, he thought of trees, and airplanes, and of his parents, he calmed, and let his mind ramble. His fingers were making headway without his attention.

"Sam is my human. You too have become human. My entity has a purpose, to protect and serve you as needed. Sam has many good traits. My entity has tried to assist Sam in every way. My entity has had many times to see this world. I have traveled with Sam on many occasions, in cars, and airplanes, in good times and in bad."

Evelyn interrupted "Sam"; her voice was calm but just. "The times that you have created more than he could handle are outweighing the good times! He's about to lose his mind! He looks calm, but he has been stretched to the limit! You have done that!" Evelyn's voice grew louder with each word.

"Sam" had backed to the wall slowly. His legs moved but seemed to be unattached. He touched the wall and only appeared to sink into the wall; his back was flat. Evelyn watched in fascination and horror at the disappearing act "Sam" was displaying. "Sam" realized that he was losing control and stepped forward and became whole again.

"EVELYN! Sit down! Now!" "Sam" glided forward, and almost came in contact with Evelyn as she backpedaled across the room. She sat on the arm chair unceremoniously, her hands clutched the chair arms, and her eyes locked on "Sam's"! Evelyn didn't want to look at "Sam," but could not look away.

The mission impossible theme was playing. "Sam" and Evelyn both broke from the concentration that had took control both of them. It played again!

"Sam" spoke first. "What is that sound? I have heard it again and again."

"It's Sam's cell phone. Where's Sam!" This time Evelyn was hysterical, standing and moving toward "Sam."

"Sam" only looked in Evelyn's direction, and his thought process sat Evelyn back in the chair. "My entity is trying to make this as painless as possible. You will cooperate!" "Sam" had to try and recover the phone from his inside coat pocket several times before being able to grip the small device. It had stopped playing the tone, and only had numbers flashing on the tiny screen. "Sam" glided across the room to Evelyn, and held the phone out to her. Evelyn remembered from her last conversation with "Sam" that she could not touch his entity, and the manner in which he had placed her into the chair made it all too real. She didn't want to touch the phone, or "Sam"!

"Take it! My entity is in control, you will not be harmed. Take this machine!" "Sam" held the phone steadfast in front of Evelyn.

Evelyn took the phone. "Sam" was cold, no heat radiated from his hand, the phone was cold. Evelyn took the phone, held it with two fingers, then took it in both hands and drew it in close to her. Evelyn never looked at the phone. She was sobbing quietly, she was terrified. "Where's Sam now?" Evelyn asked, as she felt her shoulders being pinned against the chair.

"Sam is safe. My entity could not and would not harm Sam. My entity had begun a conversation with Sam, he was less than understanding. My entity has only good plans for you and Sam. The two of you will always be my humans. My assistance will only be directed to you. My entity has plans for your friends, and all humans. My entity will make your world a far better place than it has been, ever before!"

"What the Hell do you think you are, Napoleon, or Hitler! You are going to take over the world!" Evelyn's sobs had stopped. Tears still ran down her cheeks. In her upright position in the chair she looked like a statue, with a red face and tears. "What kind of a monster have you become! Where is Sam!" Tears ran down Evelyn's cheeks; her hands could not move to wipe them away.

"My entity will get Sam here this night, but first, conversation is necessary to make sure that Sam will assist my entity in its plan to assist your world. Now as was my entity's intention, when you arrived here, to ask but a few questions of you, Evelyn. I will need you and Sam to assist in making others aware of my presence, my power, and what intentions my entity has for this world. My thought process has had many times to think of how to approach this problem. Humans are an oversensitive lot, they have had ideas for many times that will not allow them to understand. You and Sam must make humans know that my entity is here to increase their ability and to enhance their lives. There will be some sacrifices in the beginning. There will be a necessity to make those that will benefit my entity and all of mankind more available to me directly."

The phone tones began again. Evelyn still held the phone, but her arms had been pinned to the arms of the chair. "Sam" had stopped his speech, and looked at Evelyn. "It's a telephone. Answer it—be careful in what you say."

"Sam" released Evelyn's arms, and she dropped the phone. "Sam" allowed her to pick it off the floor and pinned her back to the chair. Evelyn bobbled the phone, caught it, and switched it on. "Hello. No, he's not here right now. I'm talking to an old friend, well one of Sam's old friends! Yes, that would be delightful! Oh, no problem, Sam will be delighted. You know how much fun we had the last time. I will have him call as soon as he gets here. Yes. Yes. Merry Christmas! Bye."

"Who was that, Evelyn?" "Sam" wanted to know. His hearing wasn't as good as it had been, and the phone was so small, the noise it produced was irritating.

"Just some old friends. They will be dropping by for the holiday. You will want to meet them, I'm sure. It will begin your campaign for world domination!"

"He's there right now!" James was smiling from ear to ear.

Nicole came out from the bedroom brushing her hair. She looked at James, who was smiling from ear to ear! "Who's where?"

"Their entity, he's there! I know it! Evelyn only answered my questions like he was listening, and I know! He's back, from wherever the Hell he goes to, but he's back!" James danced around the coffee table and smiled like a kid in a candy store for the first time! "When I asked if he's there, she said yes!"

"Merry Christmas, Jimmy Holly! You've finally got what you wanted for Christmas, a real live alien. That doesn't change our plans for tonight, unless of course you want to drive to Illinois! I think I'll wait on the airplane. Are you going to get ready?" Nicole brushed at her hair. She watched as James began to come back down. She was very interested as well, but would not give James the satisfaction of knowing.

"Don't call me Jimmy. But this is great. I'll have to have some sound equipment and recorders, and one of those....what am I thinking of!" James stood quiet now, his head resting in his hand, and his fingers drummed his forehead.

"You will want an infrared lens and electromagnetic scanner," Nicole said as she turned back to the bathroom.

"Yeah! Yeah, and I'll need a good camera, a video at least six megapixels. And I will need to make reservations."

"James, you've got reservations, remember?" Nicole called from the hallway as she moved to the bedroom. "And you'll need to get dressed!"

"What for?"

"Don't start with me, I'll give something you haven't planned for! Now get dressed!"

James reluctantly went to the bedroom to see his sports jacket and pants on the bed. He started to undress and was mumbling to himself. He managed to get showered and dressed in a new record time for James.

Nicole dreaded the party. She just knew James would fall into nothing but shop talk and the whole evening would be ruined. Much to her joy, James did not. Once when asked about finding any aliens lately, James has laughed it off and told them that you never know when one will show up on the front porch and introduce himself, and it will be your neighbor that you had always thought was as straight as straight could be. Nicole had enjoyed herself and she thought James had as well. It was, after all, Christmas.

Sam was free at last. He looked like a mummy that had been poorly wrapped. There were pieces of silver tape hanging off his pants, his coat, and but most that had been in contact with his skin he had removed. The adhesive had left red marks on his skin where he had turned back and forth to free himself. Sam had gotten up slowly when he had realized he was free, unzipped his coat and left it on the chair, went to the side door, and flung it open! The wind had immediately thrown the door back in his face and almost toppled him to the floor! It was cold, but he didn't care. He had to cool off. He was drenched from head to toe, and his shoes felt like they had as a child after wading in Goose Creek. He started to chill, and closed the door. The furnace was still running; the hot air was oppressive. Sam went to the thermostat and turned it back to fifty-five. The furnace ran on for a minute and shut down. It was music to Sam's ears.

Sam felt his pockets—nothing. "Sam" had taken it all. He looked around the garage and saw the Chevelle. Sam went to the office. The desk and chair were splintered and the chair had one leg sticking into the wall; it probably protruded outside. The shelves were destroyed, papers everywhere. Sam looked to the wall, just inside the door, the keys were hanging neatly, as always. Sam looked to find the Chevelle key; it of all keys was missing. But he remembered "Sam" told him there were too many pedals. Sam went to the Chevelle and opened the door. The keys were in the ignition. Sam got in and tried once, twice, the engine roared to life. He tapped the accelerator pedal a couple of times, he left it idle and retrieved his coat.

Sam flipped the light switch on and looked at his coat. It lay on a chair that he had never seen before. It was metal and had perforations to the metal. Sam picked his coat off the chair and looked at the seat and back. It was in sections, not all one piece as most chairs might be. As he walked around the chair he saw the electric cords that went to its own section. "It's a damned electric chair!" Sam thought, or had he said it out loud? Sam looked at the wires and pulled his coat on slowly. He absently pulled a few pieces of tape from his coat and pants. He reached into his pockets—no gloves.

Sam was worn out. He trudged to the overhead door and pushed the button. The door went up. Sam stood and looked at the swirling snow. He thought of Evelyn, he thought of Sara and Paula. He breathed deep and walked back to the office. The Chevelle idled patiently as Sam strode by. Sam pulled the desk away from the wall and pulled on the drawers. They were all jammed and twisted. He kicked at the desk and shook it till he thought he would fall to the floor in exhaustion. His escape had taken all his strength. Sam breathed deeply and pulled at the drawer again. It gave a little, again, a little more. Sam took the face of the drawer and yanked with both hands and all his strength. He sat down hard on the office floor; the cheap indoor outdoor carpet didn't cushion his backside much. Sam crawled to the desk and reached inside the drawer of his last attention. Sam's finger felt the barrel of the automatic. It was only a .380, but he would take it with him, for what he didn't know, but he had it.

Sam looked at the fuel gauge—three quarters of a tank. It sounded good! Sam smiled a fiendish smile and backed the car out of the parking space. The outside light gave an eerie appearance to the snow as it swirled into the garage and melted as it entered the heated interior. Sam wanted to feel the power and drive fast to get to Evelyn, but knew the roads were slick hours before. He looked at the dash clock—eight-thirty. He had been here six hours now. He didn't know what he would find, probably a burning rubble of what he had called home. He could feel his eyes begin to tear up; he wiped them. Sam drove slowly out of the garage. As the car cleared the entrance he pushed the remote button and the door started down. "Well, at least something is normal!"

The hill into the driveway was snow covered—eight inches maybe. The Chevelle bucked as Sam goosed it up the hill keeping it nosed in the right direction. No ditch on the right but a monster on the left. He goosed it again and was on Green Street Road. The Chevelle twisted to the right then left. Sam brought it back to center. "Not much traffic," he said aloud; he heard it this time. "That's alright, you'll be talking a lot on this drive!" He picked up a little speed for the upcoming hill. He looked a the speedometer—thirty-five, too fast, but he kept it going straight.

"I want Sam right now!" Evelyn yelled at "Sam."

"There is no need in being so emotional. I will retrieve Sam in a short time. Who are these friends that might help me?" "Sam's" voice never wavered; he didn't sound like a entity that had Evelyn pinned into her chair. He was gentle and his voice had the soothing tones of an old friend.

"James is a business associate of Sam's. He knows how to address issues that you have. He will be here soon!" Evelyn still had her arms free, but even with the extra leverage she was stuck.

"LISTEN TO ME!"

Evelyn quit struggling and looked at "Sam."

"I will allow you to be free, but I have conditions for this freedom. I am not going to hurt you, I am not going to hurt Sam, I will not hurt anyone. Do not try to strike me. It will do you no good, you will only come into contact with my entity and be injured. I will retrieve Sam, and we will all hold conversations. I have made plans for many times now. You cannot stop me, only assist. I have a power that I will share. This power will make the humans stronger, more efficient, better. But my entity is a danger to anyone who approaches, without my being under control. I am what you would say, electric, very electric. I would harm you without being able to stop it. Do I have your cooperation?" "Sam" was relaxed now; his tones were soothing again. He looked comfortable as he leaned against the fireplace.

Evelyn thought that he sounded sincere, but she still didn't trust him. "I will not try to run. I won't try to hit you. I will await your and Sam's return. Now, please go get Sam. Please!" Evelyn leaned forward, she hesitantly stood, she was free.

"Sam" became guarded as Evelyn rose to a standing position, but as she stood and had an appearance of awe at being free, he once again relaxed against the fireplace. The music from the lighted display on the fireplace played away on a tune that "Sam" would not recognize, but he liked the sound; it was calming. "Sam" did not look forward to the drive back to the garage. Maybe, once calmed, Sam would drive. "Sam" smiled. He liked to smile; it wasn't forced anymore, it was...natural, yes natural, his thought process agreed.

Evelyn looked to "Sam" at the fireplace and saw him smile; it was friendly, but like a storefront mannequin. It wasn't natural. Evelyn stood in the living room that she had gotten so used to. She felt like she was somewhere as a stranger for the first time. She was scared! Evelyn moved her feet, half expecting them to be frozen in the carpet. Her feet moved, both of them! She looked to "Sam." "Are you going to get Sam?"

"Yes, I will leave now." "Sam" made sure his paced steps made contact with the floor and a light swooshing sound as they skimmed the carpet, he even left light indentations in the carpet that disappeared as he walked. The sound changed as he stepped on the hardwood of the hallway. "Sam" opened the back door. Wind blew snow into the kitchen. He never looked back and stepped onto the snow, no prints left behind.

Evelyn followed "Sam" to the kitchen. She watched as "Sam" opened the door, just as anyone else would, turned the knob, pulled the door open, and closed it as anyone would. Evelyn ran to the door and watched as "Sam" crossed the driveway and opened the Mustang door. Evelyn's hands went to her mouth in a hushed gasp, as she realized that Sam left no prints in the snow.

The Mustang was almost colorless as it backed to the center of the driveway. The tires spun, then slowed, then the car backed up again. The door opened and "Sam" stepped out. He waved his arm and the snow was gone.

Evelyn gasped again, her hands still to her face, fearing he would come back. All sounds were muffled, the tires in the snow, the engine sounds, even the wind was quieter with the snow to absorb the sound. But a sound could be heard above the wind and the snow. Evelyn first thought it was the Mustang, but her vision caught a red blur, as Mother Nature held up the snow for a second, that became slow motion. Evelyn saw the red Chevelle in the driveway sliding sideways as it turned into the curve of the driveway. The slow motion was gone as the Chevelle came into the back drive and slid to a stop in front of the Mustang! "Sam" barely got the Mustang moving till he had to stop it, just barely in time to not crash into the driver's door. The Chevelle backed up, spinning its tires in the snow. It cleared the Mustang, and the door flew open! Sam had a gun in his hand!

There are times in our lives that things happen almost simultaneously; this was one of those times. Sam yelled, "Get out of my car! Now!" His hand was shaking, but no one was watching but Evelyn, and Sam didn't know that. "Get out of the car!"

"Sam" stepped from the Mustang. He gestured with his arms, as any human might, that had a gun pointed at his chest. Evelyn was out the back door and down the three steps. "Sam!"

Sam looked from "Sam" to Evelyn. He didn't expect Evelyn to be alive. Sam didn't know what to do with "Sam"! His hand holding the pistol dropped slightly, it still shook. He looked toward Evelyn as she crossed the driveway, and "Sam" bent at the waist and disappeared into the Mustang. The engine stopped. Evelyn was beside Sam. She grabbed him around the waist as she slid up to Sam. "Sam" reappeared at the door he stepped aside and closed the door.

"My entity was leaving for the garage just now to retrieve you. I see you made it here by yourself." "Sam's" thought processes noted the silver tape in various locations on Sam's pants and his coat. "Let us go in the house. My entity has no use for this weather." "Sam" turned and started for the house.

"Stop! Right there!" Sam yelled at "Sam"!

"Would you rather we stay out here and catch some virus that might be carried by all of this snow?" "Sam" kept walking and was almost to the backdoor.

Sam pointed the gun at "Sam." His hand was shaking badly. "I said stop!"

"No! Sam, he was going to get you, he just wants to talk." Evelyn had tears freezing on her cheeks. "Please don't!"

"Listen to her, Sam. The bullets wouldn't hurt me anyway, it would just PISS ME OFF! Now come into the house. Now!" "Sam" opened the door and looked at the two still standing in the driveway. He bowed slightly and waved his hand toward the house.

Sam let the gun fall to his side; he put his arm around Evelyn. "Did he hurt you?" Sam took the right hand with the gun still in his hand, and used his thumb to wipe Evelyn's tears.

"Let's go in the house." Evelyn walked with Sam, slowly. They walked past "Sam," who still held the door. Once in the kitchen Evelyn and Sam stomped their feet to get the snow off. "Sam" waked through the snow on the floor silently, as he passed to the hallway his feet made sound as he walked.

Sam dropped his coat on one of the kitchen chairs and Evelyn looked up to him. "I was so afraid he had hurt you!" She kissed his cold cheek.

"I was so afraid that he had hurt you too! Are you alright?"

"I'm fine now. I'm not sure what he wants. I'm so afraid, he really scares me!"

"Me too, Evie! Let's go in and talk with him." The two started to the living room still holding onto each other as they had in the driveway. Sam still had the pistol. He kept his finger off the trigger as he knew it was ready; for what he wasn't sure, but he was ready!

"You have a lot of guns for someone that seems so calm," "Sam" said as they entered the living room. "Why don't you put that in the drawer with the other one."

"I would rather hold onto it if you don't mind." Sam waved the pistol in the air.

"Don't piss me off! Put it away, NOW! You're liable to shoot Evelyn, and you would not want that, now would you." "Sam" had taken his coat off to reveal a shirt like one of Sam's.

Sam dropped the magazine and ejected a round from the chamber. He put the round back in the magazine and snapped it back into the pistol. Sam opened the drawer on the end table and laid it beside the other pistol, closed the drawer, then he and Evelyn sat on the couch. They huddled together like two small children about to be punished.

"Why not build a fire, Sam. It makes it more cheery." "Sam" sat in the chair by the window. He smiled.

Sam obediently opened the doors of the fireplace and set to making a fire. Evelyn sat poker straight. She knew that she had not been pinned in the chair again. Her movements to check were unnoticed by Sam, but "Sam" knew she was testing. Sam had a fire started, a small flicker of flame as the brick fire starter began to catch. The flames surged upward to catch the kindling, it licked at the wood, and it charred, darkened, then caught. Sam, and Evelyn watched the flames spread to the rest of the wood. Sam added a piece of larger wood; it compressed the kindling and immediately began to catch. No one said a word. Sam and Evelyn knew the power that was present in the room, and so did "Sam." A new fear had been installed, a power that they had not known until today! As the fire began to maintain its own growth and spread through out the fireplace, Sam returned to the couch beside Evelyn.

"Now, it's cozy, isn't it!" "Sam" held his palms toward the building fire.

Cozy! Sam thought. *Cozy Inn.* He had admitted to starting the fire at Sara's. An accident, he had expressed, but Sara needed to be out of the way. Sam knew better now, Evelyn as well; the two had found out the same information, on a day they would remember forever! How much else had he done, to or for him. He was going to ask, he was going to control his temper as well. If not for his own protection, then for Evelyn.

Cozy! Evelyn thought. *Like a pit of vipers!* She was scared, and didn't care who knew it, but she had to hold her temper, for Sam.

"Yes, cozy. I have come to like fire, the heat is something I have come to like. I didn't know why humans liked fire, but have come to enjoy it. The hotter, the better!" "Sam" turned to the center of the room and folded his hands behind him like a police officer about to give a lecture.

"You just about burned the garage down! It was so damned hot!" Sam could feel his temper rising, and leaned back on the couch. Evelyn stayed beside him.

"I've had it that hot for sometimes now. I would not destroy your 'toys,' as Evelyn called them. I have a far better thought process, when not cold. I had a time of it trying to figure out the furnace in the car." "Sam" looked at Sam and Evelyn; he folded his arms in front of his chest. "Now, I have a few questions. Number one, who are these friends of yours that can help my entity to become known by other humans? Number two, do not try and make idle threats toward my entity. You have both seen what power my entity possesses! I will not harm either of you. I have told you both, alone, and together that I would not harm you. Believe me! Unless, of course, you make an attempt to thwart my plans. My plans have been made many times in the past; they cannot be changed. The only part of the plan is remaining, is my introduction. That, Sam, you will finish for my entity. Years of dedication to you, and now to Evelyn, my entity will require some slight assistance. You may be needed for some time to continue to assure humans that this plan is designed for them. Just as I have assisted you, I will now assist them."

"Your idea of assistance is to tape me to a chair!" Sam leaned forward. Evelyn squeezed his arm. "I could have died, I was so hot!"

"If you will recall, I was to have returned. My entity would not have allowed harm to come to my human. I first off am dedicated to you! Had you sat quietly, and when my entity was finished with Evelyn, you would have been freed. Your struggles to free yourself and your arrival here caused you harm. Not I!" "Sam" stepped toward the captive audience.

Evelyn tensed beside Sam. Sam felt her stiffen against him. He started to stand; Evelyn held him in place. "After what you have told me, what did you expect me to do! Sit there while you burned this house to the ground too!" Sam's voice rose as he spoke.

"Slow, calm! Sam, you had nothing to fear. I have never told you an untruth. I have answered all questions. My entity cannot tell untruths. Now my entity would have a return of assistance, just one small assist! At that time I will no longer need either of you. My entity will not dispose of you. My entity will not abandon you, either of you." "Sam" turned to the fireplace again. It was now burning well, heat could be felt across the room.

"You will no longer need us. What the Hell does that mean?" Sam was up this time. Evelyn could not hold him back; she resisted the urge to stand with Sam.

"I do not tell you untruths, now or ever. Had you asked of the woman after the Army, my entity would have told you the truth. Enough! I have asked a question, answer."

Evelyn spoke before Sam had time to re-register the question. "That's about James and Nicole. Sam's friends from years ago. I would have thought you would have known them. They will be here late Christmas Day. They have many powerful friends in the capital. They are the ones that can help you the most! They have sources of communication throughout the country, maybe even the world."

Sam looked at Evelyn in total amazement! Why was Evelyn involving James, and Nicole? Sam had only turned his head, but now turned completely about. "James and Nicole?"

"Yes. They have the government jobs and can contact many people, with many friends, that will want to know more about 'Sam's' plan!" Evelyn tried her best smile. She was afraid "Sam" might suspect her motives, but he had turned again to the fireplace.

"Oh, yes. I had forgotten them. Christmas Day, that will be nice." Sam too tried to appear natural, but motioned to Evelyn his displeasure with his facial expressions. "I was afraid they would not get back here till later. They do have a busy schedule!"

"Christmas Day. When is this Christmas Day?" "Sam" knew it had something to do with all the decorations, and all the people, but was unsure exactly what it was. He even sounded confused. He realized this too, but it was too late to change his response.

"Two days." Evelyn spoke up.

"Two days! That might not be too long to wait; my plan is not at the end yet. Soon it will be time. These humans have been told of my entity being here?" "Sam" turned to the fire again.

"No one knows of you, except Evelyn. I have only told Evelyn of you, and you have accepted her, as she has you." Sam's voice revealed his nervousness. He wondered if "Sam" could see behind him, he never really knew. "Sam" didn't seem to acknowledge his answer.

"Sam only told me when he thought I had seen you that day, and he didn't want me to think he was crazy. You understand crazy. Right?" Evelyn looked to Sam and put her hand on his leg. She pulled Sam back to the couch.

"I understand crazy. You accused my entity of being crazy, I believe. But the difference in your lives will show you that, crazy will not define what is planned. Brilliance is the proper term in human words. Time is upon us, but two days will not interfere with plans. These people will take a few days to understand. I will need a lot of people to understand soon, and you believe these two will help my plan?" "Sam" walked to the chair and sat.

"Yes, they will be the best choice for public relations. Why don't you tell us of your plan and we could prepare them." Sam spoke with more confidence now.

"Then my entity has to prepare for their arrival. I will leave you now. I will know if you try to leave, and I will bring you back here. You do understand that. I will not be as careless the next time. You cannot escape me. Soon you will have all your time to yourself. Just the two of you. Do not cause yourselves any additional problems. Sam, if you would be good enough to move the red car I will leave now." "Sam" stood and started to the hallway. He looked back at Sam and Evelyn on the couch. "Sam, you will need to move your red car, now!"

Sam was off the couch, passed by "Sam" giving him a wide berth and out the back door. The Chevelle was used to heat and started slow in the blizzard conditions outside. It fired up and slipped and slid till Sam had it squared up in the driveway. Once back on track Sam inched it by the blue Mustang. "Sam" watched from the kitchen. He had closed the door to protect his entity from the cold, but opened the door as soon as Sam had cleared the Mustang. "Careful, Evelyn!" "Sam" said to Evelyn as he left the kitchen's warmth. He reached inside and started the car, and stood waiting for Sam.

Sam approached slowly, both from fear, and the slickness of the driveway.

"Do not cause another day, as today, to be repeated." "Sam" entered the Mustang, closed the door, and slipped down the driveway. He turned on Valentine and swung wide but brought it back under control and was gone.

Sam watched as his Mustang was driven away. He felt better that he was gone but the fear remained. As the car made the corner he felt Evelyn lean against him as she placed her arm around his waist. They stood there in the snow storm, in eight inches of snow watching in fear that "Sam" would return.

"Are you alright, Evelyn?" Sam kissed her forehead and wrapped his arm around her. She was shivering, but Sam wondered if it was from the cold, or fear! "Let's get in out of the cold." Snow had already started to accumulate on the tire marks left when "Sam" left only a few minutes before. As too in the hair of Sam and Evelyn.

IV

Nothing had been said between them. Evelyn checked the chicken, and was heating a few pieces. The potatoes and gravy was congealed but the microwave could resurrect the dead, or so Evelyn hoped. Sam returned to the living room and was fueling the fire with fresh wood. The wood popped and crackled as the fire repossessed the fireplace. Evelyn came in holding a tray with chicken, mashed potatoes and gravy, and two plates. She sat the tray beside Sam, who was sitting in front of the fireplace on the floor. She turned and headed back to the kitchen, returned with drinks, and sat across from Sam. Evelyn didn't smile, she didn't frown, she just looked at Sam. Tears hung at the corners of her eyes.

"What are we going to do, Sam?" Evelyn's eyes never moved from Sam.

"I don't know, I really don't know. I'm a grown man, and I'm helpless, and I'm scared. He has become a monster! I can't even imagine what he's talking about!" Sam looked back at Evelyn. He knew he had a look of helplessness, but that was how he felt, he was helpless. But more than anything he was scared!

"I am going to call James, see if he has any ideas. I have used up most of mine trying to get loose this afternoon. He had me duct taped to a contraption in the storage room, and it was so damned hot, the sweat is what helped me escape though. I thought I was going to die in that storage room!" Sam could still feel the his body, sticky from all the sweat, from the heat, and his efforts to get free.

Tears rolled down Evelyn's cheeks, her arms hung limp in front of her, and she began to shake. "I thought he had killed you! I thought I was next, to be killed in some sick, perverted way, or what it really was afraid of… of.. Fire!" Evelyn sobbed out of control, the tears ran in rivers down her colorless cheeks.

Sam scooted around the tray and pushed it aside at the same time; he pulled Evelyn against him. Sam rocked back and forth. Sam's mind tried to come up with answers that he didn't know the questions for. He tried to comfort Evelyn, but he didn't know how. All of these years, what had he waited for, was he alone, was this like the *War of he Worlds*, he had been here for ever. Maybe even longer than Sam? How long? He would have to call James; maybe his years of hunting aliens had prepared him. Sam and Evelyn were not prepared, and they knew it! But Evelyn's ploy had been a good one, and had bought then some time!

A tone was heard, a familiar tune, but where? "Sam, it's your phone."

Sam eased away from Evelyn in search of the cell phone. It was beside the cushion of the chair that Evelyn had been sitting in before Sam arrived. Sam pulled the cushion out of its hiding place, and the sound became instantly louder. Sam pushed the button. "Hello."

Sam seemed to collapse in the cushionless chair. "No, no, I'm alright! But it has been a day! I don't know what is going on! He's going to take over the world!" Sam motioned for Evelyn to come to his side. He was nodding his head in answer to the unheard conversation, and trying to respond. "Yeah, but… no… no you don't understand, he had me taped to a chair. Yes, I said taped! Duct tape! It took me hours to get free!" Another session of Sam gesturing with his hands and nodding. "He was here with Evelyn. He… I don't know, but he sure as Hell has us scared to death. I know it's Christmas, but we need you. No, this is not a joke. We have told him you are coming Christmas Day. Okay." Sam pushed the end button and looked at Evelyn. "He's going to talk to Nicole and try to get a flight out here tomorrow, if he can."

"I said that they were coming, but that was only a bluff! What can they do?" Evelyn wiped her eyes with the back of her hand, as more tears poured from her eyes.

"I don't know. I really don't have any idea. But it has to be better than any I might have!" Sam folded at the waist, resting his elbows on his knees. His head lay on the open palms, and slowly moved back and forth. "I'm sorry, Evie. I should have never gotten you into this, I should have just kept the secret. I was afraid that…."

"Bull! If you hadn't told me something I would have either gone nuts or had you committed. Things were moving a little off center here! I thought you had lost it! I was trying to protect you and help you but had begun to think that there was no help to be had! And then I met 'Sam.'" Evelyn was pacing now, in front of the Christmas tree. The lights flashed and the Christmas tunes played on from the fireplace decorations. Evelyn moved to the fireplace and shut off the tunes. "I don't see James knowing anything about how to improve our situation. Sam, I'm scared, really scared!"

"Yeah, so am I! I am not the big brave man; I don't know just what I am. Maybe if I had listened to the doctors years ago he would have just left. I don't know!" Sam with his head in his hands still. "There's only one thing I've noticed, he's not as powerful, like he used to be. He has become more human like! Maybe four heads are better than two, I hope!"

"Well, he seemed pretty powerful to me. He had me pinned to the chair. I couldn't move; the harder I tried the worse it got! He seemed pretty strong to me! Did he ever do that before?" Evelyn had stopped pacing and was standing in front of the fireplace looking at Sam.

"Well, he never did anything like that till today! But what I mean is that he would have known what I was doing, he would have known what James and Nicole do, he would have known a lot of things. But he said he was here now. He said he didn't cross over anymore. That I never understood anyway, but he doesn't do it anymore! Why? Where does he go? And the damn chair that he had me taped to has plugs to make it electric, it's like a damned electric chair." Sam had sat back in the cushionless chair.

"Electric chair? What are you talking about?" Evelyn picked up the cushion and handed it to Sam.

"It's got plugs on it, you know like an extension cord, but real heavy. They had plugs like the dryer, 220! I think he gets his power from the chair! I don't know how or... I don't remember all the electric outlets in the storage room. That wasn't part of the building plans; I drew those plans myself!" Sam stood and placed the cushion back in the chair. "I hadn't been there in a while. When Wes died, was killed, I..."

"What do you mean killed!" Evelyn was sitting on the arm of the couch.

"'Sam' said he had to be removed...he said he has placed people in my life and has caused things to happen...he...he started the fire... he killed Sara! It was all the things I have thought about, all the things I have been afraid to ask....he's ...I don't know anymore!" Sam was pacing now. His right hand ran through his hair, his left made gestures to someone, but no one at the same time.

"Removed! What on earth is that supposed to mean? What can be his plan? He killed Sara too! He told me that!" Evelyn started to respond Sam, but decided not.

"It was all a plan. He lured me to the garage, I don't know how! But I know it was part of a plan, his plan, whatever the Hell that is! He killed Sara...and poor little...Paula..." Sam's voice tapered away. There were tears on his cheeks. Sam stopped and looked toward Evelyn. He walked to the couch and wrapped his arm around her shoulders. Evelyn turned her cheek against his hand and gently kissed it. She laid her hand on Sam's.

"I am so very sorry, Sam. I couldn't imagine what that had to be like. I'm so sorry. But what was the reason for Wes, and who else has he killed?" Evelyn sat as she was her head still lay on Sam's hand. She gently caressed his hand.

"I thought I was confused before, but now I have no idea what the Hell's going on. Thank God you're here, Evie, I wouldn't be alive now. I fear I would have taken the easy out! Now I am scared to even make a call, to go anywhere. Maybe he knows everything like before, but...I ...I don't know."

Evelyn stood and hugged Sam. "When James and Nicole get here we will think of something, we have to, they have to! I'm so very sorry!"

Sam kissed Evelyn lightly, and moved to the fireplace. "Evie, I don't mean to be seem like that is going to affect anything between us. It's been a nightmare lately. I can't shake this fear. I guess I have never been afraid before; I knew that 'Sam' was there. I didn't see him for years, but I always knew that he wouldn't let anything happen to me. I could jump off the Empire State Building and he would save me. But now, I feel like I've been betrayed! Now the one savior I had has turned against me, he's betraying me now and God only knows how many times in the past!"

"What did James say when he called?"

"He was at a party and said he would get back with me." Sam looked off as if at something only he could see.

"A party! How is he going to help us?" Evelyn was outwardly upset. Evelyn slid to the chairs newly replaced cushion. She bounced, noticed by her only, when "Sam" had her welded to the chair earlier it had no bounce.

"I expect him to return the call as he can. This is a man that has dedicated his life to aliens, and I believe we have one! I think there is a real problem with 'Sam,' and I sure as Hell don't know what to do." Sam pulled a small piece of tape from his pant leg.

Evelyn went to Sam and held on. She thought the ride was a about to begin!

They watched the fire as it burned the wood, the colors changing, moving, no set pattern. Their lives had developed the same unknown pattern, ever changing, the direction unknown. Their lives were being eaten away, much as the wood in the fire. The life that they had discovered was eroding away. As they stood there, they held onto each other hoping that today was not their last day. The chicken got colder, again.

V

Spirit, John, had become so enrapt of his own surroundings that his problem had begun to fade in his thought process. His thought process had become a tool, an ever-present tool. He could not control it as before. Thoughts came and went as did the ripples in the lake. Beginnings of thoughts were not of his mind. They called to a time of a woman, a human woman. He was not aware of any woman! But his thoughts were there, his past was like the clouds, ever changing and moving. He tried to concentrate on the woman, but his obligation to his entities was ever present, but beginning to fade. His responsibility was to the entities, but his concern was not as devoted. Spirit did not like to be brusque, but when Energy returned he would have to arrange a correction to the problem; it could not be allowed to go on any further! The woman passed through Spirit's thoughts again. Her hair was golden, her smile...she was gone! Spirit had felt his countenance change—he had felt with his hands, the physical change—he was smiling! But what for?

Time passes. Time was never a thought of John's, only assistance. But his consciousness returned slowly. Time was not a thought, only now seemed to be of importance, his now. John, wait.... yes, John! A sunny sky! A window to his new world shone bright to the blue sky, and a speckling of clouds. He breathed deep, the air filled his lungs, it felt good! Spirit....yes...Spirit was there, distant but there.

VI

"Nicole, sweetheart, Nicole." The voice was distant, it was familiar. Nicole pulled the sheet to her neck, as if to protect her from the oncoming day. The taste in her mouth was oddly familiar. Vodka. Yes, now she remembered, the party had been good. She had liked the vodka, but the taste now was not of her liking. Her eyes fluttered, she looked to the light. It was James. She forced a smile, but only wanting to brush her teeth and gargle, in truth.

"We've got a flight to St. Louis at three o'clock this afternoon. It's nine now and we need to get ready." James was buttoning his shirt, the tails hanging outside his pants. "It's colder than ever in Illinois right now and you will need to get some winter stuff ready to take."

"What?" Nicole sat up in the bed keeping the sheet pulled to her neck.

"I got an earlier flight, we leave this afternoon,. They didn't want to change it, but with a little government persuasion they changed their minds." James left the room.

It all flooded back to Nicole, the party, the conversations. James had told her they would fly as soon as he could change the flight. She had remembered telling him he would never get the flight changed. *It's time to get up and get with it!* she thought, only a little wince of pain from her brain left over to let her know that vodka was not her friend. She sat up and called to James. "You've got to be kidding me! It's Christmas Eve. Or did I sleep through Christmas?" Nicole stretched and felt for her gown. "I'm gonna kill you one of these days, you and your harebrained schemes!"

"I talked to Sam this morning and he said he would have a four-wheel drive there to pick us up. It will only be one in the afternoon there. We will have plenty of time to figure out what's going on by then." James came back into the bedroom his shirt now tucked; he held his socks in his hand. "You seen my boots?"

"Boots! Get out of here, I can't even find my gown!" Nicole patted the blanket looking for her gown. James picked it off the floor and tossed it to her. Nicole smiled. "Get out of here!" She threw the gown back.

The morning was hectic for James and Nicole. Finding winter clothes was a magic act. They tried not to go to cold spots, and now a blizzard in Illinois. The clothes were found and packed. Nicole hadn't seen some of them in years. Some were a little out of fashion, but warmth seemed more important that fashion. James had even found his cowboy boots, dusty, but still fit, a little bit awkward with the high heels. Nicole had laughed at his John Wayne impression. The Christmas tree had been looked at more than once, the gifts neatly organized, awaiting the mornings of Christmas ceremony. That would have to be a little later this year.

"That would be great, George. I'm sorry about the late call and the holidays…." Sam's voice tapered away and he clicked the phone off.

"What are you calling George about this hour of the morning?" Evelyn tossed the rest of the KFC from the night before. Coffee was brewing, Sam was fully clothed, he had his lace-up boots on and looked ready to go. "Where are you going?"

"Nicole and James will be in this afternoon about one. And with the snow and all I told them I would pick them up. George is bringing his truck over. I figured it's better to have the four-wheel drive with all this snow. Sam looked out the back window. Snow still fell, much lighter, but still falling.

"Let me get a cup of coffee and I'll get ready."

"It's too bad out there! I'll be back as soon as they arrive." Sam looked out the window still. He didn't like the idea of driving in St. Louis in all this snow, but didn't have a choice that he could think of. His thoughts had tried to come up with a better idea, but none had appeared.

"I'm not staying here alone! I'll not be here when 'Sam' comes back, no way, Sam! If I don't go neither do you! What time do you want to leave?" Nicole poured herself a cup of coffee and looked at Sam.

She's right, Sam thought. He walked to her, kissed her on the forehead and hugged her shoulder. Her eyes were watery. Sam hugged her again and they both looked out the window. The snow fell a little more now. Now.

VII

"Sam" had a lot of problems driving back to the garage the previous night, the snow was more than the highway department could keep up with, cars had been in the ditches, and almost to include "Sam." He had never felt fear, that he could remember. Spirit was always there, but he now denied his existence. He was on his own plan now, it did not have room for looking at time past, onward. But he had felt the same fear when he had struck out on his own. The fear never really left him, but his human form had brought with it an ego, and his ego grew each and every day. He had had thoughts of leaving the car in a ditch as others had done! Soon he would not have need for a car, he would be installed as a human, God! He would never need to drive. His every want was about to be arranged. His public would know him soon, though they might need some persuading! His plan had taken that into account—no problems at all. The friends of Sam and Evelyn would insure that he was presented to the populace in accordance to his plan. His plan!

"Sam's" thought process had been overloaded, energy had been used. It was a real challenge to concentrate on opening the car, once inside the building. "Sam" had to power now. It was cold in the garage, his mind pushed the control to the highest reading, the furnace came on instantly, it followed his command, just as the humans would soon! The car ticked as it cooled. The snow began to melt from under the car and the fenders, and the body began to show outlines as the heat began the melting process. The car's color was still hidden from view, pieces of ice plopped to the floor. "Sam" floated toward the parts room. The toes of his shoes drug on the floor, causing an irritation to "Sam's" thought process. "Sam's" entity fell into the chair. Plugging the power cords in was difficult at his weakened state. Power was only a slight move away. A spark of electricity shone as the first cord became filled with power; the rest were easier. "Sam" sat without moving. Even his thought process came without design. Total loss of all surroundings came swiftly. "Sam" was in full power mode now. His entity needed it, the humans owed it to him, they would care for his every desire. Quiet. Calm. Total power!

A slight glow was seen by the deer and raccoons that night. It came out of the back windows of the garage. The animals didn't go too close, but the snow reflected the bluish glow of the night around the building. The snow continued to fall, masking the glow from most nestled behind securely locked doors.

VIII

One of George's boys followed him to Sam's to drop off the pickup truck. It only resembled a pickup truck, a full camper shell on the back and four doors. The tall tires and lifted suspension made it look more formidable than an Army tank. It had lights over the cab, and on the brush guard, all the covers had been removed for maximum lighting.

George knocked on the back door. Sam was there to open it and let George in from the cold.

"These had better be some good friends! It's colder than Hell out there, and the damn snow just doesn't quit. There will be a bunch of crazies out there too.

Why should I tell you that, you're going to be one of them!" George took off his gloves and nodded to Evelyn. "Take it slow and easy. It's a monster truck and will get you through most anything, but it's slicker than the devil out there."

"I won't hurt your baby, George!" Sam took the offered keys. "Cup of coffee?"

"No thanks. I've got to get going. Family's in for the holidays. It's crazy at my house. Don't worry about the truck, just be careful. I can get the damned truck fixed. I still think you're nuts! Merry Christmas!" George pulled his gloves on, turned his collar up, and was gone. He leaned into the west wind shouldering his way to the red truck in the driveway. George opened the passenger door, gave a short wave, and the truck backed down the driveway.

Sam looked at the keys in his hand, then out the window. He shook his head, slightly, took a drink of coffee. "Are you ready for this little excursion?" Sam turned to see Evelyn with a short stack of blankets and extra gloves, and Sam's field jacket. "Is this an arctic expedition, or what?"

"In this kind of weather you can't be too careful!" After the last night's events, it wasn't funny at all. Evelyn did not feel like smiling but she did.

"George says it has five hundred pounds of tube sand in the back and should do just fine. It looks like it should do just about anything but fly. But slipping and sliding is more in the reality of what is going to happen!" Sam took the blankets and coats from Evelyn and headed out the door. "I'll be right back!"

Evelyn followed Sam to the door. She felt the cold from outside, and pushed the door closed tightly. Evelyn watched Sam as he unlocked the back door tossing the extra coats and blankets on the seat. Sam went around the front of the truck, sliding as he went, opened the driver's door, got in and started up the truck. Sam scraped around on the truck windows; they became covered as quickly as he cleaned them. The defroster was beginning to kick in and made clear half moons on the windshield. Sam tossed the scraper back into the truck and headed back to the house. Evelyn was making a pot of coffee. She already had the thermos standing with hot water to heat the inside to keep the coffee hot. Her mind was on other matters, but a little hot coffee would make a long and dangerous journey much better. This close to the holidays, and the weather conditions, not much would be open.

Sam blew into the kitchen. Snow swirled in behind him. The door pushed closed, the wind noise was muffled now. "I know your reasons for going, and I don't want you ho stay here, but, it's going to be bad out there."

"Going to be! Now that's an understatement. I watched you try and clear windows—that was a joke. I know we have to go—did you hear me, Sam Young? We. I'm not staying here a minute longer. If 'Sam' would show up, I don't know what I would do. But I don't have to worry about that, 'cause I'm not staying here! Got it!" Evelyn poured the just-finished coffee into the thermos. "Let's get out of here before 'Sam' comes back."

They both donned their coats and started out the door. The wind blew snow into the kitchen and the curtains almost blew off the rod as they both looked one last time into the warm kitchen before entering the gale. They both looked at each other and started out. Sam opened Evelyn's door and helped her into the truck. Sam pulled the scraper out once again, and with the defroster in full gear now it didn't take long to clear the windshield. Sam opened the back door and tossed the ice-covered scraper on the floor. Evelyn could feel the cold wind on her neck; she pulled the coat tighter. Sam opened the driver's door almost as quickly as the back door closed, and hopped into the driver's seat.

"Cold!" Sam said as he got in. Sam pulled the lever to reverse and backed in beside the garage, smiled at Evelyn, shifted to drive, and they began. Sam eased down the driveway and onto Valentine Street. They moved easily, only seeing a few others out in the snow. Most all had seen the coming of the snowstorm, had finished all shopping, visiting, and parties before now. Any events on Christmas Eve would most likely be canceled, except of course the arrival of Santa at the fire station, couldn't hardly cancel that, the streets would be busy tonight. Parents trying to be in the Christmas spirit, and children in their best angelic mode. Sam only looked out the windshield and hoped for the best, not the drive, but the gathering of the alien hunters, and the alien. Sam had pretty much made his mind up the "Sam" was indeed an alien. What else could he be?

They had arrived at Sandoval without an incident. Of course at thirty-five miles per hour what could happen, but Sam knew the ditches on Route 50 were deep, and even this monster truck would not be able to get out. Not a word had been spoken. The truck slipped slightly as Sam made the stop at US 50 and US 51 with just a little slide.

"Not so bad!" Evelyn said as the truck came to a full stop. "Not many out today."

A lone red pickup passed into town with his back lowered close to the ground, most likely filled with sand or rock, but now all covered with snow. Sam watched as he crept by slowly. He looked again; the visibility had improved slightly. Sam took his foot off the brake and eased his foot on the accelerator. The truck moved forward with ease. Sam gripped the wheel tight on the turn. They moved along with ease at fifteen miles per hour.

"I'm going to go south to I-64 for the trip into St. Louis. I think if any road is passable it will be the interstate." Sam spoke as a tour guide, not expecting a reply. None given.

On the route to Centralia they saw a couple of cars on the side of the road, completely covered in snow. They had been there probably since last night. The state snow plows had banked more snow on the top of Mother Nature's serving, and they appeared as large bumps. A couple of cars in the ditch, but they too had been there for some time now. In town the streets were more slippery, and with more adventuresome people, as there was a bit of traffic. Both looked for a blue Mustang, but never said anything about it. US 51 south had not been bladed in the last few hours and had a bit of an accumulation on the road; the northbound side had been. As they approached Irvington they both tried to break the silence at the same time.

"No. No. Go right ahead," Evelyn said.

"Well, it's going to be a long drive, and I had a few questions... not questions, but statements. Oh, I don't know. Listen and jump in when you have something, I just have to talk. That may be all it is."

"About 'Sam'?"

"Yes." Sam wiped the windshield and turned the fan on high to clear the inside. "I have noticed a few things that you may not have. I mean you have only been involved with him, it, for a little while. He doesn't seem to have the control he used to. I mean he didn't know that I was coming home, he was unaware of where I was, except he had been with me. He had a lot of control when he was there!" Sam looked briefly at Evelyn and back at the road. Evelyn was looking straight out the windshield.

"Yes, I felt that control. I was scared, probably more scared than I have ever been. He said that he was going to get you. He had no idea you were on your way, or if he did he would not have been outside when you pulled in." Evelyn looked at Sam. "It's hot in here. Let me help you get that coat off."

Sam unbuttoned the outside coat and unzipped the liner. Evelyn had taken her coat off and was pulling on Sam's right sleeve. It was tight with all the clothes Sam had on but eventually pulled free, Evelyn reached around Sam and pulled the coat out from under him as well. Evelyn folded her coat and Sam's and laid them on the back seat beside the blankets and other coats and gloves. As she pulled herself back to the front seat she stopped bedside Sam and lightly kissed his cheek.

Sam thought that no matter what, no matter where this road ended up, they were together, and he liked that. The road outside was not in need of being discussed. They both knew the road conditions. The road that was about to take them somewhere; they didn't know where, that was the scary part, but they had found each other and would go together. "And the chair I told you about. I think he get his power for electricity at the garage. I think he has it set up to energize him somehow! And the biggest thing that has really been bugging me is the trip to Sandoval. What the hell was that all about?" Sam gave Evelyn a sideways glance; she was looking at him now.

"I had almost forgotten about that till he had me welded to the chair yesterday. He doesn't seem to even try, he just holds you there. It's like a magician on TV, you know there's a trick to it, but don't know what." Evelyn passed Sam a cup with hot coffee. "Watch it, it's hot!"

"Something else, he wears clothes, and drives. Can't he fly anymore, or however he got around. And he doesn't seem to pop in, but he still floats, but sometimes he walks, 'cause you can hear him. I noticed that at the garage. Look in the glove box for some paper, we need to write this stuff down. Save a lot of questions for James, later." Sam turned his driving lights on as he noticed the semi-trailer truck with his on. All the additional lights made the road ahead seem so much wider, it had narrowed down as the gloom of the cloud cover had taken most of the light away.

Evelyn pulled a notebook out of her purse and began to write. "All those lights help!" Evelyn kept writing.

"They sure make a difference don't they. We're probably illegal, but I don't see anyone stopping us today. Something else! He has to be hot now, he had the garage so damned hot I thought I was going to melt." Sam turned the wipers down to a slower speed.

"Yeah, and he wanted a fire too! He stood near the fire his entire time in the house. And he never took his coat off either." Evelyn was writing again.

IX

James locked the Jeep and looked at the rag top. He smiled to himself at the ignorance of locking a convertible! He picked up the two large suitcases, Nicole the two smaller ones. The redcap came with a cart and checked their tickets, and the ten-dollar bill, and wished them a pleasant flight. There hadn't been a lot of conversation between them as Nicole didn't feel like flying; her head wasn't bad but her stomach could have been a whole lot better! That damned vodka! The sun was hot and that wasn't helping Nicole at all.

"I hope you find this alien, and get all you want out of this trip. This trip is starting to really sound like a dead end to me. We have heard so many stories in the past, not unlike this one." Nicole burped quietly.

"That vodka got you didn't it. I've told you about the stuff! You want some coffee? You know what the food's like on the airlines." James stopped at the coffee bar and ordered a cappuccino for Nicole and a regular for himself. They continued down the concourse to gate A37 and checked in.

"These people are sincere, I don't think that they are both off the deep end. I just don't see an alien living with them part-time. They have something, but not an alien, not as all the guidelines that we have read. This story doesn't fit." Nicole drank from her cappuccino and grimaced at the sweetness, but it made her stomach feel better.

"Maybe that's what is the matter with this. It makes me worry. I have put a lot of thought into this. Maybe that's what's wrong. All these years we've looked for something to fly into our little part of the world and say, 'Take me to your leader!'

"Maybe they have lived here with us all along. Maybe we have been looking for something that doesn't exist in outer space. But right here with us, maybe in another dimension. I know it's not the same as we have looked for all these years. I just don't know! But I feel like we are about to make a discovery that we may not have been looking for, but a discovery, nonetheless!"

The speaker said it was time to board Flight 429 to St. Louis and Philadelphia. Those needing assistance would please come to the desk and would be provided help boarding now.

Nicole and James began the movement with the rest of the cattle onto the airplane that would take them to whatever story was yet to be told. James was really not worried about any fame, he just wanted to find a real true alien, the real McCoy, so to speak. The holiday crowd was all smiles and happy, many their first flight to Grandma and Grandpa's house for Christmas. Nicole was thinking about James, his proposal, number 2459, or somewhere in that order. She did love him, and when this story turned out to be a big old zero, she hoped he would not be crushed. She had seen it before, with James, and others too. They had been sucked in, and thought they had found the one, they would be famous! Only to find a nut case in the end! But in the back of her mind, this one scared her. Evelyn was not a nut case. Sam was a little eccentric, but not crazy. The story about his youth had spilled over into the real world perhaps, but she didn't think he was that out of it, yet. But this one bothered her because of that, they weren't nuts. The government had checked both of them out, and they didn't miss much. Nicole would never tell James she was scared, but she was!

They got to their seats and watched as last-minute bags were stored and the plane settled down to murmured voices as the stewardess made last-minute checks and began the safety briefing. Nicole thumbed through the magazines in the pouch on the seat in front of her.

"Nicole, what's wrong?" James patted her leg, and looked at her for some indication or the problem.

"Just my stomach, I guess. That's all." Nicole leaned back in the seat and listened as the turbine engines began to fire up. "I'll be fine. We're going to have a white Christmas!"

X

The road to St. Louis was not paved with gold, but seemed to be lined with silver as the sun tried to break through the overcast sky. The whiteness was almost unbearable to unprotected eyes. Snowfall slowed, then started anew as the sun hid again amongst the clouds, repeatedly. KSHE was playing on the radio. The announcer broke in to tell all the people out there with last-minute shopping to do, to get done. "It looks like the snow is going away! Wrong! Mother Nature is only taking a deep breath. The forecast shows heavy snow heading our way! Yeah, folks, I know what you're thinking. What have we got on the ground now? Well the National Weather Center says to be prepared for an additional six to eight inches of this wonderful white stuff before ending sometime on Christmas afternoon! Now back to our program. Just didn't want any of you caught out there!" Sam changed to KMOX for better reports, as KSHE was a rock station and generally didn't give such forecasts. KMOX gave a worst-case scenario, six to ten inches, with whiteout conditions at times. "If you don't have to be out there, get home now! This will be as bad as I have ever seen in St. Louis. St. Louis International is still open at this time. We will break into regularly scheduled programs for updates as they become available. Repeating..." Sam clicked the radio off.

"Well, we will be there in about a half hour or a little better. I told you that this might get bad. But as soon as we pick them up we will be headed home. I hope the flight is on time." The ride had not been bad. A little slow perhaps, two and a half hours to go seventy miles was a bit slow, not much traffic, but they both knew that St. Louis would be busy. The stores would be closed on Christmas Eve no later than noon and it was past that now. The highway was still clear of traffic. But the walls of snow banks on each side were growing ever higher with the passing of each snowplow. "Hang on, we've got to get over again."

The snowplow had begun to honk its air horn long and loud! Sam pulled into the left lane, that looked as though no one had traveled there. The snowplow never slowed, nor stopped its horn till it had cleared them, he was traveling at least fifty miles per hour and throwing snow at least twenty-five feet in air. The windshield was obscured for what seemed forever, and the wipers did not want to clear the snow, but slowly they did, as the truck slipped and twisted beneath them. Sam steered to the right, to the clear path created by the snowplow. The truck skidded, and back, it skidded again, Sam's foot poised above the brake. One last squirm and it began to track straight again. Evelyn and Sam both let out a sigh of relief. The wipers again began to run as designed, but banging against the snow buildup on the sides. Sam powered the window down and reached out to rake the excess snow off his side of the windshield. Evelyn worked her side as well. The cold was almost unbearable as it whistled in the open windows, both their hands were cold beyond belief at the short exposure time.

"Maybe the cold will keep 'Sam' away longer," Evelyn said flat and cold, while she blew hot breath into her cupped hands.

Sam thought that just might be an advantage to their strategy to figure out an answer to the question of how to rid themselves of the, as he had come to believe, alien! "Yeah, maybe. I love you!" Sam patted Evelyn's leg. She took his hand in hers, picked it up and kissed it gently.

"I really don't know where this is going to take us. I love you, too, Sam!" She kissed his hand again.

The large console kept them separated, and would do so the rest of, what they had thought, silently, might be their last ride! No matter what "Sam" had told them, they were scared.

XI

Conversation on the plane had been limited to small talk, which kept coming back to work. Segues were awkward, but used not the less; neither wanted to talk about where they were headed. James had been elated at the prospect of finding an "alien," but both were skeptical. Skepticism was limited in this operation; all findings were considered to be a possible landmark find! Being this close to a landmark find had been overshadowed by an underlying fear, a fear that was beyond description. Both felt it, neither spoke about it. An occasional smile would pass between them as they took turns changing the subject of the conversations.

"Ladies and gentlemen. I would like to take this time to thank you for flying with us today. I can only apologize for Mother Nature's sky today. I guess she is paving Santa's route for tonight. Please fasten your seatbelts, and I apologize in advance this will probably be a rough landing! Thanks again for flying with us. Those going on to Philadelphia please remain seated; we are going to make this a quick stop, fuel and go."

Seatbelts that had been loosened were quickly tightened. The metal click as those that had been taken off, could be heard being snapped into place again. James snapped his; the sound was almost amplified, it seemed. The seatbelt light had been on most of the flight; it had been a rough trip. The stewardesses were making last-minute preparations for the landing; their professional smiles seemed to be a little strained today. A few rows in front of Nicole and James a lady asked, "How long till we land?" as the stewardess passed by her seat.

"Only about ten minutes." A quick answer, and she was gone. She didn't want to hear any more complaints; there had been many vocal passengers on the flight already.

"Ladies and gentlemen, please prepare for landing. We will be landing at St. Louis International in approximately ten minutes. Please put your trays in the stow position, and secure any loose articles." The plane banked to the right only for a few seconds, and began to descend quickly. The engines became louder as the plane descended. The cloud cover was low, and passed the windows in ghostly passes. Only snow could be seen when the clouds were missing, gray to white, and back again. The nose of the plane angled upward and the engines' noise grew louder, as a straight track to the ground began.

Nicole squeezed James's hand tighter and tighter as they descended. She didn't look up, her head slightly bowed. The plane's landing gear made contact hard. The plane jolted, it seemed to waver from one side, and back, and the nose came down gently. A few murmured as the plane braked, a few heavy sighs could be heard. Nicole's was one of those. The brakes and the heavy reverse thrust pushed the passengers forward, but only for a second it seemed. The plane was turning. The snow that had been only a white blur was now seen through the small portholes as heavy large flakes, snowball in size! The terminal was almost obscured through the snowfall! Nicole's grip loosened.

"Are you alright?" James leaned forward to see Nicole's face.

"Yes. I just don't like to fly in bad weather." But it had been a pretty soft landing.

James knew better. It was this trip; they had flown everywhere, and it had never bothered her before. "Well, it's going to be a white Christmas all right!" James didn't know what else to say.

"Uh, huh." Nicole's only response.

Evelyn was waiting for flight 429 by herself, Sam was parking and moving as fast as he could. He had just entered the terminal and was looking at the monitors to find the right gate. The terminal was almost deserted. Flights were showing canceled to all points west, and most all other directions. Southwest 429, four minutes late. Sam breathed a sigh of relief. He hurried to the east end of the terminal and saw Evelyn there watching the corridor, just as a large group of people came into view. Sam watched as Evelyn hugged someone; he couldn't see who, but he knew. Sam saw James just over Evelyn's right shoulder.

Sam stuck his hand out to James as he approached. "Thanks for coming, it has been a little different since you were here." Sam saw that Evelyn was crying, Nicole was consoling her like an old friend. Sam and James looked at the two women and back at each other. "Let's get your luggage and get the Hell out of here. We're about to get more snow, maybe another ten inches!" Sam looked for the directions to the luggage terminals.

"Ten more inches of this? That has to be some kind of a record around here." James moved quick to stay with Sam; the women lagged behind somewhat. "Sam, slow down. I've got a bunch of questions."

"We have at least a two-and-a-half-hour drive to get home; there will be plenty of time, believe me! Here's the luggage carousal now. I've got some stories for you, stories that will not be the most pleasant. I am scared, James!" Sam stopped at the carousal; it seemed the only one in use today.

"Scared! You said that this friend had been passive, and had only helped. What happened?" James initiated the conversation, but luggage was already coming up out of the gaping hole in the middle of the carousal.

"Let's get your luggage first," Sam said flatly. Sam heard Evelyn sniffle as the women joined them.

James looked at Nicole; she only shook her head. James thought it best not to push it any further. He grabbed Nicole's suitcase as it came onto the carousal.

Chapter 14
The Beginning of the End

I

"Sam" was sure that he was powered, but it was going to take a lot of power. Soon there would four humans. He had never tried to control Sam and Evelyn at the same time, and now four! This was not part of his plan, but it had made sense to his thought process. They were government people, and could help. There were going to be those that did not understand, and those that would resist. A little demonstration would show what he could do and how powerful he was! They would help! Even if they did not want to help! His plan was almost complete. "Sam" began to pull power into the chair, the lines outside shed their ice, and the snow and ice everyone had worried about pulling down the lines began to melt. Few noticed as the snow and ice began to thaw. Power began to surge into the chair. "Sam" knew how much to pull. He could not have a fire; as much as he liked fire, he could not have a fire. Not yet! "Sam's" thought process blinked, it became passive, and his entity became comfortable. The power surge stopped. "Sam's" thought process tried to stay in control, but it slipped away, control was gone. Power was absorbed, not at the rate that "Sam" would have wanted, but absorbed slowly. His entity was resting, building power. His batteries could not be overloaded, he was energy, consciousness slipped away. Humans would have dreamed of sugar plums and Santa. "Sam" was only absorbing, nothing more, nothing less, just absorbing energy. "Sam" could not be overcharged, or overloaded, only filled.

The snow was relentless. It began as heavy and got worse. Cold had taken a grip on the Midwest, and had stopped all movement of humans. On this the most joyous of all occasions, the joy was best felt by those that did not have to go outside.

"Sam's" unconscious state did not allow any outside judgment of weather, or ice, or snow. It was not aware of the power that now flowed into his entity; it only absorbed.

II

Snow, ice, and wind were the only concerns of the foursome that had just left the terminal. The wind caught them with a gust that almost pushed them back into the warm confines of the airport. But undaunted they pushed on. The dread could almost be measured as they left the building. The parking garage had been salted, and sand on the top of the salt, as it failed. The slick surface was still there hidden under all of man's attempts to make it go away. Laughter cannot be suppressed in all instances. Nicole slipped and landed on her bottom hard; it even sounded hard, and very loud. It also broke the ice that had gripped all four of them. James laughed first. He bent to help Nicole, and found the same slick spot and fell beside her. She began to laugh. The wind blew the laughter away, but it was too much for the moment and Sam smirked, and Evelyn smiled then laughed. Nicole laughed, they all laughed!

The wind blew. With it, the snow traveled sideways through the garage, never stopping to touch the driveway. The snow was getting heavy as they got to the truck. It had followed them from the terminal and was trying to prevent them from opening the truck doors. The doors were frozen shut! They got the opposite doors open and Sam started the truck to get the heat up and running. They sat and talked about the weather and the flight. Only after the defroster had begun to do its work did the subject change. Sam scraped the windows. With the heat inside and four people the windows were short work. Sam put the gear selector in drive, and the truck and the tales of the last few days began.

"I did not know what to do. I only remembered our conversation about how maybe 'Sam' was an alien. I never really thought of that till then. I mean, I was scared, scared for my life!" Sam pulled out onto Interstate 70.

Sam and James were in the front seats. James turned in his seat to look at Sam as he spoke. "Wait! Wait just a minute! What do you mean, scared for your life!"

Sam began to tell the goings-on since they had left. Evelyn chimed in with the part of the Mustang in Centralia when she and Nicole had been shopping.

Sam ended with the garage and how "Sam" had been driving his car. James sat quietly, contemplating why he had flown halfway across the United States to talk to a nut case.

"Sam, I have to get this right in my mind. This friend, er, 'Sam' has not only taken on a new personality, he drives your car. I have trouble with that." James looked at Nicole, the look that they had passed before was now a silent message that only they knew.

"You have trouble with it! What the Hell do you think I had going on in my mind! Evelyn and I have talked about how to tell all of this. I have had many times in my life that I have been dead sure of myself. I have made deals that seemed sketchy, but I knew that they would work. I know that I am a dead man, if you can't help me!" Sam looked at James. His look would have sent him to a special home—he looked mad!

"Sam, I have to ask. Have you ever been treated for delusions?"

"James, I have saved the best for last. I am not delusional; I have an alien living with me. I didn't think of him that way. But I'm scared to death now. He physically manhandled me, and Evelyn. I was taped in a special chair that he made. He has taken on new characteristics that I have never seen. I know my ribs were broken, and he fixed them." The snow was coming down now. It was hard to see even with the driving lights.

"He has a sore spot on his side, not marks. While Sam was trying to escape and save me, 'Sam' came to me. He forced me to stay in a chair; I couldn't move." Evelyn was corroborating a story that James and Nicole were finding high on the "crazy scale."

"Wait! I have heard some stories but I have to admit that this one is getting a little out of hand! I believed in what you have told me up to this ride. I am getting a little concerned now. 'Sam' you call him, has only been good to you, and now Evelyn. But he has turned on you?" James gave Nicole the look again.

The truck hit a large piece of snow dropped by another car or truck and the bed of the truck tried to become the part to move down the road first. Sam fought it from side to side, and in slow motion the truck came back to his control. It was silent in the truck. The wind pushed it from the back; it tired to move on its own. Sam tweaked the steering wheel and it stayed in what little track there was on Interstate 64. They hadn't seen another vehicle in about an hour. Occasionally they would see red in the distance, the only two cars on the route. Sam hoped he would stay on the road, because he would follow his tracks, probably right into the median. And all of their problems would be solved. Thirty more miles to the Centralia exit. Quiet reigned inside the truck for a few minutes.

"Listen, Sam. I have been searching for the elusive 'alien' forever. Now you tell me that you have one that wears your clothes, and drives your car, and tapes you to a chair. You are serious, right?" James has regained his composure following the wild ride.

"James, I know this is hard to believe. But 'Sam' has agreed to meet with you and Nicole. Evelyn has made 'Sam' believe that you will be a good PR team to help him take over the world. He has some kind of plan to take over the world. He needs you two to tell the world about him, and agree to his takeover. He has become powerful! Very powerful! I am sorry we have involved the two of you in this, but we had nowhere to turn." Sam and Evelyn told of the incident of "Sam's" last visit.

The ride had been long. Sam was worn out from fighting the truck. The worst part was the drive to Odin. The interstate had been almost impassable, but the state routes had had little to no attention. The driving wind had drifted most roads closed, and the big four-wheel-drive had all it could handle. Slow was better, and they had gone slow; it had taken them six hours to go seventy miles. As they turned down Valentine Street in Odin, it was as though a weight had been lifted. Stories had been retold innumerable times. They had used Evelyn's notebook and made more notes. All were tired and happy to be home. Sam and Evelyn looked for the blue Mustang. The driveway was clear of any additional piles of snow that had not been there when they had left almost ten hours before. Sam pulled close to the deck and all exited form the passenger side of the truck. Sam kicked the snow away from the door, and they all entered the warmth of the kitchen. It was dark, very dark. The reflection from the street light tried to get in, only shadows were created. Evelyn moved with speed to each room and turned the lights on. She stood by the door of each room and looked to see "Sam," but not today! The cold had slowed "Sam," and that was a welcome gift for Christmas. But no one knew what was going on!

III

John had been confused; that was unacceptable, but that had been Spirit! But confusion had become part of his life now. So many things had moved in so many directions, all it seemed, at the same time! He was confused about his body, his time, his name. He had not always been Spirit, as he had first thought, but this John name had clouds surrounding it. This was an additional confusion that he wanted cleared up. His thought process...er...mind...he had a mind, he had thoughts now. He was confused with that too! He had never thought about being reprocessed, to be recycled and begin again. His mind thought that that was what had happened to him, a new life, soon he would be reassigned to a human form. That had to be what was going on, surely; Energy would begin to program him for assistance soon. But that was only more confusion. He really knew he was not to be reprogrammed. This was somehow to become his life. All and all it wasn't a bad life. As Spirit he had always had many entities to over watch, but now he only wandered and looked, and he was amazed at all he saw, all he heard, and the most amazing part was the freedom, and his new life. Life, he knew the word, but was very confused! His body kept throwing things at him that had never happened before. His hands reached up to feel his face. He was smiling again, and that brought with it a feeling inside his mind; it was a good feeling, and he liked it, he could like it, he had thoughts of likes and dislikes. There hadn't been anything he disliked, except for the human known as Energy. He had not answered all of John's questions, and he had many.

John had walked to his favorite spot, the bench by the lake. Here he could see the children. He liked to see the children; they laughed and played, and they were...they were happy! As Spirit he had had a sense of fulfillment, but not happiness. This was happy. He didn't question that, it was, and he was happy! A ball rolled up to John's bench; he bent and picked it up. It was closely followed by a little girl. The little girl had dark brown hair, a little curl at her temples, and a precious smile.

"What's your name, mister?" She stood in front of John, her hands engaged with one another as she fidgeted back and forth. But her eyes never wavered from John's.

"My name is Spirit, I mean, John. What's your name?" John looked back to her dark eyes. It caused his smile to break out even more than it had before.

"My name's Julie. You're new here aren't you." Julie jumped on the open end of the bench and wiggled to the backrest. She laid her hands in her lap, but never took her eyes from John's.

"Yes, I am new here. I've been around for a long time. But you are right, I am new here. What are doing today?" John thought her voice was a sweet as she was cute. "My name is...John."

Another little girl called to Julie. "Come on, Julie."

"Can I have my ball? We are playing kickball." Julie never moved.

John handed Julie the ball. She took it and smiled. "Nice to meet you, John." She put her little hand out to John. His hand completely covered her little hand. She pumped his hand up and down twice. "I've gotta go, but I'll see you soon." Her little hand slipped from John's and she was off the bench and running toward the other children.

As Julie ran away, John could smell the trees, he could hear the birds and ducks, he heard the rocks move as Julie ran toward the other children. John leaned against the bench. He laid his arm across the backrest, he felt the texture of the wood. The bench was old, it had been here for a long time. The rough surface told his mind not to ask, only accept. And he did.

The sky was a beautiful blue, a few clouds, and a gentle breeze caused the trees to sway ever so gently, moving in unison, but with individual life, each moved in its own direction, but together. John watched as a few humans walked past him. They smiled and nodded to John. No one entered his space, none made any gestures to invade John's area. He wanted to speak, but was unsure what to say. Confusion still held reign on his new time, life, but it was pleasant. Energy would come again, then the questions would begin, or not; it didn't seem as important as it had. Too much Spirit left in his mind to accept. He had questions, but the confusion; he was on a discovery tour of all things. He thought that maybe he would answer some questions on his own. He had after all come upon his name, John, if it was his name. But he knew that it was, but he still had questions, that being one, somehow it wasn't really that important, was it. John stood. He felt great. He began to walk, he didn't know where, but that too seemed less and less important.

IV

"Sam" had powered and had a good feeling about his new, soon-to-be-acquired humans, but the weather was working against his plan. The cold snow covering was banked against all the doors of the garage. The wind caused it to move and seemingly shift from one spot to another without regard to "Sam's" plan. "Sam" understood the weather patterns on the human world, but the irritation was great. His thought process had developed a new plan, to wait till the snow had stopped. He could move without the assistance of the car, but his human clothes could not make the trip, and his thought process had made signs to indicate that power would be lost during his time in the cold. Power, Energy, were both precious to his plan. Good form was required to make those he was about meet aware of his power. He could not be in any less than perfect form. No excuses could be made. He had to present himself as what he would become, the Power! He had watched weather here for many times; it would change. It would end, and he would begin. The additional power he had absorbed would be added to, again. His design for the chair had been a good one. It made his existence here continue; his existence would expand, it would grow. But now he was at the mercy of the weather. That was not possible, but yet it was happening!

"Sam" had taken on many imperfections of the human form he now possessed. His thought processes had become aware in the early stages, but "Sam" had ignored them, he had come to accept them. To appear human required an adjustment time. It had been slow, it had slowly infiltrated his system, it had taken many years to formulate his plan. It had also taken away from his pure energy form, small changes that could not be mapped out in "Sam's" thought process any longer. An entity is programmed to assist, not to create. The first time he made his presence known to Sam, the first time he was able to fly the small wooden airplane, he began to lose his pure form. His thought process had not known that there had been a flaw in his programming. He had been different. Now he was at the mercy of the same weather that humans suffered from. His acceptance had become his flaw. The chink in the armor, of a self-made God!

"Sam" had tried his process of rejuvenation on mice. In the beginning there had been few; with the changing weather they were many. "Sam" fed them the bird seed that Wes had had in the storeroom. They had come in to the garage, the same time the weather had grown cooler. He had inspired them with power, his power. They had grown, they had multiplied; the young needed more food to keep them alive. The food had run out. The carcasses had been removed so new mice would not be repelled by their presence. Humans would be better. He would create living arrangements for those picked to be examples for the other humans. They would be greater than any humans before! His plan had been proven many times over. Spirit had recycled many, and only minor reprogramming was required. Humans reprogrammed everything and would soon learn to reprogram themselves, under "Sam's" direct supervision, of course. "Sam" had been a good student of many things in the past times. His thought process would be clearer after powering, he required more power, but that too would come in times yet, soon. But the mice had died!

"Sam" had no reason to walk to the chair. He floated and occupied as before. His power was high now, but he would add to it again. The plugs were of little problem. In his already heightened level concentration was simple. He occupied his chair. He was only energy now, his human trappings had been dropped at the door. The clothes were not as durable as "Sam"; they showed wear from the chair. Not power efficient! "Sam's" thought process had signed. He smiled. But of course his smile was not to show. He was a pure energy now; no human traits existed in this, his real state. He could return to the human form, but chose not to. One day the humans would see him in his true form! They would fall to their knees and worship him! His thought process thought a color would be needed, RED, he liked red. But he had to return to his human form to power. That too would change in time!

"Sam" had dreams, not of puppy dogs and kitties! But of cathedrals for his worship, for humans to be awestruck at his power! "Sam's" thought process was aware that thoughts were being created without its input. It had been the impure energy, but other processes had prevented "Sam" from being aware of these signs. Plans took precedence over all other processes. Later when less activity was present, these problems would be addressed. A god could not be bothered by minor needs. All plans had been set, except the weather, a minor little problem; "Sam" could fix that later. "Sam" was being attacked by a human trait, and his human ego, his God-like aspirations, would not allow his thought process to have free reign. His thought process had tried to make him aware of the problems that loomed in the near time. "Sam" was caught between aware and asleep. His entity needed not to sleep, but did become without consciousness, and in that state his dreams appeared. His dreams, the dreams of Gods, the future as he would know it, have it. "Sam" slowly slipped away, the twilight of his day, the dawning of his entity.

The snow began anew. The cold became worse. The furnace kept the warmth inside. Cozy was "Sam," cozy in the heat. The power kept coming. He kept absorbing.

V

Evelyn made hot sandwiches, hot coffee, and hot tea. All wanted something hot. The truck had been warm, but the day had chilled their souls; they looked for a warm that was not to be found. Evelyn and Nicole had moved to the living room. Soft Christmas music played. They talked about everything but "Sam." Food and impending doom did not mix well. They did not discuss anything that wasn't happy.

Sam and James were in the kitchen still. Coats were on the back counter still. They too had tried not to discuss "Sam," but their conversation had meaning and direction. James was not afraid till now. He had been in many investigations, many that had seemed full of peril at the time, but this had scared him; he was afraid.

"It's been several hours now. I know that most of the conversations have been me. But I am sure that you have formed some sort of an opinion by now." Sam tipped his cup and drained the last of his coffee.

"Had I just met you, had you just told me the story, had you called me on the phone or online, I would have said thank you, and moved on to my next project. You have been exposed to something that I have never encountered. I have been flooded with stories of alien abduction and mind control. But I have moved on to the next story. This on the other hand has caught my attention or I wouldn't be here in all this snow on Christmas Eve! I believe you, mostly due to our earlier meeting. I will tell you that it has gotten pretty hard to believe."

Sam started to speak up, but James held him off with his hand gestures.

"Let me finish. Think about what you have told me. If you read it in a supermarket tabloid, or in your hometown newspaper, what would have thought? Don't answer yet." James was on a roll, and just gathering steam. Not because he doubted the story, but he could solve more problems on his feet. "You have to admit that it is quite a story! But I do believe you, right up to the taking the world over, that is a bit hard to swallow!"

"You can't imagine what I thought when he told me! Of course I was taped to his electric chair at the time. It was a bit easier for me to hold still and listen. I don't know what to do. You were my first thought. You don't know how much I appreciate your coming as soon as you have. I need help! The little ole invisible friend has become a monster, a monster that I don't know how to stop." Sam went to the refrigerator and got a Pepsi and offered one to James. James held his coffee cup up to indicate that he still was working on the coffee.

"You and Evelyn have placed a lot of stock in us. I have been looking forever for an honest-to-goodness alien. Now I find one and he's something out of the comic books. I can't find a little old Martian that looks like the one that's always after Bugs; I get a Godzilla." James looked into his cup and swirled the remaining coffee around the bottom of the cup. "God, I wish I didn't believe you! I wish this was just one of those little nightmares that would just fade away." James tipped up his cup and finished his coffee. He mumbled to himself as he walked to the counter. "Where's the coffee?" he ask Sam.

"Second door on the right."

"Thanks." James still mumbling. "Go and get the girls."

Sam looked at James, thought about asking who gave him the right, thought against it, and went to the living room. The two women looked at Sam, reluctantly got up and began to move slowly toward the kitchen. No one said anything, only looks of regret. The conversation in the living room had not been about the problem, but inside all knew that that was why they were here. Sam let the ladies move ahead of him and he followed them to the kitchen.

"Now, what we have is an alien, not unlike a virus. It has taken up space too long. It no longer functions to aid us." James was pouring water into the coffee pot as he spoke. "I have thought this over in my mind. It is not my first want, but seems to be the only direction that we should proceed. Evelyn, I need your notes." Only then did James turn to face his allies and friends.

Hesitantly, Evelyn left the kitchen. She looked into Sam's eyes for hope; none registered. Sam and Nicole still standing watched James for his next words of wisdom. James held his empty coffee cup on one finger and rocked it back and forth.

"Sit! This is going to be a long session! I need a little help here. I have never fought an alien before. I have thought that I might have to, that is, if I ever found one. Now it seems that I have one that makes house calls. And my first job is to engage him with my light saber, to the death! My gravest problem, I forgot to pack my light saber!" James chuckled lightly; neither Nicole nor Sam laughed. Evelyn entered the kitchen and only looked from one to the next; confusion seemed her only expression.

"People, that may have been your last chance to laugh!"

Nicole knew James was thinking; about what she had no idea, but she knew James, and he was working the room. Once the fresh coffee was flowing he would really get wound up.

Sam still waited for a punch line, or something.

Evelyn looked to Sam—no help there!

James took Evelyn's notes. "Thank you, Evelyn. Now. It seems that your little friend, soon to be mine, has changed his habits a little. One thing is that he seems cold now, right? Was he cold before?"

Evelyn moved to a chair and spoke first. "Yes. He wanted heat, and never took off his coat."

"Did he wear a coat before?" James has his pen out, poised to begin writing.

"Always before he, ah, well he had clothes on, but they were like a picture. It wasn't like he was wearing them." Sam moved to the table and sat too.

"Now he has clothes?" James flipped the sheet up and began to write on a new sheet.

"Where did he get these clothes?" Nicole asked.

"He said he had been out." Sam looked at Evelyn; Evelyn nodded her head.

"So did he buy them?" James had stopped writing, but pen ready.

"I didn't ask, but assumed he bought them. He drives now. I guess he has to buy stuff, and no one would really give him notice; it's Christmas, people are in a hurry. I saw him in town but couldn't catch up with him. I thought it was Sam. He was in the blue Mustang."

"What was he doing?" James still poised to write, but nothing had struck him as needing recorded.

"He was at a gas station, the Amoco station in Centralia. He was getting into the car, so I can only assume he had just bought gasoline." Evelyn didn't like the tone of James's voice, it was a questioning tone.

"Did anyone else see him?"

"How the Hell would I know! I didn't go to the station and ask if anyone had seen a ghost! I tried to catch up to have coffee. What kind of questions are these?" Evelyn looked ready to cry again.

"Sorry, Evelyn. He's like this when he gets rolling, just call him a stupid SOB and keep going. That is all that works for me," Nicole said and sat at the table by Evelyn.

James, never fazed by Nicole's rebuttal, began to pace. "What kind of clothes did he wear?" James spun like Sherlock Holmes about to name the murderer.

"Just like Sam's. Sam always bought his own clothes, no coordination of colors, quiet, subdued." Evelyn told herself that she would stand up to James's questioning.

"So he has paid attention to you over the years, Sam. He emulates you in dress. How about his mannerisms, how does he act?" James was writing.

"That too is like Sam. He looks like Sam ten years ago! But he looked older the last time. He looked more up to date, like Sam looks now. His wrinkles are the same, but different. You know, like his clothes had been before, no dimensions, painted on!" Evelyn got up and went to the cabinet for a coffee cup.

"You can hear him walk now. Do his clothes make any noise?" James tore the first sheet and laid it on the cabinet. He began on a new sheet. "Like when you take your coat off, it makes a noise—did his?"

"He didn't take anything off!" Sam replied. "And he bought everything at Penny's, with a credit card he made, with my name on it!"

"Oh, yeah! Yeah, when he talks now it's not like in a Godzilla movie. His voice matches his lips, and when he first came in his feet, you could hear him walk, but later, after he had gotten angry he, he kinda, floated! No sound! When he walked in the snow, he left no prints!"

"At the garage he made noise when he walked on the concrete, but when he held me in the chair he didn't!" Sam scooted closer to the table, and now he smiled, they were getting somewhere!

"He can do a lot of things, but evidently he has to make normal things happen. He's like the ghost, he doesn't touch, he can't!" James was writing, and he had a smile.

"Now wait just a minute. If he bought gas, he had to pump it. And he threw me against the wall." Sam's smile was wavering.

The Amoco has a full-service island. But I don't know which is which. But he did pick up Sam's cell phone; he gave it to me. That's when I noticed how cold he was. Oh, and when I was going to give him a hug, he backed away. He said he could touch me but I could not touch him. He said he was energy, and could not be touched. Does that make any sense?" Evelyn looked abut the others.

"And the pain in my side when he threw me against the wall. I have never broken a rib, but I can tell you that I was in immense pain! And he said he fixed me!" Sam motioned for Evelyn to pour him a cup of coffee too.

James stopped writing. "What do you mean fixed you? I remember you saying that in the truck, what do you mean?"

"I hit the wall, well not the wall, a shelf unit. A solid wood shelf unit, and it was in splinters. I know I busted something up inside. The pain was so intense

I passed out. He said he could not let me die. He fixed me! I'm still sore, and a little red, but no holes or anything. He said he had to fix a few things he had broken in the garage too." Sam took the cup from Evelyn and blew on the hot coffee. He looked at the Pepsi, and his coffee; he pushed the Pepsi aside.

"You saw him do something?" James's pen was writing slowly and looking at Sam over the top of the pad.

"I passed out. The pain was intense. I figured him to finish me off then. When I woke he had me taped up like a mummy in the electric chair—I told you about that. I had a pain, well more like an ache in my side. I didn't see anything, then he left. And he had it so damned hot in there that I thought I would melt." Sam sipped at his hot coffee.

"How did he leave?"

"I don't know. I was tied up in the chair."

"No. No, I mean, did he use the door? Or did he just disappear?"

Sam thought. "He left by the big overhead door. He drove the Mustang out of the garage and then he closed the door, but there is a remote in the garage, and all he has to do is push the button."

"And the blue Mustang was parked out back when I got home, and we both saw him drive away. He had his hands on the wheel. I mean it's not like he floats the car over the road; he drove it here, and he drove it away!" Evelyn looked to Sam for support.

"He made me move the Chevelle out of the way so he could leave! It's not like he makes himself magically appear in an old Mustang!" Sam's voice strained as he hoped for James to understand.

"Does he, as you say, 'magically appear' anymore? You said he used to." James wrote as he talked.

Sam and Evelyn looked at each other. Sam spoke first. "He hasn't in a while. Not in about a month I guess." Sam's voice tapered away, as he thought about "Sam's" new mode of travel.

"How long has he been driving?" James was writing but more slowly now.

"I can't say. Evelyn said she saw the blue Mustang in Centralia when you were here last. But I really don't know. He says he's been at it for a while. I haven't been to the garage since Wes was killed." Sam's face gave that comment away.

"Killed! Who was Wes? I've heard you mention the name but I have no connection." James stopped writing at the mention of killed.

"'Sam' said he had to be eliminated. I was a little angry at that time. I lost my temper, and that's when he threw me against the wall! I believe he did it to show me that he could. He has a temper, and I believe a mean streak that he is unaware of. He would be in some kind of therapy if he were human!" Sam watched James's expression.

"Eliminated! Mean streak, I guess so!" James moved to the table and started to sit, but had another thought. "What else has he done lately that seems out of character for him?"

"One thing that has been on my mind of some time now..." Sam paused. "Was why he sent me to Sandoval, twenty years ago. I still haven't made any connection with that. I have intended to ask but lately have been afraid of the answer." Sam drank from his cup out of habit not want.

"I had forgotten about that!" Nicole jumped into the conversation; it was the only way to be heard over James's ranting. "I had quite frankly dismissed this as another fairy tale. I had not given that much thought after we had heard it. Sorry."

"Yes! I will have to ask him when he gets here!" James was writing again. He had a good assortment of pages lying on the counter now!

"Wait just a minute!" Evelyn had entered the fray. "You're supposed to get rid if him, not become old friends! I just want him gone!" Evelyn's voice was strained, almost falsetto.

"Wait a minute. We're to help find out how to get rid of him. If he's watching we're all in trouble! Were not Ghost Busters; I don't have a thing-a-ma-gig to set into the floor and suck him in. This is a real-world bad guy that has evidently gone off the deep end, and we're here to help. I hope we can. That's what this is all about. I have been looking to make friends with an alien. I have computers that can make contact in languages that we don't even know exist. But I have never been approached by one that thinks he's God! I am in a whole new world here!" James stood awaiting a response.

"I'm sorry, James. I just thought... I don't really know what I thought. I just want him gone, and my world, what's left of it, to become normal again." Evelyn laid her head on Sam's shoulder and grasped his arm.

Sam patted her hands. "I know where she's coming from. I expected a miracle, too. After the ride today, and the last few days, I'm like a little kid that has only wanted to sleep without the monster under the bed from knowing that I'm really afraid of him. He did say that he had to remove Sara and Paula, they didn't fit into his plans!"

James stood by the table. He was amazed to think that he was plotting the end of what he had searched so long for, and Evelyn was wanting it done before he actually got to meet the villain. Part of him still believed that this "Sam" was a figment of someone's imagination. "I don't mean to upset you. I realize what you two have been through. I will do my best to eradicate this...this ...whatever he is! I don't know what to do as I really don't know what he is, not yet anyway, but I will!"

VI

"Sam" has his dreams. "Sam" would tell you that he doesn't fall prey to human emotions, habits, or needs. A thought process is trying to contact its entity without result. A mind, what ever kind, must function, it must respond to the needs and wants of its person, or whatever. The thought process of "Sam" has accomplished waking his entity from his energy lifeline. "Sam" does not understand why he has had so much trouble powering; he has the heat at full throttle and still feels the cold. "Sam" floats from the chair and enters the garage. It seems warmer there; the heat seems to enter and blow through his entity. It is good! Warm has become a necessity for "Sam." He remembers his clothes and thinks about placing them over his entity for additional warmth. But instead he will only absorb the heat from the furnace. He tries to open the door by wishing it open. The mental capabilities seem different, but he knows it's his new source of energy. If only he could return for one good power, he is sure that he would be better equipped to meet these friends of Sam. "Sam" floats to the overhead door, and after three attempts he has pushed the white button to open the door.

Snow! Snow has drifted to almost three feet at the opening of the door. "Sam" feels anger. He has no idea what anger is, except when Sam had tried to attack him, but that too was forgiven in little to no time. Humans have so many emotions; that is what is the matter with the race. The cold sinks into "Sam's" entity and he makes five attempts to push the black button. The open door has caused much heat to escape the garage; some snow has melted into small pools just inside the door. In "Sam's" efforts to close the door his entity has floated close to the concrete floor. He comes into contact with the water, and pain sears through this entity. Only once before has there been such a pain.

It moves inside and through. His mental process is declaring an emergency! "Sam's" movement is almost in the speed of light, not fast enough to get out of the already absorbed water. The door has only closed a few inches and "Sam" has half penetrated the back wall that encloses the office area. The wood becomes apparent to his thought process, the spikes of wood tear at his inner entity. The pain from his water exposure is only worse than the wood. "Sam's" thought process projects signs, Calm, Slow. "Sam" pulls his entity from the wall. The cells of the wood pull and tear at his entity. The pain is intense, but still the water has precedence, and hurts worse. Calm, Slow. He calls again, his concentration is regained, his entity sees the door only halfway closed now. He emerges from the wall. He watches the door as it continues its slow constant descent to the closed position. It finally closes with a bang. The motor runs on for a second till switching off. "Sam" wants to destroy the garage and all its contents in a maddening rage. The pain from the water contact is almost unbearable. His thought process is signing at a rate that is incomprehensible. The thought process cannot compensate for the pain. It knows that in time it will ease, and his entity must bear, and stand, the thought process now will sign its fear of the plan. The entity known as "Sam" instead chooses to return to his chair, power, and cause the pain to be lost in the process. "Sam" floats, except for a slightly visible portion of his entity that drags on the cold concrete floor into the room that houses parts, liquids and a strange metal chair. "Sam" recalls his clothes and arranges them on his entity; they afford some warmth. He has to leave the chair and plug his chair back in to make his preparation to remove the pain, or at least ignore it. The pain is easing now, but still makes his concentration to make the electrical connections difficult at best. The plugs are now in contact with the electricity. "Sam" can hear, he can almost taste the power. As his entity sits in the chair sparks fly as the water-soaked part of his entity comes in contact with the current. Calm, Slow… "Sam" obeys; he does not want to, but he does. It's some time before the sparks stop and the pains eases. By now "Sam" has become almost without desire to resist, he only complies, Calm, Slow. The thought process is in overtime trying to make the entity listen to reason, another human emotion of little value to a God!

"Sam" rests, he rests with only his plan, his only ally.

VII

The hour grows late, many options have been discussed. No plan can be founded. The enemy has evolved from a helpful little busybody, to that of an ogre that will snap a man in half on a whim. It has been discussed that Wes was eliminated. How is apparent, but was it an accident, or was "Sam" only taking credit to scare Sam? That part had worked well; Sam was scared. His company of Evelyn had been expanded to include Nicole and James, whose jury was still out at this time.

James had moved his paperwork, that had expanded, to the living room. Papers were all over the floor, and he sat in the middle of the entire array. He would pick up one and read a little, maybe mark through a line or two, or add a line or two. He arranged and rearranged till the other three had almost gone mad watching.

"He hasn't gone into the stacking faze just yet. When he does he's close to being done, well, at least within two or three hours. But you can't gauge his position till he starts to stack." Nicole elicited a slight laugh out of all but Sam. James looked up with a scowl on his face in Nicole's direction. She made a face at him. It was an inside joke that James did not feel like sharing at this time.

"I'm not a stranger here anymore. All of you might as well go to bed. Nicky, I'll be along later. Just lay me a towel out and I'll finish up here in a bit. I have an order that I have to set right before 'Sam' arrives." James never looked up, just kept sorting and resorting.

"You remember where everything is located, Nicole?" Evelyn asked, as she yawned; it was two in the morning. Evelyn looked as the mantle clock struck the hour. "Merry Christmas, everyone!" She didn't feel much like Christmas, but thought it was only appropriate; it might be the last!

"Merry Christmas," Nicole returned, a faint smile on her lips that only lasted as long as the words passed her lips.

Sam put his arm around Evelyn and kissed her cheek. They too retired, leaving James the only one to meet jolly Father Christmas.

James smiled as he heard the last of them leave the living room. *If only I knew where this garage was located. That monster truck would get me there, and I know that "Sam" is there!* James's thoughts came and went with his papers, always moving, never stale. He was excited inside, while trying to keep a stern countenance on the outside; he was excited, and it wasn't for Christmas!

His notes began to run through him before he picked up a sheet of paper. He had handled them so much they sent off waves of information that he became aware of as he sorted. No flaw in the armor of this alien could be found. All creatures great and small had a weakness, and he would find it. The sleep monster began to take its toll. James's eyes became heavy with the need for sleep. Just a little nap. James lay on his side and allowed his head to rest on his arm, he held a piece of paper that he had held many times in the evening, and now into morning. It was one of the first sheets he had written on the previous night. *Has to drive/doesn't like the cold/wears clothes/WHY!!!!* The sleep monster had taken James while he was weakened. His handwriting began to fold into itself, it became a blank sheet as his hand lay back on the carpet. As his hand felt the carpet touch, it jerked slightly, and lay back, the sleep monster had won.

Outside, the snow became lighter, never stopping, but less now than before. Christmas lights were left on, in celebration of the birth of the baby Jesus, or so Santa would not miss the house, directly related to the age of the occupants of the now dark houses. Some of the displays were elaborate, with many blinking lights, some were all but covered by the last three days of snowfall. The snow kept falling making the scenes all the more beautiful, or eerie depending on one's view.

Most all were nestled in bed, with the blankets pulled high to ward off the cold winter's night. Nicole got up and saw that James had fallen asleep. She covered him, kissed him on the forehead, stood and said quietly, "Ask me when this is over." Back to her bed she stole, not wanting to wake anyone. She smiled as she looked back to James, now covered, amongst his notes and his Christmas hopes and wishes.

VIII

Christmas morning, all was quiet at the Young house. All but James. He had woken at eight and begun Christmas breakfast. There was hot coffee, and chocolate, juices and fruit, he had the table set on the poinsettia table cloth, and all was ready for the arrival of his party of three.

Evelyn was the first to smell the coffee. She came into the kitchen with her hair slightly tousled, her Christmas robe, and her pink slippers. "You've been busy, Mr. Holly. That is fresh coffee I smell."

"Indeed it is. Have a seat." He held a chair out for Evelyn, and poured her a fresh cup of coffee. "Merry Christmas!"

"And Merry Christmas to you as well. I guess you have found a way to remove 'Sam,'" Evelyn said as she tested the flavor of the coffee.

Sam walked in about the same time, and James never answered Evelyn. "Well, you have been busy this morning!" He kissed Evelyn on the cheek.

"Not I! Mr. Holly has been the little Santa's elf this morning. Merry Christmas, Sam!" Evelyn pulled Sam to her and kissed him on the lips, ever so gently.

"That it would seem, has been caused by a plan?" Sam asked as he crossed to get coffee.

"Sometimes even suicidal people have a plan. My plan, as you want to refer to it, may have a few flaws. Let's discuss it after breakfast. You see I can make coffee, and I can set a mean table. But I can't boil water. I am about to go wish a Merry Christmas to my cook! I'll be right back!" James gave a sly smile and was off to the bedroom to wake Nicole.

"I can make a mean scrambled egg, and omelet," Evelyn said as she slipped out of her chair. She smiled at Sam.

Out of the bedroom thy heard "HO, HO, HO, and has Nicole been a good little girl?" James used his deepest voice.

"James Holly! I am just about to kick your ass. What the Hell time is it anyway!" Nicole was not a morning person!

"It's almost eight-thirty, little girl!" Then the door slammed, and James was running into the kitchen. "She'll be right along." James picked his cup up, and took a deep drink.

Evelyn got up and began to put together Christmas breakfast as she had planned before the recent exodus into unreality. Christmas stolen, apple tarts and all the fixin's were served up, almost as a last meal. The conversation had turned from the unorthodox wake up, to the continuing snowfall. No one wanted to talk about the plan, if in fact one existed. James had a smug look about him, but Nicole had seen this before and it worried her to no end. Sam and Evelyn were only willing dupes to be woven into whatever plan James might have concocted in his living room slumber.

"Okay, that was great. Now if all of you would adjourn to the living room, I want to thrill you with my next feat." James smiled, pushed back from the table, picked up his coffee, and left for the living room.

Evelyn and Sam looked at Nicole. They shared the same look of wonder. Nicole looked back as if to say "I have no idea." They all slowly moved to the living room. They came slow and cautious, fearing the plan, or lack of one, whichever was presented was fearful at best.

"Now first off, hear me out before you decide to hang me from the mistletoe. I have gone through my notes and have decided on what direction to go. I will not tell you that this will work. But it is the only direction I can think of to begin." James looked about his captive audience. "I would have started last night, but I don't know where your garage is located. I really would have, but without Sam there I would have miserably failed. This, entity he calls himself is an unknown factor. You have told me everything that you have seen and can remember. From that I have decided we need to attack first. Sam, you and I will go to your garage. He has a power source there, he has decided that is his place for now. I don't think that he has the ability to move about as before. I think he has been ejected from wherever he came from, and is at the mercy of the weather. While we, on the other hand, we have the big monster truck that will get us there."

"You want to go after him?" Sam now stood too.

"Yes. I think that it is important for him to think that we are ready to serve him and his plan to save our asses. I want him to think that we are willing to do whatever he asks. I think I can put him on the defensive. From what you have told me, he is not really sure about all the surroundings here, and is at our mercy. I have to get to know what he is all about first! I cannot formulate any kind of plan without first knowing what he is, where he's from, what he wants, and most importantly how he plans on getting it." James folded his arms and looked at the other three.

Nicole spoke first, as James thought she would. "James, I know how long you have, and me as well, looked for the ever-elusive alien. Don't commit yourself to a suicide mission that might prevent us from averting a real problem. From what Evelyn and Sam have told us, this is very serious. This is not a game to be played for high score!"

"I don't doubt what they have told me, us. When Sam and I return we will begin again. I don't have any knowledge of what we are up against. I have a PhD in anthropology, not ghost hunting. I have to be able to establish a baseline somewhere. I am lost. I have three stacks of notes, Good, Better, and Lost. My lost stack is the largest! Sam, I will need you to follow my lead; what direction it will go has yet to be figured out. I have no equipment. I'm not sure that the equipment we need has been designed. I'm scared as you all are. I really don't want to die today. I do not plan on dying today."

The other three looked at one another. No one could fault his plan, if that was what it could be called. Nicole walked to James and looked into his eyes. She placed her hands on his cheeks. "Just be careful!" Nicole kissed James long, held his cheeks a little longer, and walked to the kitchen.

Evelyn looked to Sam, and to Nicole's back as she exited the living room. Evelyn went to the kitchen as well. Nicole stood looking at the snow, less now but still falling. Evelyn sat at the table, not wanting to interrupt Nicole's solitude.

"You have an extra stocking cap? It's going to be cold out there."

"Yeah. I'll get one for you. I guess all the talk is over; it's time to go." Sam went to the bedroom to find James a stocking cap.

IX

The drive was quiet. Not many out in the snow. More than likely many sleds had been delivered by Santa the night before, but even the kids knew it was extremely cold. The truck had been slow to fire up. Sam had thought the Chevlle would be a real bear to start. Of course it wouldn't make it out of the driveway. The driveway was drifted to four feet by the creek, but the truck dug away at it slowly, and forged on to what they had no clue.

The highway had been bladed down to a sheet of ice; no pavement was to be seen. Sam kept the speed slow and steady. Green Street was a new and different experience. In all Sam's years in southern Illinois it had never snowed like this, and it was still snowing. Green Street was nothing but a series of ruts accented by drifts of three feet. The truck that had been so stable on the road back from St. Louis was now a bucking horse of less than dependable nature. Sam kept it between the ditches, but a few moments were somewhat less than safe; luck had to be riding with them. A fifteen-minute ride had already become almost an hour and fifteen minutes. James and Sam had not spoken since the last sideways hill. Now Sam was slowing on a hill and curve. James wanted to ask something, anything, just to break the silence, but he thought better. Sam turned from the road through a three-foot snowdrift onto a hill. James grabbed the sides of his seat, but he saw a garage, almost obliterated by the whiteness and the snowfall. He didn't ask, but only hoped this was Sam's garage.

"Well, we made it! I had my doubts for a while little back there! Just ignore that big ditch on your side." Sam tried to be lighthearted, he didn't think it worked.

"What ditch? This is level ground over here, you know where we are?" James looked again to see the big ditch.

"Must be full of snow!" Sam braked the truck to a sliding stop, he backed it in front of the large door and pulled it around till it was facing out again. The motor shut down with a simple twist of he key. It now was silent, only the pawing soft touch of the snow as it landed on the windshield and melted. They sat quiet and watched as the snow began to cover their view.

"Okay! I'm ready. Remember, just follow my lead!" James opened his door, the wind, and snow came in like it belonged there. Sam started to take the key, then decided to leave it; they might need it really quick, no sense having to look for it. He opened his door; the wind blew through the two open doors and traveled on. Sam led James around the side to the street door. He found the key and after a few clumsy attempts, got the door to open. The heat met them instantly. James would later recall how snow melted as the door was opened. It was insufferably hot, with the furnace still running. "'Sam'! Are you here! 'Sam'!"

The two looked at one another as though to question whether the ride they had just finished had been for naught.

"Who is your friend, Sam?" a voice not booming, but close, inquired. The voice came from the supply room.

Sam noticed that the door stood on its hinges, but just a little off, not much but a little. Sam started for the supply room. He glanced into the office, still destroyed. He paused and looked at the shelf, or at least where it had been. It now was only splinters. Sam winced as he touched his ribs. When he turned back to the supply room door, "Sam" was standing there, well not standing, but close to the floor. His clothes looked slept in, his hair perfect, but the rest of him disheveled.

James was taken aback by "Sam's" appearance, but as they watched, wrinkles disappeared, the clothes moved into a smooth line, and all thoughts of having been slept in vanished. All but one foot. The foot had a sock half on and half off; no foot and ankle could be seen. James stepped forward, sticking his hand out. "You have to be 'Sam'! Sam has told me so much about you. He said I would be amazed. Well, amaze me!" James's hand was not met by that of "Sam."

"Why are you here?" the voice still not booming, but almost.

"After I told James about you, he could not wait. I have the loan of George's truck and we thought we would come here to meet you. We left Nicole and Evelyn at the house. It's pretty cold out there." Sam was almost out of thoughts.

"I insisted! If I am to be your public relations man I need ammunition, I need facts, I need to meet you and get to know you just a bit. You're going to have to get over the shy part. You will need to meet the public, get out amongst the people, shake some hands. Sam has told me many things that I found a little hard to believe, but Sam has never lied to me. What can I say, I'm here, right!" James took out a pad of paper and a pen. "I need to ask some questions."

"What kind of human is this, Sam! I will not answer questions, I will not shake hands. I will be your God soon, and if you expect to be assisted, you will heed what you say!" The voice was booming now!

"'Sam,' wait just a minute. Today is the birthday of Jesus Christ, over 2,005 years ago. He and his Father have been worshiped since, and you think people will just give him up. Listen, we will have to do many appearances, we will have to show people what you can do. It's not easy to recreate you into a god! For one thing, your sock is down, and it doesn't show any of you! You will scare people to death; they will run away! Later maybe that won't matter, but now, you have to look good to the people that you want to impress. You can burn all those that don't believe, and more will just take their place. You want to be God! You're going to need some help. And I can do it!" James set his hands on his hips and stared at "Sam."

"Sam's" voice was normal now, almost quiet. "Is all that necessary? I will show the humans my power, they will be surprised at what I will show them. Then they will know! I want someone to show them, but all that will not be necessary." "Sam" stood still not moving; he floated a little higher from the floor. "How can you help in this plan?"

"I thought that you were already aware of what I could do? I guess Sam has not told you everything." James looked at Sam, who looked more uncomfortable as the center of attention. "I can set up television feeds to the entire world. But first you have to show the people what you can do. No one takes anything that they hear as truth. In this day and age of movies, television, and newspapers, so much is fake, it's hard to tell what is and what isn't! It has to be shown to the people, in front of them, they will have to see it firsthand."

"I thought that you had better get this information from James. I thought you might not believe me; our last meeting was not the best." Sam wanted out of the limelight, and fast; he didn't want a repeat of their last meeting.

"I know that is was somewhat difficult for you to understand. I thought my entity had explained that to your comprehension." "Sam" shifted his entity to another position, his clothes followed a split second later.

"Right there!" James jumped in!

"What are you talking about!" "Sam" found this man to be an irritant, but seemed to know what he was signing.

"Your clothes, are those real? If not you have to get some real clothes, and you have to cover up that missing ankle." James was on a roll, but on the inside he was sweating; he only hoped it didn't show, it was hot enough in here.

The pant leg pulled into a pressed pair of slacks that covered his ankle, his sock move back into its proper position. "Better?"

"Yes, but you cannot make a mistake like that. Do you have skin?" James pressed on.

"Skin? You mean an outer covering?" "Sam" asked. He sounded really interested. His clothes became crisp in appearance; he had all but his shoes. The shoes slid across the garage floor making scraping sounds; they passed effortlessly onto "Sam's" socked feet, if they were in fact feet. James had more questions now than before.

"'Sam,' listen, I need some time with you, but I need to make notes now, and begin working up a presentation. You do understand, don't you?" James was almost insulting now, he was rolling now, faster than ever before.

"I understand that you are being less than cordial. You have an arrogance that will not be tolerated by my entity!" "Sam's" voice was a little louder, but seemed to lack confidence.

"Don't take my aggressive nature for arrogance. A job like this calls out the best of me, but in a pushy sort of a manner. Please excuse me for that. I want to make you understand that I do not understand all you can do. I have to know what is in store for those that follow you, and for those that don't. People will not follow an aggressive leader. We need a new direction in this country, we need leadership, and most will follow you if they like what they see. But if you come across as a fake, or an evil man, they will shun you like the plague." James was breathing hard and fast inside.

"What can I show you that will convince you?" "Sam's" usual command of the scene was lacking luster now. "Sam's" thought process was frantically trying to break through to his conscious entity. What is this plague?

"I don't want any stage tricks. We have magicians here that can make whole buildings disappear. I want something that I can use a base line for real authority, something that shows power!" James looked at Sam; he thought he might have gone too far.

"I could make you disappear, I could make you go to your home in the past. My entity has the ability to make you burn into something less than a dot on the floor!" "Sam" had his voice back, confidence was in his voice now.

James's hands went up in front of him. "Please don't do that! Tell me, Sam told me about your sending him to his earlier years, is that difficult?" James stepped back a little.

"Sam" sensed a fear in this human, a fear he might exploit to his advantage. "It takes a lot of power and concentration, that humans might be able to develop in the future. I had to get Sam out of my way; my entity needed to make some modifications to this building, and to control his worker." "Sam" waited to see what this human had been told.

"I was told of that, but I do understand. Sam was a little less understanding I believe. There are times that require a bold step. I understand, Wes had to be removed. But why send him back to his past?" James was beginning to sweat for real now, and not just because of the heat!

He does not ask more about Wes. Does he fear me, or does he understand? "Sam's" thought process calculated, to many unknowns. "My entity understands that times past must not change. It would be too much for this fragile world to handle. The results would cause too many unknowns in the future. And he need to see that my entity had power beyond his mental abilities to understand. I needed his attention!"

Sam thought, *This is great! He doesn't even use my name now! How expendable am I!*

"Sam, were you impressed?" James had to think. He hoped Sam would help, get him some time.

"I...er...I was mostly scared! I saw people that I had known many years ago. I was lost. I thought I had been drinking again. The sudden reappearance of 'Sam' was at best difficult. I had known he was always around, but I thought I was in a *Twilight Zone* episode. I thought I was stuck there...forever! And when I returned, well I guess Evelyn and I would have never become as we are, I would have just been her boss. We would not be a couple, as now. I was impressed, but scared. I had no idea what, or why till now. The chair, was that part of the modifications? I haven't been here much since Wes died." That part stuck in his throat. James gave him the sign, or what he hoped was the sign. Sam didn't have to be asked twice to shut up, he was still scared!

"'Sam,' I'll not ask you to send me to my childhood. That's fantastic, but I need to know what you can do. Just a little demonstration." James was playing with dynamite now, and didn't even know it.

"Sam's" entity smiled, or whatever it was supposed to be. It was a vicious smile. "Let my entity show you something that I had thought of using to get to Sam's house." No holds barred, "Sam" floated to the overhead door. He stopped six feet from the door. "Open the door!" "Sam's" voice boomed.

Sam opened the door, his mind wasn't ready for anything that might happen. He wanted to leave, now! The door rolled up slowly. It seemed the cold affected everything, even the door. The chain seemed to be extra slow. Sam's mind was moving extra fast, worry about what they had let themselves in for!

"Sam" floated about four feet off the floor. The smile on his face was almost a grin now.

"Sam" looked at the snow outside. It blew in with the cold. Never a flick of an eyelid could be as fast, a light so bright that Sam and James covered their eyes. It was so quick that neither had actually covered their eyes, they hadn't even moved. Snow still came into the door, but no snow existed, to halfway up the driveway.

James waked outside. The snow fell on his shoulders, small sounds as each flake touched his shirt. James knelt and picked up driveway rock. It was dry, not hot, not wet, dry! James spun around on his right leg to look into the garage at Sam and "Sam." "Can you do that wherever… you can …how the Hell did you do that?" The rocks in James's open palm began to accumulate snow. The rocks had no heat, the snow lay on the rocks. James looked at the driveway as the snow fell; it began to reclaim the uncovered rock. "What kind of energy do you possess?"

"Pure energy. Simple and complete energy." "Sam"s entity began to fade back into the garage.

Sam looked at James with the look of a child. It asked, "Please don't ask for any more!" Sam stood quietly by the overhead door push-button control, never offering to exit the garage, nor to ask any questions, frozen with fear, almost as if waiting for the next magic trick that would kill them both, and "Sam" would still smile.

"Look at this, Sam!" James held the rocks out for Sam's inspection. Sam only looked, never moving, just waiting. "This like something out of *Star Wars*, controlled energy that can melt the snow. Can you melt the rocks together?"

"And what would that prove?" "Sam" asked quietly floating inside the garage.

"No, I mean could you?" James still held the rocks. He walked into the garage. As soon as he was inside Sam pushed the down button. The door started its downward motion. James stood looking at the rocks as if they were gold.

"I could turn this place into a blackened scar on the face of this part of the world, if that is what you would like." "Sam" had begun to descend to the floor. His pant legs had become shorter, or his legs had become longer. Nothing held his feet to his legs. As he descended the feet came to rest at the end of his pants legs, just normal now. "Power is a precious gift, one that my entity shall share with the human world. In times yet to come my entity will develop power that will run all human needs. I will be the savior of this world, unlike man who would in times yet destroy it." "Sam" spoke matter-of-factly, no sneer now, just a serious face. He turned to walk to the storage room.

"You don't know how, yet?" James asked.

"My entity will, and are you yet a disbeliever?" "Sam" took his place on the electric chair. He sat in an upright position, shoulders squared and back. "There is much wrong with this world. I shall correct all of human problems. I will only keep those that are of value to this world, and my assistants." "Sam" looked directly at James, and then shifted his gaze to Sam, and back.

Sam wanted to turn away from the gaze but couldn't. It was brief, but conveyed the threat of days past. Sam looked away after the gaze turned back to James.

"We need to sit down, we need to talk!" James did not see the same threat as Sam had.

"If you are to be the one to convey my power to other humans, then you shall. I see no reason to demonstrate anymore. I can do that many times again, with far more devastating results. Do you need to see more, or has your human thought process seen enough?"

James had not seen enough, but thought better than tempt fate any further. "No, I do understand. I will work up a presentation, and begin to make my contacts with others. They may need to see something like this, in order to understand, or not. I will try to see what I can do, first. What do you think, Sam?"

Sam was incapable of much thought. "Yeah."

"I think we will be going now, unless there is something you want to tell us." James suddenly felt a rush of fear! His awestruck mind slipped back to reality.

"When?" "Sam" saw the fear in James's eyes now, not as much as in Sam's, but it had come suddenly.

James's hands closed around the rocks. He slid them into his pocket and slipped his coat on. "Three, four days. The holidays will make it a week or more before I can make contacts. Yeah, two weeks, that would do it. Don't you think, Sam?"

Sam had his coat on already, and was pulling his gloves on now. "Yeah, at least that long, the holidays. Will you come to the house, 'Sam'?" Sam looked at the floor, not wanting to lock gazes with his namesake.

"I will, if this snow slows and the roads are scraped or melted." Smug was the shape of his smile now.

"I guess we will leave now. I've got a lot of work to do." James stuck his hand in front of "Sam." After a few seconds he dropped his hand to his pockets and pulled out his gloves and hat. "We'll probably be back in a few days. Do we need to call, or whatever?"

"No!" "Sam" knew he had impressed James; he knew Sam had told him all that had happened in the last few days. He only smiled.

James backed into Sam, jumped slightly, as did Sam. They backed together for a few steps, Sam turned first and moved for the door. James was in close pursuit. Once outside they stepped quickly for the truck. Sam had the truck started and was almost in motion before James was inside. The dry rocks crunched under the truck's tires as they pulled away.

"What the Hell were you trying for in there, to see if he could melt us down too! My God, what were you thinking? Sam pulled onto Green Street and the tuck slipped to the right. He eased on the accelerator pedal, and it came back in line. "Were you so impressed that you wanted to see more? That thing's dangerous!"

"Calm down, Sam. I know what I am doing now. I let my mind want more, and I ... I know what happened, then he said I'll keep those that are of value!

I almost lost it! He has so much power that I can't imagine. Yeah, he only melted snow, but the rocks weren't even warm, it just went away, he didn't even move. It was like there had never been any snow! What else can he do, I wonder. The driveway was dry under the truck!" James looked out the windshield now. They had been there for almost an hour and their tracks had vanished. No one else had tried the road. The wind pushed the truck back and forth as they headed north.

"Did you see the office, or what was left of it?" Sam turned the steering wheel back and forth to keep the truck under control. The ruts under the snow made driving a full-time job.

"He did that with you?"

"Yeah!" Sam touched the brake gently as the curves came up; all the white made it difficult to judge where they were located. He steered into the curve, trying to correct for the wind and the road, and not knowing what he was correcting for first. "What do you think we can do?"

"I don't know, I just don't know. Not yet, but I'll think about it, there is a way. I'm just not sure." James had his arm braced for the rough road, and bent his legs in to help the truck make the curve.

"Relax. The worst part of the day is over, I think." Sam smiled a little now. "Now all we have to do is face the girls!"

Chapter 15
The New World

I

"Sam" never gets bored, "Sam" never gets excited, "Sam" never fears, and "Sam" does not suffer from human desires. Most of the time, his new home had given him a few moments of each. One out of four, not bad. "Sam's" entity had been ignoring his thought process. It had not served his entity well, and had been discarded as not of value to the plan. Thought process had been brought out for other plans, but "Sam" was suddenly hit with logic. Logic was one of the human traits that "Sam" had thought to have been of least value. His entity's thought process had rushed to the forefront as "Sam" began to assimilate ideas. His ideas were of how to process humans for need to his plan. Need for more humans began to seem necessary. He didn't like it, but there would be many humans that would need to be removed to allow only the dedicated humans. Those needed to make the human race, a race that would grow and expand to a new world of pure energy, "Sam's" energy.

"Don't your senses sign that maybe humans are plotting to prevent your plan from becoming finished? Only so many thoughts may be processed, reason for a plan, is not enough of a plan. A decided methodology must be determined to make all parts of the plan to become. Nothing becomes without reason. My plan cannot become, without reason. My plan is complete!" "Sam" heard voices, signs had been sent. His only want was for power, more power! Had he spoken aloud again?

"What if a plan is being formulated to stop your plan? One negates the other. What then, how might you prevent their plan?"

"What plan?" "Sam" heard voices, signs, no a voice. No one else was present. Sam and his friend James had gone—no one else. They were the only humans that knew of "Sam."

"My thought process will not sign you that such a plan exists, but then I cannot tell what is in humans' minds. My powers are many, your powers, but my guidance might prevent another plan from preventing completion of the plan."

"Sam" rose from the chair. He had not yet connected the power. "Who's there?"

"No one is here. It is only your thought process, that begs to sign you measures for completion of the plan."

"I do not have thoughts, I have a process that accepts my entity's plan. I am not human! I am a god!" "Sam" floated about the office and back to the open garage. The only sound was that of the furnace. Clothing fell from "Sam" as he moved about the garage in search of the voice. When his thought process was identified as his own signs, and not that of an intruder, "Sam" slowly returned to the storage room and his chair. "My entity's plan is without flaw. My human and his friend are incapable of preventing my plan. My entity saw fear, a fear of the power I have, a fear of me! Spirit does not command my entity. I am my own entity now, not a slave to be sent to assist, no longer!"

"Sam" connected the electricity to his chair. He occupied the chair, at first stiffly, then he relaxed, he became a slight bluish glow, his thought process became inactive. Reason! The last thought processed before power began to fill his entity, his thought process still was active, but could not receive sign of acknowledgment!

II

The ride was not without trepidation, but after all the slipping and sliding, a few close calls seemed without note. On the road as another car passed by, sideways, was perhaps the worst, but the truck responded, the ditch had been shallow, and a bit of luck, they had ended up on the road again, and even headed in the right direction. Sam looked at James. They both shared a smile of Thank God, and onward with the conversation.

"Close. He seems to require assistance, the same assistance he has given all these years. I don't think he can make it on his own. He could eliminate a lot of folks till he finds the ones he likes!" James only glanced at Sam; his eyes were always facing forward. Death by entity seemed far removed; death by rolling one large four-by-four seemed immediate, and he only wanted to see it coming.

"Well, it seems that not only does he need it, he will get it if he wants it. One by one or two by two, either cooperate or die. Pretty simple way to get people to assist. Jump off the cliff and lunge to your death, or I'll toss you off! Most people will take their own chance as to be tossed off, they had a choice. Those are the ones he will get rid of. The compliant humans will be put to use, for whatever the Hell he wants!"

The truck struck a hidden piece of ice that had fallen off someone's vehicle and hidden well by the fresh snow. The truck bucked and whipped back and forth. Sam steered into the skid, and again, and once more for good measure.

Without missing a beat Sam continued. "So, Mr. Alien Hunter, what kind of alien do we have here? Has he gotten into some bad electricity, something tainted with foreign power, or what?"

James had recovered from the skids as quickly as Sam. "That might just be it!"

"What?"

"What you just said, he can't take the cold anymore. It's the electricity that has affected him! He had a power source, a source from somewhere else, not of this world! And now he has lost some of his power! Like Superman and kryptonite! He can't do it anymore. Car batteries run down in the winter because of the cold!" James looked at Sam for longer than he liked, but turned to the windshield again. He saw the overpass at Odin.

"He seems pretty powerful to me! He didn't toss you all about the office and use you as a battering ram!" Sam looked at James. He watched him face back to the windshield. Sam looked again to the front. He too saw the overpass; relief was in sight.

"That's it! Now all we have to do is find a way to make the power work for us!" James was talking to James now, he mumbled and moved his hands as though he had an invisible audience on the dash.

"Hey! Talk to me, not you! I want to hear any wits of wisdom you might have here too! I now I'm only the driver, but I am part of this too!" Sam eased up on the accelerator as the truck started up the overpass.

"Just working out a few technical problems. That's all. But I think we have bought ourselves a little time by going out there, instead of waiting on him to drive in to your house." James's hands continued their motion.

"How do you figure that?" Sam asked as the truck slipped right. He brought it back just as they passed over the top. No traffic, no one—it almost looked deserted. Lights shone through the icy windows. Few if any cars had been on the road.

Sam normally took the first left, but thought not to tempt fate and slowed more without the brake, and turned at the second left. The road was white. No one, no traffic, it was after 1:00 p.m. now. The snow was at least three feet deep in town. The truck slowed its forward motion and had to be urged on with a slight accelerator touch. They crossed the tracks and were almost home, and the relief was easy to see in their faces.

III

The women had set about making a meal. Not much else to do; it was after all, Christmas! Dinner had been planned. Nicole had been a lot of help, but one could see she had not been a made for scratch cook. Evelyn had begun shortly after the men had left with the ham, the sweet potatoes were prepared for the oven, and put in the refrigerator, to wait their turn in the oven. Pies for dessert and jello was molded into colorful little trees. The table was set, and they only had to wait on the ham in the oven.

"How did you and James meet?" Evelyn asked.

Nicole was not paying attention; her thoughts were with James, and the alien, or whatever. "What's that again?"

"I asked how you and James met." Evelyn looked up from folding napkins.

"He was on vacation, a working vacation it turned out. I had been a bit of trouble with the feds. They picked me up in Germany, tied me to a chair and proceeded to tell me about some papers I had written in college. I was being looked for, not in particular by the Watchers but by government people. They made me a deal I couldn't turn down. James and I hit it off. It was shaky in the beginning—I wanted to kill him. But I got my citizenship back, a good-paying job that I enjoyed, and here we are!" Nicole hoped Evelyn would not ask too much else.

And so went Christmas day. Every now and again one or both would look out the window, expecting the big truck to arrive at the back door. As time passed, both became less and less talkative. Conversation had all but died. The two women thought about their respective significant other, what perils had befallen them, or were they in a ditch somewhere, an accident, and more Evelyn than Nicole. What had "Sam" done to them? Were they tied up, or had he just killed them? If he uncovered their real reason for going to the garage, that was probably what had happened.

The clock over the sink registered one-thirty when they heard a car, or a truck as it turned out to have been. A big old black truck, with a blade on it headed to the dead end. The only vehicle either had seem all day. Then Nicole saw another set of headlights. The truck was all covered in snow and ice. It stopped and let the black truck back out the street. It was the men; no one else would come to the end, it was the last house on Valentine Street. The truck turned into the driveway and pulled up at the back. The truck sat for a few minutes, idling, then it shut off, doors opened revealing Sam and James. They both went to the backdoor, waiting, Evelyn thankful, and Nicole awaiting the story.

James was in first, still stomping his feet to get the snow off his boots and legs. Sam came next, going through the same procedures. James looked a Nicole and smiled sheepishly. Sam looked to Evelyn, who could hold back no longer. She wrapped her arms around Sam and laid her head on his chest.

"Was 'Sam' there?" Evelyn's head lay against Sam's cold leather coat.

James answered, "Was he! It was really something. This is a real honest-to-goodness alien. If not he was the best magician in the world!"

Evelyn helped Sam with his coat as James related the stories from the garage. Evelyn slowed with her assistance, as the stories continued. Sam took his coat and gave Evelyn a long look, and a slight nod. Sam took James coat and hung them in the kitchen closet. Sam turned to the coffee maker that had been in constant use since they had left, and poured a cup of coffee. Sam leaned against the sink letting the heat in the kitchen soak into him.

Evelyn got the ham ready, and started to put hot food on the table. Christmas dinner was about to begin. The story would not surround Santa and his reindeer today. Dinner was good and all had their fill, the pies would be cut later and the men adjourned to the living room. The women cleaned the kitchen, a quiet clean; not a lot to be discussed, most had been done over the meal.

Sam was to the point in the living room. "What can we do? No whitewash! Just how?"

"I have seen a lot at the garage today, I have seen more than I ever expected. He has power, but not what he thinks he has. I don't think he can hold off a real offensive." James fingered the garland around the fireplace.

"Offensive! What are you talking about?" Sam was rubbing his right temple; he had the beginnings of a real barnburner of a headache! "He has duct tape down pat, I'm afraid to see much else!"

"No. What I mean is that I don't think he can really be away from the electricity too long; he has to recharge a lot. I don't know what he's got there, but it looks like a bunch of 220-volt setups. I don't know what he had before, but electricity has limits, I think." James turned to Sam and sat down on the hearth.

"You think! What kind of an answer is that?" Sam was pacing and rubbing his temple.

"I hate to tell you this, but I had never met a real alien! And now I have to dispose of him. I don't know how. That's what I'm trying to tell you! I have a few ideas, do you?"

Sam massaged his temple steadily. "James, that's why I called. I thought that you might have in your years of looking, have thought about what if I find a bad one. I have no ideas at all."

"Ideas about what?" Evelyn asked as she and Nicole came into the room.

Sam put his left arm around Evelyn and continued to massage his temple. "We may be screwed about getting rid of 'Sam.' James says he has a few ideas, I have none. I have lived with 'Sam' for many years, but never had a need to get rid of him, or even try. Lately 'Sam' has become unmanageable, he is no longer what he was. He has become... I don't know what he's become!"

"I'll get your medicine." Evelyn left the living room, and so did any conversation.

Sam looked at James with Nicole standing beside him. The lights flashed, the street light shone through the window, and Sam's headache grew in intensity! Evelyn returned with pills for Sam and a glass of water. The quiet was deafening. Evelyn remained where she had given Sam the medicine. Sam paced.

Nicole spoke first, it seemed too loud, after the silence. "Well, what can we do? You two have seen a real show today, but how can we use it, what was really seen? Was there something that he did that would show a direction?"

"Sam, what have you seen him become?" James was up; he wanted to pace, but stood fast.

Sam rubbed his temple, and his right eye watered. "Change into what?"

"That's my question. Has he ever changed into anything? Something that you remember from your childhood? Anything? I don't think he can come here, I don't think he can handle the cold, I don't think he can drive because of the weather. He can do lots of stuff, and I think what he showed us is only a little show. I will bet it takes a lot of power to melt the snow, to change his shape. Did you see the way he looked when we got there? I think he is running on a pipe dream. I don't think he can pull this rule-the-world trick off. I do think he can fry all of us in a millisecond if he so desires!"

Nicole felt a shiver slide down her back at that statement. "You said you could see through him. How does he keep his clothes on, why don't they just fall off? Can he become real?"

"What do you mean real?" Evelyn asked.

"You know. Real. Like us. Skin and bones. He evidently knows something about us. He can become a shape like us, he has fingers, and evidently toes. He smiles and talks. He is like us but you could see through his leg? His ankle, right through it, just like a window. And he pulled his socks up without bending, or pulling them up with his hands, they just slid up his leg! I was talking fast and not making much sense. I took up the public relations job just as Evelyn had told him, and I think he took it, hook, line, and sinker! But I don't know how much longer I can keep it up. He's not a fool, but he does not know what I can or cannot do. But he will pick up on it quick! I just don't know." James took up the pacing, as Sam had sat down, still rubbing his temple.

"What does he look like when he's not 'Sam'?" Nicole asked.

Sam looked up with his right eye shut, still watering. "I tell you, he has never been anything but Friend, 'Sam.' I didn't even know you could see through him till today. He has always been dressed like me, my size, my shape, me! And I didn't even know that. Evelyn was the one to notice that, not me! He was always been opaque, but not clear like today."

"But he could be, right?" Evelyn asked.

James and Sam started to answer at the same time. Sam kept rubbing and motioned James on with a wave of his hand.

"I think he could! I told him that he would have to be careful not to let people see him in a transparent form. People would not think of him as a god, but a ghost! Like I said I was really talking fast, I was scared!" James stopped pacing, and looked at the others.

"So you think we could wear him down by making him do parlor tricks? Maybe he could become a pink bunny!" Sam stopped rubbing long enough to answer Nicole.

"But maybe we could find a flaw! A chink in his armor. Something, we don't have much else!" Nicole answered quickly.

"Yeah! That's a start! But we need him here, away from his power." James looked at Sam, who now looked up to meet James's gaze with his one open eye.

"You want to bring him here? How?" Evelyn's voice moved up the scale a little as she asked.

"Yes, he has to depend on us to take him back, and we have had some long sessions here, and he will want to fit in, so he will stay long. He won't fry us; he needs us right now! He will want to do most anything we ask, within reason. We can see him in action then. We will have to be careful, I don't want to give it away, but he has to really want help, he doesn't have any choice." James was happy with his thoughts, and to get to see what this alien could do!

Sam's headache had improved. He looked to Evelyn. She had the deer-in-the-headlights look! Nicole watched Evelyn, then Sam, and back.

"You got a plan, James?" Sam asked.

"Not really. Or do you want me to lie to you?" James was still pacing. "Tomorrow."

"Tomorrow," Sam repeated.

Chapter 16
A Beginning?

I

James had a plan! Everyone was elated! What was the plan, what was to happen? That was yet to be determined. That, or the lack of that, made for a quiet breakfast. Sleep had been difficult for all. Nicole was the only one without anticipation. Coffee, biscuits and scrambled eggs were consumed in silence. Each in turn looked at all the others, on the side trying not to be seen. The worry was there, the fear was more apparent in Evelyn and Sam, but James also showed a slight fear. Eyes glanced back and forth, all heads concentrated on the meal, maybe the last meal.

Sam finished eating. He put on his coat and while pulling on his gloves, he said "It's time, I'm going to start the truck and let it warm a bit." He turned and was gone.

"It's stopped snowing!" Evelyn looked out the window over the sink.

"Good." James started to get his coat on. "That ride yesterday was a bear. I hope for a better one today."

Sam came in stomping his feet. "It started. It is cold out there! But it has stopped snowing. We are ready and will be back in a couple of hours. It's going to be icy out there and we will go slow."

"And it might take a little talking to get 'Sam' to come with us too. And he may not, I just don't know, we will play it by the minute." James looked at Sam. "Ready?"

"No. But do we have a choice?" Sam looked at James with dead eyes.

"No."

"We would like to know what your plan is before you go." Evelyn looked at Sam. They had discussed it in bed the night before.

"Me too,' Nicole chimed in.

"I don't exactly have one. This is right off the cuff. Let me get him here first. It will be obvious or it will be panicked, I don't know just yet. Don't look at me like that, just bear with me a bit." James pushed by Sam, and was out the door.

Sam shrugged his shoulders, walked to Evelyn and kissed her on the cheek. "I love you!" He turned and was gone, behind James.

"What the Hell was that!" Nicole exclaimed.

"He's your partner, not mine. If you don't know, I'm sure I don't." Evelyn started to clean the table from the meager breakfast.

"All of you are afraid. I feel left out. I'm running on fear that's not my own, and that creates panic, I'm real close!" Nicole began to help clear the table.

James was sitting on the passenger seat, belted in. He watched as Sam crossed in front of the truck. The door opened and Sam got in. The blower on the heater was beginning to clear the windshield. The whiteness was brilliant. The sun shone like in the summer, but no heat could be felt from the blazing ball. It was 9:30, and the day's plans were only a mere sketch in James's mind, and he was the planner. Sam was trying to find the right words to begin his conversation. Sam slid the windshield wiper control to low. The wipers hesitated, then began their duty and ground away at the snow and ice. "Do we, or should I say, you have a plan?"

"Yes and no! The yes part is still unclear. Will he come with us? I think so. Will he be able to detect an insurrection? Maybe. Will he do as we ask? I don't know. That's about as far out as my plan goes. Not much. But I will make leaping advances if he does all that we ask." The wipers had managed a hole in front of each of its passengers.

Sam got had the scraper in his hand, got out and began to assist the wipers. Between Sam, the wipers, and the defroster the windshield began to clear again. Sam worked the side windows now.

James had thoughts, and he had opinions; none made a lot of sense right now. He felt guilty that all of them thought he had a plan. He first had to develop a pattern, a pattern of little facts about "Sam," then tonight he could make a real plan. Today he was to get to know "Sam." His first and only alien. He had to know where he was from, he had to know if there were others, and where they were, why were they not here too! Then, sadly he had to find a way to change this alien's mind; he had to keep him for evaluation. But no one could know what he was about to try. And as far as what he was about to try, that was true, he had no idea! Sam had the windows clean, and got back behind the steering wheel.

Sam looked at James once, no response, and he began to back the truck into the remains of last night's turnaround spot. "You don't have a plan do you."

"Not really, but I will have soon enough. You did well yesterday. Follow my lead again, and we will have this alien bagged and tagged!"

The roads were icy. It was slick. The sun had made all ruts like valleys. The truck seemed to be riding on nothing but the frame, it jolted and bounced, new or not rattles became more and more the sounds of the day. When they got to Highway 50 it had been plowed, basically a wide lane. If they met someone it would be tight. The snow had been pushed aside, leaving the remaining snow compressed into a slick hard pack. Sam lightly touched the gas and the truck was sideways. He steered back and forth, the truck slowly came back into alignment. They started up the overpass, the tires spun, and grabbed, it slipped from side to side. Sam gave James a look of dread as they climbed over the top. The road lay before them in a jagged, snow-walled ribbon. It looked wider, in places. Wishful thinking. Sam unzipped his coat a little, as the heater, still running full, had begun to heat the cab.

The ride was eventful! The road was littered with cars in the snow banks and ditches. It was ten times as slick as previously, ten times worse than either had thought. Conversation had been held to a minimum as the truck slid in all directions but straight!

James had begun as they approached the last mile. "I know you're busy, but we can't let him know how bad it is out here. Play along with like it is always this bad and nothing new. Just follow my lead." James had a death grip on the door pull as Sam turned into the driveway. It had a few inches of snow but not bad. James exhaled full, and took in his first real breath of the ride.

Sam killed the engine and slumped over the wheel. "Act like it's always like this, now that's gong to be some acting! You had better be in high form, your BS will go far longer than my acting. I will try not to look scared to death of the possibility of having to drive three more times on this road today!" Sam never looked at James, he just got out and zipped his coat back to the top.

James followed suit with his coat as well, and they slowly trudged toward the side door. Sam turned the knob and pushed the door open. The heat was welcome from the outside, but it didn't take long to realize it was like the tropics in the garage. "'Sam,' are you here?" *Stupid thought, stupid question,* Sam thought.

"But of course." "Sam's" voice returned, not too loud, not too low, just right. "What brings you out in such short time?"

"It's not me, it's James, he has a lot of questions that I could not answer. He asked and asked, and I told him it would be best to ask you direct." Sam felt rubbery inside, but he kept up a good front.

"James, you have sign for my entity?" "Sam" asked, to the point.

"Yes, I do. You do mean questions?" James stuck his hand out, knowing "Sam" would not take it, but he wanted it to appear normal and natural. James let his hand drop, in response to no move by "Sam" to take it. "Nicole and I need to ask a lot of questions in order to get going on this. We need to make sure we have all the details of what we are selling."

"Selling! You are not selling me, you are to present me to humankind!" "Sam" showed a little irritation to being sold.

"No! No, that's not meant to be literal, but we must sell you and your image first. Then we can sell your product—I mean, what it is that you can do for mankind. But you see you have only known Sam. Now you didn't have to do anything to make Sam like you. He was a kid. But you now have to deal with skeptical adults! There are people that will believe that you are only another magician, that has a new name, and will not take you seriously." James had his hands going, he was rolling already.

"If they do not believe they will not be needed! No problem, simple solution!" "Sam" was not buying.

"They will infect others, as people begin to disappear, others will wonder. They will be led in the wrong direction by your trying to assist them. People need to know the good side of you, and learn the work that has sent you to assist them. You may be able to assist, but you will meet with much resistance. You will have to explain your assistance. Humans will run, they will hide, they will defy your every attempt. We have to sell you to humankind first. They need direction. But they need to be led, not forced. There will not be enough left over to lead. And you will not have the best prospects. You will have to settle for those of less desirable character than if they can see your plan, after they know that you are only to assist them in making a better place for them to live. They need a leader, not a tyrant; a leader, not an ogre!" James had to stop to breathe. He was rolling, and he was making "Sam" look worried.

"They will accept my plan. Will they follow one who has to be presented, as you say?" "Sam" floated two inches off the floor; it was obvious that he was unaware.

"Look, 'Sam'! You are floating again. Magicians make tigers float, and they make things appear. You cannot be less than a human god. You have to be like humans! Like humans with special powers. Not like a magician. You have to be among the humans, just like them, then we will tell them, no show them what you, with your special powers can do. Then and only then will they accept you as you are now. Then they will understand. Humans are fickle. They have to know what is best first." James looked at "Sam," he looked hard at what shown as eyes. "Do you understand?"

"Ask your questions." "Sam" looked back at James just as hard.

"Get your coat, and let's go." James never faltered; he turned to the door and started away.

"Go. Go where?" "Sam" had not stopped floating.

"To Sam's house, that's where Nicole and Evelyn are now. It's far more comfortable there. And we can all help you with your own little problems, like floating!" James stopped and looked back at "Sam." His look showed demand; he had gotten in too deep, he thought at first.

"I have not been driving as long as most humans, and the snow is very trying on my skills at the car. I cannot leave just yet." "Sam" was backpedaling now.

"Sam and I will bring you back later. But we must find all your little problems, get you to start to control yourself first. I understand that it will not be an easy task, but we must. It will be good for Evelyn to see you again; she asked about you earlier. And my partner Nicole has yet to meet you. Are you shy? I know I am a little difficult to deal with at times, for that I apologize. But it's the way I make my money, I have to be hard. Get your coat, it's cold out there." Once again James pushed "Sam" as hard as he could, he wanted a reaction.

"Sam, you will return me to this place in time?" "Sam" was bending.

"Of course. It will be no problem." Sam had been afraid his voice might not be there when he needed it. It came out clear and normal, he thought, he hoped.

"I have no other coat." "Sam" was unsure now; his voice had given him away.

"The truck is warm. We will put you up front, you'll be fine." Sam's acting was pouring out now, he hoped.

James led as he had attempted, before, now "Sam" then Sam. Just three good old boys out for a ride in the snow. The snow crunched as they walked, a noise they had not heard when they arrived, at least didn't hear. Now it was overbearing, but none from "Sam."

"Just like now, you need to make foot prints in the snow, you are floating again. You have to stop the floating and be a human." James was almost a nag now.

"I will try and do better, later—the cold, it is difficult." "Sam" floated into the front seat. The seat did not show any weight on it at all. James saw as he got in the door behind "Sam."

Sam started the truck, and pushed the heater control to high. It was cool as it started. "Sam's" legs seemed to shrink away from the cool air, but began to fill out as the temperature increased. Sam turned the truck around and headed out the driveway. On Green Street the truck slipped and slid as it had on the way in. "Sam" looked out the windshield, eyes not moving, almost glassy.

"The girls will have a good meal laid on, I just imagine. That ham was delicious! I don't get too much home cooking with Nicole. She's like me, we eat out a lot, and frozen stuff. After this trip I will have different view of frozen though. I have been cold since I got off the airplane!" James kept his conversation moving, like it was an everyday occurrence to have an unknown entity on board.

"Yeah, hot food will be nice; breakfast was a little light. 'Sam,' have you ever eaten anything? We have been together for many years, and I have never seen you eat anything." Sam had picked up on the direction of James's conversation. "What is a normal holiday feast in Arizona, James?"

"It's all the same. I have been in other countries that don't seem to have any kind of idea what is good food, or maybe we just don't like their food. But there are all kinds of food from all over the world that have special meaning, I guess. We just try and get home cooking, or at least American food, wherever we travel. Sometimes that is a difficult task in itself." James rattled on. He paused for "Sam" to have time to enter into the conversation.

"Most foods are cooked, correct?" "Sam" asked, his eyes still glued to the road ahead, or at least directed that way.

"Of course! I guess fruits, and some vegetables are eaten raw," James said, and paused for "Sam."

"Raw? Not prepared? Why must you consume food so often?" "Sam" asked. The questions seemed rather stupid for one who was not new to his surroundings.

"Where have you been all these years?" James asked, almost in a laughable voice.

"Energy is the basis for my entity, consumable food stuffs is not necessary!" "Sam's" voice almost boomed inside the confines of the truck cab.

Sam cringed, and pulled the wheel as he did so. The truck responded by allowing the rear to slide and slip back and forth. The rear movement told Sam to pay better attention to what he was supposed to be doing, not to "one up" his entity.

"Hey! Calm down a bit! That voice of yours will crack the glass! We don't mean anything by asking. We, or at least I have no idea on what is normal for you, and what's not. I have to ask a lot of questions in the next few hours that you might consider to be stupid. But how else am I to know? We all are getting to know you, more today than yesterday, and more yet tomorrow. We are, as you say, only here to assist." James had an inner smile that he hoped "Sam" could not see.

"I have developed a few traits from humans. My thought process has a difficult time in proper responses to questioning. I have only assisted, and now have a greater plan. To be trifled with details is not my entity's normal purpose. Answer I will, but I do not understand all of your questions. My thought process will become more clear on answers as it feels they are in direct design to my plan." "Sam" was cold, he was irritated, he was angry, but these were traits that he had only begun to recognize, Calm, Slow, Control entered "Sam's" thought process.

The road had gotten more treacherous than on the ride out. Speed was at a bare minimum. The sun had caused the snow pack to become an icy ribbon to take advantage of any lack of concentration of the best of drivers. The truck was not nimble. It lacked any grace; it was only a means to transport from one place to another. The amenities inside only made one feel comfortable on their ride to instant death. One minor glitch could prove to be the last. Sam and James knew that they could walk to nearby houses to get out of the cold, that is of course if they could walk. "Sam" was another question. The cold made him uncomfortable, but what else it did to him they did not know, and did not want to find out! The truck slipped and slid its way toward Odin. A large state truck was in the ditch shortly after the turn toward Odin. They stopped but all on board had deserted the now unusable snow plow. James and Sam looked at one another in wonder of what wonderful road lay ahead, or had they already traveled the worst part. Only time would reveal that secret. The wind blew the snow, and it drifted as they watched. Any clear sections left from recent plowing had begun to drift over. Sam checked his fuel—a half tank. He pushed the switch to its second position and the fuel gauge showed a little over three quarters. The second tank was in the rear and was left for more weight and better traction. Sam put the switch back in place to keep the weight in the rear for traction. The overpass could be seen in the distance, as Mother Nature allowed the wind to die down on occasions. They knew their progress was slow, but they were progressing, at least in direction of their vehicle. Conversation had become James and Sam, small talk to keep their minds off the road and its presently deteriorating condition, and the next trip that would only be worse.

The threesome had spent many minutes in anticipation of arrival. James and Sam in wonderment of what they would discover next about their companion's personality and powers. "Sam's" thought process was trying to make a decision as to why he had agreed to become a part of this farce. He was the all powerful, he had the ability to put a stop to all of these foolish questions. He was uncertain, but very certain, at the same time he knew that he would prevail!

The overpass shined like it was chrome steel. It reflected the sun's light and the headlights as they approached. All of this too spotlighted the little blue car's valiant, but ineffective ability to negotiate the overpass. The truck came a stop. The little jerks and jolts reminded them they were still on an ice skating rink.

"What seems the problem with the little car?" "Sam" asked, as cold as the surrounding air.

"He's too little, no traction on the ice. We will have try and push him, before he gets stuck in one of the snow banks on either side. Are you ready for this, James?" Sam had his hand on the door handle.

"I guess so! This is going to be a joke, he can't move and we can't walk." James opened his door while pulling on his gloves. Sam followed.

The two rescuers used the truck's front fenders to inch their way the front bumper, where they found a grip. James and Sam looked at on another and laughed, the first smiles of the day, real smiles. Sam looked to "Sam" and saw no change in the stern face he wore. James took a step and fell face forward on the snow-covered pavement. Sam laughed. James was not amused in the beginning, but joined in as he tried to get up.

"We might as well wait till they get stuck and try to get by them, they will never make the top. I'm not sure I can even get up!" James was laughing loudly now, and Sam was sliding all around the bumper trying to stay standing upright.

A sudden bright light completely encompassed both James and Sam, the little blue car's front tires found purchase, tire smoke rolled like a top fuel dragster, and the blue car was up and over the top in a flash. James found himself lying on hard cold asphalt. Sam became stable so quickly that he almost fell. The smiles left their faces and the two looked at one another. Laughter ceased. James stood and brushed himself off. Sam stood erect and looked at "Sam." No change in the look of determination on his face, no smile, his eyes did not blink. The two would-be rescuers move toward their respective doors.

"Nice job, 'Sam,'" James said as he got in and closed out the cold.

"Assistance is many forms that are determined by my thought process. The little car would not have made the hilltop with the ice and snow." "Sam" never turned his head, never made any indication that making dry roads in the winter was out of place.

Sam pulled the shift lever to drive and the truck was off to the top of the overpass, just as any other day. Sam had accelerated as they moved up the hill, but saw snow at the top. He lightly tapped the brakes, and the truck slowed. The downhill side had not been touched by whatever "Sam" had used to clear the snow. In front of them was a small blue car just past the bottom of the overpass, sideways and kicking snow up with its front tires. They had kept speed up to the other side of the hill, and were suffering the results now. Sam chuckled as he saw the small car, and hoped he had slowed enough to make his turn, or could avoid the small car if he indeed stayed in his present position. The small car corrected and moved on down Highway 50. Sam decided the second turn would be his best choice, and proceeded on his present course.

"How do you do that, 'Sam'?" James asked again, trying to get "Sam" out of his sullen mood before arriving at Sam's house.

"I do not want it there anymore, and it is not." "Sam's" look brightened slightly. He knew the ride was about to end; he was glad for that far more than James and Sam would ever know.

Sam and James prodding laughed about the surprise the little blue car must have had to have been suddenly launched over the overpass. "A Kodak moment indeed!" James had said. They both laughed. It was a forced laugh, not something they wanted to do, only because at the time it seemed necessary. "Sam" never looked at either one; he could not see the worried looks on both of their faces. "Sam's" eyes never moved, never blinked, only watched, but seeing what?

In town as small as it was, human life had emerged, kids making snowmen, new sleds were bogged down in the deep snow. People were, as always, adjusting, and trying to make the best of the time at hand. Some driveways were in the process of being cleared, at least an effort was being made, but not much headway with the deep snow. They had nowhere to go when cleared, but their piece of the world would be ready to use, if and when the roads were cleared. Plumes of white vapors were in front of all, children and adults alike. They laughed and waved as the four-wheel-drive plowed through the streets.

Many four-wheel-drive trucks would be sold in the upcoming weeks; they would not be caught like this again!

A car was stuck on O'fallon, so they drove to the next available street that connected with Valentine. Only one set of tracks were vaguely visible, they slowly made their way to Sam's house, where Christmas lights could be seen on the tree in the living room as they turned into the driveway.

"I love to drive in the snow. We haven't had this much in a while!" Sam tried to sound like he had enjoyed the drive; his voice gave way to the truth, but "Sam" never indicated he knew. Sam saw Evelyn looking out the back door as the truck came to a sliding stop. One of the girls had shoveled the snow away on the deck to a large rectangle in the driveway. They now occupied that rectangle.

II
Christmas Begins

"They are here!" Evelyn turned to Nicole and exclaimed. No happiness in her voice, although she was relieved that they had gotten back as soon as they had. Dread filled her mind and heart. This could be very bad, and most likely would be worse than her fears. Evelyn saw all three figures in the truck. The sun revealed that there were two Sams and a James; two had left and three had returned. She stood by the door, her hand on the cold knob. Doors opened and all three got out, "Sam" being the most graceful as he did not touch the cleared spot. He floated to the door first.

Nicole made an audible gasp as she saw "Sam" maneuver the steps without touching them, his form seemed unaffected by the wind. He moved without any movement of his extremities, his eyes only looked forward as he approached the door. Evelyn automatically opened the door, and "Sam" was in the kitchen. James and Sam came lightly stomping their feet to remove the snow from their boots.

"Hi, 'Sam.' This is Nicole White. Proper introductions. Nicole, this is 'Sam,' just 'Sam,' I have never heard another name, and in actuality we named him 'Sam,' because of how much he looks like Sam!" Evelyn looked from one to another. She had run out of words.

Nicole and Evelyn had decided they would react to "Sam" as any other person. But "Sam's" exit from the truck had begun a new set of rules that had not been outlined as yet. Nicole stuck her hand out to greet "Sam." Her forward motion and extended hand caused "Sam" to move back slightly. Nicole saw that "Sam" did not intend to shake her hand and she let it fall to her side.

"Well, 'Sam.' Sam and Evelyn have told me so many things about you. James has had the opportunity to have already met you, so now is my time to get to know you." Nicole had stumbled through her words. She still saw that "Sam" floated a few inches above the floor.

"Do you have a fire in the other room? I do not like to be cold." "Sam"s' lips moved, but a little slow for the voice, out of sync. Nicole watched in amazement that all had been told true.

"Yes...yes we do. I thought you might be cold after that long drive." Evelyn directed "Sam" with her right hand.

"Sam" moved toward the living room. His legs moved silently, but his feet did not touch the floor yet. Sam and James watched the scene unfold, as they took off their coats. James looked at the wide-eyed Nicole as "Sam" exited the kitchen. She had a painted-on smile, one that James had never seen. She only looked back to James, and changed her gaze to include Sam. James and Sam walked toward the hallway. As they passed the women they both took a hand as if to lead them to whatever awaited them in the living room. As they came through the archway, "Sam" could be seen in front of the fireplace, his back to the room, and the incoming four.

Nicole took a set nearest to "Sam," by the Christmas tree. Her eyes were glued to his feet, which almost touched the floor. She inspected his clothing. It now appeared to be more normal. His hair, graying, not as much as Sam's but still there was a noticeable likeness. "'Sam,' I have a few questions, if you don't mind."

"Sam" turned to Nicole and he looked into her eyes. His eyes seemed softer now, his facial appearance now softer too. "Everyone has questions. James is never without a question on his lips. Time is passing as my entity answers questions. Go ahead, I have found humans require answers."

"Do you never touch the ground, or anything?"

James butted in. "I have told 'Sam' that he will have to begin to look more human. He is going to have to walk, not float about. I didn't say anything as we came in, 'cause he doesn't like the cold. But I have told him about that!"

"Sam" placed his feet on the carpet. Nicole could see the carpet move with his apparent weight. "Sam" grimaced like a small child caught with his hand in the cookie jar!

"Oh I see, I didn't mean to cause you any additional problems. Well that's settled, but you will have to be so careful not to float when others are around. Sam and Evelyn have had many times with you, and we don't have long to come up with a plan, so, we will be asking a lot of questions. I hope you don't mind." Nicole backed off and let James take the lead.

"I believe the girls have lunch about ready. Would you care for anything, 'Sam'?"

James knew better but asked anyway; he wanted to see the response.

"Nothing. Thank you." "Sam" didn't like the questions, but required assistance in getting his entity known, and James seemed to have a plan, so he would endure, even though he would like to occupy James, and drain him of all his energy, and watch him slowly disappear!

"Do we want to have lunch in here? We could be far more comfortable, and that way "Sam" can sit by the fire," Evelyn asked. All nodded their approval. Evelyn set about getting the trays, and setting them up by the archway.

James and Nicole were supposed to be the experts, so they remained in the living room, while Sam helped Evelyn. All was planned, but what to do next? James had seen what "Sam" could do while seemingly not trying. He had his careful approach planned.

"'Sam,' what made you come to the decision to manage human life forms, and to take control of this little planet? Have other entities done this on other worlds?" James sat on the couch and began taking notes. His notes had nothing to do with his questions.

"I know of no other worlds, I know of no other plan. My entity has been with Sam for many years, in assisting Sam. Wasted energy, and wasted lives have been seen. My entity will instruct humans on the proper conservation of energy. Humans will become self-sustaining, energy will become a fuel for future time. Humans waste energy at an alarming rate. They use systems to manage health, doctors, and medicine. I will instruct humans on wasted human energy. Every human contains energy. This energy is allowed to become fallow in older humans, and wasted. It could be recycled into humans, extending life force, and energy ten times yet to come." "Sam" had a little James in him, their egos were marked by the same showmanship.

"Some humans will have to be…sacrificed?" Nicole asked.

"Not sacrificed. Recycled, returned to useable energy, energy to assist other humans, those that have vision for time yet to happen." "Sam's" hands were behind him, in a statesman stance. His coat fell open to reveal a light brown turtleneck sweater.

"They will be recycled? How can you recycle a human life?" Nicole did not want to sound the way she had, but the idea of humans being killed to help his world didn't set well with Nicole.

"By occupying a human form, all energy can be absorbed into my entity and recycled into other humans. This additional energy is capable of being perpetuated into additional humans over and over. The meager life of one human will assist a human of normal energy to go forward to create, and perform many times beyond human capability." "Sam" now had his best smile on his face. He had practiced it in the bathroom of Sam's garage many time now. And he liked to smile!

"How will you pick the humans that will become part of this master race?" James had not heard till now the plan, a plan out of some science fiction story yet to be told.

"That is a process that you will assist my entity to emplace at a much more efficient pace than my entity's original plan." "Sam" still smiled.

"We will? How will we do that? I thought our job was to assist in presentation of you to the public. To make you a known entity." James was into a plan he had not anticipated.

"Lunch, everyone. Just make up all you want. What's not eaten will go to the dog, as soon as we get one." Evelyn had not heard the questions or answers, but could see the looks on the other three. Sam had only been in the living room for a few minutes before Evelyn and had a look of terror on his face.

"We have a lot of work to do, just to make you presentable to the public. Look at the way you float about." James pointed to "Sam's" present position, about one inch off the floor. "You have to understand, Mr. John Q. Public will think you are evil, just because you are different. If asked what you eat, and you tell them electricity, they're going to freak out! They will run from you like you have smallpox! They will not believe anything you say. If one hundred humans tried to get away from you, and you didn't want them to leave, could you stop all of them, without killing them?" James thought the ice had been getting pretty thin, but he had to see what "Sam" would tell him.

"Yes. Is smallpox worse than the plague?"

"They are only expressions of bad diseases. How? And why?"

"They would be of no value. I would occupy all of them. They would not leave!" "Sam"s voice raised considerable.

"I said without killing them," James asked again.

"They would not be killed, they would become recycled." "Sam's" smile wasn't as broad; it was barely a smile, more of a sneer!

"That's killing them! You have to understand. In this country, we have those that consider any incursion into their space, into what they consider abnormal, will not be tolerated. This is abnormal. What would you do with the bodies? How could you hide the fact that one hundred humans are dead now?" James was asking the questions, but was liking the answers less and less.

"No bodies would exist. When recycled, nothing is discarded, total recycling. Re-programming would begin in the receiving humans, immediately." "Sam" had thought out his answers well. His thought process was in high gear now.

"Wait, wait one moment. Re-programming! When does that take place?" Sam jumped into the questioning.

"Sam" turned to face the new questioner. "Immediately following recycling." "Sam" never faltered. He answered flatly. His smile was back.

All listening, almost shuddered, all were listening. Evelyn was caught pouring glasses, and filled one over the top. She broke the quiet. "Damned!" One word, one word that held more meaning then any wanted to admit. Evelyn was off to the kitchen to get towels. Sam followed. Nicole adjusted her position. James just gawked at "Sam."

"You're willing to just end lives, and use the lives to recreate your new world?" Nicole stated just as flat as "Sam" had been.

"Yes."

"Okay. Now we need to get on to how we are going to present you to the public." Nicole was less than interested in how he was going to perform the recycling, or the re-programming. She had decided the situation needed to move on.

"Sam" thought it was about time that a plan was started. Questioning him was of no value to their plan. "That is what I was brought here for, correct? It is time we moved on to your plan."

"Yes. That is what we are here for." Although all wanted to hear more, they felt recycling was their next stop. They wanted to hear more; it's human nature to hear the worst that might happen to them, and possibly soon, if their plan was not liked! "What we need to know, more about what you do. I mean how do you energize? How long must you energize? What does it do to you? Any problems? Do you have an alternate power source?" James was digging a hole he hoped he could rationalize himself out of.

"What importance is that to you?" "Sam" became defensive.

"What I mean is, do you have any after effects? Do you have to recover after you energize?" James could feel sweat in between his shoulder blades.

"I sometimes have sparks that fly about as I begin to recreate myself." "Sam" felt in control, a human trait, but he didn't even notice.

"Recreate yourself?" James looked at "Sam." *Now a new problem, what the Hell does recreate mean?* James thought to himself.

"I have little satellite energies that sometimes orbit around my entity following my power stages, usually from a large amount of energy being absorbed in a short time. I can control most of it. It seems that I can create them but have to allow time to pass to make them stop." "Sam" was being honest.

"Can you show me what you mean? That may sound foolish but I don't really understand," Nicole asked.

"Sam" suddenly had small spark lights that began to orbit around him in a elliptical manner, two, then three, then none. "I created those. When I recreate my entity, energy has been absorbed to give me new power, it becomes one with my entity and recreates my entity. Anytime I remake myself into human form, or to my entity I have small sparks, I believe you call it static electricity, harmless, but following recreation uncontrollable."

"Those little sparks are harmless? We cold touch them?" Nicole asked. She was fascinated as James was at the alien's ability.

"Sam" rekindled the sparks and allowed Nicole to place her hand in one's path. Nicole was shy in her being able to thrust her hand into the path at first. Slowly she placed her hand into the expected path. It passed through her as though her hand was not there. Nicole could feel the hair on the nape of her neck rise and fall back as the spark passed through her hand. She took her hand away and looked at it. She rubbed the palm—nothing remaining, no marks, no feeling or loss of feeling.

"That will sometimes happen." "Sam" had his smile in place now, almost a pleasant smile, not his usual sneer. "Sam" did not notice he was hovering just off the carpet again. He was gloating over his parlor trick; he liked to be in the spotlight!

"You are not touching the floor, again!" James raised his voice this time to emphasize his position and to throw "Sam" off guard. His position was emphasized, and so was "Sam's" scowl.

"How can you expect my entity to manage all of these trivial little jobs? You haven't even shown my entity what you are going to do to present me to humans!" "Sam's" voice was a little louder, just enough to show his disapproval.

"That's what they are doing," Sam said. "Humans are a different lot in life, than you. You have a lot of power in your world. We do not. We are made to conform and exist by an attainable standard. You have no such standards. If you want us to make you ready for presentation to the population of this world, then pay attention." Sam was at the food table. He wasn't really hungry, but thought it would look normal, so he continued to prepare his plate. "We have little to no power to fight you. You are going to make this a better place to live. We only want to help, that's all."

Evelyn had cleaned up the spill and had been standing and watching. Now she entered into the fray. "You told me just a few short weeks ago that you were here to assist. Now it is our time to assist you. To return the assistance you have given Sam, and now me." Evelyn had a very sincere look on her face, not scared anymore.

"Please let us assist," Nicole told "Sam"

"My entity lacks human emotions, no human traits. Assistance to create a more powerful human life is what my entity is trying to accomplish. I… I am sorry." "Sam" had had much difficulty to say that.

"There are people in this town that would burn this house to the ground, if they knew who you were. They are afraid. I was afraid. I still am. You could destroy all of us in a blink of your eye! We have only been trying to make your plan work. We are going to make your plan work, by making our plan work, together." James was running now.

"Burn this to the ground!" hadn't set well with Sam. He tried not to let it show, but Evelyn saw it in his eyes.

"Sam" had liked the "burn this to the ground." The fire would be nice; he liked fire. It had been a long time now, but there would be more fires, but not here, and now. He needed their help, maybe.

All had stopped, all had thought their individual thoughts. Two and two is four, to one. But was it simple math? The four hoped so. James and Nicole had sought out an alien, they had actively looked to find one, they had seen many graves of prehistoric man, all of the animals that had surrounded him. Now the future was within their grasp. They would be real, because their alien was real! Not a theory, not a maybe, a real alien! Nicole would be famous, James would be famous! They would write books, lectures, they would finally get what they had so long looked to find. Nicole would accept James's offer, maybe a kid. James would not have to read all of those obscure letters. He would still continue on. "Sam" would assist him to become the most famous of all men. The first to cross the barrier, to have found a man from another world. What world?

III

John wondered. His thoughts could not go far from what he still perceived as his duty. *Duty, to what? I don't even know who I am, and this place, where is this place?* John had caught himself wondering more. His memories had named him. They were cloudy skies that covered the blue of the heavens. And Energy was a total mystery to him. This man, nice enough, had almost refused to tell him more! John had walked for hours in one direction, or so he had thought. Only to find himself back at the same bench. The evening was beginning to start, shadows had just begun. The house where he had stayed was only a short walk from here. Food would be there, and a quiet existence. Was this his ever, his time to be. To be what, he had wondered. He stood and decided it would be nice to lie on the bed. He had walked many steps, only to find himself back where he had begun.

John waved to Julie. She had a puppy running after her. She laughed and danced in circles, and then was off to who knew where. John only saw her here. Maybe in a child's mind that was good. John had been an entity, his job had been important to...to...well, it had been his job, and he had done it well...he thought. Now he was left to his own, to do what. Nothing looked as though it needed to be recycled or reprogrammed. John walked. He had gotten good at walking, especially for someone so new with legs and feet, feet that had a slight ache to them.

The path turned to the right, it passed by a small brook that bubbled and babbled and flowed back to the woods. The light was falling over John's shoulder, and lighted his way. The light was slowly going away as he made the turn to the house. Lights were on inside the house. *How nice,* John thought. *Now the house is ready for me to come in, and become part of what it is, whatever that is.* His pace slowed as he approached. Someone was moving about inside. Maybe Energy, maybe another such as he. The thoughts made his mind race! It also gave him reason to stop. Maybe it was not his house, maybe he had been using someone else's house. Maybe it was another wanderer, someone like himself. Or maybe he has lost his way and it was time to move on to another place. A place not yet revealed to him, by his memory, or Energy, or whatever. John stopped and watched. He could only see shadows, images to cause his mind to move from one possibility to another. The shadow moved from one room to another, the shadows grew around him as well. John looked to the sky. Stars were beginning to shine. He stepped forward, his walk slow, his heart worried about the meeting that was about to happen.

At the door John stopped. He wanted to open the door and ask who was there, friend or foe. His hand found the door handle, it turned in his grip, he pushed the door open. Inside he could smell food, he hadn't been able to identify food odors as of yet, but whatever it was smelled good! He stepped inside.

"John. I was about to look for you!" She turned from the table and came to John and kissed him on the cheek. "Supper is about ready."

"I am new to this world. You seem to know me by my name. Where are we? And I must ask, who are you?" John was still standing, door open, and a slight warmth had settled across his cheek where she had kissed him.

The blond-haired woman stopped, looked to John. "I am Phyllis. I was told that you would take time to remember. Your job had been so long here, but all will come back, I have been assured of that." Phyllis set the two glasses on the table. She returned to John, and placed her arms around his neck and looked into his eyes. "Welcome home." Phyllis kissed John on the lips gently.

John searched his mind. He smiled, he was confused. He walked to the table with Phyllis and sat down. Phyllis bowed her head. John did the same.

IV

"Sam" had decided it was good what they were dong for him. He would do as they asked. His plan had not made preparations for such nonsense. But his plan had not been completed as yet. The last part was to be a fluid-in-motion plan, to give and take, to make it all come together, so it was still a plan, and this was part of it.

Nicole had pulled the coffee table into the center of the room, and all but Sam had sat on the floor and were eating. Sam had sat on the couch and had his food on the end table. Sam had stoked the fire, and added some more wood to the fireplace to keep the fire as warm as ever. Outside the day grew on. It was as cold as it had been. The sun had darkened, and the wind still blew. The fireplace had become "Sam's" retreat. He had been asked to join in the meal and to sit with the others, but he had declined. "Sam" stood. He had stood motionless for hours, answering nonsense questions, but he had answered as best he could. His entity had been a very smart entity; it had gotten around the likes of Spirit and had beaten him. "Sam" was now his own master. He would soon be the master of all, with the minor assistance of these four humans. He watched as they ate and laughed. He smiled on the occasion they looked his direction.

Evelyn had been up and refilled all the glasses. She turned to "Sam." "Are you sure you don't want anything to eat? We have tons of food. Doesn't the smell make you hungry?" Evelyn held a cookie in her hand, and a cup of coffee.

"Sam" had been answering questions all day and it only seemed to his thought process to answer this one as well. "My entity does not smell. Odors are perceived, no attachment is given. Only noted. Odors are categorized for future reference, but are used to recall instances or places."

"You are missing a great part of the day. Today I actually cooked, I don't do a lot of that, and the holiday smells of ham and pie are what makes the day. The birthday of our savior is today. We celebrate and have friends and family together to celebrate." Evelyn still held the cookie, and sipped from her coffee.

"I heard what you said, 'Sam.' Something I have meant to ask, but was afraid to ask. Now I need to know, and I don't feel it to be offensive to ask anymore." James was hedging, testing "Sam."

"Humans are so slow to ask. If you have a question ask it and move on. Time is not to be wasted either!" "Sam" looked at James; he too had a cup with coffee.

Nicole and Sam looked to the gathering in the middle of the room. It was quiet, only the crackling of the wood remained.

"Well, I … Sam, and I have talked. When you threw him into the wall, at the garage, he said he still has a sore spot. Well, he said you told him you fixed him. How do you know what to fix? Do you have X-ray vision or what? What I wonder is, how did you know what to fix! Or was he even hurt?" James had stumbled through that question.

"It's still tender, it doesn't hurt, but it is still tender!" Sam added before "Sam" could answer.

"My entity knew damage had been done. Blood was present and a bone was protruding. I occupied Sam's body, and recreated Sam as before. Ribs. Yes. Ribs were broken. My entity has studied with Sam for many years and understands the makeup of humans' structures. My entity has better control of foolishness like happened there. My entity still assists Sam, now Evelyn, and you and Nicole as well. My entity has first to assist humans. That is why my plan is to be completed to assist all humans. Repair was necessary to enable Sam to continue in time." "Sam" looked to his assembled human audience. All were silent, all looked to him, all would look to him soon, not just these four, all humans. "Sam" smiled and waited for the next foolish question.

"What's inside you?" Evelyn asked.

"What do you mean?" "Sam" asked back.

Evelyn started to push on "Sam's" arm. She stopped. "I am sorry. I almost touched you."

"Go ahead if you must. I am in control and no harm will befall you." "Sam" enjoyed being the center of these humans' attention.

Evelyn reached out again. Her hand pushed into a pillow, little to no resistance, mostly clothing. Nothing!

"Sam" smiled. "When I know you are to touch me, I can control my energy."

"That's part of what I'm talking about." James stepped in front of Evelyn. "Can you make yourself like us, you know, solid?"

"What would I do that for?" "Sam" asked, his voice normal now.

"Well, because you are standing in solid rock right now!" James pointed with his empty hand, at "Sam's" feet inside the hearth.

"Sam" had not felt his feet and legs come into contact with the stone. He looked to see what he had done, and eased back out of the hearth to assume normal position. All watched in amazement as he moved out of the stone. "Sam" had not done this as easily lately, it had been easy in time past, but that was before. He put his best smile in place.

Let me see something, or first I have to ask something. James pacing as his habit had become, especially of late, he didn't just pace he walked fast and pivoted, turned and back again. What's inside of you?

What's inside of me? "Sam" had brushed this off earlier, he could not understand asking again.

Yes! If a camera takes your picture and you are talking, what will it show? James stopped in front of "Sam" and looked into his apparently non-blinking eyes.

I do not know, darkness, as would be seen of your mouth. I have teeth. "Sam" a little taken aback, he could not understand the questioning.

"Sam, do you have a digital camera?" James pivoted to face Sam.

"Yes I do. I take pictures of properties..."

"Get it if you would. 'Sam,' I will show you how easy it will be for someone to know you are not of this world." James paced again.

Evelyn looked to Nicole, who shrugged; she had no clue. Sam came back checking the battery of the camera, and he pressed the flash to make sure it worked. Sam handed the camera to James.

Now "Sam" I want you to start talking, just ignore me. James flashed the camera toward "Sam" and moved about him in a circle.

"Sam" turned to watch, and then began to speak; the words matched his lips now. "I really have no idea what this is all about, but I will cooperate to prove what ever point you have, as invalid."

James snapped six pictures of "Sam" as he spoke. The little camera flashed each time. That made "Sam" uneasy at first, then he relaxed.

"How much more should I say, or should I start over?" "Sam" turned to look at James.

James was reviewing the pictures as "Sam" turned to face him. James held the camera to "Sam." "Now look at these pictures I have just taken. There will be many photographers at each and every news conference. They will almost drive you nuts, and when they hear what you have in mind, they will follow you everywhere."

"Sam" looked at the pictures. He saw what James had told him; there was nothing inside him, only a light, beyond his teeth, nothing but light. "What does this prove?"

"That you need some work, if we can. Are you able to change what is inside?" Nicole had picked up on the line James was working.

"Sam" handed the camera to Sam, who was careful not to touch his hand. Sam and Evelyn looked at the pictures. The light was the most overpowering image on the picture. It was like looking at the sun, the sun surrounded by teeth!

Nicole asked Evelyn to take a picture of her mouth to show "Sam." Evelyn took several, and handed the camera back to "Sam." "Sam" twisted the camera in many directions looking for a flaw in James's argument, but he knew they were right. He had been so careful in his outer makeup shell.

Before "Sam" had a chance to argue James began anew. "Can you change that? Can you make it so you could have skin on the outside? Can you make it so you could eat? Not a meal, just snacks, so you would appear relaxed?" James was chasing, he was trying to save his ass, he thought he was about to run out of ammunition. "You said you could burn the garage to the ground, and if you wanted it would only leave a charred spot on the face of the earth, right!"

Sam flinched at the thought of the garage charred like Sara's house. Sam slipped his arm around Evelyn; she could feel the tenseness in Sam.

"Yes. I could do that." "Sam's" figure became stiff, as did his voice.

"Then try this!" James gave "Sam" a cookie decorated with a green tree, with garland and bulbs.

"You are serious about this?"

"Yes I am. First make the inside of our mouth so it won't just drop in. You have to have a mouth, a cavity to chew food and swallow." James had stopped pacing and stood before "Sam" defiantly!

"Sam" looked back at James. The stare was like looking into a grave. The pupils did not move, the eyes did not reflect the light, only darkness. "Sam" smiled and looked at the others. "This might take time, my entity has not seen a reason for this modification. But I will try, I will make adjustments to my form." "Sam" closed his dead eyes. Light slipped through the space between his eyelids. The eyelids seemed to move, but not move at the same time. Minutes passed, no one spoke, all eyes were too busy watching to allow any thoughts to be used for speaking.

"Now, better?" "Sam" opened his mouth and tilted his head back. It was like a painting of a throat, like you would see in a doctor's office. "Sam" took the cookie and inserted half of it in his mouth. He chewed so they could see his teeth in action. He swallowed with an audible swallowing sound. He then opened his mouth and stuck out his tongue, like a child playing show and tell. When he closed his mouth, he smiled, a Cheshire cat smile. "Not too bad. I will have to put taste into my thought process for further enjoyment of food!"

James had rolled the dice; what for he didn't know. "Sam" had been able to meet and match all his requests, although he was floating about an inch high now. Evelyn had watched, and had a thought; she wondered if the disciples had asked Jesus to play show and tell! Evelyn laughed!

Everyone looked at Evelyn as though she had yelled fire. "Sorry. I just had a thought." She covered her mouth, and snickered again.

The others did not see Evelyn's joke till days later when she would recall it at dinner. Even Sam scowled at Evelyn's outburst, which only made her laugh louder. She went to the kitchen as her laugh got louder.

"That's good. No. that's great! Now pull up your pant leg!" James could not believe that he had been outfoxed. He needed to find a flaw; time was running out. If not today, soon. James was scared.

"Sam's" pant leg rose unassisted, to reveal pale skin, with short, curly, brown hair. "Sam" smiled and stared at James, who turned his face away. "Sam" pulled his shirt out of his pants to reveal an abdomen that would have passed for Sam's. But no one wanted to compare slightly round bellies.

"What would you have my entity to do now? Is this not like the magician that you said I should not imitate?" "Sam" was proud; his ego flashed before all but Evelyn.

Mid-afternoon sun came in the window to reveal friends playing charades. Most were inside, and would not have thought anything of the Young household. They had time to play new Christmas games; toys were enjoyed by all. Football played on some televisions, others were still outside in the freezing cold covered in ice and snow, but those were young, and had no perception of cold; they were having too much fun! The city grader was making numerous passes trying to clear streets for normal life to begin. The sun shone bright in the front yard of the Young house. And Sam went to the kitchen to see what the Hell Evelyn found so funny!

Evelyn and Sam reentered the living room. Her fit of laughter had passed. "Now 'Sam,' you must learn to become socially acceptable!" Evelyn said as she entered the living room.

"What now?" "Sam" asked.

"You must learn how to act. Your plan may take a little longer to put in place. And you will have to meet people till that time. You will undoubtedly have to meet lots of news reporters and officials. You will have to become socially proper," Evelyn said. She still had the image of Jesus at the last supper with his mouth open playing show and tell; she stifled a laugh.

"What will this involve?" "Sam" asked. His smile had waned.

James spoke first. "Instead of standing all the time, you will need to sit and hold conversations, small talk, your plan. You will be expected to show courtesies in most all meetings. It is customary."

"I do not need to be socially accepted, I will be worshiped as your new God! This is unnecessary for my entity to perform. Eating and speaking and walking are now part of my entity's abilities, all of which are unnecessary!" "Sam's" voice had risen, and so had most pulse rates.

"'Sam,' I have never tried to make myself as smart as the others here. But I can tell you that to make a plan that will make the whole world bow down to you will take some time. Do you have any memory of Viet Nam? How far away was that? Are you aware of distance? Have you any concept of 'world'? It's a big damned place. It will take time. But it will have to be quick. Any part of you that is not accepted will be used to make people not want to accept your plan. You may be able to make some do your bidding, but others will have to coerced into believing. I am sure. But you have promised Sam and I life together, forever, and for that I will try and help." Evelyn leaned against Sam and hugged him, and laid her head against his chest.

"My plan may, in fact, take time. I have understood that. But is it necessary for my entity to perform all these little changes, on a day-by-day time?" "Sam's" smile was replaced by a look of fear.

"If I am to get my Sam, and you are to rule the world, no matter your reason, you will. I have seen what you can do, I will admit it scares me. I am fearful that you will destroy us four when you are finished with us. I will do all you ask." Evelyn's arms were still around Sam.

James was impressed with Evelyn's oration. He had wished he had spoken the words; he too had the same feelings.

"How will I develop these social abilities?" "Sam" was floating again.

"We will teach you. Today we will begin. The little things must become normal, like not floating, sitting on the couch. Having a cookie." Evelyn moved away from Sam, and to the couch. She motioned for "Sam" to join her.

"Sam's" concentration was better, but he still floated to the couch. His legs moved, but his feet did not mark the carpet as he did so. He sat on the couch, and the cushion imprinted with his form.

"Cross your legs and relax. Do you ever relax?" James asked.

"I become placid when I power. I have not been relaxed as much here as before," "Sam" told James while looking at Evelyn. Evelyn had been truthful with "Sam." There was the one time she had tried to mentally challenge "Sam," but that was forgiven. "Sam" liked Evelyn, better than Sara, but that would never be told to Sam.

Nicole asked, "Where were you before? I mean what planet? Does it have a name?"

"I am from here. My entity was dispatched to assist Sam at his birth. Many entities are dispatched, programmed, and continue to assist." "Sam" was going to explain more, but James broke into the conversation.

"There are more of you?"

"Many entities, many children, not all have an entity now. More children than entities. That is part of what is wrong with this planet. There have become too many humans to allow energy to be useful. Entities are not social creatures as are humans. Associations are not made. We provide assistance to perform; that is why an entity is programmed."

"Where do you come from?" James asked again.

"I am from here. I have existed for Sam's life beside him. Only when power is needed do I return."

"That's what I keep asking—where do you go to power? You leave here, and go where?" James was frustrated. His line of questioning was strictly for his benefit now.

"I cross over. I go nowhere. Now I need not to cross over; energy is now completed here." "Sam" tried to cross his legs like Evelyn, but was having some difficulty keeping form to his legs, and keeping his legs crossed. It distracted him, as well as the other four present. "Sam" put his feet on the floor and laid his hands on his lap. "This is the only planet, world, that my entity has ever visited."

"You said visited. Where do you go, no, how do you travel? What kind of a craft, what kind of vehicle?" James's voice had raised and he was pacing again.

"No vehicle. No travel, just crossing over. My entity only has to process the thoughts and cross over to the place. It's a place but nowhere. It is only in my entity's thought process. It exists for recharging, and recycling, and reprogramming. No travel, no vehicle, only thought and energy." "Sam" was getting tired of being badgered, his facial expressions only came into play when he was very agitated.

"Now you will need to try and eat a few snacks. The meetings will have coffee, or drinks of some kind. And generally something to eat, small cakes, rolls, donuts, something of the kind." Evelyn had continued on her social grace classes.

James and Nicole were interested in who and where, and most of all how. And now the revelation of many more entities! The questions were more than James's mind could conjure now. He had pad and pen. He was categorizing questions as Evelyn continued to talk. "Sam" was calm with Evelyn, something that was good, but it was not solving any problems. And it was not satisfying the need, the need to know what kind of alien they had amongst them.

"Stop! Now! My entity has meet all your expectations, I have answered all your questions, you have told me to learn to relax! I am trying!" The voice boomed throughout all their heads. It was like broken glass inside their head! "Sam" floated above the couch. His eyes glowed now. He seemed to grow in height and width. "Stop!"

All conversation ended. James dropped his pen and paper. "Sam" moved about the room with incredible speed. The room filled with light so bright that all had to shield their eyes. The room seemed to grow, the fireplace glowed from the roaring fire, the flames licked at the stone, on the fireplace, and the heat became intense. "Sam's" form circled the room faster and faster! Then, slowly, so slow, "Sam" came back to stand in front of the fireplace. He began to deflate, he shrank before their eyes. Clothes began to loosen and look like clothes instead of a shroud. "Sam's" eyes went from light to dark. His face began to take on a human form. "My entity will have conversation with Evelyn. I will relax, and I will ask questions, now!"

All eyes turned to Evelyn, still sitting quietly on the couch. Evelyn looked back to each. Her eyes gave way to her inner thoughts that she had betrayed the others and had set back the reason for the day. Moisture had begun to collect in Evelyn's eyes. Still afraid, but now, of who? No sound but the crackling of the fire dying back to normal, the heat slowly dissipated, tears ran down Evelyn's cheeks.

"Sam" returned to the couch and sat beside Evelyn. "My entity has the power to eliminate all of you, this house, the cars outside. My power can do more than melt snow from the road. Do not play me for a human. I will have my plan in place soon, you will find me to be a forgiving God! My entity is programmed to assist. Your time to assist my entity is short. Do not shorten it more by trying to outsmart my entity! I will wreak revenge on your human forms as none has seen before!" The voice inside Sam, James and Nicole's heads tried to shatter their skulls it was so loud, and boomed inside their heads. Evelyn sat quietly. She too heard the voice, but it was normal, and heard through her ears, not her mind. "Sam" touched Evelyn's cheek. The touch was warm, no shock, and gentle. Evelyn reached to "Sam's" and laid hers on his. Sparks flew from her touch. She pulled her hand back as fast as she could, but the energy had already surged through her hand up her arm and to her shoulders! Evelyn screamed; she threw her body sideways away from any contact with "Sam."

Sam started for Evelyn, who was curled up at the opposite end of the couch. Sam was lifted and forced against the wall beside the archway. Nicole gasped. James stood his place not moving. Sam held against the wall, his feet inches from the floor, he could not move, could not talk. "Sam" released Sam, he fell to the floor.

"Evelyn, I have told you that you cannot touch my entity. I may touch you. As for the rest of you, do not be foolish. Find seats, and we will conduct a social evening, as the manner I will need to complete my plan. Conduct yourselves as humans, not as fools. Now, Evelyn, if you will instruct my entity in the social graces that you were referring to before. All of you may need to be instructed as well."

Sam got off the floor slowly. He looked at "Sam" with contempt in his eyes. James moved to his side. "Easy now, Sam. Are you alright?"

"Yeah, I'm fine." Sam walked to Evelyn. He touched her cheeks with his hands. "Are you alright?"

Evelyn sniffed once and nodded her head. She watched "Sam."

"Evelyn, can I get you something?" Nicole asked.

Evelyn sniffed again. "No, I'm fine. I forgot, I'm sorry."

Conversation with "Sam" began again. James asked a few more questions about "Sam's" programming, but stayed away from where he was from. Sam followed Evelyn to the kitchen to make sure she was indeed alright. Nicole sat in the middle of the room looking into the fire, her knees drawn up and her arms wrapped around them.

Evelyn explained to "Sam" that she would put away the food, and they would continue in a few minutes. "Sam" had nodded agreement and continued answering a few of James's questions. The darkness was coming soon, shadows had grown long on the Young front lawn. The grader had been by several times and the street light made odd shadows from the snow piled beside the road. The snow reflected the light in streaks. The trees cast long finger shadows. Clouds of snow blew by the front window making shadows as it did as well. The wind was getting stronger as nightfall approached.

Evelyn had put away most of the food from the long table in the living room, Sam had helped while trying to get Evelyn to answer questions. Everyone had questions, but Sam wasn't getting any answers. "You have to get him to answer some of the questions. He's just babbling now, he thinks it's funny. After you talked to him he got nice, and he tosses me against the wall. You have a chance!"

"Sam, I don't have a chance of getting anything out of him, none of us do! He is going to do what he wants, can't you see that! We, you and me, and I guess James and Nicole stand a chance of getting out of this alive; we can live, we can go on. I can't do anything for the rest of the world! I can't see his ever making this work. But I do see that he has a lot of power; he just might. I can't do anything more. Maybe someone else can, but I can't. Don't you see that?" Evelyn was putting sliced cake and cookies and some Chex Mix on a platter.

Sam grabbed Evelyn's arm and turned her around. "You've got to try! Tell him next time we are together you have some questions, but will wait till then. Humor him! He likes you! Anything, till James gets something together." Evelyn pulled away from Sam.

"Next time. How many more times are we going to play this game? We have to save ourselves, if we can. Once upon a time might have been the beginning. All I want is for us to live happily ever after." Evelyn turned to Sam. "We can't beat him, maybe later, but not now!" Evelyn began to cry, Sam pulled her against him.

"Evie, don't cry. We'll try again next time. He will want more and more." Sam smoothed Evelyn's hair and held her to him.

Evelyn opened the refrigerator door and took out the magnum of champagne. "Take this, Sam. It was meant for Christmas Eve. We may as well celebrate now, it might be the last time."

Sam took the magnum of champagne. Evelyn picked up the tray and started for the living room. Sam looked at the large bottle and then to Evelyn as she left the kitchen. Sam shook his head from side to side and followed.

It's getting late. James turned on the music on the fireplace. Evelyn set the tray on the coffee table and pushed it back to its place in front of the couch. "Sam" watched as she spread out napkins and moved a few items on the tray. "Sam has the champagne. We were going to have it on Christmas Eve, but that didn't happen. Tonight we are about to begin new lives, I think. 'Sam,' we are going to have a little celebration with you, and this way you get to see how to be socially acceptable at the same time."

James looked at the magnum Sam was holding. "That should just about do all of us. Could you get a bigger bottle, Evelyn?

"It's supposed to be good champagne, the man said. It might be a little big. But we are celebrating, right!" Evelyn just looked at James.

"Well the party seems to be ready to begin!" Nicole said. "You need some help with that bottle, big boy!" Nicole looked at Sam.

"It has been a while since I opened on of these things, but I think I can handle it! 'Sam,' you are not used to all the little things here just yet. So let me advise you that this thing is going off like a cannon shot!" Sam smiled. He should have let it go but thought better; he didn't want "Sam" burning the place down!

"What will?" "Sam" tensed. His cushion wasn't showing any weight, no indentation.

"Relax! That's what you said, remember? The carbonation will cause the cork to pop, and it will be rather loud!" Nicole told "Sam." She had spun around on the carpet, but retained the same position. She had rejoined the living, she hoped living.

James didn't like the way Evelyn had taken over, but she had insured more time, more time for James to find the answers that "Sam" was holding back. He was from somewhere, and it sure as Hell wasn't the earth! But the moment had been salvaged from the raw edge that had been displayed. James would hold back and let Evelyn have her little tea party; he would have the next day. He would inform "Sam" that he would have to cooperate if he was to be presented properly.

"Now, 'Sam,' there are simple rules that make it easy. You take what you want, and you nibble; you don't push it into your face and inhale it." Evelyn giggled; she was really laughing at "Sam" and his cookie experience earlier. "If you haven't gotten an odor sensor, you will need one; this stuff is good! Food smells good so we eat it, it is a simple deal. That's why we try and make things look good, make them look good to eat! You have never eaten, except a cookie.

This will all be new to you, but I don't think you will gain any weight!" Evelyn giggled again. She had a job now, and it took her mind off of what had just happened, and what might yet happen.

"Why do people eat all these little things? Do they provide any energy?" "Sam" had his worried look again.

"Quite frankly, all the sugar content is full of energy! It's also full of calories. That's why I don't do a lot of this stuff, except at holidays. And this is a celebration! So chow down and enjoy." Nicole smiled at "Sam." She was afraid, but thought the friendly atmosphere would save them for another day.

Sam was less than happy with all the twists and turns of the day, but had begun to see a light at the end of the tunnel, so to speak. Maybe something could be, would be done to stop this maniac. He would play along. He hadn't been able to follow James's lead, as they had discussed; James hadn't had a lead. It had been like the blind leading the blind!

The only one not blind, it seemed, was "Sam." And his little plan seemed to be a nightmare. He had already done more damage than he had ever done good for Sam. He had admitted to his killings; Sara, and Paula might have been an accident, but Wes had not been, and how many others had he tried his horrible experiments on! How many had died, that had just disappeared?

"Sam. Are you alright?" James asked.

"Yeah, I guess so. Not much of a plan here is there." Sam looked at James. He saw the same look of doom in James's face too! "I guess we join the party."

"I suppose so. Cold night in Illinois, not much else to do, huh." James was at a loss for words too, and he didn't like being that way.

"I haven't any champagne glasses, so we have an assorted variety here, some wine, some shot glasses, and so on. We make toasts, to celebrate whatever. We lightly touch glasses, and drink to whatever we are celebrating." Evelyn had "Sam's" undivided attention.

Sam worked with the champagne. It was down to removing the cork. He twisted and turned. "Sam" watched with fascination that humans went to all the trouble to make a nothing time into something, something he was yet to understand. Soon they all would celebrate his entity, he was to be their celebration, their God. Thought processes were all alive. All four humans had thoughts, but they had been sidelined for lack of an answer. So as humans generally do, laugh in the face of disaster, they had decided to join, of now. "Sam's" thought process had many plans, but now was only concerned with getting this lesson over, and continuing his plan.

"Sam" tried a cookie. His nibbling was going to take some work. The cookie was fragile and seemed to crumble too easily, and it was gone, simple. But he would appease these humans as long as needed, then they too would be sent away, out of his plan. "Sam" would let them live; they were being helpful and were assisting his entity. "Sam" remembered the years before; his assisting had been fun, now theirs was too!

The cork was loosed. As with most champagne it was loud; only the best of the best could open one without the loud report. Sam had been quick and started to pour before the champagne had had time to overflow. Sam filled all the glasses and set the bottle on the coffee table. The liquid rushed toward the top, but fell short of overflowing.

All but "Sam" had a glass in their hands. They laughed and asked to what they should toast. Evelyn spoke up. "To a better world!"

Evelyn held a glass for "Sam" to take from her, slightly frightened, but held the glass with only the slightest shake. "Sam" looked at the miniature bubbles as they rose from the bottom. He smiled.

"Remember I can touch you." "Sam" took the glass carefully from Evelyn. He held it up to examine it more. All the glasses came together with a slight clink. "Sam" looked up at the sound. He extended his glass, another clink.

Evelyn had just graduated her first etiquette student. They all smiled in unison. "To a better world!" They all drank from their glasses. "Sam" had hesitated. "Go ahead!" In unison again.

"Sam" smiled. "To a better world." He tipped his glass as he had watched others. His mouth opened. All saw that "Sam" had let the inner lining of his mouth go back to just energy; it glowed. All smiles left the foursome. All had taken a step backward. "Sam" was still a monster, "Sam" was still not of this world. The laughter died away as they watched, and wondered what was next for each of them.

"Sam" had a smile on his lips as the liquid fell from the glass into his entity. It poured like a glass of water into a five-gallon pail. Then "Sam" fell back to the couch. He sprung from the couch like the cushion was an ejection seat. He stepped through the table like it was not there; the pants and shoes, with socks still inside, did not. "Sam's" hands and arms arched behind his growing back, his back arched and his coat and shirt fell away. His form was a light blue, only slightly visible. His entity flew about the room. It could be easily tracked as it moved at an ever-increasing speed, by the light inside! The light grew and grew. It seemed to pulse with a life of its own, the light became brighter and brighter. The humans shielded their eyes—the worst was about to happen! All of the dread had come to pass, now! All was over and they were being forced to watch their own doom! A copper odor came to each nose in the room, the light became unbearable, then as all became aware the end was near, a loud pop was heard. The window by the tree cracked loud. It did not explode, just cracked, leaving a small hole in the very middle of the glass.

Evelyn cried; Nicole was near tears; James and Sam looked to one another expecting to watch the other ablaze, but none came. Only the wind whistling in the small hole in the window could be heard. Each looked about their own immediate area for signs of something, they did not know what, so they were extra cautious.

Only the music from the garland on the fireplace was heard. All were on the floor. All looked about the room for the next outburst. They looked for "Sam." The copper odor was dissipating, and the music played on!

Sam looked at his hands, then arms and scanned the area. James followed suit. Nicole looked at her glass and then to Evelyn, whose tears had stopped, leaving only wet reminders on her cheeks. Evelyn got up from in front of the couch and walked to the window. Through the cracks, Christmas lights could be seen down the street, and the garland on the fireplace still played Christmas tunes.

Sam turned to the archway, looked in the hall, then slipped to the kitchen. He looked out the kitchen window—just snow and shadows. "He's not in here!" Sam heard other doors being opened and closed. It was like being a child and playing hide and seek. All doors were opened, closets, and Nicole even opened the medicine cabinets. No "Sam"!

After looking in and around everything in the house they all converged in the living room again.

"I'm going to the garage. I will not be happy till I know he is not there!" Sam started for the kitchen.

"Sam! I'm going too!" Evelyn called.

"That truck seats four—we're all going, Sam!" James called.

"It's going to be tricky on the road tonight. You all don't have to go." Sam had turned and was looking at the gathered crew. It was a fear, fear that they had all been dealt a bad poker hand, the fear that it was not over. Only postponed!

"Sam Young, you're not leaving me here. I may not be your wife yet, but let me tell you, I'm not staying here." Evelyn had her hands on her hips in defiance.

"Get all the warm stuff you've got. I'll go and start the truck." Sam began to get his coat and gloves on. He went out and started the truck, and got the heater cranked up to warm the inside, and get the crystals of ice off the windshield.

Before Sam could get back in the house all were coming out the back door to meet him. Sam got everyone inside and he scraped the windows clean.

Sam got in behind the steering wheel and looked around the cab. "Well, I have no kind of an idea what the Hell just happened, and if 'Sam' is at the garage don't be surprised. Just be aware, you wanted to go too." All nodded in return, and Sam started the truck on its way.

The road had been partially cleared, and a lot of calcium chloride had been spread. There were still a lot of slick spots but the drive was only a half hour, and they were parked in the garage driveway. The women noted that there was not a lot of snow on the driveway as they parked.

"Sam and I will go in and if he's not there we'll be right back." James tried to be in control, but a mutiny had already been formed.

"Mr. Holly, back off with the orders. I'm not waiting here; we will go in together or not at all!" Nicole informed James.

Sam led the foursome around the side. The door, still not locked, opened to a hot summer-like atmosphere. No one really noticed as they went through each room, they pulled up canvas coverings and looked in all the cars. The last place was the storage room. The chair sat idly, waiting. It looked like a chamber awaiting an execution. The chair was still unplugged. Sam kicked the electric cords away, half expecting them to come to life. No "Sam," not a sign of anything out of place since James and Sam had last visited.

"Let's go home. I think I need to make a toast." Sam switched the lights off as they left by the side door and turned the thermostat back to sixty. Sam pulled the door closed, tried the lock; it worked, it was locked this time.

Back in the truck they had all begun to feel the cold. Sam turned the fan on the heater. "Where the Hell did he go?" Sam asked James.

"That, my friend, is the million-dollar question! I have no idea. But Evelyn, you, my dear, are the heroine of the day. I was really pissed that you had occupied 'Sam's' time with your tea party. But I am thankful that you did."

James looked to the back of the truck and smiled a warm, real smile. They all smiled, but wondered if "Sam" would be at the house when they returned.

The drive back to Sam's house was a little longer than the ride out—not much, about a forty-minute ride. Sam's driving was a little less reckless. James looked at Sam, and they exited together; the girls were not far behind. Another thorough search, and still no "Sam." They toasted "To a better world" and finished the champagne. Sam taped a piece of cardboard across the cracked window. The night was upon them; in actuality the early morning was upon them. Slowly they all retired, but most had a rough night. The wind made an uneasy sleep that night. Eyes opened with each creak or wail of the wind.

No one could believe what had happened, whatever it had been! Each had developed a theory, and each expected "Sam" to reappear at any time.

Chapter 17

I
A Better World!

John woke early. He slipped away, and left Phyllis asleep. He had begun to remember more. Phyllis was his wife, from when, that had still been his question. Phyllis could not give many answers, except the she had waited, but she did not know how long. John had only been confused with answers, and had quit asking questions. John walked up the hill and headed for his bench. He knew Energy would be there. John was not disappointed. He saw Energy sitting and watching the ducks in their early morning fishing ritual.

"Morning, John," Energy said as John approached. He never turned to see John, he just knew it was him.

"I have a few questions. Don't wander away or disappear. I need to know a few things," John said as he sat beside Energy.

"Go right ahead, John. I waited till your mind began to bloom. There was a period of adjustment. I could not tell you before, you would not have believed me," Energy said.

"You have that right! I want to know who you are?" John looked at the ducks paddling along.

"Does that make a difference?"

"I once was an entity, and now I'm not. I am not sure how you did that, but it all makes a difference."

Energy turned on the bench to face John. "Let me tell you how you came to be. Once upon a time you were a regular human. Yes, you were a human. When you came to me, I saw a man that had been good, worked hard, and was dedicated. You became an entity as many before you. You were, and are a patient man. You were sent to assist other entities, in their assistance to humans. Do you remember all of this?" Energy asked.

"Yes, but it is as though it seems to be fading away. I have to concentrate to remember all, but it is still there. I knew you would be here this morning. I have not told Phyllis any of this yet. She too seems confused about time and places." John looked at Energy.

Energy looked back to John and smiled. "Today is probably our last meeting like this. That is part of the plan. None of this is by accident. Come with me." Energy stood and walked to the lake. The ducks quacked their way along the bank just out of their sight.

The reflection of the water was rippled by the gentle breeze, but as they stood there, the ripples cleared and a picture appeared, a house with five people, a fire and a tree with lights. That caused a stir in John's mind, of something, but he wasn't quite sure what. The people were having a good time it appeared as all had something in their hands to eat and to drink.

"Who are these people?" John asked.

"Who they are is of no consequence. Just watch."

The scene played out in front of them. All five people tipped their glasses and drank, one slower than the rest. The last drank, and suddenly light filled the room, women cried and men cowered as the last disappeared. The room became normal again, and the picture returned to a rippled lake.

"What happened?"

"Do you remember your problem? It is no longer a problem. As I told you before, humans are a resourceful race. I can't say that they removed the problem for good. Problems arise from time to time. This one was only a problem for a while." Energy turned toward the bench.

John looked at the water again and saw nothing. He turned to catch up with Energy before he could slip away again. Energy was sitting as before, on the bench. "What just happened? And what do you mean only a little while? This has gone on for many times!"

"Time is forever, John. Your time is now forever. Your problems will be few. I know your memory will return in short times. You will not remember this meeting long. When people come here, they have had the times of trial. They have come here because they have been devoted to what is right. As you are, John. You will not remember those times either. Your time here is in reward for that dedication and devotion." Energy stood.

"No! You have not answered my question." John stood facing Energy.

"Who am I?"

"Yes! I must know." John looked searchingly at Energy.

"I am known by many names. I have been around for many times. I have been known as God, Mohammad, and many names that you have never heard or would remember. This is of no value to this conversation."

"But I expected a great and powerful man, someone that was not to trifle himself with the likes of me. You are the same as I, you have the same appearance. Surely you cannot expect me to believe that you are my God!"

"Why not, John? Why should I be something untouchable, would I then be accepted as a god? Or would people fear me, would they not approach me? I am here to tell you of the one thing in your mind that would not disappear. I have come to make your mind rest. Why do I have to be something that is not real? Why do I have to be something that cannot touch and feel? Why?" The man looked satisfied as he turned away.

"Don't go. I have many questions, and now I probably have even more."

"Yes, John, of that I am sure. This is your home now. You and Phyllis can roam to wherever you like, or you can live out all time here. You will not remember much of this conversation, or of that as an angel, but you have done well. I thank you! Give my best to your wife, if you can remember. Goodbye, John." He walked away, as any normal man would.

John began to remember many things, but there was always a cloudy place, and he would remember in the time between the dark and the light. He and Phyllis live happily, still devoted to a God that neither would ever meet. They knew it was heaven, because they were together. They never remembered much in their past, long time past didn't mean much to them. As time passed even short time past began to mean little,;only tomorrow was looked forward to each night as they began to drift off into a sound sleep. John had dreams from time to time, but he never remembered them. Just as well. Each day was enjoyed more, and never were two angels ever happier! They spoke of God, of angels, of heaven. Never were they told, and never did they know they too were angels.

II

Sam and Evelyn took James and Nicole to St. Louis for the fight to Arizona. Most of the ice had melted by then. The snow storm had been a record breaker.

It would be long remembered by many. Especially by the four; they had met an angel, and would never know it. Times are not all made for the average man. The average man would not accept anything that he could not touch or see. But these four had seen many things that would last them a lifetime. Nothing spectacular, but enough to put fear into their dreams for years to come. Nicole and James got away from the Watchers and became real anthropologists.

Sam and Evelyn were married on April Fools Day! They went on together in the only thing they knew, buying and selling. It became a more aboveboard business. And they still got a Christmas card from Nicole and James, usually shortly after Christmas.

I do not know how this tale will be accepted, I have written this for my pleasure. It has not been as easily written as I thought it would be. If you have read it and enjoyed it, I am pleased. If my views on religion seem a bit off center, then they must be. In the end it is a story. It involves a lot of my thoughts. I have worked long on this tale; it has been a joy for me. I hope if you have gotten this far you have enjoyed it too.